PRAISE FOR THE

absolutely LOVE the Grace Macallan series ... modern, gritty and always a rollercoaster of a read. The crimes are always incredibly dark and the characterisation intense. The author often provides a backstory to characters major and minor ... offering an insight into what drives or motivates each character, whether it be a cop or a criminal.'

Anne Bonny Book Reviews

'Ritchie certainly knows how to spin a yarn ... criminal nasties, family feuding, ambition, corruption, a fit-up and an investigation of omission, police complicity, informers, low-level enforcers, sexuality, friendship, empire on the wane, murder, kidnap ... and after a breathless few hundred pages – eventually some chickens coming home to roost. Ritchie goes onto the list of top Scottish authors I enjoy.'

Col's Criminal Library

wonderfully gripping story from start until finish! This fast-paced tale of Detective Grace Macallan's chase after the criminal gangs of Scotland's underworld leads the reader on a page-turning journey.'

Jera's Jamboree

With a strong and determined central protagonist, tense action and truly dramatic storylines, as a reader you are faced with a very different view of life in two of Scotland's most iconic cities – Edinburgh and Glasgow.'

Jen Med's Book Reviews

OUR LITTLE SECRETS

Also by Peter Ritchie

Cause of Death
Evidence of Death
Shores of Death
Where No Shadows Fall

OUR LITTLE SECRETS

PETER RITCHIE

BLACK & WHITE PUBLISHING

First published in 2019
by Black & White Publishing Ltd
Nautical House, 104 Commercial Street
Edinburgh, EH6 6NF

1 3 5 7 9 10 8 6 4 2   19 20 21 22

ISBN: 978 1 78530 241 1

A CIP catalogue record for this book is available
from the British Library.

Typeset by Iolaire, Newtonmore
Printed and bound by CPI Group (UK) Ltd, Croydon, CR0 4YY

*For the men and women out there
in the dark places who keep us safe.*

PROLOGUE

It felt as if the muscles and tendons of both shoulders were being ripped out slowly, the balls forced from their sockets as the men each pushed hard against an elbow to straighten his arms behind him. The pain should have been excruciating, but strangely enough there was nothing, and from that moment he was aware only of the wind whipping through his hair and the deathly quiet. His mind, like his ruined body, had passed that point of no return where fear had been replaced by an almost dreamlike state. He didn't give a fuck because there was no point, and he realised that they couldn't hurt him any more. The bastards who thought they controlled him were wrong.

Despite this state of mind, he was aware of a problem that needed to be resolved, which was that his whole body was hanging forward by about twenty degrees and seemed to be defying the laws of gravity. In fact, that wasn't really the problem at all; when it came down to it, the problem was that his feet were on a ledge, and the rubbish-strewn ground was way too far below him for Lady Luck to hand out any form of landing that wouldn't kill him. No chance of an expert parachute roll before springing to his feet like an acrobat and sticking two fingers up at them; with his luck, he'd land in a pile of Doberman shit. He was fucked and had always been fucked; he just hadn't realised it before. They were five (or was it a hundred?) storeys up on top of a disused industrial building in the middle of a wasteland which seemed to stretch out to the horizon without a break. It looked like those pictures of a World War One battlefield. He thought there would be a few seconds' flying and then it would all be over. Not so bad after what the bastards had already done to him.

'It's time tae go, son.' He said it through the blood that kept filling his mouth. For the first time in his life he was absolutely sure what he wanted to do. That was it: the meaning of life – the moment where you realised it was just another scene from Monty Python. Fragmented thoughts were fighting with each other to make it into the conscious part of his brain and he remembered the old line from *The Lion King*: 'I laugh in the face of danger.' People did it and found strength. There was an old school pal who was a genuine good guy, had never harmed a fly, who just kept smiling and saying 'fuck it' before he died of cancer. He'd hardly ever cursed in his life, so it had real effect. 'Fuck it' made sense to him after that. It gave meaning to what was left – he understood it – and the best bit was that the bastards who'd spent the afternoon taking lumps out of him didn't. How good was that?

They were so strong they didn't have to grip him hard, and instead of concentrating they were taking the piss out of him and hee-hawing to each other at his distress. They both froze for a moment, wondering why a man with his coupon rearranged and hanging over the edge of a tall building was laughing.

Dominic Grainger looked round and discovered it

was his brothers holding his arms. Where had they come from? He took them by complete surprise and stepped over the side onto thin air. They weren't prepared and he slipped through their greasy paws like the wind. He closed his eyes and flew like a bird. No one could touch him now.

1

A few months earlier

Davy McGill, or 'Tonto' as he was better known, ran like fuck across Gorgie Road in Edinburgh, his lungs burning with the combination of high-intensity activity and the fact that Pete the Pole was chasing him with a large axe. He'd got the name Tonto from his love of Indian food and his almost encyclopedic knowledge of the cuisine; it was the only thing apart from the Jambos that he'd studied in depth.

'I fucking slice you up!' The Pole had screamed it a few times now and Tonto knew for certain that if the boy caught him that's exactly what he'd do. The Pole was nuts and everyone had warned him not to deal with the radge, who was built like Superman and consumed so many steroids that he was in serious danger of exploding one day.

They were hard times for Tonto, although it was never anything else, and he was dealing to anyone who could boost his wages. The previous couple of years had been reasonable enough by his own shite standards, selling dope or stolen gear around the city or wherever he could punt it. At one time, he'd done a bit of work and bought his gear from the Flemings in Leith, but they'd been sent to gangster heaven, so he started working for the Graingers, who basically ran the west side of the city and were still expanding.

A bit of part-time dealing supplemented his earnings with them, which never seemed to be enough. It wasn't that Tonto was any worse off than most of the guys in his position, and his spending habits were limited to a few bets on the nags, bevvies when he could and following the Jambos. The truth was that working at the bottom end of a gangster's team didn't really pay that well and all that stuff in the movies about the glamour, well, that was just shite. He wasn't exactly Prince Charming anyway, pish poor with the ladies and only tended to score when some inebriated female was in a worse state than him. And as for his flat ... well, it was cold and barely furnished; it certainly didn't have a 'home sweet home' sign hanging anywhere.

Apart from that, the stair he lived on was inhabited by drunks, junkies and bampots, and sometimes all three wrapped up in the same human form. However, as he was always staggering around the edge of the poverty line anyway, he spent most of his waking hours on the streets hunting for new ways to earn, so his domestic situation didn't really matter much to him. The Graingers paid him for the odd dope run and dealing, but he was way down the pecking order, and he often wondered if he'd ever get to be a real gangster, whatever the fuck that was.

The Graingers were okay as long as everything was hunky-dory but seriously violent bastards if there was trouble. Their old man was Dublin Irish, a small-time gangster who'd come to Scotland to try to make a better life. It hadn't taken him long to discover he was just back in the old one with a slightly different view from the front door. To appease his second wife, who'd said she couldn't tolerate the idea of living off illegal income, he ended up in a shite job feeding the scaffy's lorry but determined his boys would do better. That had partly worked: his eldest son, Dominic, realised early on that his father looked old before his time and decided that he preferred success, and quickly. It just wasn't the kind of success his stepmother had envisaged. But as his generation had been told that greed was good, she tried to believe perhaps it wasn't all his fault.

He started to build his own gang and mini-empire in the concrete heroin fields of Broomhouse and Wester Hailes and his stepmother only started to forgive him when he bought them a decent home in Inverleith. She got through life by pretending the boy wasn't what he was, though his dad was secretly quite proud of him. And although the house was enough for his parents, Dominic wanted nothing less than it all, the result being that by the time he was in his twenties he was respected even by the bad bastards. Something marked him out as different, just a bit savvier than the normal career gangster.

He'd realised that eventually even the best of them took a fall – they always got that little bit too greedy and stood under a big fuck-off light that shouted, 'Arrest me!' He'd seen it and learned the lesson. As quickly as he could turn illegal wonga into legal wonga he invested in legit businesses, and he was good at it. Most of the investments thrived and he had a gift for negotiation with other businessmen, whether they were on the right side or the wrong side of the law. On the surface, he positioned himself squarely in the middle of the legit business and let his younger brothers carry on with the villainy. That way he spread the risks, and although his siblings always came to him for decisions, he'd put firewalls between him and the crime side of the business to keep reasonably safe. It didn't make him completely fireproof, just safer than most, and it would take pretty determined law to come after him.

That was the secret – make yourself really fucking difficult to catch and most of the time it'll put the law off coming after you. He took care of the finances from the crime side for his brothers, and they were happy to leave it to his skills in washing their profits.

At least that's how it should have worked.

2

For Tonto, everything had been running smoothly for a couple of years, but then a substantial wad of gear he was looking after for the Graingers went missing from a safe stash in circumstances that stank like a jakey's oxter. He'd constructed a false hide at the bottom of his mother's coal bunker and some bastard had chored it in the night. He hadn't told another soul where it was, yet someone knew, and no way was it a lucky guess. The Graingers, well, they weren't happy because that was one of the jobs they gave him: looking after gear and keeping it safe till it was dealt, sold on or traded. They were even less happy when, a few days later, the cops took out a large stash from another numpty who, like Tonto, was paid to look after it and take the fall if necessary. The numpty had taken the fall for them alright; nevertheless, they'd lost a shitload of money. The problem was that Tonto's stash had just disappeared, whereas the other numpty was arrested. The Graingers could understand the arrest, but they couldn't understand how the gear Tonto was minding was just chored. Whatever it was all about, they'd taken a serious hit and they lacked a sense of humour in these kinds of situations.

The certainty that someone inside was at it always sent panic through a gang because everyone was a dishonest bastard at heart. This resulted in Tonto having to work extra hard to convince the Graingers to give him a break. Their decision to add to all his financial problems by taxing him meant he had to work harder than ever, which was why he ended up selling on the side to people like Pete the Pole. In fact, the tax meant he was earning hee-haw from any work he was doing for the Graingers and so it became almost impossible for him to keep ahead of his debts.

Tonto's first couple of deliveries to the Pole had gone okay because the mad bastard had taken his medication. But on the third visit the crazy fuck was off his tits, sitting in a darkened room because he'd smashed everything up, including the light fittings. He badly wanted to hurt someone, so when Tonto came to the door for money the Pole didn't have, it just made his day, and what followed became a little bit of local history.

3

Tonto ignored the car horns and various threats from motorists burning their brakes to avoid him. As often as the Pole repeated his threat to slice him up, Tonto would say 'Oh God!' – as if the big man in the sky had any intention of helping him – or could hear him, for that matter. Unfortunately, his leg muscles were starting to burn, and what energy had been available in this young man whose main exercise of the day was pressing lift buttons was fast draining away. The Pole was gaining as Tonto gasped his way down Wheatfield Street towards the gates of Tynecastle Stadium, the hallowed or hated ground of Heart of Midlothian Football Club, depending on which side of the city you saw as yours. By luck, and certainly not by design, the Jambos were playing a midweek game in an hour and the few fans who had started to mill around the area took in the drama. Some were horrified; a couple of the more pished variety screamed encouragement to Tonto and the Pole.

'Ah hope the boy in the front's a Hibee!' was one of the more unsympathetic shouts, although Tonto wasn't taking it in. Instead, he was concentrating on the Police Scotland uniforms gathering at the main gate, who were thinking they were in for just another night as glorified doormen.

Tonto tried to scream for help, but nothing came out except a feeble 'Huuuph'. Sadly, the decibel level was way below what would have alerted the forces of law and order, who were probably his only chance of surviving.

Unfortunately for Tonto the two uniforms at the gate were probably the least likely in all of Police Scotland's ranks to give a Donald Duck what happened to him. The older of the two PCs was Billy Denholm, or FT as he was better known to his long-suffering colleagues. The handle 'FT' didn't come from a passion for following the business news in the *Financial Times* but from his attitude to every order or request he received. 'Fuck that' was his standard reply, sometimes under his breath, depending on the rank of the officer giving it out. In a way, it summed up his whole wasted life. He was one of those characters who'd made an art form out of avoiding work and yet talked himself up as Edinburgh's version of Taggart. Those stories were strictly for his civilian friends because the job knew exactly what he was made of.

The second and much younger cop idolised FT, thought that his teachings were gospel and was busy morphing from a promising recruit to someone who just carried a uniform. It wasn't Tonto's day, and there was worse to come.

The potentially violent drama moving quickly towards the stadium gates seemed to create an invisible shock wave that raced ahead, rippling over the alarm senses of the early-bird fans, a few locals and the polis. Many of them felt it before they saw it: the change in noise level some distance from them as jaws collectively dropped and a hundred conversations stopped mid-sentence. Some people froze at the passing drama, transfixed not so much by Tonto sprinting in a way unique to the hunted animal but by the shiny axe that every cell in the fleeing man's body was trying to avoid.

The sight of the Pole, almost naked apart from his Mickey Mouse boxers, would have been comical had he not intended to spill his target's brains all over the outer perimeter of Tynecastle Stadium. No one really noticed the pants, but a neutral and safe observer would have been interested in the varying reactions of the dozens of witnesses ahead of and behind the two men, who were now no more than five metres apart and closing. Some people turned into living statues: one man had a handful of greasy chips halfway to his gob and stayed like that for almost twenty seconds till his brain switched on again. There were people who dived for cover as a natural reaction to danger, and there were a few mercenary characters who saw an opportunity when it came their way. They whipped out their iPhones to capture an incident that would tickle their pals on social media and might even bring in a few bob from one of the news outlets. The ones that started videoing were in for a real treat, because no sooner had Constable Denholm sensed then identified the fast-approaching horror story than he made the decision that a tactical withdrawal was in his best interests.

Denholm didn't wait for his young partner. For someone at least a couple of stone overweight and whose idea of aerobic exercise was walking to the boozer rather than getting a bus, he took off with remarkable pace, yelling, 'Get tae fuck,' as he went.

Tonto couldn't believe what he was seeing. For a moment, the sight of the uniforms was like all his best Christmases rolled into one, and then it became an unfolding nightmare as one of them took off along Wheatfield Place, thirty metres ahead of him. His heart, which was under near-critical strain, sank a little further as the younger of the two uniforms stared at him and they made eye contact for the briefest of moments. Tonto believed, because he had to, that this fit-looking young guy with shoulders like a middleweight boxer was his last remaining hope. His legs felt as if molten lead was pouring through his veins and he knew that he was slowing, in contrast to the madness that consumed the Pole and drove him on like an Audi TT on rocket fuel.

He was closing on the young policeman and rescue when he realised that the cop had been swivelling his head from Pete the Pole to the escaping arse of his supposed partner, who hadn't taken a moment to worry about his health and safety. A couple of the witnesses who were nearby would later testify that the young cop mimicked Denholm's favourite catchphrase 'Fuck that' in a loud voice before taking off and pounding away in the same direction as his mentor.

The witnesses, and especially those with their iPhones running, knew they were onto gold dust – if they could take pictures of fleeing cops plus the mad bastard axing the boy he was after then there was pay dirt at the end of it.

Tonto made something like an agonised groan as he swerved left into Wheatfield Place, well behind the young cop and a long way behind his partner. He tried to pump some energy into his engine, but he was failing, and he heard the sound of the Pole's feet hitting the street with an almost rhythmic beat. The Pole knew all he had to do was wait till his quarry ran out of juice – then it was time for some open-skull surgery.

It was as if white noise was drowning out Tonto's hearing, but just above the roar he could hear some drunken twat shouting, 'Gon yersel', big man.' He realised the Jambo bastard was encouraging the Pole. Tonto had been a diehard Hearts man since he was old enough to hurl abuse at the Hibees and here was a maroon brother encouraging his annihilation!

If he'd been able to stop long enough for breath he'd have lamped the bastard in the nuts, but that wasn't going to happen. He could actually hear the Pole's lungs pumping oxygen round his body like an Olympic sprinter, and he was so close that Tonto finally accepted he was about to die. He'd always been convinced that he carried bad luck about with him like a physical blemish. Other people saw it too and it was a regular piss-take. Much as he laughed it off, in his heart he believed it, and that he was cursed in some way.

The moment arrived as it always does, when enough is enough and it's just better to get it over with than draw out the agony of waiting for the red card. Time to switch off, lie down and in a few moments the pain would be over.

He let his body turn to loose jelly just as a trailing foot hit the edge of one of the old cobbles and he sprawled onto the deck like a drunk. The Pole was ready to strike, but Tonto's collapse meant he was actually too close and he had to jump over the groaning figure on the deck to put the brakes on. He turned, grinned and showed the space where his two front teeth had been removed over a drugs debt.

Tonto looked up and somehow found the strength to say, 'Please ... ' as he squeezed his eyes up into knots, waiting for the first blow. Remarkably, that moment of delay he'd caused by collapsing saved his life. He'd got lucky at last, although he would never see it that way.

The Pole took another moment to consider which part of his victim to bury the axe in and two dozen iPhones zoomed in on the action.

'Armed police!' It was said loud and clear. The Pole hadn't even heard the police personnel carrier arrive with an armed response team. He'd been enjoying it all just too much.

The watching film-makers groaned almost in unison

and hoped that at least if the mad bastard didn't do the boy on the floor then the polis would riddle the axeman.

'Fack yo!' The Pole gobbed a greaser in the general direction of the police team pointing an array of firepower at his torso. The guns never wavered and the Pole spat on Tonto just as he raised his head again and the mess ran down his forehead into his eyes. It didn't matter; it seemed like he was going to survive. He looked round at the marksmen and had never been so happy to see the law in his puff.

The Pole decided that he wasn't going to die that day and threw the axe to the side. He knew the drill, stuck his hands up and, staring at the cops, got down slowly, first onto his knees, then his belly. He rested the side of his head on the cold surface of the road no more than four feet from Tonto. He grinned all the way from one ear to the other.

'I come back and fackin' kill you someday.' He looked like he meant it, and Tonto grinned in return because he was going to live.

'It'll be a fuckin' while, son.' But Tonto's problem was that he could never see that far ahead. He should have realised that there was more bad luck waiting in the shape of an ounce of high-quality Charlie in his left-hand jacket pocket.

The firearms team were all over the Pole and it turned out that although the two uniformed officers at the gates had legged it, there were a couple of concerned citizens who'd called in the incident while Tonto was still being chased along Gorgie Road. He had two slices of luck because the firearms team were close and just happened to be travelling through the area when the call came in. There was more to it than that, but a little player like him never saw the big picture till it fell on his napper like seagull shite.

4

'Yer a lucky wee bastard, Tonto. Never thought I'd say that.' One of the firearms men knew him from his days on the beat in the West End.

Tonto hated his nickname and would normally have kicked off if anyone called him it to his face, but today the polis were his saviours, so he definitely did not want to fuck them around – not for the time being anyway. He still had that rush of elation that follows a near-death experience; he was flying and even liked the polis at that precise moment. The medics had given him a hot, sweet tea and it looked like spring had arrived early. Tonto had never really thought about the natural world apart from his nights with his ex-burd Chantelle, who he always said was the closest thing to a dog walking on two legs. He told that joke over and over till Chantelle's old man heard about it and punched his pus in.

He was in a nice moment, drinking the tea and realising that he was still alive, back from the dead even, and as he looked up at the sky, Tonto seemed to be seeing his environment for the first time. The weather had been freezing the country's balls off for months, but today

17

the sun had been showing its face and there was still warmth in its early-evening glow. It was as if nature was trying to make up for the overlong pish winter. Shafts of almost copper-coloured light split by small, harmless altocumulus clouds looked like great spotlights, and after the terror of the chase the world was back at peace. He smiled almost dreamily at the nearest firearms cop, who sneered back, frustrated as he always was that he hadn't been able to shoot someone at last.

'What happens now, Officer?' Tonto had never called a lawman officer in his puff, but given how he felt, it was time to show a little respect after hating the bastards all his life. It was a moment and a half, but as his survival instinct began beating its way back to life, he realised he'd been chummy with them long enough and wanted to get the fuck away from the uniforms.

'Tell you what happens, Tonto. You're all mine, pal.'

The sound of the female voice behind him drew his attention – the phrase 'you're all mine' when there was law about usually meant trouble. He swivelled round and faced Detective Inspector Janet Hadden.

'Who the fuck are you then, hen?' He was looking straight into the steel-grey eyes of a woman who on any other day would have pushed a lot of the right buttons for him. Unfortunately, he might have been better trying to outrun the mad fucking Pole.

5

DI Hadden was regarded in the job as a cold fish but supremely efficient at getting results. 'Cold' didn't quite hit the accurate temperature description where she was concerned, and she was known as the Ice Queen for good reason. She just didn't mix well; in fact, she didn't deign to mix because she despised people – both men and women, but particularly other women. She turned up at the odd piss-up for appearances' sake; that is, to counteract the almost inevitable view in the police culture that a single woman avoiding social contact could mean only one thing: she was a lesbian. Like everything about her, there was the legend and then the reality. The truth was that sex meant nothing to her, and certainly not as something that would be part of an emotional relationship. She'd only had a few brief encounters: one with an influential female boss that confirmed her promotion to sergeant then inspector. When the same boss realised Hadden had played her like a child, she cut off all contact. She had to keep it quiet because Hadden knew too much and had sucked out every little dark secret she'd kept well away from her professional reputation.

The others were different and a bit off the wall. A couple of times she'd changed her appearance as much as she could, jumped on a train to Glasgow and trawled the bars for the wrong kind of guys: gangsters. Although she'd only managed it a couple of times, they'd been the real deal, and she'd even recognised one of them from criminal intelligence bulletins she'd read. They were crude, foul-mouthed and only wanted a short, absolutely meaningless relationship – and they got it. The thrill of risking her career and her own safety made her feel alive. The sex didn't worry her because she felt nothing.

One of the men was still so pissed in the morning that she'd even dipped his wallet and taken his mobile phone before heading back to Queen Street station, grinning all the way. She'd extracted some top-class intelligence from the phone and claimed it had come from one of her sources. It helped develop the reputation that she might be cold but by God was she fucking efficient.

Becoming a bent bastard hadn't happened overnight, but eventually it seemed to become the only logical option that could work for her career prospects. She'd looked at so many of her colleagues and seen them as nothing more than pre-programmed robots who'd complete their service, work in some pish job for a few years, then die. Life was meaningless without risk and she'd had to find other ways to feel that she existed at all. Danger and risk were vital.

Having tried every extreme sport there is, Hadden discovered that after the first thrill of jumping out of an aeroplane or diving among sharks there was nothing. It had become harder and harder to trigger the adrenalin rush that made it all worthwhile; so, slowly, corruption had replaced the legitimate sports and become the oxygen she needed to live. It was all she had left and she'd decided that it wasn't monetary gain that was important, only how it could propel her to the top.

There was success, no doubt, but her lack of empathy had caused her a problem she just hadn't planned for: despite the benefits from the encounter that had resulted in her first couple of promotions, she just couldn't win over her bosses. A subliminal message had flickered around the force and however hard she tried, she simply couldn't overcome other people's natural instincts. No one could point the finger at hard evidence, and, particularly in such a politically correct age, she was safe but stuck. Realising this, she decided she needed to cut a new path to the top. She engineered a sideways move to the source-handling unit and was determined to recruit gold-plated informants who would give her career the lift-off she craved. It hurt like fuck that she was surrounded by so many incompetents and someone like her was stuck at the inspector rank. She watched the self-satisfied looks of the men and women who had been the promotion opposition till they ran past her at speed. She could have killed them for those expressions that said 'look at me' every time she passed them in a station and they expected her to say 'sir' or 'ma'am' just for the privilege of being in their presence.

At night in her flat she would stare at the spectacular view across the Forth and grind her teeth at the injustice of it all. She had the plan – all she had to do was make it happen.

Sometimes in the night she would wake, frightened, dribbles of sweat trailing down between her shoulder blades. It was the same dream over and over again: she stood on cliffs that were so high she could hardly see the waves crashing over the rocks in a fog of chaotic spray. She was wearing a chief's uniform and regalia, but they were no more than rags almost devoid of colour. On the horizon, there was a line of fire and in the dream she imagined that she was the only person left alive after some great event. She looked over her shoulder and it was as if there was nothing but a black wall behind her, stretching all the way into the far distance. She was on an immense stage, then she felt the cliff giving way below her and she would scream as she fell, even though no one was listening.

6

'Anyone searched this man?' Hadden barked towards the firearms team.

The lead officer told her they'd done a rough pat for concealed weapons; he didn't want to get it wrong with this woman, but the search had been cursory, probably too fucking cursory. Fortunately for him, it suited her purposes, although she couldn't actually say that. The fact that Tonto was being chased, and therefore the victim, didn't mean he wasn't carrying something he shouldn't have in his possession. He was a ned being chased by a ned and that was the point.

Tonto felt reality cramp his stomach and suddenly his bladder decided it was about to explode. He wondered how that had happened; he hadn't worked out that fear had just kicked him in the goolies. The high had peaked, stalled for a few minutes then he nosedived back into the real world, and although he didn't mean to, he pissed himself. In the cooling shadows of the stadium his groin area steamed like an old coffee machine just to complete his humiliation. The firearms team variously screwed up their faces or guffawed, but Hadden stared straight at him and was pleased with the result. A ned wetting himself in public didn't make her laugh or wince – it was just a positive result as far as she was concerned. It meant he was scared, and scared was good. The realisation that a substantial bag of Charlie stuck down his pants might be about to come into the light had clearly added an unsustainable pressure on his bladder.

'Any chance of a toilet break, chief?' Tonto directed his words towards the firearms officer who'd wanted to shoot him a few minutes earlier and was bored now. Even though the bastard looked disappointed for some reason, he thought he might have more joy than with the female pig who'd dropped into the scene.

'A bit fuckin' late, Tonto.' The firearms officer sneered at his humiliation but secretly loved witnessing it.

'I'll tell you when you get a break, Davy. I'll tell you exactly what to do and when to do it.' Hadden walked as close as she could get without it being indecent and stared hard into his eyes.

Tonto felt like a child and it was as if he was being assaulted. He tried to take a step back, but the bitch had her front foot just behind his heel, so as soon as he moved, he landed on his arse and the pain of hitting the cobbles on his tail took all his breath away. 'What the fuck?' It was all he could say, but he knew that what had started off as a normal day, became a terrifying day and then a joyous one had all turned to rat shit – in other words, back to normal. He knew the drill and what was coming next.

Hadden stared down at him and showed him her perfect teeth, but it wasn't a smile. It was a predator baring its fangs just before it ripped half your arse off for dinner. She nodded to a couple of the uniforms. 'Get a towel and put it under his arse in my car. I want a word with him.'

They stuck him in the back of Hadden's unmarked wheels and she slipped into the front seat and adjusted the rear-view mirror so she could talk without turning her head. He saw her eyes lock on to his before she spoke. Her nose wrinkled for a moment at the stink from his soaking trousers, but she was made of hard material, and that was no more than a moment. She wanted something and that was all that mattered.

'You're carrying, Davy. Now don't fuck around or try and stick it down the back of the seat or, I promise you, it's the pokey and no favours. If you want, I'll get a couple of those hairy-arsed gunfighters to come and do it the hard way. Or, of course, you can just hand it over and save all this nonsense.' Hadden said it in the way that only someone who knew she was right could have done.

'So some bastard grassed me up then?' Tonto knew when the game was a bogey, stuck his hand under his belt into his wet briefs, extracted the bag and offered it to Hadden. She turned and did the teeth thing again, pulled on a rubber glove and held it up between them.

'We've been followin' you, Davy. You're fucked, and I'd say there's a few years in Saughton coming with the contents of that bag plus your previous.'

He thought about the last time he was inside and the time before that. It was fucking horrible; it terrified him. Those endless nights, the low-level noise of suffering from every cell and the nightmares shared by them all, punctuated by the occasional scream from someone's dream terrors. Added to which there was the fucking noise people made to kill the endless boredom. Men who stared at him, hardly seeming to blink, so strong were the feelings that stirred them. Long-term prisoners deprived of the scent and touch of a woman realising that in their isolation they were attracted to other men. It came as a shock to some and a revelation to others.

Hadden broke the distraction of his memories. She opened her window and called to a couple of bored uniforms, 'Get him locked up and I'll see him at the factory.' They seemed happy to oblige and pulled him out of the car as if he'd been accused of murder instead of being the victim of the drama such a short time earlier. As they walked him towards a van, Tonto turned and stared at Hadden, and wondered why he had started shivering.

7

Tonto clasped his hands together over the table and looked around every few seconds as if something would change in the almost-bare, windowless interview room. He'd been in plenty of these soulless boxes in his time and usually he just took it on the chin, said hee-haw and did his time. He was brought up to say nothing to the law, and the offers he'd had in the past for a deal if he grassed up a few people were met with a deafie.

But each time he went inside it just got harder and harder. The days behind the doors were like a lingering death, especially on that last stretch where his co-pilot had been a manky bastard; just remembering the guy made him want to spew his ring up. He tried to block out the memories of what the perv had wanted and tried to do to him night after night. The perv was what he was, though, and to make it worse he was a strong, violent man who could take the likes of Tonto with an arm tied up. Eventually the screws had him moved, but the prison nightmares were locked into his brain and erupted every so often.

He'd lost something of his youthful self, who at one

time had almost looked forward to the inevitable stretch inside as if it was just a holiday minus the bevvy and a bit of female company. Young as he still was, his old, ever-optimistic nature was gone already and it was frightening. He spent more time staring at the broken old men in the bars who'd been just like him, and he realised the future wasn't as far off as he'd imagined only a few years earlier. The time inside had aged him, maybe not in his body but in his mind, which was full of doubt, and no matter what he did there he had an underlying suspicion that there was no happy ending for him. The brash teenager who had just wanted to get a name on the street was gone and the thought of prison was like something that was forever on the horizon. He was a criminal, so he knew almost everything he did to make a living might again lead him through those gates that crashed behind you every time you moved from section to section.

'Are you fucking listening?'

The sound of Hadden's voice snapped his attention back into place and he caught her eyes again. The woman scared him and he couldn't figure out why. He'd never been afraid of a woman before and he'd met a few radge females in his time. Hadden was something else: she looked like she was carved out of some sub-zero material; even her skin looked chilled and white in the harsh light of the interview room. He was sure she could see right inside his napper and examine all those little dark places he kept to himself.

'We've been on your arse for a while, Davy, and you're so thick you never saw a thing.'

Hadden opened a packet of chewing gum and unwrapped a piece, taking a moment to let the words sink in nice and slow. She left the implications for a bit and let them ferment – he'd worry about the mistakes, what they might have seen and heard. She knew letting his imagination run riot was all in her favour; stoking up paranoia and letting it do the job for her was one of her favourite tactics. She leaned forward and he recoiled as if she was about to stab him or draw back her lips to expose a couple of vampire fangs.

'That's fuckin' out of order, by the way.' He tried a bit of defence, but his voice let him down. The tone was too high and the warble of fear gave the show away. Tonto was shitting bricks, and trying to mount a counter-attack had only exposed his anxiety and hopeless position. The older and wiser neds always said to keep it shut, because once you'd opened your gob, the bizzies would stick their arm in and pull out your guts.

'Look, Davy. You see a recorder in here or anyone else but me?' She was leading him to the slaughter, and he was following her every time she tugged the rope.

'Well, no. What's the score then?' His eyes widened as the bait dangled just in front of him.

That was exactly what she wanted to hear. She'd shown him the tiniest glimmer of light and he was blinded by it. The man was a fucking cretin and she wanted to smile, but it wasn't time yet.

'You had enough dope on you to put you to the High Court. Correct?' She waited – watched him open his mouth slowly and start to nibble at the bait.

He nodded a couple of times as if he had no choice. 'Aye. Fair dos.' He was a man looking for a break and she played with him like a cat with a three-legged mouse.

'Well, I want something, and to be honest I can live without sticking you in the pokey. In other words, Davy, I can make this go away.' She sat back again, letting the words ferment.

In the past this would have been the point where Tonto would have said, 'No fuckin' way am I grassin',' but that had been in a different life before those nights in the cell with the perv. He knew what was coming and the combination of prison memories and this woman fucking with his brain was just too much. Tonto sat up and swallowed the bait whole, almost begging for more of the same.

'Okay, what's the Hampden then?' He opened his mouth and eyelids at the same time, and she saw the non-verbals were flashing green and all good to go.

'You work for the Grainger boys. Correct?' There was no point in using their Christian names because they both knew who she was speaking about. 'Now they interest me. So basically, Davy, you sign on with me, I keep you nice and safe and all I want to know is what the boys are up to. Added bonus is there's no risk. Don't want you to be in danger or anything else. Just be my eyes and ears and I'll take them out another way.' She kept it slow and easy, left little quiet breaks in the offer, let him think, avoid panic. She leaned forward and acted out a friendly smile. 'It's a good offer, Davy, and you get paid decent money.' She waited again and watched him swallow the bait camouflaging a great big poisonous hook.

'They'll cut ma baws off if it goes tits up.' He looked beaten. It was the old dilemma of 'do you want shot in the left arse cheek or the right one?' Fucked if you do and fucked if you don't. 'What happens next then?'

'Tell the truth, Davy, it's Dominic I want. But the younger brothers will do as well.' She smiled but injected some warmth this time to kid him on they might become friends.

'I've got fuck all goin' wi' Dominic. He's the big man. Disnae get his hands durty. Know what I mean? I only work wi' the brothers. The story is that Dom runs the show but well back. Know what I mean?'

Hadden reeled him in and gutted him. The cocaine would go into the private stash she kept well hidden for a rainy day or in case she needed to fit someone up. It had all come together nicely.

Tonto shook his head a few times, but he kept reminding himself that at least he didn't have to go back behind those doors. The Pole was dubbed up; Hadden promised him that the mad bastard wouldn't see the light of day for years. In any case, he'd likely end up in Carstairs with a bit of luck and would probably spend his days assaulting staff and adding to his time. He was that kind of turbo-charged bampot who acted regardless of the consequences; a kind of Polish Charles Bronson with a dash of Scots senseless violence thrown in.

Tonto walked out of the station a few hours later and headed for the boozer. His shoulders slumped and he stared at the pavement a few feet in front of him all the way to the bar, where he ordered his first drink, promising himself that he'd get wrecked before heading to the rat box he called home. He'd been mesmerised by the process of becoming a covert human intelligence source or CHIS. Hadden had called in another bizzie and they did it all nice and official. She'd told him he was an agent, had explained how it would work and he'd felt like his world would never be the same again. And he was right.

Inside the station he'd just wanted to cooperate and get the fuck away, but as soon as he walked back into the cold night air it was as if someone had loaded a stone-filled rucksack onto his back. He'd signed on as a grass, and if he made the slightest mistake or said the wrong thing with a few drinks in him, he was dead meat. He'd seen what had happened to the odd rat in the past, and if the Graingers ever got to know then it was goodbye cruel world.

He stood in his usual spot in the boozer and realised that the Graingers would hear about the drama outside

Tynecastle and want to know what had happened in the station. Christ, the whole fucking world would know what had happened with the bizzies who'd deserted their post then the gunfighters arriving on the scene like the cavalry. He looked up at the telly, gulping his beer, and the next thing he was snorting it through his nose when he saw the Sky News clip of the first cop belting away from the scene.

'Fuck's sake, Davy, are you pished?' The barman looked annoyed and with good reason because what had sprayed through Tonto's nasal passages had splattered the bar. He hadn't paid attention to the news clip and hadn't yet realised that Tonto had been part of the chaos outside Tynecastle.

'Sorry, pal. Bit of a heid cauld.' It was all he could think of and would do for the time being.

He guessed that his name wouldn't come out in the press just yet, but the grapevine would provide the story to the streets so the Graingers would find out. He knew the cops who'd been there would blab as soon as they hit the boozers because it was a great story. That was fair enough – he was the one being chased, but the Graingers would know he was delivering gear, so the first question they'd ask was: where the fuck was the dope they'd supplied him with?

The next question they'd ask was: if the pigs had hold of him, did they find the gear, and if they did then why the fuck was he not on a lie down?

The only thing he could say was that he'd dumped it when the cavalry arrived on the scene and it was gone when he went back to look for it. It might work, but he knew exactly what Sean and Paul Grainger would say before they even opened their gobs. They acted like they were the Krays, and if it hadn't been for Dominic they would have run out of control years ago.

The trouble was that Dominic stayed well away from the limelight. The younger brothers would demand payment regardless, and up the tax he was already struggling to pay. That was if he was lucky – because if losing the first stash was bad enough, losing a second was trouble.

The way things worked in crime-land, even if they couldn't prove something, it would annoy them, and anything else that went wrong would be his fault, even if he was in Magaluf when it happened. There wouldn't be a third chance if he survived this, because that was way too generous in his world. Gangsters always needed someone to blame. It was a funny old day, but a drink had to come first and he had to work hard to numb his worries for a few hours. He gave it his best shot and wired right into the bevvy.

8

Grace Macallan stared out of the boozer window in Stockbridge, not far from her office on the second floor of the old Lothian and Borders Police HQ in Fettes Avenue. The architecture of the old building looked uninspiring, especially as it sat almost in the shadow of the splendid Fettes College, which represented the dreams of men who saw a different future for Scotland. Fettes, as the former HQ had always been known, had changed from being the epicentre of sometimes frantic activity to just another office in the national police service, or Police Scotland, which the cynics claimed was just a disguised takeover by dark forces in Weegie land. The transformation had been so complete that it was as if the building was a relic of a time that had already long gone.

The world was changing too fast now; the daily bulletins on war and the sea of human tragedy heading to Europe made Macallan worry about her own children, who were growing up too fast. When she was in her office, she would stare across the playing fields and the school opposite, remembering those first days after she'd arrived, almost broken from her experience in Northern

Ireland. Her old life during the Troubles seemed like an experience that belonged to someone else, and in a way, that was true. The woman who'd fought PIRA, and sometimes her own side, was a person she thought about less and less. That soul was a lonely character who'd thought that the job mattered more than her sanity. Skirting alcoholism at times and torn apart by betrayal in her personal and professional life, she'd rebuilt her world in Edinburgh. Married to a man she'd forgiven and mother of two children, she now had a life she wanted. Even though her demons came back from time to time, she could face them, understand why they were there, and she knew she was a match for them because there were other people in her life who mattered more than those fading nightmares.

'Cheer up, Grace. I mean, you could be a Rangers supporter and then you'd be entitled to be depressed!' Mick Harkins liked to talk football to Macallan just to wind her up, because he knew she wasn't interested. She was having her monthly meet with her old friend and ex-colleague. It had become a form of therapy over the years, and it was easy to unload to the man who'd become her confessor.

Harkins hadn't exactly left the force covered in glory, but his sins hadn't resulted in charges, and he was regarded in the force as like an old Rottweiler who still looked scary but had lost its teeth and couldn't really do much harm to them now. That wasn't an accurate summation of the man; Harkins kept his ears to the ground and, like most old detectives, he would never really retire. He'd spent a lifetime nosing into other people's sins and it was too hard to give up.

Grace had stayed faithful to him; he was one of the few people she could really unload on, and it was simple: he cared about her. He was probably one of the few real friends she'd ever had. They couldn't have explained it to anyone else, but it didn't matter – it was what it was. The real compliment was that neither of them could really imagine that only a few years before they hadn't even known each other. Grace had arrived after being driven out of the PSNI following a death in custody. She was almost broken by the events in Northern Ireland and the dark memories of the Troubles. She had been Mick's boss when she was given the Major Crime Team, and he had looked after her. He was pensioned out after almost being killed and narrowly avoided being charged with corruption. But it wasn't brown envelopes that had been the problem. Mick Harkins had operated under the principle of noble cause and had decided early in his career that the law often didn't provide justice – so he applied his own interpretation of the concept.

'Sorry, Mick. Just this world at the moment. I worry about the kids and what's going to happen to them and their children.'

'You always think too much. People have been worrying about the same thing since Adam told Eve to put some clothes on. Come on – drink up.'

He tilted his beer and smacked his lips after it, as he always did with his first pint. Although he'd slowed up over the years, he still took more than the average man. The main difference was that almost every morning now he woke up and knew what he'd done the night before, which he should have regarded as progress. It might have been for his partner but, perhaps perversely, Harkins missed those days with the inevitable morning hangover and its cure, which had always been a bacon roll with enough brown sauce to drown him. Most of his progress was due to his relationship with Felicity Young, a senior analyst with Police Scotland who had worked for Grace in the past, as well as now in her new role in counter-corruption.

'I'm just going to do another few years then it's done with. The kids are growing so fast it scares me. I feel as if they'll be in school then grown up and I won't have spent much time with them. I haven't got enough service in for a full pension, but Jack's doing really well with the books. Can you imagine that?' She cheered up as her mind drifted away from the world and she realised it wasn't fair just to sit and bleat to Harkins, who never really worried about the big events. His world was limited to his passions of crime, beer, football and, although he would never say it publicly, Young, who he was certain had kept him from an early appointment with the Co-op undertakers.

'You know what, Grace, you've nothing to prove now, so stop worrying about all the problems in the world and concentrate on the positives. Christ, when the time comes you can live where you want and do something new. So ... forget the worries and get the drinks in. It's your round as usual.'

'Okay, no more woes, but I don't really want that much in life. I'm happiest in the house in Northern Ireland. That's where we're at home and I think we'll just settle there when I go. I love it here in Edinburgh and think we can keep both homes, so all I have to give up is the job. That's it. Now tell me a story, one from those days.'

He lifted his glass and made one up. It was absolute cobblers, but she loved it and sat with her mouth slightly open like a child listening to – and believing – a fairy story.

9

Janet Hadden was pleased with the way things were going. She'd identified Tonto weeks before as the wanker she needed to get a closer look at the inside of the Graingers' team and what they were up to. If she could report on a top and growing team then it would push her profile up where she wanted to be. The Pole chasing Tonto had been a nice bit of divine intervention. He was reporting back already only a couple of weeks after she'd signed him up and arranged his first payment. The younger Graingers had given him a hard time, and at one point he was convinced they were going to cut him up when a knife had been produced. But in the end, they'd only slapped him around a bit and dropped a new and heavier tax on him, which meant he was in one piece and still in the game, but had run out of lives.

Tonto looked at the money Hadden had given him with disbelief: it was the easiest he'd ever made and for almost no effort. He just filled in who all the players were in the Graingers' outfit and the names of a couple of third-division dealers who sourced their gear from the team. Hadden told him they'd do a bit of work on the dealers and if they took them out, there would be a nice bonus for him.

Tonto hadn't worked out that Hadden was just using him as a disposable pawn in her game of chess. He never understood that every time he handed over information a rope tightened around his skinny little neck. Quite the reverse. Hadden had explained to him that he was an agent for the police, and while at first he felt like he'd stepped in dog shit and had betrayed just about the only code he'd ever followed in his life – *don't talk to the law* – gradually his imagination started to run ahead of reality and he began to like the term 'agent'. It felt dangerous – on the edge – and brought in some decent cash, and he was actually starting to enjoy the new life. It felt like he meant something, and when Hadden saw what was happening she exploited every moment of his self-delusion.

Dominic Grainger was her real target. He was the man who knew everyone from the right side of the law in his business dealings and the wrong side of the law from his other career, existing in that amorphous area in the middle: that dark place where there was no clarity in what was legal or illegal, where smart men made fortunes and stuck the single finger up to anyone who questioned the morality of what they did. Hadden knew if there was some way to recruit Dominic Grainger as a CHIS then she was back in the game. That would be the real prize. She couldn't be arsed pissing around with little rats like the Tontos of this world. He had his purpose and could feed them decent stuff that would get a few dealers and couriers jailed, but it was mere bread and butter. Dominic Grainger, well, he was in Barcelona's first eleven.

She'd checked and found he wasn't registered to anyone else as an informant, and as far as she knew no one had tried, so no problems there. It was obvious what her pitch had to be – if he wanted to maintain his position as a real operator, he would need to get some friendly law on his side. The players with longevity knew there had to be a bit of quid pro quo to let them spend every Christmas at home.

She knew enough about him to know he was a smart guy and she wondered why he hadn't taken out some Police Scotland insurance already. She knew that the Graingers had taken a hit when their second haul of drugs was found. Tonto's had been intentional but the second was pure luck, although the gangsters had no way of knowing that. Criminals always suspected a rat first, and they had to because most of the time it was the truth. Tonto was just someone who could confirm and add to a lot of the intelligence they had that needed hardening up. Plus, he could toss them a few arrests along the way and that always cheered up the figures, which kept the bean counters happy for a while.

Hadden had manufactured the loss of Tonto's stash during the surveillance she'd been running on him. It had been her intention to keep him under observation for a while before she went for recruitment, and these operations always threw up useful tools to use against the target. Sometimes there was a real bonus where they identified criminal activity, which was exactly what had happened with McGill. The team watching him were sure they'd identified his drugs stash and where it was at his mother's house. The problem for Hadden was that if it was taken out by the surveillance team then there was no choice but to lock up Tonto and that would fuck up her plan. Her solution was to get hold of a useless small-time dealer she was running, tell him exactly where Tonto's gear was and let him know he was free to raid it.

'You've done the business for us, so this is a little bonus,' she'd told the dealer, who was only too happy to fill his boots – stealing from other dealers was like skinning a few notes off the Revenue for a straight peg. Absolutely fine if you could get away with it.

Hadden knew that if Tonto lost the gear he was supposed to be holding for the Graingers it would put him in a hard place and they would at least suspect he might be the grass for the other loss. The dealer showed his appreciation the same night by emptying Tonto's hide. It was more than he'd ever had his hands on, all gratis, and it was done and dusted without a hitch – even the next-door neighbour's Alsatian had slept through the theft.

Hadden was beginning to think the gods were definitely on her side as each time she made a move, it worked perfectly. There was, nevertheless, always a worry if it was all too smooth, because that just wasn't how investigation, or in her case corruption, worked. There was always a problem; something inevitably went wrong when you were in the game and the winner was always the best prepared when that inevitable crisis occurred.

She relaxed a bit when she read the latest report from the financial team she had looking at Dominic Grainger to see what he was worth, and, more importantly, where his money was going. It looked like he was shuffling cash all over the place and what surprised her was that it had become just a bit too obvious for a smart operator. It had the smell of problems, and if so then that was a bonus.

The stink in her nose suggested that he might be trying to cope with debt of some kind. She'd seen it all before, on the surface all chrome and glitz but underneath just another pile of crap. Some of the biggest financial institutions in the world had crumbled during the crash so why not Dominic Grainger? But if there was a problem, what was it? There wasn't enough for a case – just suspicion – but that would do for what she had in mind.

Joe Public imagined that informants were all criminals who had to talk, but the source units had their mitts on people in all walks of society, including a lot of professional men and women. The financial boys had already identified a crooked accountant who was doing some work for Grainger, and the gods just kept on smiling, because he was a CHIS who'd been on the books for years, since he'd been spared the ignominy of appearing in court for ripping off an eighty-year-old widow. He had been given the choice of signing on or going to prison and taking his chances surviving his sentence in a world he was never equipped for. He made a wise decision, and because he was in the habit of taking on work for some of Scotland's premier villains, he was an extremely useful source. His wasn't used too often in case his cover was blown; they didn't want to find him floating in his own blood. His clients were like that when things went wrong.

Despite not knowing him, Hadden made the approach to the accountant, who hadn't spoken to a police handler for a while and was naively hoping they might have forgotten him. His life was back on track, the debts that had nearly led to his ruin had been paid off and his wife had forgiven him and come back into his life.

When Hadden sat down opposite him, he felt the nerves ripple through the length of his body; he just didn't want to be involved again, and when she told him it was Dominic Grainger she was interested in, he decided enough was enough. Only in his mid-fifties but a bit old-fashioned in his thinking, the man hadn't quite moved into the twenty-first century and the new order of things. He was the son of a respected QC who had given him the gift of the best education only to end up disappointed in the final product. Nevertheless, the accountant carried all his father's ancient prejudices – and two of them were sitting opposite him in the form of DI Janet

Hadden. First of all, she was a woman, whose place was at home as far as he was concerned, and secondly, she was a police officer, which meant she was probably a bit thick. The officers who'd threatened him and signed him on originally were thugs and had frightened him, but life had moved on and he wasn't having it.

'I'm very sorry, Officer Haddock, but—'

She knew where this was going and grinned as she stuck her palm up to stop him mid-sentence.

'The name's Hadden and it's in your best interests to remember it from now on.' She paused for effect, lowered her hand and gave him the reptile grin that said *do not fuck with me*, then when she saw his Adam's apple bounce a couple of times, she continued, 'Carry on, please – I'm enjoying this.'

He struggled for a reply but decided to try taking control one more time, because this wasn't going to plan. 'Look, I have a different life now. I've helped you people enough and I want nothing further to do with the police. So please go and get your information somewhere else.' He sat back, feeling rather pleased at the way he'd recovered the situation, until something in Hadden's rictus seemed to freeze his balls and he squirmed in his chair because he knew she wasn't going to turn and run.

She leaned forward, resting her forearms on the desk while she considered the accountant as if he was a minor problem, no more significant than an annoying piece of lint on her coat: should she swipe it or pick it off?

'You just don't get it, my friend, do you?' She pulled out a piece of chewing gum, pushed it into her mouth and sighed as if a child had just tested her patience. 'If I go away from here empty-handed, I'm going to dig into what Dominic's been up to. If I find you've had any hand in, erm, let's say washing his money, then I'll come back with a couple of hairy-arsed detectives and strip this place back to the bare wood. At which point you go straight to the pokey and no fucking deals this time. I'll make it my business to ruin you. Then when the judge passes sentence, I'll get in touch with a few of the bams you've helped us put away over the years and see if they want to share a cell with you.'

She took the gum out of her mouth. 'I only like it when you get the sweet taste.'

She rolled it a few times between her fingers and stuck it under the rim of his solid-oak antique desk. 'No one'll see it there.'

She winked and bared the death grin to frighten him even more. 'You choose. Personally, I don't give a shit, because I hate accountants.'

She sat back, sighed again and looked at her watch for a moment as if she was timing him.

'Oh, by the way. You're an intelligent man and should have realised that we gather new intelligence every day . . . and when it's someone like you, we don't forget. You have certain tastes when you're browsing.' She winked like a co-conspirator. 'Like them young, eh?'

As the nerves in his face began a chaotic twitching display, she paused, almost disappointed that it had been so easy to get the upper hand, then watched him slump back in his leather seat and shrink a couple of sizes.

The accountant rolled over like a puppy and admitted that he was doing the business for Grainger. He described to her how Dominic was skimming a lot of money from the business and said he was sure that the rest of the family didn't know. He'd realised from what he'd seen that Grainger had expensive tastes and, like the accountant, was shite when it came to gambling. His other problem was a taste for expensive women. He was paying heavy-duty rent for a piece of class property in the West End and, as a particular woman's name cropped

44

up in regular payments, he guessed she was part of his problems. From what he'd seen, it seemed most likely she was a high-end escort.

The accountant used to fantasise about being able to afford any woman he wanted, but he would never have that freedom of choice again. Even though all the things that used to give him pleasure and brought ruin were in the past, he sometimes wished he could do it all just once more. Nowadays, staring at his computer screen and watching the abuse of children was the only thing that he looked forward to for relief from his mundane existence.

It was just perfect. Hadden would have been prepared to just cold-call Dominic Grainger to see if they could turn him because sometimes that was all it took, even with the worst of them. But this was gravy – now she had something to pitch at him if he told her to 'get to Falkirk'.

When she walked out of the accountant's office, she turned her face up to the sky and felt cool droplets of rain wash over her face. Everything was beautiful and her plan gave her a thrill she felt nowhere else in her life.

She bought a paper and headed for George Street, where she planned to sit with a long cold drink and read the latest bad news about uncontrolled immigration and the Tories going for each other's throats over Europe. The bad news that disturbed the dreams of most citizens just fascinated her, and the depravity of the terrorists who dominated the news in their black balaclavas just made her curious. She felt no hatred towards them because, like her, they were just trying to make their mark on the world. She would relax for a couple of hours with a drink before heading for her apartment, where she would work out her approach to Dominic Grainger.

She was down to the sports pages when an expensively dressed type who was trying too hard to conceal his baldness sauntered over as if he was George Clooney himself and offered her a drink. The detective lifted her face towards him and gave him full eye contact without speaking. Hadden never spoke, just waited. Eventually his smile started to wobble and he was aware of the muscles in his face refusing control.

'Fucking weirdo.' It was all he could think of saying before he walked back to the bar and guffawed with his friends, who all looked like him, give or take the comb-over. She guessed they worked in finance from the stench of money on them and the way they acted. She wondered what the collective noun for arsehole was.

After another half hour, the nether of arseholes (she'd decided 'nether' worked as the collective word) were well pissed and she watched the big one who'd tried it on head for the bog downstairs. It was time to move; she picked up her things and pushed through the drinkers who'd reached that mid-evening noise level just short of collective shouting.

The man felt like his bladder was stretched to bursting point and sighed with relief when he played the stream around the urinal bowl. He was glad the bog was empty and he could enjoy that wonderful feeling of release.

His bladder was half-empty when Hadden kicked the back of his left knee. Losing his balance, he almost fell backwards, but his attacker had the collar of his jacket, and when she kicked the back of the other knee there was little resistance and he went down like a bag of shite because he was so pissed.

'What the . . . ?' was all he got out before she pushed his face forward with enough force to break his nose when he slammed into the bowl. He slid down onto the floor and forgot to stop pissing. A couple of minutes later one of his rat-arsed colleagues came into the bog and found him out for the count under the bloodstained urinal.

'Twat.' His drinking buddy had come into the lav to

try to ingratiate himself with the arsehole who happened to be his line manager. He couldn't stand the bastard, who loved to walk over everyone unfortunate enough to be on his team, and his mouth tightened with disgust at what he thought he saw – just another piss-head who'd fallen over.

Unfortunately, this piss-head had seniority, so he had to pretend to like him. He'd spent the night gritting his teeth at the man's loud-mouthing in the bar and felt nothing but contempt for him and the mess he'd made on the floor. Worse still, he asked himself whether he needed to help the fuckwit when what he really wanted to do was whack the guy in the balls just for good measure.

Still, every crisis throws up opportunities so, as at every modern-day incident, a camera phone was produced to record the details of the damage, which would go online the first chance he got. Well, it was just too good an opportunity.

He slipped back out of the toilet and left his unconscious boss where he was. When the ambulance arrived, he was raving about being attacked, but as far as everyone was concerned he'd fallen over pissed – just another drunk trying to make an excuse, and his 'friends' would never let him forget it.

Janet Hadden had made their night, although that had never been her intention.

10

When Dominic Grainger first met Jude Hamilton they'd been drawn to each other by the fact that they were both physically attractive people, and until they were married that was all they seemed to need to fulfil their relationship. She used to tell friends that it was like an electric shock when she first saw him. He had no striking features, but everything being in exactly the right shape and proportion made him stand out.

He was average height with auburn hair that was almost unfashionable. Swept hard back from his forehead with sideboards down to the bottom of his ears, it should have looked so last century, but somehow it worked, even though it was obvious that he spent far too much time on it for a 'real' man. His Irish roots had been sprinkled with a touch of Spanish, so his skin was more olive than the Scots version of white and he never needed to go near a sunbed, while his eyes were deep brown – almost black from a distance. His teeth weren't quite perfect because the left incisor seemed to protrude slightly, but again all it did was give him a certain charm. He spent a lot of time in front of the mirror working on the expressions he used to maximum effect.

They both said 'I love you' a few times, never meaning it for a moment but thinking it was a statement that needed to be made from time to time, especially in public. Each of them had been having a great time in their respective fast lanes and had taken up with each other in much the same way as they might have acquired the latest fashion accessory, so perhaps it shouldn't have come as such a surprise to Jude that it was only about a fortnight after they'd taken their vows at the obligatory glitzy wedding that she'd found him in their bed with one of her closest friends.

It was at that point that this couple who led lives of no depth realised they didn't really know each other all that well. In fact, there was definite evidence that their joining together in holy matrimony had revealed they didn't much like each other once they saw beyond the looks and highly developed appreciation of expensive fashion.

After the 'bedroom incident' they continued to live in the same house but started to lead separate lives, both understanding that someday they'd have to get divorced. A kind of phoney war existed where major conflict was coming but full-scale combat operations hadn't quite broken out yet because both of them were constrained for different reasons. Those constraints originated from secrets that could ruin them and any plans they might have for the future.

It all started to go wrong only a few days after the wedding, and before the incident with her friend, when Jude discovered she was pregnant. A huge overdose of champagne plus high-quality cocaine a few weeks earlier had resulted in an uncharacteristic and complete loss of control one evening. It was ironic, because in most respects they looked after their respective bodies, maintaining memberships at the most fashionable gym in the city and rarely drinking to excess. They'd thought they were having a ball and that the world belonged to them, until it had all gone to rat shit after the party at the home of a friend who had less regard for his health and didn't mind a bit of recreational substance abuse. It shouldn't have been that much of a surprise because shifting coke was where the friend made his living. He'd convinced them to go for it because 'everyone does it now', and they'd had the night of all nights – then, in the morning, the crash of all crashes.

In two short weeks the honeymoon was over, replaced by quiet contempt, though the pregnancy, as quickly and surprisingly as it came to their notice, ended when she miscarried. It was a result both of them were happy with, as they could stop pretending they were delighted at the news that she was carrying.

The fact that neither of them felt even a moment's sadness for their unborn child exposed them for what they really were – selfish, shallow people who didn't give a fuck about each other or anyone else; who hid behind glossy images that were entirely false – and what was left in the way of feelings for each other deteriorated in a few short months into raw hatred. The phoney war was over and now they were going for each other's exposed throats.

Part of the complication was that Jude Hamilton was the daughter of a semi-retired but well-respected gangster, Arthur Hamilton (or Big Arthur as he was better known), and Grainger didn't need bad blood with the father-in-law who could still create a shitstorm if he was brought into the issue. For different reasons, they kept their problems out of his sight – or so they thought – and Jude swore to Grainger that she was going nowhere for the time being. 'You can fuck right off but I'm staying,' she told him. 'You're the genius who decided to screw the bridesmaid two weeks into the marriage.'

It was after that statement that she lobbed a couple of expensive ornaments at him to prove she meant business. They missed and smashed on the wall, but he got the message.

'You can fuck off whenever you like but I want it all. You hear me? I want the house and everything that goes with it.' Hamilton had almost come to enjoy despising him and had made up her mind to cripple the bastard where it would really hurt, so the contents of his wallet and all he owned were her target and no more than she deserved – at least as far as she was concerned.

She'd come to regard him as a heartless bastard who'd rewritten history to fit his version of their problems: he'd suggested 'getting rid of it' when she first realised she was pregnant (although she'd erased from her memory the fact that a termination would have suited her as well). The idea of stretch marks and nappies had filled her with dread, and they weren't the image that she liked to present to the world. After remembering various real and imagined instances of his callousness, she came to the conclusion that this was just another man who'd used and abused her, and she was fucked if she wasn't going to have her revenge. In her self-delusion, she forgot that her husband was a crook and being devious was part of his toolkit. Hamilton hadn't soiled the marriage bed as he definitely had, but she had her own guilty secrets, which weren't as well hidden as she might have thought.

Dominic had been in a corner after the incident with the bridesmaid, but he knew he had no option but to fight back.

'I'm going nowhere,' he told her every time the subject of the division of property came up. 'This fuckin' place cost me seven hundred grand, so no way am I leaving.'

Although he was the one who'd been caught in the act, he knew it was still not far off a score draw, because he'd discovered that her morals had turned out to be no better than his. He had been stunned for about ten minutes after he found out that she was going at it as if the Tory government was about to ban sex for the general public. But after pulling himself together, he'd realised that her father, a proud racist, would go into meltdown if he learned she also had a taste for black men.

Grainger immediately invested in a private detective to get solid evidence, and the man duly came home with bacon and all the trimmings in the form of some nice pictures of her in a variety of compromising positions that would be enough to give her old man a fatal stroke. Grainger stashed them safely away.

It was a war of attrition, and with each passing day they hated each other a little bit more. It was the domestic equivalent of the Cold War concept of mutually assured destruction, or MAD as it was known in the days when the West and the Soviet Union pointed hundreds of nuclear missiles at each other.

In fact, both of them shared a passion for picking up strangers and forgetting them the next day, although Dominic had one expensive hooker he loved to entertain every couple of weeks. She was a stunner who went on the game for big money, and she took every penny she could screw out of him. Although he felt ashamed because she didn't even pretend that she liked him, for some reason she excited him in ways he could never have imagined. As far as the hooker was concerned, he could have died in front of her and it wouldn't matter a toss. This was just part of the mess that passed for Dominic Grainger's personal life.

For Dominic and Hamilton, it could only last so long, as the venom in both their hearts boiled with the growing rage they felt for each other. At first, she held the upper hand and almost got her result, but when he confronted her with the evidence that she'd hooked up with the occasional black man, the game had changed. She had ground her teeth when he showed her the photos but was rendered impotent for the time being.

'How would Big Arthur like that, Jude? Sure he'd love this one.' Grainger had pointed to his favourite, where she'd thought there was no one watching them in the back of her car. 'You could ask one of them over for a nice dinner with the old man.'

He knew it was a pyrrhic victory, but at least it kept him even with her in the poison stakes. Her father adored her, but Grainger knew if he found out, he would never forgive her for this little indulgence. When they had their rare conversations, they looked at each other and saw the same empty life; both were searching for something that didn't exist, but they were addicts and addicts don't do logic.

So Grainger trawled the upmarket boozers for women who were sometimes married, bored and wanted the kind of thing men like him could provide. He had looks, desire and a complete lack of morals – all he wanted was to meet, satisfy himself and forget whoever he was with as soon as possible. The hooker was the only one he came back for again and again. There was no point in forming relationships when the world seemed to be filled with so many souls like him trawling for adventure.

Grainger had become slightly bored with it though and had started to look for women with something different to offer, although he didn't quite know what that would mean.

11

Janet Hadden sat at the end of the bar she knew Grainger used on a regular basis. It was in the heart of Edinburgh's West End and a favourite for married men trying to pull women half their age or, if that failed, the older models who were always good for a laugh. There were some intelligence notes on his habits, but they were vague, and she was proved right when she recruited Tonto. There was enough talk within the Graingers' team to give her a pretty clear picture of Dominic's hobby at the weekends. Tonto had never met Dominic Grainger or been near him, but he'd seen him around with his brothers often enough, and in any organisation the staff talk, exchange gossip about the bosses. Tonto was all ears now he was working part-time for Police Scotland, and he'd given Hadden a mine of information on all the Graingers, though mostly on Dominic's younger brothers, Paul and Sean. He had nothing about Dominic that related to crime, but she got what she wanted in what he liked doing and his off-duty habits. The guy was a rabbit where women were concerned and that suited her perfectly.

Hadden had been in the same boozer the previous

couple of nights as well, hoping that Grainger would appear. It wasn't by the book – not even close to the book. What she was doing might have worked in the period covered by *Life on Mars*, but she was operating alone and in dangerous territory. By the book, she would have had a surveillance team on Grainger, picked her time to talk to him, and the rules meant she would have to be partnered up for corroboration. It was the thrill again, the one thing that made her feel alive, and her spine tingled when she weighed up all those laws she was breaking.

The other legal option was pulling in Grainger as a suspect, work the oracle on him about possible money laundering and then make the offer to recruit him rather than shoving him in a cell. But they didn't have solid evidence – only a suspicion that he was washing money. She was short on weapons to fire at him, but the thought of the pokey could make the best of them sweat. That one might have worked because he was one of those rare creatures in his game who hadn't done hard time inside. The reality of existence inside the high walls was that it crushed the spirit – any romantic vision of happy cons only existed in TV comedy. Hadden wasn't interested in any of that though; all she wanted was to play the game she'd invented.

She stared at the mirror behind the bar and a small smile turned up the sides of her mouth when she saw her reflection. Anyone who knew her would have to have spent some time staring before possibly working out it was her: the wig and gold-rimmed glasses worked a treat and looked natural. She was pleased with it, liking this version of herself, and in that bar at that time she looked like a piece of class material.

There was always the possibility that he might just ignore her, but she was on her own and there weren't too many women who looked like her or had the confidence to carry off the act. He would have to at least notice her; after all, that was why he was there – to spot his next victim and make his move. If push came to shove, she'd just walk up to him and make him an offer he couldn't refuse.

Grainger had walked in the door on his own and scanned the bar area, partly because he was a professional criminal and liked to know what was in the same room as him in case any of it was labelled 'pork product'. Hadden was dressed just about right to send out all the signals required to attract predators and Grainger wasn't the only one in the bar.

It was Friday night and a few business suits were there pretending they weren't married. She wore the black suit she kept for court and those special occasions; it had cost a fortune and made for an attractive business look. Her high-cut cheekbones and steel-grey eyes gave her a look all of her own, and if nothing else he couldn't miss her. She could never be described as beautiful, but there was something in the plain, clean lines of her face and almost boyish body.

From a distance, the Cruella de Vil features could give her a *do-not-approach* look, but the hairpiece plus glasses softened her appearance, and she had the ability to act or lie like a trained thespian. Over time, people who knew and worked with her always sensed something dark in her nature, which she was aware of, so she'd learned to adopt faces or camouflage whenever it was required. So much of what she said and did was a lie, like the briefcase she was carrying – it had fuck all inside but completed the picture for the evening.

Grainger wandered slowly to the opposite end of the bar and ordered a beer, while his head swivelled back and forward through an arc, digesting as much visual information as he could. The bar was near to full with West End office staff trying to relieve the endless boredom of jobs that forced them to stare at computer screens for most of the day. The noise level was up and a few older men started to appear minus their wedding rings, hoping that the soft lights would shave a few years off their real age.

Grainger chewed the fat with a couple of mid-level drug dealers who he really couldn't be arsed with but who gave him a bit of human cover as he scanned the bar for what might be available. He caught his reflection in the mirror behind the bar and it pleased him. He was a good-looking man; there was no doubt about that in his own mind, and some lines of premature grey in his hair gave him a nice touch of sophistication. With his deep brown eyes that seemed to smile, and like the woman at the end of the bar who was watching his every move, he could act the part when it came to the opposite sex.

It was all a game, but it was becoming dull; even though his last few visits to the West End had been successful, they'd left him feeling empty and it gnawed at his mind. Even the hooker he used was starting to get to him: he felt nothing but shame when he was finished with her, and her contempt made him feel angry and humiliated. He needed something different, but the problem was finding it in the bars he trawled. If picking up women was starting to bore him, he wondered what he would or could do to replace the thrill that part of his life had once offered.

The two dealers were flattered that a premier-league name like Grainger would spend time with them, not realising he barely registered a word they said. He saw nothing that interested him and decided he needed to move around the bar to see what else was on show. The place was starting to heave, and he knew from experience that something interesting could be concealed in among the crowd. That was how he thought of women, as some*things* rather than some*ones*.

'Need to go for a slash, boys. Might put some business your way next time,' he lied as he moved away from the dealers before they had time to say *au revoir*.

As he made his way through the throng, Grainger decided that if there was nothing doing he'd head for George Street, and anyway he'd had enough of the two dealers trying to get their tongues up his arse.

He'd given up and was almost behind Janet Hadden when he glanced to his left to cop another look at his profile and caught her reflection staring down at a newspaper on the bar. Bingo! She was on her own and was definitely not part of the usual crowd – different, no doubt about it. He had her as a serious business type, maybe a lawyer with the tin flute she was wearing. Grainger had never bagged a lawyer so that would be a first.

He carried on to the bogs, washed his hands and checked himself out in the mirror, feeling the buzz that maybe he was onto something. He'd seen enough to decide she would be a challenge, but that was fine by him. He seriously needed a distraction because, unlike in popular fiction, sometimes being head of a criminal organisation could be a full-time pain in the arse with all the problems that cropped up, like keeping ahead of the law or out of range of your competitors.

Grainger knew that just appearing next to her at the bar then pretending to make casual conversation was too obvious, especially as she had the look of a smart piece of work. She could be waiting for someone, but that seemed unlikely given the time she'd spent there, and she definitely had that look of someone comfortable with their own company. Being a criminal, direct action tended to be stitched into his nature, so he thought *what the fuck* and went back to the bar to make his move.

'Can I buy you a drink? We look like the only two people on our own in here.' He leaned on the bar and spoke to the side of her head; she still seemed to be studying the middle pages of *The Scotsman*.

She looked round slowly, no smile, and studied him for a moment as if he was an interesting problem. 'Why?'

She met his eyes and for a moment he felt uncomfortable, which was unusual for a man who could take the decision to bury someone in concrete without a moment's doubt. It passed; he was definitely interested and wanted to know who she was. He fell back into his role.

'Why not? You look interesting, it's Friday night and we're both on our own.' Grainger had decided that, for a change, a straight, upfront approach was the best method, as she definitely didn't look like someone who would appreciate a pile of bullshit.

'Don't you have any friends to play with?' She seemed to be unfazed by him. He felt uncomfortable again and Hadden realised she might be playing the cool bitch too far, so she broke into a pretend warm smile to show she was kidding. It worked and he took the lie.

'Are you going to stand there giving me your good side or are you going to sit down and buy me a drink?' She folded the paper and pushed it into the leather bag on top of the briefcase beside her glass.

Grainger felt that twinge again that he wasn't quite in control. He eased his concerns by guessing that she was a high-flyer and one of those modern women who thought they were equal to men. Maybe in her world, but no fucking way in his. But that made the game more interesting. The women he'd been with in the previous weeks had simply accepted he was good-looking and groomed to perfection, and therefore not all bad. That was enough for what they wanted. If Grainger was asked or tried to remember, he wouldn't have been able to recount anything of interest that had been said with any of those women, but this one wasn't in that bracket, and when she opened her mouth, it was as if every word counted.

'What do I call you when I've bought the drink?' He stuck an arm up to the barman, who knew who he was and ignored the punters who'd been waiting patiently for service. 'Large G&T.' She smiled again.

He ordered the same for himself while a mug waiting for a drink opened his gob to the barman. 'What the fuck? I'm waitin' here for fuckin' ages an' the wank gets it first!'

The mug was about three stone overweight and trying to impress the woman from his office he'd been trying to cowp for ages. He'd had a few, delusion had set in and he thought he'd turned into a hard man without any training.

The barman winked at Grainger before leaning over the bar and speaking quietly to the mug. Even at a distance Hadden watched the poor guy pale and try valiantly to control his shakes. His date saw it too, shared the humiliation and promised herself she'd make a reasonable excuse and get the hell away from him permanently.

'Impressive.' Hadden's lips twitched but she really wasn't that impressed. He could tell – there was no more than mild amusement registering after a little show that would have had most women he knew interested, if not drooling at the display of influence.

They avoided the incident with the mug, made small talk and Grainger felt a surge of excitement he had been missing for a while. He was back on form and it was as if there was no one else in the bar. The woman was class and he'd been on the money with that assessment; also, she kept a lot back and didn't do the usual thing of trying to tell her life story in five minutes, as if he was remotely interested. In this case though, he was interested and drawn to her. He usually went straight for the kill but knew this one required some foreplay, plus a bit of respect. When he formed the word respect in his head it startled him for a moment, because a man like Dominic Grainger didn't really do respect where women were concerned.

'How about a bite to eat somewhere a bit quieter?' He felt good, elated even, and like an athlete right in the zone, everything he did was bang on. She smiled and seemed amused again when he tried humour and gave him a lot of eye contact, although for a moment it was as if she was examining him and looking straight into the back of his brain. He noticed her hands: almost white, with smooth, unblemished skin that he wanted to feel against his face. It was crazy, and although he was only on his third drink, he felt intoxicated.

'I'm starving, but we go Dutch or no deal. Where do you want to go? Or tell you what – surprise me, Dominic. I'm just off to the girls' room.' She squeezed his forearm and it sent a tremor the length of his body.

When she left him, Grainger was buzzing and did what all modern human beings do and checked his phone. He scanned down the messages that were all crap and then tossed his head back to look in the mirror as if an alarm had just gone off in his head. How the fuck did she know his name was Dominic? He'd given her his middle name, Patrick, during the small talk.

'What the fuck?' He said it in no more than a whisper as he thought about those subliminal flashes he'd experienced when they were talking. Those moments where it was almost as if she'd approached him and not the other way round. His mind began to spin: he was a criminal and always vulnerable. What passed as normal activities in life for Dominic Grainger could put him in prison for a long time if the law got past his defences. Worse still, there were people close to him who would put him in the ground if they knew what he'd been doing with the profits – and that was just his brothers. That was all before competitors, and a good example was his bastard of a father-in-law, Big Arthur. He'd been in much the same game as the Graingers, although he was almost retired from crime and his legitimate businesses kept his lifestyle and a large home in Spain going strong. Big Arthur kept the peace because of his daughter's union with a son-in-law he despised, but in his other life, he would have torn Dominic Grainger's throat out for going near his only girl.

He'd let his defences down and he felt heat spread through his body, sweat popping through his skin in reaction to a mixture of stress and fear. *Who the fuck was this woman*? he thought, shaking his head and trying to pull himself together. Maybe she was just someone who'd fancied him and seen him round the bars on some other night when he had someone else to fill his attention. She could have just asked the guy serving. *That must be it*, he thought and chewed his lip, trying to regain a sense of proportion. He stuck his hand up in the air and called the barman, who came right over. Grainger was a heavy tipper and someone who mattered, and the barman would have given his eye teeth to work for him.

'The female I'm with. You know her?' He slipped a twenty over the bar and the barman saw a thin sheen of sweat glisten on his face. He decided that Grainger must be in heat.

'New one on me, Mr Grainger. Been in the last couple of nights on her own and doesn't say much. Nice – very nice – but a bit serious.'

Grainger nodded and saw her walking slowly back towards the bar. There was just a hint of swing in her hips and, despite his anxiety, he really had a thing for her look. He remembered who he was, emptied his glass in one and signalled for refills. He took a couple of deep breaths and felt the booze steady him up. If it was some kind of fucking honey trap then he'd be ready if someone was going to take a shot. He moved his left hand round to the back of his jacket and pressed his hand against the hard length of the blade sheathed inside his belt.

Hadden saw the tiny lines of tension round his mouth and eyes, but she'd been expecting that. Dropping his name had been no accident. She'd trained in martial arts since her teens and knew that balance was everything in a tussle. You had to keep your opponent off balance wherever you could – and Grainger was off balance by a mile. She'd make her play and then it would all be down to how he reacted, but for a man with such a reputation she saw what she so often saw in the so-called stronger sex: weakness covered up by layers of bravado and a willingness to hurt others. Time and time again she was surprised by the frailty of men, and she was equipped to exploit those failings wherever she needed to.

12

Janet Hadden had been born into a family who'd farmed the beautiful border land round Melrose for generations, and in many ways her childhood had been idyllic, with almost no dramas or tragedies to mar her early years. Her parents were model citizens and her mother could have been used for advertising baking products. They loved their three sons and Janet, who was the youngest by quite a few years. Once the surprise of a late pregnancy had worn off, for the parents and the shocked existing children, the new arrival was a happy addition. Her brothers were typical Borders boys who wanted to follow their father onto the farm and, like him, worshipped the game of rugby. In almost every way they were a very happy and absolutely normal family. Why Hadden had turned out the way she did was down to the gods or something in her ancestral genes.

Life on an affluent farm should have been the ideal platform for any child, but even as an infant Hadden was different. Extremely bright to the point of being annoying, she devoured books and learning, but despite being part of a healthy, happy, noisy family household, she was a solitary child, and it was as if the word *dour* had been created just for her. She shunned other children in favour of her books and her thoughts, which she just wouldn't share with her family, despite their best efforts. Her parents worried, but Janet never caused any problems apart from failing to return the love and affection they tried to offer her every day. The brothers were sanguine about their little sister's eccentricities and like all young men tended to see what they thought was the funny side of it.

She eventually took to sport like an addict and excelled at everything she did. However, it was on the sports field that another side of her personality showed its face. She was competitive, but even the description 'fiercely competitive' didn't cover it, and it was after the second incident on the hockey pitch when an opponent was badly hurt that alarm bells began to ring. A call from the head teacher and a tense meeting made Hadden's parents realise that their daughter was never going to be someone who loved easily or would be loved by others. They had to live with the veiled comments of friends and acquaintances, whose common agreement was that Janet Hadden was a 'strange yin'. It certainly bothered her parents, but for the girl herself it mattered not, and she moved on, almost relentless in her studies and love of sport. She did the sensible thing and ditched the hockey stick for martial arts, where her passion for sticking it hard to opponents could be put to best use.

As a teenager, she'd had an athlete's figure, broad shoulders and an almost boyish face, which despite being superficially attractive rarely displayed warmth. She never spent any time on make-up and her auburn hair was always cut short and flattened into her head. Her clothes were simple but suited her shape and, on the rare occasions she managed a smile, she could swing a few heads her way. Boys meant almost nothing to her, but she learned that women had power over the hormones raging through their young veins and it was just something else she needed to learn. She made sure she learned it well, discarding those young men along the way as if they were the detritus left over from an education she didn't necessarily want but saw as necessary for her future development.

After gaining a first-class degree in English from Edinburgh University, Hadden announced to her parents that she wouldn't be living at home again and had applied to join the police. Lothian and Borders accepted her and she excelled throughout her probation, leaving the competition in her wake. She wanted to get into criminal investigation as soon as she could in order to fulfil her early ambition of specialising in covert work. What she wanted she had to get, and her early days were all success until her lack of skill as a team player was identified. Since this wasn't a new problem, she adapted, pretending that she actually liked people; hence her habit of turning up at the odd piss-up to make sure she was seen as one of the boys.

'Adapt and survive' could have been her motto, as it was her answer to everything, whether it was when boredom started to plague her or when her career stalled; in every case she would decide to steer a fresh course, which increasingly included breaking the rules to give her the thrills that were missing from her life. Martial arts had kept her satisfied for a long time, and she could inflict some pain, but that sedative for her urges eventually wore off and she ached for stimulus in her life. Other people reacted to births, deaths and marriages with emotions she could only watch and struggle to understand. Normal life or great events just left her cold, and she struggled to understand what it was that touched most of the human race. Though not all of them, because people like her were sprinkled among society like aliens in the midst of everyday life.

13

'You look tense, Dominic. Let's forget the middle name, eh?'

She pulled the stool away from the bar and sat down with just the hint of a smile. His face was tight and he was still struggling to make sense of it. No one took the piss out of Dominic Grainger, and he wasn't used to someone toying with him, which was exactly what this woman was doing. She was not only calm, he could see she was enjoying every minute, which meant she was either a complete bampot or someone with a plan – and she was way ahead of him if that was the case.

'What's the fucking game here?' He was angry but for some reason still attracted to her, and he didn't want to make the wrong move. He couldn't just walk away because this wasn't two hairy detectives arriving at his door with a warrant; there was a game in play, and he needed to know what it was before he acted.

What was clear was that someone had been studying him, and he didn't like it. He wouldn't have hesitated to act and hurt whoever needed to be damaged if there was a good business case, but it was way too early for that. In addition, he was a careful man and had only one conviction for assault, which was way back in his teens. More than willing to dish out violence when it was necessary, he nevertheless always ensured that it was away from the light, where there were no witnesses apart from his own people and the victim. Grainger had ordered the killing of a couple of unmourned people in the past, but they'd deserved it, so he'd never lost a minute's sleep over the act. His brothers were harder still and had done a fair bit of time, but he was always careful about staying in the shadows and most detectives would have struggled to recognise him by sight, although his name was well known in the city and beyond.

The barman placed the drinks in front of them, saw Grainger's face and decided that it wasn't time for a laugh and a joke.

'My name's Janet Hadden – DI Janet Hadden – and I've been interested in you for quite a while, Dominic.' She bared her teeth in a false smile and tipped back a mouthful of her cold G&T. She was in no rush and waited for his response.

Grainger's face darkened and he looked round the bar to see if there were any other law in the place. He knew a few off-duty detectives trawled it on a Friday night looking for something to take their minds off the crimes they dealt with every day. There was no one who looked like the force, but that didn't mean they weren't there.

She saw what he was doing and why. 'If this was official would I be sitting here on my own?' she asked. 'I'd have brought some heavies with me, lifted you and had a long chat back at the ranch about money laundering.'

She'd thrown the dice with that comment because she had no hard evidence of his activities, nothing she could use. Even though the accountant had backed it up, that was another unauthorised visit.

She pointed to his drink. 'Go on, before it gets too warm.'

He lifted the glass and looked round the bar again as his mind went into overdrive trying to make sense of what might be happening. Maybe she wasn't a cop and this was all a set-up. There didn't seem to be anyone who was obvious muscle in the bar, but that didn't mean there wasn't a van outside ready to drive him to his final resting place.

Hadden saw him struggling with the situation.

'I'm on my own,' she told him. 'This is all off the record, and all I want is to talk to you and see if we can work out some business that benefits both of us.' She held his forearm for a moment, as if she was reassuring a frightened child.

His mouth was a tight, straight line and he barely held his temper in check. 'How the fuck do I know you're the law? This is definitely not the way it works.'

She took out her warrant card and flipped it open on her lap to avoid any of the punters or the barman seeing it. 'Tell you what, let's grab that table over in the corner there and we can talk. They say the safest place to negotiate is a crowded bar with plenty noise and drink going down. We could have gone to the flat you rent down in St Vincent Place, but I'm not sure we trust each other yet. Maybe later.'

She watched his face tighten again as he wondered how anyone but the women he picked up and used knew about the flat. For a moment, he pictured her in the flat with his hands round her throat as he squeezed the life out of her.

She picked up her drink and headed for the free table just vacated by a couple who'd decided to go their separate ways. She knew he'd follow her and, at least for the moment, she had his full and undivided attention.

Grainger scanned the bar again and although he couldn't see anyone backing up Hadden, his instincts were all on high alert. He knew it was just the stress of the unknown and he was looking for something or someone who probably wasn't there. It was one of the constant problems for any criminal regardless of their position at the top of the tree or in the gutter – a dull ache in the back of your mind that it could all go south in a heartbeat; that feeling that the law were listening, on their way to get you or just building a case.

There were four chairs round the table, but he went for the one opposite Hadden.

'Okay, you seem to know why we're both here so talk. I'm all ears.'

He'd regained some composure. If it was just an approach for money by a greedy detective then fair enough – he might be able to do the business with her as well. If it was some kind of set-up by other criminals then he was safe enough in a boozer with a couple of hundred punters looking on. What threw him was that it was a female making this play, as he thought corruption was the domain of the male detectives; a bent sow would be something new.

'It's simple really: we've enough information or evidence, if you like, to draw your guts out through your nostrils.' That wasn't strictly true, but she knew that Grainger couldn't know one way or the other. The tactic worked a lot of the time and was always worth a throw.

'You've been laundering an awful lot of money, though I suppose it comes with the job. Now I know a smart lawyer can make a fight of it, but the thing is this: skimming off the top is really going to piss off those cuddly little brothers of yours.' She waited and let her words sink in while she sipped her drink.

Grainger sat back as if he'd been punched in the chest.

He was the top man, the captain of his own ship, but his brothers Sean and Paul were street fighters and their Irish blood showed when it came to a bit of action. They just loved a tussle. Hadden wasn't just pulling ideas out of the sky. He'd been ripping the arse out of the profits, and his brothers would kick off if they knew. He'd been sweating blood for long enough, worrying constantly about a problem that had almost run out of control. Grainger was a gambler, and trying to win it back day after day had made it almost unsustainable. On top of that, his expensive tastes, showing off to the women he met, cost him an arm and a leg, plus other vital bits of his carcass for that matter. He rented the flat in St Vincent Place that he really didn't need and definitely couldn't afford just to feed his ego, and the money and resultant debts had become a mind-fuck drug that had formed a big black hole, sucking him into its core.

Hadden ran a finger across the sweat on his forehead, taking him by surprise, and his colour paled a little.

'You're nervous – good.' She said it with a smile. 'You've got the picture. Now we can do it the hard way – win or lose I still get my wages in the bank every month and the business goes on. However, my guess is that if your brothers find out – and they will' – she winked as if they'd shared an intimate moment – 'it would mean a little war with the boys that you'd have to win. Worst-case scenario is . . .' She hesitated. 'Well, guess I don't need to explain that one to you, but it tends to end in us searching for the body.'

Grainger was no mug, and because of the worries over his finances he'd run a lot of options through his head before the detective had walked into his life. Up to that moment he'd believed his bitch of a wife was the straw that might break the camel's back. Part of her revenge package was she'd been spending his money as if there was no tomorrow, and he could do nothing about it because he didn't want her getting her old man involved in the poisonous mix. That was the ace up her sleeve.

Grainger was already in a corner, needed breathing space, and now he had Hadden with either something to offer or perhaps a ton of shit to drop into his life. Whatever she was there for wasn't on the table yet, and he had no option but to listen. Although he was in no position of strength, he guessed correctly that she didn't know the full extent of his problems – otherwise she could easily have piled even more pressure on him.

'What do you want?' He leaned forward dejectedly with his elbows on the table. The cocky swagger that he'd been displaying like a beast in heat was gone, and although he wasn't quite defeated, he was open for business. She read the non-verbals and almost imperceptibly nodded in response to what she saw.

'Simple really. You operate at the top. Hardly a conviction to your name. You deal with the top men and they respect you as a businessman, so for all intents and purposes that's what you are most of the time. You have pals in the Scottish Parliament and are chummy with a few councillors round the old country. So you're the go-to guy if someone needs a favour or to be pointed in the right direction.'

She waved over to the barman for refills.

He turned up his face slightly to look directly at her, saw something in her that made him sweat a bit more and wondered how to win back some control. He couldn't have been in a worse position if she was squeezing a handful of his balls under the table. 'And?' He could guess what the 'and' was but he needed to hear it all the same.

'The "and" is that I want you to sign on with me. I want you as my eyes and ears when I need them.'

'A grass?'

She smiled because they nearly always said the same thing when an approach was made. He wiped the back of his hand across his chin in a nervous gesture.

'This isn't London in the seventies, Dominic. We call them agents now, or the official title is covert human intelligence source. CHIS for most people. All nice and official, lots of protection and even the working detectives have no idea who you are – only a couple of us in my unit. You feed me and I feed you back. It's a two-way process. There's money in it, but despite your financial problems I'd guess that what we pay wouldn't be the incentive for you. I'm offering you a bye as far as arrest and possible conviction goes. Plus, your sweet little brothers stay in the dark, at least for now. The big bonus is I can keep my gang off your back, and if the spotlight does fall on you for any reason, I can let you know how and when to keep your head down.'

It was the strangest feeling, because he was still wildly attracted to her despite the fact she might take his life apart if she was genuine, but he was satisfied that this was no act and she was real enough . . . too real for that matter.

Grainger had reached that point where panic seemed to make no sense and his heart rate slowed to an almost normal rhythm. His business brain clicked in as he accepted that this was just another piece of trading and negotiation that needed to be dealt with. The costs of failure would be catastrophic, but it was a business deal and he knew how that worked. In a way, it might solve a problem he'd wrestled with for long enough.

In the crime game, the men who survived to pick up their pensions were the ones who had diplomatic skills and covered all the angles. The killers and radge merchants tended to be wiped out or end up doing fifteen in the HMPs because they had no strategic skills – and wouldn't have known what the word strategic meant anyway. Grainger had wrestled with the idea that as the business grew, he'd picked up contacts in almost all walks of life except the police. He knew that was a gap in his security and that the wise men in his game had lines into the force; the smart villains would talk about taking out fully comprehensive insurance, which of course made sense to the deeper thinkers. Christ, it made so much sense to get a friendly in the job, because Joe Public paid a lot of tax to put people like him and his brothers away. Every so often the police needed to put big scalps inside and he didn't want to be one of them. Despite what he was doing, he ran a good business and perhaps this problem could be turned to positive effect.

'How would this work then?' He wrapped his hand round the glass and felt the cold seep into his flesh. Grainger saw the pupils in the woman's eyes dilate and he wondered if it was a sign of her small victory or interest in him.

Hadden felt her skin tingle, not with any attraction to the good-looking man opposite but at the thought that everything she touched recently seemed to have worked, and the roll continued. She'd never felt more alive – if she could land Grainger then she had the big prize in the palm of her hand. A man like him could toss her the occasional major scalp, which would turn her into a rising star again. She believed in her soul that it was her right. Guilt was something that only troubled her in her dreams.

She explained calmly how it all worked and a couple of times she watched his eyebrows kick up in an involuntary gesture. He was surprised how straightforward it could be and realised he was dealing with a real pro who definitely knew her business. The fact that she was bent law and female did nothing but impress him – he knew it took extra-hard balls to carry that one off.

'Now, the last thing . . . this meeting is unofficial. It didn't happen, right?'

He nodded but was confused.

She continued, 'The official way is that I'll approach you again but with another officer. Official means two have to be involved. It's the law. Remember that we're breaking the fucking law now. Understand?'

He got it and she leaned in close to the table. 'You act like we've never met; we do all this again and you agree to come on board. Right?'

He nodded.

'We do the paperwork and then we're ready to go. In reality, you and I will meet off the record. You tell me what you've got and I'll tell you what we want. If you have something of interest, I come back with the co-handler and you tell us only what I've cleared you to say.'

'Can I ask a question?' He admired the play and saw it all now – it was just one businessman playing the game with another one. 'What if I want something?'

'Then ask. I might tell you to fuck off, but if you don't ask, you don't get. Just make sure that if you want something you ask me on my own and not with the co-handler. Got it?'

She almost had him in the bag, and there was a bonus ball because she could see he was still attracted to her despite the revelation. That gave her all the extra leverage she needed.

'Let's have one for the road and we'll make an arrangement for next week when the co-handler and I can cold-call you somewhere and get it sealed up.'

She felt the effects of the drinks she'd already had as one side of her brain told her to go home with game, set and match while the other side told her she just couldn't lose, whatever she did. That was her first mistake in a while.

The moon and the stars sat exactly where they were in the night sky and everything should have been as it was, but Hadden had forgotten the lesson that all successful gamblers know: every run comes to an end; it's inevitable. She was good, very good, at what she did, but like the man opposite, you could never really let your guard down or some horrible bastard would stab you in the eye.

Grainger was still trying to work out whether he could get her to his flat. The thought of strangling her had passed, however, and he had something else in mind. She knew exactly what that was and toyed with the idea of giving him some hope that he'd get what he wanted (but always in the future), and they were both so preoccupied they failed to notice that they were being watched.

14

The two guys blended perfectly with the clientele in the bar. They'd taken care to look the part, were one hundred per cent smart but casual and a few thirty-something girls had given them all the signals they needed, but still they'd carried on talking to each other as if there was no one else in the bar. Their admirers lost interest and decided they had to be gay. In fact, they were real pros and just doing the job Grainger's father-in-law, Arthur Hamilton, had asked them to do.

When Big Arthur asked for a job to be done, there couldn't be any distractions. He demanded loyalty and no fuck-ups. For that he was a top payer and a good boss. The 'big man', as he was sometimes known, was virtu- ally retired these days, having operated in a different era when the only gangs that mattered were almost all in the west, with a few scattered through the Central Belt. He was one of the rare breed who had worked all over the country, but Arthur, together with the old Scotland of his younger and middle years, was fading into history, and when he walked past the Parliament building for his morning exercise or saw Wee Nicola tearing up the opposition, he shook his head and remembered the days when a burd like the First Minister would have got a slap in the pus and told to get back in the kitchen.

Hamilton wore a razor scar that ran from his temple to his jawbone and he displayed it as a badge of honour that had been earned doing it the hard way to the top. It was a sign that said, 'Do you want to fuck with the man who survived this and beat his attacker into a career in a wheelchair?'

He was a big man with a full head of short, salt-and-pepper hair. His eyes were clear blue and he looked fifteen years younger than his actual age of sixty-five. For the last decade or more, he'd lived well on the profits of his business and an overblown vanity had seen to it that he took good care of himself: he trained in the gym, played golf a couple of times a week and was careful with his diet.

Health-wise, high blood pressure was a bit of a problem, but when he saw the state of most of his contemporaries he reckoned he'd done pretty well. His wife was gone so all that was left was his only girl Judith, or Jude as she'd always been known. She was the only person in the world he'd ever felt he really loved, and as long as she was happy, so was he. Even as the years passed and she learned to despise him, he still ached for her.

The day she told him she was seeing Dominic Grainger, and that it was serious, was the first time in years he'd felt like hurting someone. He'd never met Grainger, knowing him only by sight, but he knew enough about the family to judge that a Grainger was wrong for his little girl. The irony that his daughter hated him and the reasons for that were airbrushed from his mind, apart from at those moments when what he'd done would rip into his conscious mind like gunfire.

Although Hamilton was semi-retired, he was smart

enough to know you never left the game completely – men like him knew too much, and there was always someone who might come back to square up a perceived wrong that had lain dormant for years. It meant that he kept his hand in, followed the news on the men and women in the game, who was playing for big numbers and, more importantly, he kept hold of all his friendly contacts. He knew he might have to call on them again if he needed to come out of retirement. He'd seen the result where a couple of his own generation had done nothing more than stare at the sun as they drank themselves into oblivion on the Costa Crime. Sometimes these men were visited and put into the permanent sleep because someone decided to settle old scores or make sure their secrets died with them. Hamilton had made up his mind that just wasn't going to happen to him, so he was always ready if anyone wanted to try their hand.

As for his son-in-law, well, he wanted better for his girl, despite there being much to admire in the Young Turk, who, in his swagger, was a lot like Hamilton himself at that age. He'd climbed to the top quickly and, as soon as he was able, had started to open up legit businesses to complement the illegal side. But it made no difference – the boy was a gangster and he'd never settle with that. Rows had followed and his daughter had given him an ultimatum.

'I go with him and if you make this an issue you'll never see me again. You can't buy me with money. You know that. And don't forget our little secret, Dad.'

When she said the word *Dad* her mouth twisted as if something foul was on her lips. The words made him reel, which was exactly what she'd wanted. He'd tried to forget what he'd done to her mother, but she'd seen enough of it through her child's eyes and it couldn't be cleaned from the slate. The screams, the sounds of pain and walking in to see the big man standing over her sobbing mother with a leather belt hanging from his hand had left her corrupted, and he was responsible.

It had been a classic situation: when Jude Hamilton hit sixteen and suddenly realised that she could take control and exert power, she'd turned on her father and told him no more hurting her mother. Perhaps not surprisingly, his wife had died well before her time, and Jude had nearly choked at the funeral as her father played the part of the loyal, grieving husband laying to rest a woman who had loved him right back. She realised that it was all a lie, that everything people believed about him was a smokescreen for the cruel bastard who just happened to be her father. It was still their little secret and she'd keep it that way, as long as she could squeeze what she wanted from the man with the gold-plated reputation for loving his family above all else.

The truth was that those emotions were only bestowed on the girl whose innocence he'd stolen. He genuinely felt so much love for his daughter, even when the memory visited him in the dark hours. He would see it again and again as if he was an onlooker at a crime scene: the small confused girl in the doorway, eyes wide and holding her favourite toy as she stared at her mother lying like a beaten doll with him towering over her; later, lifting her head from the pillow as he came into her room, sat on the bed and told her it was alright and it was their secret – that her mother was bad and needed to be punished.

Then came the school years when Jude realised that what had happened was foul, dreaded that it would be discovered and that she would be marked for life as soiled goods, the daughter of an animal. Then as a teenager she'd learned to hate properly. She'd watched the men who worked and dealt with her father bow and scrape to him, treat him as above ordinary beings. But she could bring him down anytime she wanted. It might destroy her as well, but he was vain and lived the lie with style – the truth would kill him, and it was a weapon she kept reminding him she had if she needed it.

15

The two men in the bar worked for a friend in Glasgow who was still in the game and owed Hamilton more than he could pay back. Whenever Big Arthur needed pros, they were available from his old friend.

The two Weegie hoods saw all they needed to see and even managed a couple of photographs of Dominic Grainger and the unknown woman. They really wanted to watch them head off to a hotel or wherever he did the business so they could call it a night plus a result. This was the second time they'd watched him, and the last time he'd taken his pick-up to the flat in St Vincent Place. They had enough now, and Big Arthur would be pleased; well, maybe pleased wasn't the right word.

They watched Grainger and Hadden in deep conversation, in two minds about staying or calling it a day. Big Arthur would always have questions and they would have to have answers, so they hung on to see where they would go if the woman who was with Grainger was game for a laugh. If they'd known who she really was, they would have been on a bonus from the big man. As far as they were concerned, she looked like someone who mattered when compared with the last woman he'd picked up, but that meant nothing at that moment in time.

As near as dammit the night was more or less following the pattern they'd hoped for. However, their best-laid plans were about to go belly up, while the consequences of one too many drinks would alter Hadden's night and future in ways that she could never have predicted or imagined.

The overweight mouth who had complained at the bar earlier had discovered his balls again, helped on by necking several drinks rapidly. That was his solution to getting over his humiliation in front of the woman he fancied. She'd made her excuses and left halfway through his feeble attempt at explaining why he hadn't sorted out either the barman or Grainger. Some people just can't help being an arse, and by the time he was well on his way to being fully pissed he realised that Grainger being some sort of name meant fuck all to him. He'd been in the TA a few years earlier and still remembered some moves. Unfortunately, he'd forgotten that the lads in the Terriers had thought he was an arsehole as well.

He kept glancing over at Grainger, a good-looking guy in a sharp suit with a female who looked the absolute business, and it gnawed at his bones. The injustice of it all. His eyelids drooped and the room seemed to be spinning slightly, but it was time to act.

He walked too close to the table where Grainger was adding up the proposal that had been made to him. Normally he would have spotted what was coming a mile off but he was preoccupied by the fact that signing up as a police informant seemed to make sense.

'Hope she gies ye the clap, man.' The guy followed his words up by tipping the remains of his pint in Grainger's lap.

It wasn't the sort of insult Grainger responded to; his style was to make arrangements to get a private face-to-face with such people and sort it so there was no risk of a conviction. He wouldn't risk anything in front of witnesses and had made an art form of staying out of the light. This meant there shouldn't have been a problem – the bouncers were already on their way and they fully intended to impress Grainger with what they would do to the guy. In fact, nobody expected what happened next.

Hadden was on her feet before the twat could even start grinning, chopped the outside edge of her hand across the area of his Adam's apple and he went down as if he'd been hit by an axe. The action was so quick that hardly anyone saw it, and he was out of the game.

Hadden stood over him, her chest heaving with rage as she resisted the temptation to drive her fingers into his eyes. She'd been in total control and then the idiot had stepped into something he didn't understand.

Grainger looked at her and said, 'For fuck's sake,' quietly. He knew and understood violence, but he also saw something in her that he thought only existed on the male side of the fence.

She looked at him and tried to control herself, almost embarrassed that she'd exposed her other self, the side she couldn't always control. It was like a demon living under her skin, ready to erupt at any moment. There were two people inside Janet Hadden grappling for dominance, and in the rare moments she knew it was happening, it could terrify her or turn her into someone who could hurt and destroy without a flicker of emotion.

'Is there a problem?' She glared at him when she said it and all she'd achieved with him looked like it was hanging on a very loose nail. Grainger saw something that could be exploited and he regained a large slice of his confidence.

'Not for me.'

He stared at her and waited as he dabbed his lap with some napkins. He nodded to the bouncers, who were waiting for his signal. They dragged the idiot to his feet as he struggled to get the breath past his aching windpipe.

'Don't be gentle with him, boys. Catch you later for a drink.'

Both the heavies looked delighted and saw it as a possible opportunity for future employment with the Graingers, which wasn't to be sniffed at. They'd make sure the culprit would hurt where it mattered, so his suffering was far from over.

'I think we need to fuck off before we attract any more attention,' Grainger said calmly as he watched her try to put back the mask she'd been wearing earlier. There was something like fear and confusion in her eyes for a moment, but it passed quickly as she buried the demon. She nodded and they headed for the door.

Arthur Hamilton's two watchers stared at what had unfolded and had uttered the same expletives as Grainger at almost the same time. They were hard bastards, but the speed the woman had moved to take out the drunk was something to behold. They looked at each other and shrugged, gulping what was left of the drinks, and headed for the door to see where they'd gone.

They were too late; Grainger and Hadden were already in the back of a taxi and away when they opened the door into the cold night air. But they weren't too upset because they were confident Big Arthur would be interested in this latest story, plus they had a photo of the skirt. Someone had to know a bitch with that temper and fighting ability.

What was puzzling was that she looked classy – what did that mean? But it wasn't for them to worry about – as far as they were concerned it was for Big Arthur to decide what happened next.

16

'What was that all about? He was a fucking mouth an' the bouncers had it all in hand.' Grainger wanted an answer and wondered where this new relationship was heading.

Hadden had regained her face and cool. She knew she'd made a wrong move and that Grainger would use it if he could. They were on even ground now and it was a case of who could take control again.

'Don't worry about it. Shit happens and it makes no difference to what we do. Let's get back to your little problem.' She smiled the way she had back in the bar and in that moment Grainger knew he was dealing with someone who was unpredictable. Like most criminals, he didn't like unpredictable because it could land you in the tin pail or fertilising an unmarked grave. He decided to hold it there and let her do the talking, seeing as the law was right on his case and that had to be resolved. What had happened in the bar told him he needed to wait and see if the cool, steely woman who'd reeled him in at the bar came back to life again or whether he should worry about the one who'd made a brief appearance disabling the arsehole. The answers might give him a handful of aces or ruin his day.

'Where we going then, chief?' the taxi driver called over his shoulder, thinking what a handsome couple they were.

She jumped out at Waterloo Place and told Grainger she'd get in touch with him later in the week and they'd follow the script she'd presented in the bar. She kissed him on the cheek before she stepped out onto the pavement and smiled back at him.

'Nice-looking girl.' The taxi driver was only trying to be polite when he said it.

'Dangerous, my friend.'

'What was that, chief?'

'Yes, she is.'

Grainger leaned his head back on the seat and closed his eyes for a moment, wondering what he'd let himself in for.

17

'She did fuckin' what?' Big Arthur Hamilton liked clarity and wondered for a moment whether the two boys he'd brought through to watch his son-in-law had gone on the piss, but he was well aware of his own reputation and he'd been assured they were pros.

'That's it all, Mr Hamilton,' the older of the two Weegies said, shrugging. The other one chewed his lip because something about the job didn't feel right. Grainger was what he was, but who the fuck was the woman with the Jackie Chan hand skills? He'd noticed her himself before Grainger came into the bar and thought she was a bit tidy, and when he'd seen her in close-up a couple of times on the way to the cludgie, that had only served to confirm she looked top drawer.

It wasn't just her obvious style – the first time he'd walked past the two of them, Grainger looked like he'd just been told he had cancer and was staring at the woman as if she'd delivered a terminal prognosis. Grainger had been Mr Cool himself the first time they watched him pick up, and when he came into the bar the next time he was the same. That was how he'd been described to them before the job, so what the fuck had upset him after meeting who they presumed was a complete stranger? It was all gut feelings and probably wouldn't make sense to Big Arthur, who wanted facts, so he kept it shut and chewed his lip as the other boy talked.

'Need us for anythin' else, Mr Hamilton?' the older Glasgow boy asked, praying they were done with this and could get back to normal service in their own city.

'Tell me somethin', boys.' Hamilton looked between them and saw them tense up; a hard question from a boss could often be the prelude to a punch in the pus for neglect of duty. They didn't want hard questions, just to fuck off back to the Wild West.

'How many women in our game have you seen who looked like her and handled herself the way she did? Know what I mean?' It was a fair question and they looked at each other, but the answer was obvious.

'No' many. In fact, none, now you mention it, Mr Hamilton.' They both shrugged again and waited, happy that it was an easy question with no blame attached.

'Aye, that's what I thought as well.' Hamilton looked troubled. He was sharp, knew the game and had an expert's nose when something was rotten. He was going to slip them a bonus and tell them he'd have a think about it. That's when a small light went on in the younger Weegie's napper. He'd still been worrying about the woman when the trace of another story ran through his head. It was probably fuck all, but he had a feeling that if he didn't clear his chest on this it might backfire later.

'Wan wee thing, Mr Hamilton. Maybe nuthin' . . . '

The older Weegie looked annoyed because he always did the talking.

'Wee things can turn into big things, son. Go ahead.' Big Arthur leaned forward, elbows on the table and knew something was coming. He felt it in his water.

'Well, our boss's boy got ripped off a few months ago. Apparently a real classy burd and had an east-coast accent. Maybe Edinburgh. Said when they were on the job it turned out she had a wig, an' she had glasses as well. Dressed the same and on her own when he picked her up. Bitch chores his wallet an' phone. He was fuckin' ragin', by the way. A few of us were sent round the boozers tryin' to get a line on her. Probably nuthin', Mr Hamilton.'

He suddenly wished he hadn't mentioned it; he knew his partner was pissed off with him for coming up with something interesting.

Hamilton wasn't annoyed at all and studied the two ambitious young gangsters. It should have been just what the boy said – probably nuthin' – but he trusted his instincts, and there was something here. Lesser men missed small things but not Big Arthur Hamilton. When there was a problem, the clues were usually available if you knew the right place to look.

'Show the laddie the photos you took an' get back to me pronto. An', boys, there's a wee bonus in the envelopes on the table there.'

He stared at their backs as they left the room, stuffing the money into their jackets. Something bad was on its way and he'd have to be ready. He'd been heading to full retirement but now there was a mess to confront. The fault lay with the bastard who'd married his daughter.

He'd heard rumours that Dominic Grainger was at it, and he'd acted even though Jude treated him with contempt. Why hadn't she said something? No matter how she felt about him, if she needed help or money, she could still ask without a shred of guilt. He wondered whether she knew what he was up to.

Of course, she might be playing her own game – and maybe with Big Arthur himself. She had reason, and every day of his life he dreaded the moment she might decide to disclose in front of his family or friends – or to the law. The thought made his skin heat up and sweat. The guilt was an awful weight to carry and if she ever chose her moment to destroy him, it would create a firestorm. How long would what he'd done remain their little secret? He asked himself the question every day.

Before the two Glasgow boys had even arrived back at Queen Street station, Hamilton had spoken to their boss and told him what he wanted. He didn't expect any arguments, even though it concerned the man's son. 'I want it done right away. This is important. Agreed?'

There was no argument from the Glasgow end; the man owed Hamilton big time, and a major chunk of his business came through their lasting friendship.

Hamilton put the phone down and wondered why it mattered. He'd identified the fact that his son-in-law was fucking around already so the women involved shouldn't have made any difference, but for some reason this last one did. He didn't know why but it did.

Two hours later he got the call back and a definite ID that the woman who'd been with Grainger in Edinburgh had ripped off his friend's son in Glasgow.

He put the phone down and stared out of his study window. It had been cold and wet, but he saw the summer flowers were well through and it was going to be another year where they couldn't figure out what season it was. He sighed, absent-mindedly scratching his chin, and wondered whether he should just leave it all alone. Was he going to open one cupboard too many and expose his own skeletons?

He stared at the TV screen above his desk. The sound was down but it didn't matter; the news never changed from all bad and he watched a picture of crying children – it was Syria again. He clicked the off button and thought he'd stop watching the news because it was too fucking depressing.

He picked up the phone and called a private investigator he used periodically and asked him to come round to discuss a job. For the time being, he'd keep eyes on Grainger and see if he could find out if shagging was just a hobby for his son-in-law or whether something else was going on. He was obsessed with getting him out of his daughter's life but had to tread carefully to avoid the mess turning against him.

He squeezed his eyes tight, rubbed his temples with the heels of his hands and wondered again how much his daughter knew about his business. He was never sure if it was all just his imagination or the fear of what she knew already.

Despite what had happened, he would have cut his arm off to make her smile and love him again.

He remembered watching TV one evening when the subject of domestic violence came up and Jude was in the room with him. She had swung her head round and her eyes had flared with loathing. In front of the family she would be completely different and put her arms round his neck so that everyone called her a daddy's girl. It was a kind of slow-burn torture; she wanted to make her revenge last. He knew she was biding her time – Dominic Grainger was just another form of punishment, a way to hurt him – but what was her endgame?

18

The detective was with him two hours after the call. Hamilton paid top whack and didn't care how the job was done; in fact, that was why he employed a man regarded by almost everyone who knew him as a scumbag with absolutely no morals. He used Frankie Mason because he did the business, no matter what was required, was value for money and nearly always got a result. Mason knew what crossing a man like Hamilton meant and had a machete scar the length of his back to prove it, gained after an indiscretion years earlier where he'd opened his mouth about a man who didn't do forgiveness.

Mason started life as an average Maryhill ned and spent ten years in the army before joining a dodgy private investigation company in Glasgow that bent every law ever invented, and he was impressive in the role. The scar was a gift from the managing director, after he'd got pissed and mouthed off in a bar that his boss was a wanker. It was probably a blessing in disguise because he'd learned the trade, or at least the way they did it, packed up and moved to Edinburgh, where he thought there might be a gap in the market. It took years, but he got there and now he was the go-to guy for most of the top men in the east. Big Arthur was his number-one client and he'd do whatever the man wanted, because Hamilton didn't care what he paid if he got the right result.

Mason stared at the photograph Hamilton had given him of the woman with Dominic Grainger and suppressed a leer. Without thinking, he picked at his nose and wiped it on his jacket. Luckily Big Arthur was distracted or he would have dug into Mason. He was meticulous about hygiene and had problems sitting anywhere near the creep, who definitely had problems in that area. However, being a talented, old-school criminal, he knew that needs must and he'd had to tolerate some unpleasant people in the past to be successful.

Mason could definitely be classed as unpleasant. He was just under six foot with a frame that had been fairly muscular in his army days but had diminished through a poor diet and lack of use. He smoked too much, drank too much and had worked out pretty early on that no woman in her right mind would have anything to do with him, so grooming had never become one of his strong points. The saving grace was that he had been a good-looking man in his day, and on the odd occasions he scrubbed, up he was almost presentable.

'Very nice-looking woman, I must say. Very nice indeed. So you want me to find her?'

Hamilton pushed some coffee towards Mason in an old mug that he would toss away after the detective had used it. 'No. Or at least that's not the starting point. I want you to watch Dominic to see if he meets up with this female again, or any other female for that matter. Cards on the table: I know he's fuckin' around, an' you'll know he's married to my girl. I've already got the goods on the bastard but want a bit more. If this skirt comes back on the scene, though, I want you to find out who she is. You don't need to know why, but that would be a bonus.'

He sat back and watched Mason slurp the coffee noisily and wondered whether the detective deliberately tried to revolt people. He had to know he was a pig. Hamilton squirmed a bit in his chair and waited.

'I'll have to spend a lot of hours on a job like this and might see hee-haw. You know how it goes. Surveillance is expensive, Mr Hamilton.'

'Fuck the expense. Just do it an' let me know at the end of the first week how it's goin' and we'll take it from there. I might just pull the plug on it but let's see.' He fidgeted with a pen. Mason was just such an annoying, horrible bastard. He had no pre cons but hadn't a redeeming factor to his name.

What got to him was that a man like Mason had no sense of what he was and, particularly in his case, how he offended people just by being in the same room with them. Big Arthur was guilty of some dark and awful crimes that might yet drag him down, but it was a flaw that he couldn't help – that's how he made sense of it. Men like Mason didn't have to be disgusting, but they chose to be so, and it made Hamilton want to chew his nails.

In his own career in crime he'd done good things at the same time as the villainy. He'd looked after his parents, his friends and was a gold mine for local charities. He knew that his legacy might burn in flames if the truth came out, but men like Mason would never suffer for anything they did, and he was almost jealous when he thought about it. As far as he was concerned, Mason was a poisonous insect who crawled out in the dark to hunt and disappeared once his victims had been poisoned or devoured. Trouble was, every so often he needed the bastard.

'If you have his phone number that could help. Might

be able to do something with that as well.' Mason scratched his groin absent-mindedly when he made the suggestion and Hamilton squirmed a bit more. He checked his phone, scribbled the number down on a Post-it and handed it over.

'Handy to have your lassie's as well so if they call each other I can know who's who.'

Big Arthur gave him a hard look and his instinct was to say 'fuck off', but he knew it made sense and complied.

'Anythin' else, Frankie?' Hamilton asked. 'Need to shoot.' What he really meant was he wanted the detective gone and the first thing he'd do was wash in boiling water.

Mason stuck out his hand for a shake and Hamilton put his hand palm up.

'Had a bit of a bug. Don't want to pass it on.' It was a lie, of course; the truth was that the bastard was probably immune from the bugs that ravaged everyone else.

Mason smiled, wiped his hand on his jacket to remove the ever-present film of sweat and said he'd be in touch.

It wouldn't have happened in the glory days when Hamilton would never have gone outside his own team to be sure of security, but he had no full-time muscle or specialists now and had to hire men like Mason. The risks from a grass inside the team weren't so much of a problem now because the days of trafficking shitloads of H, counterfeit goods and women were long gone, and it would be almost impossible for the bizzies to make a case now. The bodies he'd buried weren't making a comeback, and in truth he couldn't remember exactly where any of them were now. Anyway, he'd always thought that the men he'd killed deserved it, and that was the game. 'If you don't want risk, don't be a fucking gangster,' was a phrase he used over and over again.

Half an hour later, Hamilton nodded off in his favourite

chair. In the dream that came he was a child, the room pitch dark but with a single, four-paned window that glowed white opposite his bed. The light didn't enter the room and he was terrified but didn't know why. Then a shaft of light threw a line across his bed and eyes as a door was opened a few inches.

'Arthur.'

It was almost indiscernible: a whisper, a soft voice that said his name.

'Arthur.'

He tried to remember why he should be afraid, but it wouldn't come; all he knew was that he was in danger, and he screamed for his mother over and over again.

He woke gasping air into his lungs and remembered it was that same dream again. Always the same.

Half an hour later he gave in as his eyes started to flicker; he was knackered and headed for his bed.

19

Dominic Grainger had an office in among the Georgian splendour of Edinburgh's West End. It had cost a bomb, but his legitimate businesses had been doing well enough. Fortunately, the property recovery happened ahead of time in Edinburgh and saved him from a complete train wreck. His siblings complained about the extravagance of an office in the most expensive area in the capital, but it gave the business a professional face, and he knew better than they ever would that was important if questions were asked.

There was another difference: they were traditional gangsters in every sense, whereas Dominic was more like those despised bankers than he could have imagined. At least he'd spread some of the risks over a wide area of investments, kept a few mid- and senior-level civil servants sweet so he knew where new opportunities would arrive in the city, particularly where property development might rise from the dust. He'd made sure the business supported good causes, and cancer charities had good reason to shake the hand of Dominic Grainger for his efforts.

The complication was balancing the criminal and legitimate arms of the business. At various times of stress, one had supported the other when it was required. It had worked during the pre-recession boom days, but on top of everything else his extravagance and gambling addictions were now running out of control and he was struggling to hold his nerve when he thought about the true state of their finances. The problem was all down to him, and when he thought about the size of some of his bets it made the nerves in his gut rattle.

He'd been stressed out since his meeting with Janet Hadden, had spent the following days working out all the angles he could and had come to the conclusion that he had to be positive. It could work, and he knew the men who mattered in this world had their fingers in all the pies. Maybe it had been forced on him, but the best option was to treat it as an opportunity, and it could be.

One thing he was sure of was that he couldn't let this woman have all the handles of control – she was a strange one, and it would be interesting to see her in action when it was official and she was in the company of another detective. He still wanted her – if anything, the desire in him was growing stronger – but he knew it could cloud his judgement when he might need it most.

She'd called him on Monday morning, sounding businesslike, and told him who she was, which meant someone was listening, and said she wanted to ask him some questions. They'd then agreed that she would call into his office the following Thursday with her colleague – their first official meeting – as she'd outlined during that first night together.

Since then, they'd also set up a safe phone system where he would use a clean pay-as-you-go mobile to talk to her, and it was that they were using now.

'When we meet officially to exchange information it'll

be on neutral ground,' she told him. 'Somewhere out of the city, or we can arrange a hotel room at our expense.' She let that one hang in the air, *we* meaning herself and her co-handler, but she knew what would be going through his mind. That was fair enough. 'The unofficial meets we'll arrange at the time and either at a hotel or your flat. Wherever, that's your expense.'

He raised his eyebrows. He was going to have to pay to be a fucking rat. 'Do you get embarrassed at all?'

'Why the fuck would I get embarrassed?'

They both let that one hang in the air.

'I've got a meeting with my brothers this afternoon and they're getting edgy. We've had some property stolen recently and they think there's a security problem somewhere inside the business. Just something we need to take care of.'

He was throwing out his own line to see how she reacted. He was talking about the loss of dope consignments but without detail; there was no way she was going to do him any favours yet when he'd given her nothing but a drink in a bar. Hadden still held the best cards, but the deal had to have some give as well as take and he had to play his cards with a poker face.

'I need to tell them something about the other night. They'll hear what happened in the bar. They drink there as well. Weird if I don't mention it to them.'

'Go ahead – but no names, no pack drill, right?' She was giving an order and didn't want discussion.

'Fair enough. See you Thursday.'

'That's it. See you then.' She put down the phone and thought *so far so good*.

Grainger put the phone in his pocket, stepped over to the window and watched a hailstorm thrash the cars parked out in the street. The sky was a variety of fat black and cobalt clouds rattling over the old city. He felt it again: the conflict inside, the overwhelming desire for her, but also an image of squeezing her throat till the capillaries in her skin and eyes ruptured, a myriad of petechial haemorrhages erupting as she died at his hands. He let out a long breath and shook as he saw the image fade in his mind.

He opened the cabinet in the corner of the office, took out the twenty-year-old malt and half-filled the glass before throwing it over his throat. The impact on his acid-filled stomach almost made him retch and he sat down, his sight blurred for a moment as he let the nascent panic attack subside.

'Everything's fucked.' He said it through instinct and knew there would be no happy ending, whatever he did. There were too many lies to bury without trace.

20

Sean and Paul Grainger walked into the office and Dominic stood up, grinning at the boys. He'd survived his panic attack and pulled himself together as far as he could. He needed to put on a show because his brothers would smell the least hint of nerves on his part. They were his half-brothers, much younger than him and the result of his mother dying before her time and his old man eventually marrying his second wife. Dominic never took to his new stepmother, through no fault of her own, and when the boys came along he struggled with the additions to the family. They got on well enough, but there was a distance between them that tended to show when a problem came up; most of the time, though, they were like friends rather than brothers. They would go to Easter Road, scream at the Hibees and neck beers after the game like so many other young guys. But when they fell out it was always hard, and there was a resentment caused by a set of circumstances that had nothing directly to do with any of them. As the eldest, Dominic took the lead on everything where a decision had to be made, and although it was perfect sense, it bothered the younger brothers, especially Paul, who always wanted more. The older he got, the more he felt Dominic had too much control.

Their father had been a criminal – not a very good one, being more muscle than brain – but he had taught them the trade. Dominic had inherited his mother's looks and brain and the younger brothers their father's temper and tendency for unnecessary violence.

The office meeting was a regular event; unless there was a crisis they met up at least once a week to chew the fat. There were a lot of arms to the business, so communication was needed to keep things stable.

'How's it going?' Dominic pulled some beers from a bucket of ice and flipped the tops off the bottles. He knew what they liked and always had them ready.

'All good, Dom.' Sean Grainger was the youngest of the brothers and easy-going unless his temper caught fire. He grabbed the beer and necked half the bottle in one go. Paul grunted and sipped his brew without saying too much. Dominic could tell something was bothering him, but that wasn't unusual – there was always something bothering Paul.

'Any problems your end?' Dominic said easily – it was his usual opening line when they met.

'Still no joy on the gear we've lost. It fuckin' bothers me this.' The question had fired Paul up, but then he never took much lighting either. 'Then that numpty Tonto losin' the package when the Pole chased him.' Paul said it through gritted teeth, the old temper simmering. He was pissed off because something was going wrong and he couldn't make up his mind whether it was bad luck or a human problem, intentional or otherwise.

The story with Pete the Pole and Tonto had already become legend, even making the Scottish news. The uniforms fucking off had made front-page, laugh-out-loud headlines as the papers indulged every piss-take possible, with one rag suggesting that they were looking at the cops concerned for the sprint event in the next Olympics. The mobile phone shots were hoot of the week on Facebook and the Chief Constable had said in private he wanted them hanged, drawn and quartered. Of course, that comment was leaked to the press and had just added fuel to the raging fire that was Police Scotland's already battered image.

'It's the fourth loss in the last few weeks. Don't like it one bit, Dom.' Paul pulled on the e-cigarette that wasn't helping his craving for the real thing. He cursed, put it on his brother's desk and pulled out a twenty-pack of cancer sticks. He lit up and closed his eyes with relief when the drug hit his bloodstream.

'Might be just a bad run; shit happens in this business.' Dominic tried to calm his brother's frayed nerves and turned to his other sibling. 'What do you think?'

'Not sure.' Sean was the closest of the two to Dominic. 'Seems funny the two dealers we supply getting done at the same time. That has to be some fucker talkin'. Might just be another pissed-off wee dealer. Hard to say, but we've drawn a blank so far. Tonto's on a final warnin' and top tax. If he loses anythin' else then it's time to have him in.'

Paul's face was red with suppressed anger. 'Fuckin' right he's in!'

Dominic didn't like the way Paul was acting one bit and wondered if he'd been powdering his nose again. He had the look even though he claimed to have been clean for over a year.

The office phone rang. Dominic lifted it with a heavy sensation in his gut; something chewed at his nerves, and it was as if a number of crisis indicators were all moving into negative territory. One of Paul's team was looking to speak to him and it had to be important if he was inter-

rupting the brothers' meeting. After saying 'What?' Paul
went quiet for the next minute.

About an hour before they'd started the meeting
another of their couriers was travelling back from Leeds
with twenty kilos of H concealed in a suitcase in the back
of a hired Beamer. The courier was a tried-and-tested
carrier, ex drugs squad, bunged out of the force for an
off-duty skirmish in a Glasgow bar that had resulted in
a decorated soldier losing an eye. He looked the part,
dressed as a businessman, and it should have been a
breeze. He knew all about surveillance and countermeas-
ures, but it had made no difference that day.

The Leeds suppliers were the main targets in a National
Crime Squad operation south of the border. The NCS
hadn't a scooby about Scots couriers or Scots involvement, but they were close to taking out the English team
thanks to an undercover officer working inside and
reporting successfully. It was simply coincidence that
the Jock appeared at a meeting the UC was attending
and took a suitcase away to his overnight hotel. The UC
clocked the Beamer number and relayed it back to his
ranch, and the NCS team leader decided there would be
no harm getting a routine pull on the Jock well north of
the border – if the man was dirty then it was all good
evidence for their own case when the time came. A Scottish traffic patrol car stopped the guy, who made it easy
by doing ninety in a sixty area. Not very professional, but
the courier had got pissed in the hotel the night before
and wanted to get home and rest his hangover. Shit
happens and he'd been arrested when they searched the
car and found the goodies.

'I'll be there shortly and you better get on this fuckin'
mess now, you hear me?' Paul had lost it completely,
almost screaming down the phone, before he stood up
and threw the handset across the office.

'That doesn't do anyone any good, Paul. Sit down and I'll get you a drink.' Dominic's face darkened; he knew troubled times were about to get worse. Sean shrunk a little into his seat and left the talking to his older siblings. He never got anywhere with Paul anyway, and few people did once he'd made up his mind about a problem.

'Tell me what's up. We always work it out,' Dominic said as calmly as possible.

Paul's chest was heaving with rage – he needed somewhere to put it till he could give some of his team a hard time. He glared at Dominic and it was obvious that despite whatever shreds of brotherly love they might once have had, they were heading in different directions. Dominic realised that he should have taken it on a long time ago; he'd seen it coming but parked it. That was a mistake, but who wanted civil war with brothers? They were always the worst and bloodiest enemies.

Paul sat down and lit another cigarette. The stress level in the room was on red and Sean knew that whatever was happening was going to be a pain in the arse. He followed his brother's example and lit one up for himself, despite having been stopped for a month.

Paul told them what had happened to the courier, sucking in the tobacco smoke between sentences as if it was saving his life. 'That's it.' He spat it out: 'We have a fuckin' grass somewhere an' it'll bring us down at this rate. I'm tellin' you, the fuckin' bizzies are probably on our case, has to be. Twenty fuckin' kilos. We promised half to that Weegie bastard Greig Young. He'll really see the fuckin' funny side.'

'Greig Young?' Dominic sat up, his mouth tightening into a straight line. 'When did we start doing business with him? He's just all bad news. You didn't think to run this past me?'

He picked up a pen and started to tap the end of it on

the desk. Dominic was the calmest of the brothers, but he felt the heat rising – their troubles seemed to be mounting by the day. The problem with Greig Young was that he was permanently in conflict with other criminals. He was so unreliable that he constantly let people down, refused to pay for goods and would even rip off people he was dealing with. No ordinary decent criminals, or ODCs as they were known in the game, would touch him with a stick. Yet Paul Grainger had.

'It's fuck all to do wi' you, Dominic?' Paul used his full name because he was pissed off, not that anyone needed a clue. 'You stay well away from the hard stuff, leavin' us to take all the risks, an' we agreed we run this side of the business. So what's your problem? While we're at it . . . what about you, brother? Think it's a secret what happened at the boozer?'

Paul had calmed and enjoyed watching Dominic squirm in his chair.

'You fuck around every weekend wi' anythin' that has a skirt an' a pulse. Now some tart you've picked up half-murders a punter. Fuck's sake, you should remember you're still married to Big Arthur's wee girl. Do we need him on your case at the moment? Jesus!'

Paul sat back; his anger had been released and for a few seconds they sat quietly eye to eye, digesting what had happened, what had been said and what was to come.

'I was going to tell you about it. Christ, I didn't know she was Bruce fucking Lee's sister.'

It would have struck anyone listening that there was a marked difference in the way Dominic and his brothers spoke. The younger men used the language, inflections and dropped Gs of most of the east-coast population. It was education – Dominic had excelled at school and was unusual in his trade in that he'd gone on to university. His father had been a bit of an arse but he'd promised his first wife that her only son would be educated as far as he could. Dominic had sailed through, but his father had made no such commitment for his other sons and it was another wedge driven between them through no fault of their own.

Dominic looked sheepish, for once on the back foot. It was simple – he had no answer to an obvious truth. He needed fresh cards and he grabbed the only ones available.

'Look, I've managed to bend a top suit. Early doors but they should be able to give us an inside line on what the fuck's happening. If there's something going on, then we should know what the problem is.'

He sat back and wondered if he'd made the right move. He'd spent his life mostly getting it right, but now he felt there were forces backing him into a corner with no escape routes.

'A cop? How did this happen? Think we should have been in on this one, eh?' Paul looked round at his younger brother for the first time. He normally didn't wait for his okay but he wanted to show that Dominic was becoming isolated. Sean didn't really want to take sides but when he was forced there was only one, although not necessarily the best choice.

'Yeah, you should've mentioned this. We should agree. This could be a set-up.' Sean sat back; he'd said all he needed to.

'It's sound.' Dominic had to win this one. 'This cop's as bent as a nine-pound note. It's about money. We keep the suit in readies and we get a pass on the business. I'll test it this week and let's see what we get.'

He left it there. It was enough but his stomach cramped because he wasn't even sure he could deliver. Given the mood he was in, if Paul found out he was skimming a fortune out of the business, there would be blood.

Paul nodded slowly and smiled but there was nothing pleasant or brotherly in the expression. 'Let's see then, but this better work. Tell you what, find out if the runner that's been lifted talks to the bizzies. He's sound as a pound and hates the fuckin' force. Never forgave the bastards. Never know, though, so let's see if your wee pal can tell us.'

He stood up – the meeting was over. 'We need to get on this now and see what we can find out.' He turned to Sean: 'Find out all who knew about this run and we'll start from there. What a fuckin' life, eh?'

He shook his head and turned away without another word to his older brother. Sean at least offered a nod and the trace of a smile as they left.

Dominic tapped the desk with his phone and prayed that Janet Hadden could come up with a solution to what he'd just used as a lifeline.

21

Frankie Mason was a happy bunny, and like the scavenger he was, he could smell something rotten a long way off. When Hamilton hired someone outside to do a job it was important, and not for a charitable cause. Mason worked on one principle: that nothing was sacred and he would do whatever it took to do the job. He didn't like people too much, plus people didn't like him, and that was okay as far as he was concerned. The job was all he had – there was no wife, no children and his social life consisted of standing on his own at the end of whatever bar he was in. That was where he could be with the thing he really enjoyed: a good beer.

Doing the job gave him access to people like Big Arthur, and being asked to do something for men of status gave him something he couldn't get in his private life. They needed him for his special form of expertise, and they came to him because he was one of the best in the business. Most private detectives played at it and couldn't do much more than amateur surveillance or proving somebody's wife or husband was playing away. Mason could look deep into a target's secrets and probe the places they wanted to keep hidden. Over the years he'd developed a network of people who owed him or he'd corrupted, and it wasn't unusual for him to blackmail the odd punter to get what he wanted. For a man who seemed so out of kilter with society, he didn't worry about much and slept easily, although only for a few hours a night.

The request from Hamilton was, on the face of it, routine in some respects: see who his son-in-law was with and report back. He hadn't been told why the woman in the photograph was important and his nose twitched at that one. Half the time he was hired, the client would only give him part of the story because they had their own secrets, but when it was a gangster, their intentions could well end up with some punter needing surgery – and that was if they were lucky. Mason made it his business to find out all he could, including whatever it was the client was hiding, because you never knew whether it might be useful down the line.

Part of his success came from being a creep, and there was always a bit of a buzz in having the inside story on the men who mattered. At the same time, it could end up as good business – he'd built up an extensive knowledge of who was doing what, and he'd been able to sell the odd gem to rivals in commerce or crime. It was delicate stuff, and if he ever fucked up with the wrong men then he could fall off a very high cliff and onto a very hard place. Other people's secrets were another of his few pleasures, and he tried as far as possible only to use the ones that wouldn't blow up in his face.

Mason used a subcontractor to help him with the eyes on Dominic Grainger. They split shifts and took turn about watching him, which wasn't too difficult because he spent most of the day in his office with only a walk round to Princes Street Gardens on the odd lunchtime. If the information was correct, he lived quietly enough during the week and his weekend started on Thursday nights. The subcontractor Mason used was from Paisley. He'd known him in the army and the guy didn't care who the target was, just liked earning. He was sound as a pound and could watch a target all day without ever getting bored.

It took Mason a couple of days to tie down the phone records from his contacts inside the phone companies. With the clampdown, plus bad press about phone hacking, things had become a bit tighter, but there were always greedy bastards who'd sell their granny for a price, and Mason invested heavily in finding and recruiting bent souls in the right places. He had the call lists for Dominic and his wife, but as Hamilton wasn't pressing him too hard for a quick result, he hadn't yet started work on the subscribers.

The subcontractor was in place on Grainger, and Mason thought it was time to get a bit of background. He looked at the photos again on his laptop. He was a sleazeball but he had a tremendous ability to recall information, and even what might have seemed liked trivia was stored in case it was ever needed. He knew that in his trade, knowledge was power and the way to bonus payments.

One of his pastimes was to wander the bars of Edinburgh, upmarket and dives in equal measure. That's where he would pick up bits of information, watch and listen in to conversations. He could spot the couples playing away a mile off, and he learned, even from these small, almost insignificant, moments. It took him no more than a few minutes to recognise the bar where the photos had been taken – and he should have because he'd spent enough time there himself. It was a frustrating place because a lot of the punters went there to pick up or be picked up. At one time, he thought he'd try it himself because he'd witnessed so many successful pulls and thought that even he might have a chance. All he'd managed to do was prove to himself that he was almost unsellable to the opposite sex without paying for the privilege.

In the end, he was successful only once, pulling a woman who amazed him by being attractive, beautifully well dressed and had a flat in the West End. But that was as good as it got and he ended up with just more disappointment. It turned out she was a member of the fruitcake family and the grin on his face when she'd handcuffed him to the bed soon disappeared when she announced she was right into S&M and to 'shut the fuck up and take it like a man'. He still winced when he remembered her displaying her favourite equipment and telling him what she was going to do with them.

Mason pushed the doors open in the middle of the afternoon, when the late lunches had gone and the early drinkers were still in their offices watching the clock.

'The gaffer in?' he said to a girl cleaning the top of the bar with a cloth that looked like it could give the whole of Edinburgh an unpleasant stomach bug.

She never answered, just chewed her gum and lifted a phone. 'Punter wants ye.'

She paused, chewing slowly as someone at the other end spoke then shook her head. Whatever had been said annoyed her, but then working for the minimum wage meant everything annoyed her.

'Please yersel',' she sneered into the phone and looked at Mason, chewing even harder. 'He says take a seat.'

She turned away and started spreading the bugs across the bar top again.

He waited for a few minutes like a stookie, working out that she wasn't going to ask him if he wanted anything to drink.

'Any chance, hen? Pint maybe?'

She looked up, understood the question and sighed. The girl eventually poured the beer and Mason took the seat where he thought Dominic Grainger had been sitting with Miss X when the photos were taken. The barman who had served Grainger and the woman emerged from the door behind the bar and looked disappointed when he saw who it was.

'Jesus, thought you'd've retired to the south of Spain by now.' He kept the piss-take mild by street standards because, much as he disliked Mason, the only reason he wasn't locked up himself was that it suited the detective's purposes at the time.

'Sure you'd be happy for me if that was the case, son. Have a wee seat.' He could see the barman's face give the occasional twitch as he tried too hard to look relaxed.

A couple of years earlier Mason had been employed by the owner to find out who was stealing from the business. He'd done a good job, identifying a couple of staff ripping the pish out of the system. But he'd also discovered the owner's younger brother's hobby was looking at pictures of young children in the scuddie. He let the boy know exactly what he knew and that he would do him a favour by keeping it between them as long as it suited him. It was the kind of thing the detective liked to store up for a rainy day – and it always rained in Scotland. It was simple really – Mason just wanted to know what had happened in the bar with Grainger and the female with the deadly hands.

'It was weird. She was the real thing – definitely not yer average burd, know what I mean?'

'You ever seen her before?'

'She was in two nights before, but never before that. Only time I've seen the woman and I'd remember. Widnae mind a wee shot, masel'.'

The boy's hands were shaking as he tried too hard

114

to please Mason. He was sitting opposite the man who could train-crash his life in a moment and he'd be a pariah. Sex offenders were registered and segregated in the tin pail in case some mad fucker did unto them what they would have done unto those frightened kids on their screens.

'You stick to the kiddie porn, son; that's where your heart is.' Mason grinned; he loved watching the fear in the young man's eyes. 'Tell me everything you remember.'

He sat back and listened carefully to what he was being told. Maybe there was nothing in it and she was just some high-class bitch who did martial arts. Christ, she wouldn't be the only one in the world. She was on her own, though, and why was Grainger concerned when he'd asked the barman if he knew who she was? According to the gibbering boy, Grainger had never given a fuck who the women were any other time.

He described going to serve them another drink and backing off because Grainger looked like he'd been kicked in the goolies. What was that about, and why was an arrogant bastard like Grainger so worried about a female he'd known for about twenty minutes?

Mason scratched the three-day stubble on his chin and decided he had to find out who she was, never mind Big Arthur's needs. He wanted to know her secrets so he could store it away in his rainy-day box.

'The CCTV still working?' he asked.

It was working perfectly and it still had the recording he needed. Mason took it back to the dump off Leith Walk that he called home, which also functioned as his office. He ran the recording again and again, stopping several times to stare at various angles of the woman with Grainger. He watched her coming into the bar and he saw it: the way she sat, the way she glanced up every so often, pretending to read her paper, and how she had chosen the best seat to watch the door behind her in the mirror. Was he imagining it?

He went over it again and again. She was watching and waiting. Whoever she was, she was waiting for Grainger, and at some point, she'd delivered a message that he hadn't wanted to hear. The assault on the twat was there as well – almost off camera but enough to tell him she operated on a hair trigger, and that was interesting.

Mason spent time watching the way she walked, moved, the small involuntary habits that are hard to disguise. By the end of the afternoon he was happy and intrigued. He stared at the still frame again with her face looking back at him.

'Christ, I'd give her one myself.' He leered and scratched the stubble on the side of his face again. 'Lookin' forward to meetin' you, hen.'

He switched everything off and called the subcontractor, but there had been very little activity at Grainger's office. He was in there but there'd been no visitors, and only the postman had been at the office door.

22

Tonto was pissed off. Janet Hadden shrugged; she was getting bored trying to reassure him that there was nothing to worry about.

'The Graingers are taxin' me tae death. Fuckin' Paul looks at me funny – he's convinced I'm a grass.' He was stressed up to the eyeballs, and he felt like there was pressure everywhere he looked.

'Well, you *are* a grass, Davy. I mean, what the fuck did you think you were at the end of the day?' It was taboo to tell a CHIS this, and she would never have said it in front of a co-handler. It was a hanging offence, and when the whole informant system had been taken out of the dark ages into the caring, sharing modern world, it was decided that the old terms for an informant were derogatory and counterproductive. Words like grass, rat, tout and squeak were consigned to the same dump as the flared trousers on *Life on Mars*. Human sources would be made to feel included and part of a greater cause. As far as Hadden was concerned it was fine for the management meetings, but a rat was a rat, even when you put a little sheriff's badge on it and told it you cared. She fucking hated rats, but you had to live alongside the horrible little bastards.

'I thought I was doin' the business for you. You said I was worth my weight to the force. All of a sudden it goes quiet. I mean, I'm gettin' a bit nervous. Just tell me what the score is here.'

He tore the beer mat he was fiddling with into smaller and smaller pieces till there was nothing left to tear. When he'd finished taking his stress out on the piece of cardboard, he picked up the one Hadden had been using and got to work on that. It started to irritate her, and she really wanted to be on her way. They'd spent an hour parked in a Glasgow boozer because Tonto had been through delivering some samples of counterfeit goods that had been offered by the Graingers to a Loyalist team from Belfast. Apparently, they wanted a shitload of moody gear if the Graingers were interested in delivering. Tonto had shown it to Hadden, who'd looked bored, tried her best to give him a pat on the back but told him she wasn't that interested.

'I'll make a note of it. If they buy in bulk get back to me and we'll see what we can do, alright?'

'Do I get a pay-off for this then?' Tonto couldn't hide the stress in his voice; he felt like he might have just had a using by the detective. It hurt after the elation of feeling that he'd been part of her gang.

'Afraid not.' She tapped the table with the ends of her fingers in a rhythmic beat. 'I need to go.'

Tonto looked and felt gutted. He'd really believed they'd become friends, and he was excited about doing work for someone other than the bastards who controlled the crime business in the city. It was a fucking liberty. He'd been putting his faith in someone who was turning out to be no different from the bandits on his side of the fence. Christ, he wouldn't have put it past her to have arranged for the Pole to chase him through Gorgie. *Was the mad bastard a grass as well*? he wondered.

The problem was that he couldn't see the big picture, and of course he could never have guessed what was going on in Hadden's mind. No one could. She wanted someone like Tonto inside where he could tell her if what the intelligence suggested about the Graingers was anywhere near true. Fill in the names and who did what job – couriers, dealers, anything he could get. He could never fill in the big-business gaps, but he was a scout, the pathfinder telling Hadden it was okay to proceed. He'd done that and she'd made her move on Dominic, which, apart from the incident in the pub, had gone to plan. Ideally, by the end of the week she'd have Dominic signed up and Tonto would still be inside the gang if she needed to back up a story. Two sources were always better than one, because everyone lied to a certain extent.

At some stage, Hadden would have to make a choice and decide on her medium-term tactics. She had a dilemma: did she run Dominic for as long as possible, regardless of the dangers that held for her, or get him locked up at the first opportunity? The Graingers were top tier and eventually there would be questions on whether the force was protecting someone who was as bad or worse than the people he'd provided information on. That was how it used to work, and she knew that prior to the unified force, there had been some dark secrets where poisonous characters were protected for all the wrong reasons. The gangsters flung a few numpties to the force concerned, who ignored bigger crimes and crowed over their solved-crime figures.

Although she wasn't feeling remotely sorry about her treatment of Tonto, Hadden realised she was being too hard on him. She couldn't risk him walking out on her, because she would need him for something in the future, so she relented, smiled and slipped fifty notes across the table squeezed inside her hand in case anyone was eyeballing.

'Here, have a wee drink, and if the counterfeits look good I'm sure there'll be a bonus.' She thought the PSNI might be happy to tie up some heavy-duty Loyalist boys, which couldn't do her any harm.

Tonto, easily pleased, visibly relaxed as if it had all been a wind-up and he was back on board as the sheriff's deputy. *Christ*, she thought, *I'll have to buy him a fucking badge at this rate*.

The money was her own – an official payment would have had to be authorised above her rank, witnessed and signed for at the handover. She didn't care about money; her lifestyle was fairly simple and she had more than she needed. There was nothing in her life but the game and, hopefully, the promotions to come. For a few moments, she forgot Tonto was sitting opposite her and imagined being behind a desk in a big fuck-off office grinding her competitors into the carpet.

'Is that okay?'

Tonto had asked her something, but she'd drifted off. 'Sorry, I was thinking of something. You lost me for a minute there.'

'I'm saying they're talking about another big run to make up the loss. Paul's ragin' an' wants Sean to take charge of it. They've said it's "need to know" for this one but Sean's the man in charge so that might help you. Eh? What do you think?'

'That's interesting. Would Sean do the run himself?'

As Tonto talked, Hadden considered her options. At some point, she might have to dismantle the Graingers' business and that would be a huge result on its own. If the youngest Grainger could be taken out without Dominic pointing the finger at her, it would put him under enormous pressure, drive Paul halfway up the wall and she could apply pressure at will. It could give her even greater control over the situation. Played the right way, she could drive the knife into Dominic's back ever so slowly and he wouldn't even know it was her hand guiding the blade. It was complex and dangerous. She felt a strange sensation, which was almost sexual.

Tonto stared at her, thinking she looked like someone thirty seconds after their first hit of smack, and asked if she was okay.

'I'm fine, Davy.' She came back down and smiled at him as if they were partners in a great plan. Tonto couldn't have understood that what she was imagining was the possibility that at some stage in the future he would make a perfect sacrifice in the game.

'Tell you what,' she added, 'even if it is need to know, bell me if there's anything that looks like they're moving to do the run. Guess it would be a fair amount of gear if he goes himself.'

'Definitely.' He was excited by Hadden's obvious interest in the job, and the thought that he might contribute to the fall of a top man like Sean Grainger gave him his own form of thrill. There was just a moment of doubt, because Tonto knew that although the brothers had given him a hard time over the loss of gear, Sean wasn't the worst guy in the world. But that doubt lasted no more than the briefest moment before he said 'fuck it' to himself. Tonto also knew that in God's great creation he was pond life and chances were he'd never rise above that level. The conversations he'd had with the detective proved that. The Graingers were taxing him to fucking death and here was a chance to exact his own form of revenge. He could never shove it in their faces, but he could watch from the sidelines and gloat when they felt what the guys who worked and took the prison time for them had to endure time and time again.

Tonto was experiencing a kind of epiphany. All his life he'd staggered from one personal problem to another. He'd had no chance as a kid, underperforming at school because all his friends were like him: the future they aimed for was there on display in gangster films and the life displayed through drama and print. Sharp clothes, fast cars and women who just turned up and performed because you were a name. He was a young man and on his second term inside when he realised that he was just like all the other poor bastards who were exploited by the police and the gangsters. There was no honour among thieves, just survival in a world where your mate could cut your face open if the gaffer told him to or you could be tossed to the bizzies as a form of human titbit. He shook his head every time he heard that some poor sod running gear up the road had been taken out by the law. It was always the same with these arrests – some pot luck, some good detective work by the bizzies or the guy's boss throwing the detectives a diversionary bone.

'Any chance of a lift back?' he asked, guessing there was no chance. He was on the money.

'Christ, think what you're saying! You get spotted in the wrong place with the wrong person, in other words me, then your current problems will seem like a fucking blessing.' She saw him look down at the table with a worn expression. She knew guys like Tonto were kicked in the Henrys every day of their lives. He'd just handed her the chance of a cheap shot at one of the Graingers and he might pick up something else to firm up the job. She wanted to get back and organise a job but she needed to keep him on board.

'All I'm thinking of is keeping you safe. We can't afford even one mistake with these people.' She was careful to say 'we' so he would know they were working together. 'Okay?'

He looked up and nodded.

'Right, I need to go. Anything, and I mean anything . . . just get back to me on the number.'

She stood up and headed for the door.

Tonto stared at her back and wondered where this one would go. He was pretty sure it wouldn't be a happy ending, but he was getting to the stage where he didn't much give a fuck any more. If this was his life and future, he wondered what it was for. He looked at an old guy sitting in the corner on his own, aged before his time, his right hand shaking as he carefully lifted the beer to his mouth and sipped a little from the top. The beer was only a quarter gone and the old boy had already had it on the table when Tonto had taken his seat nearly an hour before. He'd seen the same kind of punter often enough in the boozers, sitting there all morning and afternoon nursing what bevvy he could afford and remembering or regretting the days when he was Tonto's age.

Tonto picked up his paper and stepped out into a blustery south wind, blinking at the punters walking past the boozer with no idea who he was and what he was involved in. They had their own lives and problems – why would they care about him?

A couple walked past clasping hands and the girl turned to her boyfriend, laughing out loud at some story he'd told her. He was grinning at her and they really seemed to like each other. Imagine that, he thought. Even if they didn't have another thing in their lives, they had each other. He shook his head, turned and went back into the bar to sit opposite the old boy.

'Fancy a game o' doms, pal? Beers are on me, right?'

The old boy looked puzzled for a few seconds then grinned; it was Christmas come early. Human contact and a bevvy thrown in for good measure. 'Nae bother, pal.' The old boy looked at his drink. 'Any chance o' a wee goldie on the side, son?'

Tonto smiled and nodded. 'Have what you want, pal.'

Tonto and the old boy spent the next three hours getting totally pissed and the fifty quid Hadden had given him was well and truly arsed. The old boy turned out to have done three big stretches in Bar L. Serious assault, attempted murder and an armed robbery, which meant years inside that had taken him from his late thirties till what felt like the start of old age.

The last question Tonto asked him before they started talking drunk shite was: 'Any regrets?'

The question annoyed the old boy but only for a minute. 'Regrets, son? What dae ye see here? When I walked oot the gates the last time Glesgae wis gone, son. Men I knew were like me. Fucked either wi' time inside or the drink. Rangers were relegated an' I hadnae a fuckin' clue whit anyone wis talkin' aboot. Regret it every fuckin' day.'

Tonto looked at the old man as if he was a ghost come back from his own future. When they split up, he gave the old boy his last tenner.

'What's yer name?' Tonto asked him, having suddenly realised they'd talked for hours without monikers.

'Davy – always known as Davy, son.'

The old boy headed off; Tonto's tenner would see him through the next day in the pub and the few hours they'd been together would be a happy memory for him. Every day he'd look at the boozer door and hope that Tonto would walk into his life again.

23

On the way back to Edinburgh, Hadden started the ball rolling. She decided to pass off the meet she'd just had with Tonto as a chance encounter and would get a co-handler to go back and see him. They'd get the information on Sean Grainger and the possible run south.

The next morning, she called Tonto and even with her lack of empathy thought he sounded a bit flat. Nevertheless, she told him they needed to meet right away to get the same info in front of the co-handler. She warned him to say it was an accidental meet the day before. 'We keep the co-handler in the dark a bit. That way I can do you the odd favour for free. Right?'

Tonto said okay as if there was a choice. He wasn't quite sure what it all meant but he'd seen enough of Hadden to know she was no saint.

The meet was as sweet as a nut and the co-handler didn't pick up any problem vibes. In fact, Hadden was that good she nearly had Tonto convinced that their meeting the previous day had been a figment of his imagination. She could have acted for a living.

*

Back at the station, she organised a meet with the head of a specialist team, and a surveillance operation was set up on Sean Grainger within hours. The timing was perfect as they'd hardly had eyes on him before he picked up a hired car, which immediately got the surveillance team buzzing. A hired car was exactly what they were looking for as an indicator that the job or something else was good to go.

Hadden got the feedback and sat back in her office chair. It felt good, all so good. If someone like Sean Grainger could be taken with a load of gear, there were all sorts of possibilities. He might talk and turn himself over as a source. It happened, brothers informing on brothers. Who knew? If he was caught there would be a range of options and all of them would be good for her.

She was called into her chief inspector's office and gave a rundown on her progress so far. He was impressed, no doubt about it. He felt it impossible to warm to her, but she seemed to be someone who'd come home with the prize, and success for her was even more success for him. That's how the game worked.

'You're not letting the grass grow under your feet, Janet,' he told her. 'Impressed, very impressed.'

He was a tosser who was only in his post for a quick spell, a tick in the box before moving onwards and upwards towards executive level, and he probably hadn't seen an angry man or woman in his service. She hid her contempt and swore he would be one of the first she'd humiliate someday. He wouldn't last five seconds in a darkened room with her, and it almost made her choke to think that this was the kind of man who'd have a leading role in a world full of threats. She knew she was equipped to take on the dangers coming from so many dark places. Fire with fire: she knew what was required even if they didn't.

'Thank you, sir. Appreciate that and just want to do the best I can. I'll keep you informed.'

She went back to her office and settled into her chair to wait.

Her boss thought he might have misjudged her, that like him she wanted to do things properly. She certainly had nice legs, and that had really impressed him.

As it started to get dark Hadden got the call that Sean Grainger had left his flat, was in the hired car and the surveillance team had watched him meet up with his brother Paul for half an hour in a hotel near the Gyle shopping complex. A footman had been deployed to the hotel and watched the brothers in conversation before they split up, with Sean Grainger heading for the motorway.

All good as far as Hadden was concerned, and exactly how she expected the scenario to pan out if it was, in fact, the prelude to a run for more gear.

24

Frankie Mason was making progress and the job felt like it was stacked with possibilities. He smirked at the sheets of paper spread chaotically on the desk in front of him. He'd been speaking to bent contacts in the phone companies for hours and was now working his way through the lists of subscribers who'd been in contact with both Dominic Grainger and his wife. A list of names was building, but apart from the obvious ones like Dominic's brothers, he didn't know who anyone was yet, and it was a shitload of work to get checks done on who some of these people were. Over the years he'd built a substantial intelligence system of his own and recorded every detail he'd came across. It helped, but he still needed inside info, which often cost money, so it was always better if he could blackmail some fucker in a prime position to feed him what he needed.

He felt like he was staring through the keyhole into a bedroom that was currently in deep shade. Everything would become clear once he'd worked the information – all bought and paid for by people who'd sold their integrity to the detective. He was made for the age of greed and information technology, because all he had to do was find the dealers in the market. Mason loved every minute of what he was discovering and was so excited when a picture came into focus that he would scratch his face in a nervous gesture. It was something he could never control, and when he was really high he would do it till he bled. He kept his nails as short as possible to avoid the problem; they were still clarty though.

It was fair outside, but Mason didn't care what the weather was like, and in a way, he preferred the colder miserable months, because he'd rather cover up than wear light clothing, which showed up his rather scraggy frame.

He was being fed the subscribers to the phone numbers from his sources and at first it seemed as if there was nothing too interesting. But he knew he had to be patient and sooner or later the ripple would show, that little hint that something was there and all you had to do was reach out and grab it. All of life's routine would be there covering the traces of dark little secrets.

Mason had seen it time and time again when he was following people day after day and all they would seem to do was go to the shops, the game, gyms and all the other things that filled people's lives. The worst gangsters were just the same: so much of what they did was just what everyone else did to put food on the table and interact with friends. Then it would come out of nowhere.

There were jobs where he'd spent days wondering at the sheer agonising routine of someone's life and then suddenly they'd look around as if they knew they were being watched, but they didn't. It was that gesture before the job lived up to expectations – the moment before they turned into the hotel where they were meeting the other half of their affair, or perhaps the sauna where their favourite escort brought them relief. All the pillars of society thinking no one knew their secrets.

He remembered the elder of the kirk driving all the way to another city to spend the day tucked up with a rent boy. His wife thought he was seeing another woman and the shock of what Mason described had nearly killed her. You just never knew about people. Except that Frankie Mason did – and as far as he was concerned they were like him, just less obvious in what they were.

He was working on Dominic Grainger's number first. It was a busy phone, which was what he expected from a man who ran a successful business. Gradually the patterns began to show in the way his life moved through the weekly cycles. It was remarkable how the phone traffic alone of a modern man or woman could draw a fairly accurate outline of what they were and how their lives functioned. In time, Mason knew what time of the morning Dominic Grainger started to tick; he couldn't say what time he was up but he knew that a man like him would start taking and making calls fairly early. He could see a number that he called every morning around 8.30 a.m. and it turned out to be a landline in his office. Mason decided to get the billing for that number as well, though Grainger was likely just checking with an assistant of some kind, making sure there were no problems.

The routine was crucial, because once you knew the routine you had a large part of the map that made up that person's life. It surrounded the black hole, that dark space where the secrets were concealed. Knowing what he did already about Grainger, it was a nap that the assistant would be female and a looker.

Mason called the subcontractor to check whether he could confirm that his assessment was close to the mark.

'Fuckin' right. She's in there before him in the mornin' from what I can see so far. When our boy arrives, she appears about ten minutes later an' toddles along to the local coffee shop for the caffeine. A wee belter she is. Too good for you but just my type.'

The subcontractor was still laughing when Mason put down the phone, because he wasn't interested in the joke or the female, just in confirming what he thought, and he was pleased he was on the money so far. It meant that, to a great extent, Grainger would be predictable, and that was almost always the case.

Mason had looked at hundreds of cases in his time, and if he'd learned nothing else it was that men really were creatures of habit. Even the ones like Grainger, who were supposed to be so interesting. As for the assistant, she would be like a packet of paper tissues – required every so often but that's all. Grainger would be doing the business with her during office hours, and love and affection wouldn't come into it. These arrangements usually suited both parties unless feelings came into the equation. He couldn't imagine that would be an issue with Grainger, who he was sure was a heartless bastard even on a good day.

But for the moment, none of it mattered – it was simply another space to fill in on the map. He'd find out who she was and it would probably be another item for the rainy-day box. Whoever she was, she would know a lot about the business, so it was just possible he might need to dig her out at some stage. For a minute, the thought crossed his mind that she might be married or in a relationship, which would be ideal if she was as tidy as she sounded. Prime for a bit of blackmail.

'Another time, Frankie,' he muttered as he wiped away the little trail of dribble at the corner of his mouth.

Hours looking at Grainger's phone traffic eventually made Mason's brain hurt, and by late afternoon the pain had reached his neck, which meant it was time for a break, with a beer or two included. But it was at that point that the Belfast number caught his attention. On its own it didn't mean anything, though, and when he checked the subscriber it turned out to be a bar in the city. Although he was on the point of getting up from the seat to stretch, he decided to make one last check to finish that one off. He called another ex-army source who'd settled in Northern Ireland, married a local and drove taxis for a living. It was remarkable how many squaddies had lived through the hard times there but decided to settle once the peace process had taken hold. Mason had served two tours there with the man and, like all taxi drivers, the guy was an encyclopedia for what was going on in his city. He was one of Mason's best sources over there and was paid a flat fee for each enquiry Mason sent him.

As he rang up the number he rolled his shoulders to ease off the tension in his muscles.

'How the fuck's it goin', soldier?' They were always the first words Mason used when he called the boy; it had been agreed between them the year before that this would prove there was no problem Mason's end and someone didn't have the terminal end of a gun at his head. They'd both served in an army intelligence unit that still looked like it might be dragged into the light over there. Despite the passing years, there were still calls and claims about government collusion with the paramilitaries, and the suspicions about their activities wouldn't go away. They both knew that there might still be an early-morning knock at the door someday, so they were careful.

'How's it goin' there, Frankie? How's the Hibees doin'?' The taxi driver was a football fanatic and there always had to be a starter about the game. Mason had lost interest in football years earlier but pretended he still cared.

'Game's shite now, pal; we might as well hand it to the Hoops at the beginnin' of the season.'

Mason felt that was enough about the state of the Scottish game and moved it on. He asked the taxi driver about the pub. He had the name but nothing else. For some reason, the pub name bothered him and rang a distant bell from the past. He hadn't googled it because he knew that in Belfast there was always the possibility that there was a story not on open sources, and he wanted it straight from someone who knew the score.

'Fuck's sake, what you want there?'

Mason forgot about his neck and shoulders. There was a story; it might be nothing to do with what Big Arthur wanted, but that wasn't the point. The man was paying for his time whether he knew it or not. Mason always told his clients that there was a lot of research involved, that it was expensive, and nine times out of ten they were happy with that explanation. It amused him to think how many of them would be pissed off if they knew exactly how deeply he looked into their lives.

'What about it?' Mason picked up a pen with the end chewed to a pulp.

'Bandit country. Hard-line Loyalist territory. You do not stop in there for a pint wearing a Celtic scarf.' The taxi driver always had to bring the game into an answer.

'How hard-line?'

'Most of them are just plain fuckin' gangsters now, or maybe they always were. You know the types: they fly the flag, wind the local youth up to throw shit at the uniforms and hate the green side as hard as ever. They're identikit villains: shaved head, tattoos and steroids with their porridge. Anyone in particular?'

'Not at the moment. Just came up on some billing. Might be nothing. I'll come back to you if it shows up again. You okay to sniff around if necessary?'

'Within reason. Those boys don't fuck around, but if it's just local info then no problem. Always happy to get a contribution to payin' my sports channel, know what I mean? Let me know.'

Mason leaned back in his chair and stared at the notes he'd made. He looked at the word Loyalist – he'd drawn a circle round it. There it was: the first little window into a part of Dominic Grainger's life. Might be nothing, but he'd put a few quid on the contrary.

He stretched his neck, tilted it backwards and heard something click. Why would a Grainger, who came from Irish Catholic stock, be dealing with Loyalists? Of course, in business or crime some people forgot where they came from. Not those Loyalists though. Mason knew enough about Northern Ireland to know that God and country mattered, regardless of what the peacemakers said or thought.

It was all promising, and he stood to take another look at the photo of the woman who'd been with Dominic Grainger in the pub. He'd enlarged it, printed it off and it was hanging on the wall behind his seat. He picked up half a chocolate digestive that had been lying on the desk for a couple of days and chewed it absent-mindedly; the fact that it was horrendously soft and that crumbs were coating the front of his shirt didn't even register. 'Wonder who the fuck you are, darlin'?' he murmured as he stared at the photo.

The phone rang, startling him and he sat back down to answer it. It was the subcontractor.

'He's away from the office. The assistant left just after him. Want me to stay on him?'

'Take him wherever he goes and stay with him. If you get him settled let me know an' I'll take over for a few hours an' call it a night here. Want to finish the phone stuff then we'll go on him full-time come Thursday. We might need to bring in another set of eyes for this one, or are you okay with this?'

'Brand new, an' no worries my end, pal. Get back to you in a bit when I see where he's goin'.'

He called in again about an hour later.

'Bookies for a couple of bets and then straight to the casino. Looks like our boy likes a flutter.'

Mason grinned. It was midweek and two gambling points in one late afternoon meant something. That kind of habit might turn out to be a wee bonus. It was always a positive if they could identify a weakness. He couldn't be sure, but it was looking very much like a good start. The signs were there, and he'd almost ignored a couple of subscribers in the list he'd looked at. They were other bookies.

'Lookin' good, Frankie boy,' he muttered to himself. 'Lookin' good.'

Mason felt the high of opening up a can of worms and seeing the little bastards trying to avoid the light.

He decided that he'd give the beer a miss after all because he'd need a clear head over the next few days. There was serious work to be done. He googled the pub in Belfast to see what open sources said and there was a lot of reporting, but nothing more than the taxi driver had told him. Casual drinkers just didn't go in there. It was a den in heavy-duty Prod territory so reporters or nosey bastards would find their teeth on the floor if they even looked in the window.

Mason shook his head and wondered if the Troubles were really over. He hadn't been there since he'd left the army and still had nightmares about his time in Belfast. He knew the Loyalist paramilitaries up close and personal, had seen what they could do – and even for a man carrying the weight of many sins, they scared the shit out of him.

'Fuckin' Belfast,' he muttered.

He gave the picture of the woman one last look before he headed for the chippy.

25

Sean Grainger was pissed off, seriously pissed off. Things were going wrong and none of them, including his older brothers, were used to it. They were only realising it now, but the truth was they'd probably had it too easy. In sporting terms, they weren't match fit. When they'd first started to make their mark in the city, Dominic had always picked the right plan and had perfect timing for every occasion. Looking back, even when they'd had to use violence, there hadn't been too much in the way of opposition, and the bloodshed was usually short if not sweet. They'd worked on and occupied a fairly clear pitch apart from some other up-and-comers. The Fleming clan, who'd controlled most of the drugs trade, had been almost wiped out just as the Graingers were flexing their muscles. The men who'd killed the Flemings ended up in the ground themselves, so the east coast saw a whole new generation enter the criminal landscape.

The Campbells from Leith were almost replicas of the Graingers and filled the void round the north side of the city. Some young gangsters might have seen this as a reason to start a pissing competition, but Dominic and

Colin Campbell knew each other well enough, and above all else they were strategic thinkers; in other words, they were modern villains. Instead of a trial of strength, they decided to cooperate with each other when it suited. There was enough for everyone, although the old-timers might not have thought it was 'the right way', considering the avoidance of violent confrontation a weakness. This outlook, however, saved some broken skulls and unnecessary expense. There had been the odd tension between the organisations, but so far they'd worked it out. Half the time it would be a bam from each side running into each other, then there'd be the inevitable piss-take, one of the off-duty troops would get 'the heid' and all hell would break loose. All solvable.

Sean had just left his older brother Paul and couldn't get the logic of what he was about to do. They were losing gear to the law, and some unfortunate circumstances, like the adventures of Tonto and the mad fucking Pole, suggested their business was becoming something from a comedy script. They just couldn't work out whether there was a leak or if it was just a run of bad luck. Sean usually followed whatever Paul decided. He'd never wanted a top slot; he knew his own limitations and following his elder brothers suited him just fine.

The problem, or one of the problems that was taking on arms and legs, was that Paul was becoming obsessed by Dominic's place at the head of the game. It had always made sense to Sean that Dominic was in overall charge when the big decisions needed to be made. Apart from the very odd occasion, Paul and Sean ran the illegal side and Dominic made a bundle on straight business. Sometimes they'd consult or use one side of the business to support the other, but that was kept to a minimum. Dominic always had the last say on the big decisions, and someone had to lead. That had worked well – only a class-act financial investigation would identify the money trails, and Dominic had taken responsibility for washing the profits.

The links were there – it couldn't be avoided – but they'd been as careful as it was possible to be. Paul acknowledged, at least to himself, that Dominic had always played a great game, made them a bundle and had ten times the nous he had for administration. Dominic certainly didn't have his brother's talent for violence, but he made sure the profits were laundered properly. They'd been building a decent early-retirement pension until the recession had changed the economic outlook for the family. That being said, his brothers were completely unaware of how much their fortunes had changed for the worse.

Everything had been sweet till the losses started, and now they were down twenty kilos and a talented courier who might or might not be talking to the Gendarmes. A lot of money had been tied up in that lost gear, but there was more to it than that. It was the twenty-first century and a brand name was everything in the modern world. The Graingers had been triple A and now this. Class-act gangsters didn't like doing business with teams who were attracting an awful lot of attention from the law and losing commodity on a weekly basis. That kind of shit could be highly contagious – suddenly old pals and long-term clients stopped answering the phone or asking for deals.

Even if there wasn't a rat, everyone who knew them would presume it was just that, or else there was a major-crime team all over their case and it was just a matter of time before the walls caved in. Big arrests created waves, and those former friends and clients wouldn't want to be in the path of a fucking Scottish tsunami. There were no written contracts on the crime side, or binding regulations, so someone could just say 'fuck the Graingers' and that would be the end of the matter. Like every other business, there had to be a sensible cash flow or else the wheels could easily start grinding to a halt and reserves could be eaten up like chips off a roulette table.

What the younger brothers didn't know – and what kept Dominic awake at night – was that Dominic's own cash flow problems had forced him to use the legal business for all the wrong reasons, which was the very thing they'd always tried to avoid. Mixing the two sides up could leave them badly exposed.

Dominic had built up a creditable reputation on the transport and logistics side of the legal business, enabling them to compete with some of the big names and often coming off best. Because of his cash flow problems, he'd agreed to do a few favours for the wrong people, moving their commodities with no questions asked. He could charge top whack for these special consignments and it always went straight into his pocket. He hated mixing lawful and bent, but he was a pragmatist and only started the 'specials' to cover his cash shortfalls. His visits to the casinos were almost out of control, and he knew he was standing in a deep hole and digging like fuck. Every morning he swore there'd be no more casino or bookies, but by the time he left the office in the afternoon, he knew he would do it again. It was a slow-hanging noose that closed a fraction at a time, but the outcome would always be the same in the end. Although his brothers still didn't know, it had to be only a matter of time, because nothing remained secret in their world. They would piss blood when they found out, and while he'd tried repeatedly to come up with a cover story for that inevitable confrontation, there was just nothing there to be found.

26

Sean Grainger gunned the engine and headed towards the motorway. He lit up another cigarette as he tried to work out if there was something he was missing. He was heading south to Leeds to pick up another load of H, but what was chewing his balls was that he was supposed to be management, not number one or two but next in line. That should have involved fringe benefits such as not taking unnecessary risks – that's why they paid the numpties. Fair enough they were taking serious hits, but for some reason Paul had told him he was doing the run and that there was no discussion on other options. He'd given him some old shit that he was the only one he could trust, and they'd kept this one watertight so the chance of being grassed was unlikely. But it all felt like that old promise to get in touch after a one-night stand – only even less believable.

'What the fuck are you up to, Paul?' Sean said it out loud into the empty car because he was definitely missing the point. He was a tough bastard, the toughest of the brothers, but had only half the brainpower and never felt up to questioning them or arguing the toss because they were normally way ahead in their thinking. If there was one thing that got to Sean, though, it was being humiliated for being thick. If it was one of the boys he could just rap them across the pus, but with his brother he backed off and kept his thoughts to himself because he was normally wrong. He knew he wasn't that bright, but he kept coming back to the conclusion that Paul had decided he must be the leak and that's why he was being sent on a test run. It was the old witch-trial logic: if he wasn't pulled by the law then he was a grass and if he was pulled he was innocent, but his arse would end up in HMP Saughton for his troubles.

He thumped the dashboard with the edge of his closed fist. 'Fuck it.'

He could have just forced the issue with Paul, but that would have set his brother off on a tangent. If he argued, Paul would still think it stank of disloyalty, and in any case, he was going off his trolley and back on the coke. It was a fucking rat trap all ways.

He checked his mirror every couple of minutes. The motorway was quiet by normal standards and there was nothing obvious on his tail. The Leeds team had said they would do the handover at a service station on the outskirts of the city. They knew the last courier had been arrested on the way back to Scotland and were having their own concerns about whether the Jocks were bringing the problem or it was somewhere near their own door. In a way, they were having their own version of the same crisis because two minor couriers who worked for them and a dealer had been taken out by the law. They were giving the Graingers the benefit of the doubt because their own cash flows were being hit and they needed to keep goodwill wherever it existed.

As Sean Grainger crossed the border onto English soil, the Police Scotland surveillance team leader was as happy as a pig in shit because all was going to plan. Tonto wasn't supposed to have known about the job, but Sean had bumped his gums to some of the team in the boozer. He was bumping his gums just too often about Paul because he needed someone to listen to him. His team had looked interested and nodded at the right time. Paul was a highly strung nutjob who was pissing everyone off, and Sean knew the boys would agree. He just didn't have the grey matter to work out that if there was a leak, it might be one of those sympathetic nodding heads. Tonto had experienced a mild rush when Sean hadn't turned up as usual for the morning meet and prayed that he was on his way south. Hadden would be pleased, and if she was pleased it was all gravy for him. A few of the boys had heard the same story as he had, so nothing could come directly back to him.

A few miles south of the border, the NCA team took over the surveillance and kept well back from Grainger, who'd relaxed a bit, deciding there was definitely nothing to worry about behind him.

As the car travelled south, taking all the correct directions for Leeds, the NCA team were high – it looked good for another meet with their own targets. If that was the case, they would be getting close to moving in and making the arrests. They had technical devices in play and knew that a large importation was on its way to the UK, and they wanted to tie the Leeds mob to it. It was a big one going to a team in Liverpool, and the Leeds mob were on for a third of the load – close to one hundred kilos. They would let this Jock pick up and run north of the border again, where he could be intercepted if all was going well.

Sean Grainger made the call about an hour from the service station. The voice at the other end of the line told him it was all good and the handover was on when he arrived. He was told where to park and given a description of the car and driver who'd meet him. The NCA picked up every word from their technical interceptions and it was relayed to the surveillance teams, including the Police Scotland unit. Hadden got the message twenty minutes later, leaned back in her seat and smiled. She picked up the phone and called Dominic Grainger. He answered after a couple of rings.

'We okay for tomorrow?'

'Absolutely. See you then and nothing changed in the script?'

'Nothing. Just I'll have someone with me so we both need to act the part.'

She put the phone down, closed her eyes and decided to stay in the office till the surveillance operation was resolved one way or the other.

Sean Grainger had that feeling of being a long way from home, therefore all problems were left behind in Edinburgh. It was self-imposed delusion, and he was trying to rid himself of the nagging worries about the situation with the business and Paul acting the arse. The thought that his brother might suspect him of being a grass made him grind his teeth after all he'd done for the mad bastard. He supposed there was some logic in such thoughts, because so often it was someone close who was feeding the bizzies with the ammunition to bring you down. So often the last person you would suspect turned Judas because the pigs had managed to dig up dirt somewhere, and then it was that straight choice to either turn or take your chances in front of the guy in a wig. Often enough he'd heard the old-timers talking about the days when there was real loyalty to the boss or team you worked for, and he supposed it might have been partly true. Trouble was, now people were all material and weak. The difference in those old days was that unless you were a boss, those gangsters didn't have that much whether they were outside or inside. Life was generally shit, and some even took the time away as a relief from the wife and kids they couldn't afford. A kind of career break.

Sean made a final stop in a service station; he was well ahead of time for the meet so decided to relax for half an hour and down some coffee. He found a seat where he could eyeball most of the service area in case there was anyone giving him too much attention. By the time he was partway through a doughy 500-calorie bun, he'd finished half the first coffee and ordered a second.

He saw nothing obvious – everyone just seemed like they were miserable and in the last place on God's earth they wanted to be. A couple two tables away were arguing like fuck, and the female kept raising her voice a little at a time till it was just short of a full-scale shouting session. The guy, on the other hand, kept it low, almost begging her to calm down.

'We'll find the money somewhere,' he kept insisting.

Everybody was tuned into the drama, although they pretended it wasn't happening, and there was a real bonus when the female had just had enough, tossed what looked like a cappuccino into the boy's gob and that did it: he stood up and whacked her full force round the chops. Her head seem to rattle for a few seconds and the place almost came to a stop. It was written all over the boy's face: *What the fuck have I just done?* A couple of security guys seemed to appear out of the ground and grappled him to the floor, at which point the female, who'd recovered her mojo, tried to kick him while he was restrained and helpless.

It was a classic. Sean could barely stop himself from laughing and the little drama lifted his mood completely. He picked up his phone and called Paul.

'Speak.' It was always Paul's first and only word when he answered the phone. He'd picked it up from watching a film about the Mafia – it seemed the way a top man should answer a call.

'I'm nearly there, everything good so far and checked in wi' our friends down here. A bit early so havin' a break before the meet. Everything okay your end?'

'What the fuck would be wrong, Sean?'

The anger was there again for no good reason and he wished he'd never made the call, but it was the way they'd always done things.

'I mean, unless some fucker has tipped off the bizzies then there's fuck all to worry about, brother. That's the case, isn't it?' Paul asked.

It was there in his voice again. His brother was even more paranoid than usual, and now it was obvious Paul thought he might be the grass. It stuck in his craw because all he'd ever done was follow his brothers and do whatever was asked. So much for fucking loyalty – it was too much and even Sean Grainger had limits.

'You get a fuckin' grip, brother. I'm stickin' my arse up as a target an' you're givin' me snash.'

It was a once-in-a-blue-moon job for Sean to lose the place with Paul, but he'd had just about all he could take. He had never let his brothers down that he was aware of. Of the three, he was the one who seemed to have the best nature, though if violence was required Sean could do it with bells on. He was all Irish when it came to a square go, and what he lacked in physical bulk he made up for in every other sense. He was a heavyweight in a middleweight's frame.

'You and I need to talk because I'm done if you keep this up. And by the way, you need to stop wi' the white snuff – it's turnin' you into a complete arse.'

The phone went quiet for a few moments as Paul

absorbed his brother's words. Sean wished he'd been a bit more diplomatic, but what the fuck? He was about to pick up enough gear to put him inside till middle age if things went wrong.

'Well, let's just see how this goes.' Paul's voice had lost all the heat and dropped somewhere just above freezing point. 'You been takin' brave lessons, Sean? Want big brother's job maybe?'

Sean had wasted his time – there was no dealing with Paul when he was in this type of mood – and he decided he would face him up when he got back. 'We'll talk in the mornin', an' I want Dominic there.'

It was as if he'd burned Paul with a cigarette end. 'Oh, it's you an' fuckin' Dom now, eh? I knew there was somethin' goin' on.'

Sean stabbed the 'end' button on the phone and felt his hands shaking.

A few yards away a surveillance officer relayed back to his team that the target had been on the blower and looked upset about something. The fact that he'd made the call was recorded in the surveillance log that ran on every operation. It was there so every event could be recalled and, if necessary, might become evidence.

Sean headed back to the car and for a moment considered turning in the other direction, heading back up the road and telling Paul he was out of the game. Sean had thought about it often enough; he did what he did because of his surname, but in his heart of hearts he wished he was a million miles from what they did as a business. The longer he went on, the less he liked it, and the all-pervading feeling that wouldn't leave him now was that the whole thing was coming apart.

There was no real evidence to feel that way, and he did understand the losses might still have been shit luck rather than anything else. He'd heard about other teams who'd had a bad run against them and then everything had gone back to normal, and the vast majority of guys in the business were never really touched by the law. There were just too many people involved in it; the plod could only do so much at a time and their big operations could take years and still fall apart in court.

So the law of averages was that if a gangster didn't get too greedy, they should be able to survive. But then the bizzies did have to get a result in the bag every so often to justify their existence, and Sean – like everyone else – knew that it would always be some poor bastard's turn to go down the swanny – that was just how the world turned. The constant worry was that no one really knew if they might be next – apart from the ones who had the right detectives in the right place, of course.

Sean set off and headed for the city, thinking he would finish this job and when he got back it would be face-to-face time with his brothers – and if necessary he would walk away. Dominic had been putting a lot of dosh away for the three of them so maybe it was time to cash in and find a different way to live this life. He was single, no debts, no wife or kids, so how hard could it be to start again somewhere? He stopped worrying and hardly looked in the mirror on the rest of the journey.

Sean arrived at the service station and circled the car park a couple of times till he saw the guy nod him into a space beside the 4x4 that had been described to him. They both knew how it worked: the first rule was *do not give the other guy an advantage*. He may be about to rob the fuck out of you, so be careful and make sure the dosh and gear were handed over at exactly the same time. Then head off before any nosey bastard took an interest.

The Leeds team knew exactly what they were doing

and had even picked the place to park because the CCTV there didn't cover that one patch of concrete. They hardly spoke a word, and Sean shoved the soft luggage bag containing the gear into the back of the car. He had a look round and saw nothing to spook him, but of course he knew it was pointless worrying once you had the gear. If the bizzies did appear then you were fucked anyway.

As he headed back up the road, he wasn't to know that the surveillance commander had told his base team to let the Scots know their man was on the way back up the road and there would be a handover to them near the border.

When Sean was thirty miles from Berwick, he called Dominic. It was unusual – although they got on well enough he rarely called on anything other than urgent business – and when Dominic picked up, he thought something had to be wrong.

'What's up?'

'Just been south to take care of some business, Dom. Just thought I'd give you a call.' He paused, wondering if he was going over a line with no way of stepping back. 'It's Paul. Worried about the man. Can we meet up?'

'Wait a minute. What the fuck are you down there for? Thought that's why we pay the staff good wages. Is he losin' his marbles or what?' Dominic didn't like this one bit. With all that had happened, Paul had decided to throw the dice, with his youngest brother taking all the risks.

'Jesus! Have you got cargo?' He gripped the phone tight and felt his gut knot up.

'Big one.'

'For fuck's sake, I said I had someone inside. Couldn't he wait? Jesus! Straight back, Sean, and unload it as soon as you get up the road. Come to the office first thing.'

After he'd rung off, Sean chewed his lip during the

miles to the border, wishing he'd called Dominic before the run. It all felt wrong.

Torness power station appeared on his right and he watched the south shoreline of the Forth open up in front of him. He decided to take the scenic route and turned off to head along the coast road past the beautiful little coastal town of North Berwick and the picture-postcard villages on the way to the city. He was almost there, and he was pretty sure that if there had been a problem it would have happened before then.

He slowed to make sure he was within the speed limit and looked for all the world like just another smartly dressed businessman in a Beamer on his way home or heading to one of the endless top-end golf clubs along that stretch of coast.

He saw the village of Gullane just ahead at the same time that he noticed the police road check. He fought the urge to turn around and bolt. It had to be just some bizzies doing routine shite, and they looked placid enough as he slowed down.

The first one strolled towards the car, and as he was rolling the window down, the cop smiled broadly. He relaxed again, just for that brief moment before they came at him from every direction. Plain clothes. He stepped out of the car, turned around and put his hands on the roof before they asked. As they grabbed him, he cursed Paul under his breath and swore he'd knock his fucking lights out if he ever got the chance. Two of the plain-clothes team just couldn't wipe the grin off their faces when they started searching him.

'Crap day, Sean, eh? Bet you were all sweaty, nearly back up the road brand new, then we come along.' He was obviously a loudmouth; the other plainer looked pissed off and told him to shut up.

Even though he wasn't that bright, Sean didn't miss

why the pig was annoyed. Loudmouth had already given him enough to say this was definitely no accidental pull, and 'back up the road' meant they must have known he'd been on a run south. He wanted to say 'fuck' to confirm he was annoyed, but he was programmed to shut it as far as the law were concerned, although just a little arrogance was always in order.

He turned his head to face the loud bastard and smiled, a nice friendly one just to show that he didn't give a fuck, or at least to appear that way. 'Always happy to help the polis, an' sure this is just a wee misunderstandin', Officer. By the way, how's your mother – still on the game?'

That worked a treat. Loudmouth grabbed Sean's face and squeezed because he could. As Grainger's wrists were already handcuffed behind him, there wasn't much he could do but stare straight into the pig's eyes and show the bastard he was a rank coward – so that was what he did, until the other plainer grabbed his partner's arm and pulled him away from Grainger, who put the smile on again and kept eye contact.

'Okay, smart-arse, let's see what's in the back and then we'll get you locked up for a long time, eh?'

The pig looked like this was the best day of his life; it was obvious he couldn't wait for the climax to the afternoon's show. One or two locals had started to wander near to the cordon that had been set up and a couple of cars heading west were backing up on the coast road. They could have turned and easily found an alternative route, but they didn't want to miss the show, given they already had a great view.

Sean picked up another hint from the cops: they didn't look inside the car but headed straight for the boot. Another clue that they knew exactly what had happened. He realised that at least in part, Paul had been right, and there was no doubt that they had a spy somewhere in the camp or else the bizzies had bugged them. Either way, they had a problem, but Sean had the mother and father of them all. Without a miracle, he was away for years, and Paul had fired him right into the dock. There was nothing he could do for the moment but tough it out, and he was fucked if he would show the loudmouth that he couldn't take it.

'Bring him round to the boot.'

Two uniforms had him by the arms and walked him round to face the bastard's grinning coupon again.

'Here we go.' He gave Sean the words of the caution and seemed delighted with himself and the day so far. It was obvious that the other plain-clothes cops had much the same opinion of Loudmouth as Sean – he saw their gritted teeth and the expressions that said, 'For fuck's sake, get on with it.'

It turned out Loudmouth was the DS and team leader. He opened the boot and grabbed the handles of the soft luggage bag.

'Now, Mr Grainger. What do you say is in this bag?' He grinned at the other cops, who stayed deadpan.

'Never seen it in my life before, Officer. You must have planted it, I guess. I heard stories about these things but never guessed the police actually did it.'

That pissed off Loudmouth, who wanted Grainger to break like a child. That's what always gave him the jollies.

'Smart-arse, eh? Not so fuckin' smart, though, are we?'

He put the bag on the ground, went down on one knee and opened it up. The fat packages were there and looked the part, but the mood changed when the pig squeezed the bag in his hand and his face puckered up in confusion. He looked at his partner and then sniffed the bag. His face gradually froze as he made a small cut in one and then raked among the sausages, lots and lots of sausages – and unless Sean was wrong, they had to be porkers.

The cops looked round at each other as Loudmouth started to lose it. For a moment, he thought that it couldn't be happening and what he was looking at had to be a very clever concealment.

He ripped open a couple of the sausages but they just contained pork. His face paled as he stood up slowly and seemed unable to decide what his next move or words should be. He was no more surprised than Sean Grainger, who just couldn't keep it straight. It was a set-up, a great big beautiful set-up. After cursing his brother, Sean realised just what he'd done: he'd thrown the rat, whoever he was, the bait of a big prize – one of the Graingers – and they hadn't been able to resist it.

'What in the name o' fuck is this bag o' shite?' Loudmouth was stamping his left foot, barely able to contain his rage and trying to figure out how he'd ended up looking like Police Scotland's twat of the month.

'Well, I'd say it was a bag of sausages, Officer, definitely not a bag of shite.' Sean could have kissed Paul at that moment. Although he knew his brother was still half off his trolley, this was a moment and he was glad he was here to see it.

They took Sean in, to give him what they thought was a hard time and on the way into the back of the van Loudmouth whacked him a shot when there were no eyes on him.

Sean turned to the cop with a trickle of blood on the side of his mouth. 'Is that it? Is that your best shot?'

He spat some blood onto Loudmouth's right shoe, sat in the back of the van and closed his eyes.

They held him for no more than a couple of hours before a detective super closed it down and told them to toss Grainger back onto the street. The super walked along the corridor, opened the door of Janet Hadden's office and found her chewing the end off a pencil as she tried to figure out exactly what had happened. It had all being going so well, so fucking well, and then this. It couldn't be Tonto, she thought, because this was all too ambitious for him. So what was it?

The super always just walked in without bothering to knock. He had a reputation as someone who was permanently in a foul mood about something, and the fuck-up with Sean Grainger was right up his alley in more ways than one.

Hadden just managed to say the word 'Sir' but didn't get as far as 'Do you want a coffee?' when he lit the building up and tore some lumps out of her. He'd authorised the job and was boss of the unit who'd run the operation. He was waiting and hoping for another promotion and all the signs had been good. He had one more rank in him before he retired but this kind of situation could be the difference between success and failure. His competitors would certainly make sure that they extracted all the mileage possible from what was already being called the Great Sausage Caper by the troops, who just loved someone else's fuck-up. It would fit very easily into the all-time jobs-gone-wrong legends and various hoots from the past.

'I want a report, Inspector. You hear me? A full report on exactly what went wrong here today and what the implications are. A blind man can see that this was a massive set-up, so what or who has been exposed? Do we have sources at risk because of this? Someone certainly suspected a source, and it looks like they've just proved it at our expense. You'd just better hope the press don't get a hold of this or we'll be a laughing stock again. I swear to fucking God this place is going to the dogs.'

He slammed the door behind him and Hadden stared into the wall.

The super had been right on one account: they'd been set up and she had to figure what had been compromised. Tonto had definitely told her that a few of the team knew that Sean was going south and she could use that. She had to think through what she was going to say to Dominic. Her original plan was that Sean would be locked up and she'd be able to turn various screws on him, but that was all down the tubes so she needed fresh cover. Dominic wasn't going to be happy, and she couldn't be sure whether he'd been involved in the set-up himself, but she thought it was unlikely. It sounded like Paul's work – he'd been obsessed with the possibility they had a rat under their feet.

She had the night to think it over but she'd just taken a giant hit and was still shaking after the humiliation poured over her in buckets by the super. Hadden bit right through the pencil she was gnawing and spat the fragments onto the desk. She held what was left of it like a knife and smashed it into the desktop again and again, pulverising it till it was only the edge of her hand pummelling the surface.

'Fucking superintendent. We'll see. We'll just fucking see.'

She promised herself that there would be a reckoning with the bastard. It was typical: if it was a success it was his, and if it went belly up it was someone else's problem. The way of the world – shit always falls downwards.

As Hadden worried, Sean got back to his flat and poured a treble shot of spiced rum. It was his favourite drink, although he usually saved it for weekends or after the game. This was up there with the Hibees humping the Jambos – a bit special. Given that for a few minutes earlier in the day he'd been convinced he was on his way to Saughton for a lot of years, he couldn't have felt more relieved. He picked up the phone and punched in Paul's number. It rang a few times before it was picked up.

'Speak.'

This time the word made Sean smile. 'You bastard. You any idea what you did to me? The bizzies are pissed, brother. Very, very pissed. Must admit I'm impressed. And pork sausages – that's fuckin' inspired!'

'See, you didn't trust your big brother. All fuckin' aggression.' It came straight out of the phone that Paul thought he was the dug's baws and then some.

'Listen, we don't know where the leak is and could even be this thing we're speakin' on. Know what I mean? Meet in the mornin' and take it from there. Okay?'

'Quite right, brother, see you then.'

Paul called the Leeds number on a safe phone and told them what had happened. 'One way or another they know we're workin' together, so guess you're gettin' attention, my friend.'

The Leeds man sounded hacked off but thanked Grainger and said they'd do a spring clean.

Sean filled up another treble but didn't get to the bottom of it before he fell asleep. He'd been through a full roller-coaster journey all in one day and his imagination and nerves had been stretched to their limit. The hit from the rum and the elation in the moments he realised he wasn't going away for a decade had exhausted him.

He slept deeply, but just before his eyes flickered in those moments before sleep he thought that a corner had been turned and things were going to be alright.

27

Tonto got the call from one of the team in the morning. The guy was high and knew exactly what the set-up meant.

'They're lookin' for a grass, Davy. Somebody's gonnae get it tight. It's a fuckin' certainty an' Paul'll be lookin' straight at us.' The guy was coming apart. Tonto knew the boy was swallowing a shitload of speed, and he was another one already on a yellow card with the Graingers. He was a good boy, but since his mother had popped her clogs the year before, he'd just fallen off a cliff.

'It's fine,' Tonto tried to reassure him, but he knew this brought suspicion even nearer to him. The bonus, for what it was worth, was that Sean mouthing off had given him some cover – there had been half a dozen guys in the boozer the day Sean had been spilling his guts.

'Sean's been openin' his gob all over the place so it could be anybody. Maybe the bizzies have tapped his phone.'

It was the line that came out every time there was a problem for a gang. Everyone was convinced that the police were listening in to their phones. Even daft wee housebreakers would talk in code, as if the power of the state was turned towards them rather than the terrorist threat.

'It'll be fine. See you at the ranch.'

Tonto put the phone down and it immediately started ringing again. It was Paul, who wanted everyone to meet in the 'office', which was an old workshop they owned just off Gorgie Road. They used it as an office more than anything and rarely for storage of gear. They knew the bizzies would probably have it on their intelligence systems, so it was only used for meets or, at most, short-term storage of chored gear that was going to be moved straight on.

Tonto arrived at the workshop half an hour after the call, his head thumping from the volume of lager he'd consumed the previous night. He had been drinking for Scotland and was beginning to think the habit was running out of control. It didn't matter what he did, though, and regardless of his daily hangovers, by late afternoon he felt like the only thing that mattered was that sensation when he gulped back his first of the day. There was no other way to unload, no one to talk to unless he counted Hadden, and he was beginning to wonder what that particular relationship was going to do for his long-term health. He had the shakes and wondered if he could look Paul or Sean in the eye and not give away what he was. Hadden had said, as if he needed reminding, that he was a grass – the lowest form of humanity. For a while he'd completely gone with the idea that he was an agent, a CHIS, because it sounded good, but now reality had crashed through the roof and he was back to basics.

Paul Grainger's face was tight with suppressed rage. He was with Sean when the team started to arrive, and each time one of the boys came through the door and tried to talk he just blanked them. He sat behind an old desk and stared straight ahead as Sean took a seat at the side of the desk and hardly moved his eyes from his shoelaces. Tonto lit a cigarette and sat as far away from Paul as he could get. There was an old bench that was as uncomfortable as fuck but would do for the time being. When everyone was in, Paul stubbed out the remains of his smoke.

'Well, some fucker make the tea then, eh?' His voice was half its normal volume and even in tone. All the boys apart from Sean jumped at the same time in an attempt to do something to please the man who everyone in the room knew was on the trail of a rodent. Maybe he'd already done it and it was just a case of finding some poor fucker guilty, then carrying out the sentence of the court. The mood he'd been in lately meant it was pretty sure to be the ultimate deterrent.

Paul then seemed to come to life, starting a speech about what he was going to do when he found the person who was working for the bizzies, and despite his early control, he started to lose it the more he spoke. Before the boys had arrived, Sean had disclosed that he'd said too much in the pub, so apart from the team, God knows who else knew – because they could never keep it shut.

It made no difference to Paul in one respect. He was pissed off at Sean, who'd partly fucked up what should have been a great job, but he knew they were close to finding the rat, and chances were, it was still someone in the meeting. He'd told him to mention the run only to two of the team, including Tonto, and if Sean had only kept his gob shut, it would have meant either Tonto or the other boy was the grass – or they were bugged up to the eyeballs. That would have been enough: they could have tortured Tonto and the other suspect till they got the truth, then dropped whoever turned out to be Roland off the Forth Road Bridge before spring-cleaning for bugs. Job done – or it should have been.

'Just get this straight. When I find out – an' I will – I'll fuckin' string the bastard up by his thumbs. You hear me?'

He almost screamed the last question and thumped the desk. They all nodded, in no doubt. Tonto thought he was going to wet himself; it felt like his stomach had turned to water.

Paul scanned the room back and forward, locking onto each of them to look inside their heads. He wanted to see if he could identify who was carrying the lie, who was the traitor.

'Right, you've all got jobs today so get fuckin' out there.'

They stood up as one and headed for the door without seeming to rush.

'Oh, by the way . . . ' It was Paul again. 'When I find out who this is, you're all invited to the show.' He managed a grin. It was no happy smile, just a confirmation that he meant every word he said. No one in the meeting doubted it.

Sean walked out with them to get a breath of air, still feeling shattered after the events of the day before.

'I'll be back in a second, just goin' along the road for some smokes,' he told Paul. His brother nodded, still imagining what he'd do when he found out who the rat was. When Sean had told him that he'd gobbed to the whole team, he'd been pissed off, but it was what it was, and they'd find the bastard eventually; it would just take a little longer. Paul didn't say it to his brother, but he *had* suspected him, although now he was pretty sure that he, at least, was clean. Tonto still bothered him, as did the whole thing with the Pole and what had happened after the incident. It was just a matter of waiting and watching, letting things cool off a bit then throwing some fresh bait. He knew that rats ate anything – it was a well-known fact.

Tonto felt like he was going to throw up and empty his bowels all at the same time. He scanned the road both ways, wondering where the fuck he could make it to. He couldn't have used the cludgie in the workshop because Paul would have seen it as a mark: the fear of the man who'd let them all down. He saw the boozer sign and, although it was only minutes away, the way his guts felt, it could have been the other side of the city. This was an emergency, and he didn't even know if he could make it that far before nature took its course. He started to jog, grabbed the base of his stomach and it was as if time slowed down. He was sure he couldn't hold it.

Sean walked out behind his team and blinked into the sunshine. He had smokes already; he just wanted to be clear of Paul for a couple of minutes before he went back in. He was annoyed that he'd bumped his gums to the team and it was just confirmation that it was the family name that gave Sean a bit of privilege and not much else. Paul had been pissed off when he'd told him but, surprisingly, not as bad as Sean had expected. His brother was always full of surprises though.

He lit up, heard a couple of the guys laughing and looked to see what the big joke could be after the crisis meeting they'd just attended. Tonto was jogging across the road, holding his gut with one hand. Sean had noticed that the boy had looked the colour of slate inside but knew he liked the swally just a bit too much. It might be nothing – Christ, who didn't get a bad gut sometimes, especially given the amount of Indian food that boy ate?

Sean pulled on the cigarette and ran his fingers through his hair. He blew the smoke out on a long stream, watching Tonto pull the pub door open and disappear inside. He stared in the direction of the pub for a minute, nodded a couple of times and made a note to keep a close one on Tonto. His brother already had his suspicions and maybe he was right again. Sean had never been that sure and thought Paul was homing in on the boy as an easy target after the thing with the Pole. And if they convicted the wrong person and the rat was still in place, then that was an even worse proposition.

He took his time with the smoke because not only was he knackered with it all, he had a bastard of a headache.

Sean returned to the workshop a few minutes later and, thankfully, Paul seemed to have got it all together again. You just never knew where you were with the man, he thought. He was either high as a fucking kite or convinced the world was conspiring against him.

'What now then?' he asked. 'Think the boys got the message loud and clear?'

Paul looked at his brother long and hard, his brain working too many scenarios. 'Well, you arranged a meet with Dom, remember?'

He waited for Sean to reply. He didn't need the meet, but then why not? They were in the middle of a crisis so maybe it was best to clear the air.

'I'll call a taxi.'

28

Dominic Grainger had already heard what had happened, as Sean had called him on the way to the meet at the workshop. Whether he was pissed off at Paul or not, the set-up with the bizzies had worked, and despite what was being arranged with Janet Hadden, it looked like there might be another source inside his brother's side of the business. Dominic still thought that Paul could have achieved the same objective with a bit more subtlety. His brother had thrown a handful of crap into the faces of the bizzies and that wasn't always the best way to do it. They'd be determined that a rematch took place after the humiliation, and those bastards had long memories.

He was also full of questions about his own situation, the first of which was: did Janet Hadden know about the run to Leeds? She had to – it was her fucking job. He didn't trust her anyway, but this put him even more on his guard. He was playing a game without knowing what the rules were . . . And what the fuck happened if he lost?

He stared out of the window and sipped a strong black espresso his assistant had brought in for him. Same time, same order each morning. It gave his brain the kick it needed to get the day started. Hadden wasn't due to turn up till later and his brothers were on their way first thing. He had to change the plan after the events of the previous day.

He called the number Hadden had given him for their unofficial contact.

'Dominic, what's up?' She tried to be as matter-of-fact as possible but had half-expected a reaction.

'You telling me you don't know? What the fuck do you take me for?' He'd intended to keep the conversation businesslike but there'd been too many problems building, and now this.

'It's not what you think. Easy to explain. Listen, why don't we cancel the official bit today. I'll tell the guy I was coming with that there's a change of plan for the moment; he won't question it. We can meet and clear this up before we move on. How does that sound?'

'Just what I was thinking.' For some reason, and despite his deep mistrust of Hadden, he still felt a stirring both physically and emotionally, and once again it threw him. How could such mistrust, almost fear, go hand in hand with attraction?

They agreed to meet in a bar not too far from his St Vincent Place flat. He put the phone down and squeezed the bridge of his nose; even though it was still early in the day he felt weary. Everything felt heavy and the coffee hadn't given him the usual boost he expected.

The phone rang again and he looked at it for a moment, wondering whether to let it be. He didn't want to speak to anyone because he already had enough on his mind for the day. His brothers were on their way and that was probably the maximum he could cope with for one morning.

Paul would be full of it: if anything, it would make

him even more bolshy as far as Dominic's position was concerned. He knew in his guts that at some stage they were going to go head-to-head. It was suicidal, but it was the way of the world. Paul wanted more, always more, and there was never enough for some people.

He felt his heart race when he thought about the money problems, frightened to even think about how far down he was with the debt that was building with almost a will of its own. His luck seemed to have turned to shit. When he went to the casino, it was as if the tables, croupiers and dealers were all conspiring together to rip the cash from him. It was that old thing that when you're down, luck seems to fuck off into someone else's life, and he watched the dealers frown at his losses. They knew the signs when the regulars with a problem were breaking in front of their eyes.

The big losers would stare at the empty space where there had been a pile of chips as if they could be given back in a sympathetic gesture. Dealers tried to look understanding when they heard a customer say, 'Tomorrow's another day,' as if that was all it was and all it took. But in Dominic's case the gods had deserted him, his only solace being the women he pulled and impressed as if it was all good.

The phone rang and when he picked it up it all got worse in the space of a few words. It was his wife, Jude.

'Listen, Dominic. I need to tell you that I've got my lawyers involved. I've had enough of this shit and it's time to sort it out. I suggest you do the same. I'd like to say I'm sorry about this, but actually I'm not.' His wife's voice was ice-cold, and he knew her well enough to understand that this wasn't up for argument, but he was human and his emotions were already being tested to the limit.

'Hang on a minute.' He closed his eyes for a moment

and mouthed 'fuck'. He needed this call like he needed a dose of the clap. 'We should talk about this, Jude. Christ, all we're doing is giving these fucking lawyers money for old rope.' What he said was pointless and he knew it.

'We can talk, but what good will that do? Please surprise me with an answer. We've had all the chances to talk and what have you done about it? Absolutely fuck all as usual. Too busy picking up fresh meat. Christ, you disgust me!'

It was always the same, one insult drew retaliation and so it went on. He was already in a foul mood and sanctimony from a woman who seemed to be matching him pull for pull was the last thing he needed. 'You have some fucking nerve. Okay, I got it all wrong, but . . . Christ, you're throwing it about like the slag you are.'

She cut him off in the middle of that one and he cursed himself for losing it again. It happened every time, but lawyers sticking their fat fingers into his business could be the next nightmare keeping him awake at night. The pressure would be coming from three sides now and there was a danger that he might lose control of the situation.

The door opened and his brothers walked in. Jude answered him just as they sat down.

'By the way, if you want to tell all to my dad, go ahead – do your best and see if I fucking care.' She put the phone down before he could say anything else.

For a moment, he did nothing. Her words had surprised him. He'd always thought that was his ace card.

Eventually he put the phone down on the desk and tried to pretend he was calm, that he couldn't feel the thundering beat of the pulse in his neck.

He'd been right on the money about Paul. As soon as he'd breezed through the door he was full of it, even more than usual, and if he'd been a pain in the arse before, it was probably about to get worse. He'd scored a goal against the bizzies and it would be talked about, and do his reputation in the trade no harm at all. Sean grinned but Dominic thought he looked tired, though he probably deserved to after what he'd been through.

Paul ran over what had happened, his eyes bright, the pupils dilated like black holes, as he told the story. He was pleased with himself, no doubt about it. Sean stayed quiet and only came in at the end.

'I fucked up – spoke to the boys about the run. Nothing I can do about it now.' It was what it was and neither Paul nor Dominic said anything that would rub salt into that particular wound.

'No great harm. It happens and a lesson for the future, eh?' Paul said it without an edge to his voice and he meant it.

'Only thing I'd say is that the bizzies aren't going to forget this one. They'll look for payback if they get a chance.' Dominic wanted to say more, but his relationship with Paul was on a hair trigger and there was no need to apply pressure to a loaded weapon. 'What now then?' Dominic directed the question to Paul, as he was the one making the play.

'You mentioned havin' a line into the force. That still stand?' Paul looked his older brother straight in the eye as if he was watching prey, waiting for the slightest wrong move.

'Absolutely, meet arranged for later. First things first though. I just hooked this guy up and I need to test him.' He said 'him', which left the possibilities wide open – mentioning a woman could have made it more difficult to cover. 'Was going to test the guy about your runner they lifted. See if he's talked.' He felt that would do for the moment and hopefully keep Paul quiet for the time being. 'Where do you go now if there is a grass?'

'No if. It's happened. Problem is the guy has to be spooked. They know we're lookin' for them and have to be sweatin' blood. Guess they'll keep quiet for a bit in case it goes tits up again.'

Paul flipped a cigarette into his mouth. It was another little trick copied from an American gangster film and he waited, wanting to see what Dominic's reaction would be. He was pretty sure Sean was sound, but everyone else was a suspect, including his older brother, till it was cleared up. As far as he was aware, his older brother shouldn't have known about the run south, which would rule him out, but it was always possible one of their team was feeding him from the inside.

'There's always the possibility that you're being bugged, Paul. It's the twenty-first century and the bastards do it all the time now. Who knows? Think it would be worth paying for a security firm to sweep everything? Maybe get some new phones. What do you think?' He turned to Sean, who as usual had to be forced into the conversation.

He looked sheepish and, given that he'd fucked up by opening his mouth at the wrong time, didn't really feel entitled, but his brothers waited for his reaction. For different reasons, they would always try to bring Sean into the discussions, even though his opinion rarely swayed them. They were both safe from Sean – he would never be a threat – so they both played him in order to draw him onside if they could. They treated him like a swing voter, and although he was loyal to Paul first, he knew the business would only work with Dominic at the head. If Paul ever took over he'd declare war on every competitor, including the Campbells.

'No' sure. Whatever or whoever it is, this is close. Good idea to get the place swept. See there's a Weegie team in the news. At the High Court and they bugged them to fuck. Seems the way they do it now. Think it's worth asking if you have this bizzie on the inside. Could be worth their weight.'

Paul and Dominic both nodded. There wasn't much else to say till Dominic had spoken to his mole, so they agreed to wait till he'd had the meet and then take it from there.

As the meeting wound up, Dominic thought he'd got off lightly and had maybe even bought a bit of time to straighten something out, at least on their problem (which just left him with all the other ones). That thought lasted till Paul got to the door and turned.

'By the way, Dom, want to chew the fat over a bit of expansion in the business. Chance to make some serious profit.'

'What?' It was all Dominic could say; his stomach churned again and he already had indigestion. He never got indigestion.

'Movin' some pros.' Paul grinned as if they were discussing football. 'Few contacts in Glasgow and south of the border makin' megabucks movin' girls round the country.'

'Pros?' Dominic could only manage the one word again.

'Aye, pros. You know what they are: tits an' arse ... Fuck's sake.'

Paul grinned as he watched the lines form on his brother's forehead. He knew trafficking women was far too real life for him, but times were changing and Paul Grainger was just the man to bring about that change.

'We'll speak in the mornin'. You've got enough to worry about, eh, Dom?' He closed the door behind him.

Dominic saw the problems just pile up in front of him. He wondered what Paul meant by 'you've got enough to worry about'. The bastard was trying to wind him up, and he was throwing the first dice in whatever fucked-up game he was playing.

Paul wanted to go into the sewers to make money. Trafficking women would take them into a business where gangsters from all over Europe cooperated or fought. This was a game where one wrong move had professional killers slicing your face off, or, if they were really pissed, doing the same to your family. This was a move into a European super-league and Dominic knew they weren't equipped for that kind of business. It would draw even more attention from the law – as if they hadn't enough problems as it was.

'Jesus Christ,' he muttered and called his assistant. 'When you're out for coffee will you get me some indigestion tabs?'

'You don't get indigestion.' She was right, up to a point.

'I do now.'

29

Dominic left the office a bit earlier than usual and had arranged to meet Hadden later on. He needed to clear his head and think through what was coming his way but struggled trying to work out what he should deal with first.

He decided to walk along to the nearest bookies, have just the one bet and limit it to fifty quid. Putting a bet on always gave him that brief high of expectation that something wonderful might happen. It was almost the same with the women he picked up, hoping that all his failures would be forgotten when he hit the jackpot.

He pulled up his collar against the cold. Scotland had, even by its own shite standards, suffered a long, wet and miserable winter and now it had pissed down half the summer. It dawned on him that he hadn't had a decent holiday in the sun for an age and he imagined himself on a long white beach with nothing to do but soak it all up.

Suddenly she was there again: Janet Hadden, there in his imagination. 'Fucking weird,' he muttered to himself.

His attention was grabbed by a piss-head on the other side of the road who was swaying on the edge of the kerb, one eye closed as he tried to focus and navigate his way safely across. He almost envied the guy for being pissed, all his worries gone for a few hours.

He turned off and stepped into the warm blast of air in the bookies. A couple of the regulars nodded and went back to the lines of information on the screens.

The subcontractor stayed well behind Grainger because he was pretty certain about where he was headed anyway. The boy liked a bet, and sure enough that's exactly where he ended up. He noted the slumped shoulders and the dragging feet – the boy looked down and was definitely somewhere else in his head. He called Frankie Mason.

'He's away from the office and back to the bookies. The boy looks fucked off, for want of a better word. The two brothers were there earlier, or take it was them. The two guys who were there certainly match the descriptions you gave me. Anyway, what do you want me to do?'

'Stay with him. I'm workin' on some phone stuff here. If anythin' interestin' happens get back to me an' I'll come to you. If he just heads back to his flat I'll take over and you can knock off till the mornin'. That okay with you?'

'You're payin' the wages, my friend, so I'm happy.'

Mason had identified more of the phone subscribers. There was an escort service that came up a few times; he knew the guy who ran it and he would try and track down whether the calls were business or pleasure. The pimp who ran the girls would sell his granny for profit and Mason had used a couple of the girls himself. It shouldn't be hard to find the girl or girls Grainger had used. He knew most guys had their favourites.

He sat back and wondered again about the Belfast number. *What was that about?* he wondered. All he knew was that a contact was there. It had to be heavy-duty business, but it was difficult to see what more he could do with it in the absence of more information. He'd get a result for Arthur Hamilton, but he was going well beyond the parameters of the contract. It would be necessary to get into someone a bit closer to Grainger, and he knew he'd have to stay on his toes: those Ulster prods didn't fuck about if someone sniffed the air anywhere near their business.

Fuck it, he thought. There was something there – secrets – and he wanted to know what they were. He pulled a cold beer from the fridge and ran his finger down the side of the bottle, watching the line of clear glass trail behind his finger. If the subcontractor drew a blank he might call up the escort service and get one of the girls over to his flat. He enjoyed it when they saw the state of his place. It was a fucking midden, but that's how he liked it.

His phone buzzed into life again.

'He's away from the bookies but definitely not headin' home. Still in the New Town, walking along Howe Street. Seems to know where he's goin' and looks a bit perkier than when he went into the bookies. What do you want me to do?'

'Stay on him an' I'll be there as soon as.'

Mason stuck the phone in his pocket. *Where you off to, Dominic?* he thought. A smile crossed his face. *Fuckin' love this game.*

He put down the half-empty beer and grabbed his car keys.

Dominic Grainger felt just that bit lighter on his feet and his mood had lifted. A donkey that should have been entertaining children on a beach had caught his eye, and at odds of 25–1, he'd plonked fifty quid on it to win. Somebody had pressed the donkey's go-faster button and the thing had ended up winning. Grainger had punched the air and seen it as a good omen that blues skies were ahead. That's what addicted gamblers did.

The bookie nodded at Grainger's back as he left the shop, stuffing the readies into his pocket. He knew how it worked: the money in the punter's mitt was only away for a short break, because serious gamblers like Grainger were on a merry-go-round. Occasionally they had their slice of luck, but the main result was that they became even more addicted to the game. It was there in black and white, and all you needed to do was google it or use the common sense that God didn't give to everyone. The bookie always fucking wins.

Hadden did it properly. She used her tradecraft and gave Grainger the exact time she'd arrive at the bar. She told him that he should be there fifteen minutes later. She wanted to make sure it was safe and pick her seat. His flat was out of the question for the time being, as there was always the risk he'd set up a recording of the meet. What she was doing was risky enough without that particular nightmare scenario. She'd stick on the wig and glasses just in case. The bar was upmarket and she knew it well enough. It was full of locals. No scum and lots of discussion about Brexit and golf.

Grainger didn't get the importance of what she'd said and was still enjoying the moment he'd scored a beauty against the bookies when he arrived at the pub door at the same time she did. She hissed through her teeth and resisted the temptation to tell him to fucking pay attention to what she said. If they walked into the pub together, Sod's Law might come into play and someone who knew one of them might be sitting in the bar for the first time in their lives. It happened. Arriving separately would have meant they could ignore each other if necessary.

Hadden paused for a moment, caught in two minds,

until she realised there was little choice, and although she should have just fucked off, the previous day's events meant this little meeting had the word crisis written all over it. She nodded and they walked in together.

The subcontractor had a special gift in that even after a long, almost uneventful day he stayed on his toes. There hadn't been much time to take in the obvious meet with the female, but he'd not only clocked it, he'd also registered her discomfort. Did they meet by accident or design? It didn't matter, a meet was a meet. He managed to get a picture – not a great one but better than nothing.

Mason joined the subcontractor ten minutes later and looked more than interested when he was told what had happened at the door. As he stared at the photograph on the subcontractor's phone, he felt his heart take a couple of extra bumps, as if he'd overdosed on espresso. It was impossible to clearly identify the woman from the range the picture had been taken; nevertheless, she was familiar, and he knew where from, but he had to be sure.

'You can take off, son. Good job. I'll stay in the car. I just need to see them up close when they leave. That'll do me for the night.'

The subcontractor left and said he'd be on station first thing in the morning, and Mason manoeuvred the car till he found a spot where he could safely cover the front of the boozer.

After setting up his camera he relaxed. It was top kit, and with a bit of luck he'd get a decent shot of the woman. It was all good. He had a feeling they wouldn't be too long in there, whatever it was they were up to.

30

Janet Hadden had to work hard at pretending she was happy with the situation. It was awkward but she had to get the project back on track. Problems appeared all the time and her job was to solve them within the rules. That's what they taught at the college so it had to be true. *Like fuck,* she'd thought the first time she'd heard some dewy-eyed instructor tell it to the congregation. It depended on the problem; what she was creating and dealing with wasn't in the textbooks.

She breathed a sigh of relief that at least the place was fairly quiet but not too quiet, and there was a rerun of an old game on the box that was generating just enough noise level to cover what they were about to discuss.

She looked up when she ordered the drinks at the bar to see Lionel Messi and his Barcelona mob sticking it right up the opposition again; their manager's face looked like he'd swallowed some bleach. Every face in the pub was concentrating on the genius of the little Argentinian and wishing he was a Scot. At least it made it easier for her to talk business.

She sat down with the drinks she'd insisted on buying

175

to prove it was no longer a man's world. He half-smiled; the bulge of the notes in his pocket still felt good. His high hadn't worn off yet, but he needed some answers and, more importantly, some serious help.

'What happened yesterday? You had to know about it. Was the plan to take my brother out and then come for me?' He lifted his beer and waited. He was calm enough and had accepted there was a set of confusing and potentially dangerous problems on his doorstep. His choice was simple: take them on or at least one of them would ruin either his finances, his reputation or his health. Possibly all of them together. The woman opposite could provide answers and possible solutions, but there was nothing simple about her or what she was doing.

He waited while she took a stiff shot of her wine. The glass was half-empty when she put it back on the table and she definitely wasn't bothering to savour it. Like him, she needed the hit, but he had no idea what she was up to or dealing with and that was another problem. He knew he wouldn't get all the answers, but he was determined she wasn't pulling his strings for free this night.

He looked round as a collective murmur of admiration greeted Messi sticking a second beauty round a flapping goalkeeper.

Hadden shook her head at the TV. 'Man's a genius.'

It wasn't what he'd expected her to say.

'Didn't take you for a football fan?'

'Love it, especially the way that wee man plays it.'

For the first time, she seemed to have taken her mask off and he felt like he was speaking to someone a bit nearer reality.

'Anyway, to get back to the question. Yes, I knew about it, and what do you expect? It's my job but I didn't have all the levers in my hands.'

She'd decided earlier that a bit of truth should precede

the lie. There was no point in trying to convince him that she'd had no idea as that would have insulted his intelligence.

Then she delivered the lie. 'Thing is, it was nothing to do with me or my section. We knew your brother was going south of the border, but where did the information come from? The NCA have been running a job on your pals down in Leeds and they picked up the story. They passed it up to a team here. I don't have any control over how they handle it.'

She picked up the drink and finished what was left in the glass. She watched his face colour and realised he was about to unload on her. She stuck her hand up: 'Let me finish.'

He sat back again and gave her the floor.

'If we'd started our arrangement already then there might have been things I could have done. Understand?' Her face had tightened; she was in no mood to engage in a slanging match. She would lay down the guidelines and he would have to take it or leave it. But she knew exactly what he'd do. He had no choice.

Grainger tried to analyse what she'd said but there wasn't enough time to pick over it. 'Okay, I get that.' As far as he could work out, what she said made sense. There was no reason the information couldn't come from south of the border. These things happened, so it was what it was and they needed to talk about the future. She took over.

'Okay, you've had your answer. Now tell me – what the fuck was the bag of sausages about and where did that little plan spring from? I'm presuming you don't have someone else on my side, so what happened?' She waved to the barman for the same again.

Grainger knew that it was worth being as straight as possible on that one: it was an obvious set-up and something near the truth would give nothing away or an advantage. 'My brother Paul is . . . ' He hesitated for a moment and Hadden came in with an answer before he could.

'He's unstable; that's how he's described on our side.'

He nodded. That sounded a diplomatic but pretty accurate description of his brother. Despite his mistrust of Hadden, he felt they were in the process of forming some kind of relationship. They might have different ideas about what that was, but they were locked in now and both had feelers out hoping for a response that would suit them individually.

'Okay, he's manic about leaks.' He couldn't help smiling at the thought that manic didn't quite cover it. 'There've been a few problems recently and he's convinced we have a security problem. You understand his business isn't necessarily mine?'

She stopped him again and he knew it all sounded a bit limp. 'Look. I've told you already this isn't evidence gathering, and cards on the table, what I'm doing could land me in the shit. What you're doing could land you in the pokey or under concrete. Can we just cut the nonsense? We're both here for entirely selfish reasons, and in my case, it's fuck all to do with the reputation of Police Scotland.'

If he needed proof that she was a bit different, she'd just delivered it on a plate. Even so, he had to stay cautious and move one step at a time to avoid the traps that might be set for him. He could work with her proposal up to a point.

'We've lost a lot of gear so far, but then you know that. Just for the record, we do operate separately, although I do help my brothers out. Paul is convinced your side already have someone inside our business. I have a growing issue with Paul, and to tell the truth, it's getting out of hand. You already know about my money problems and now my wife's bringing in the lawyers. I don't know how long I can hold it all together.' It was an awful lot of truth; he seemed almost deflated after saying it, and the enormity of what he might be facing seemed to hit home with the act of disclosing it to the enemy.

'So we need to help each other out here, Dominic. Correct?'

He nodded as she lifted her glass and held it ready for a clink, sighed, raised his beer and tapped sides with her wine glass. 'To the future.'

It was her turn to nod.

'I've told them I've a source inside the force. No names, no pack drill. I had to buy time. I need a favour. A big, fat fucking favour so I can put Paul back in his box. He's full of it after taking the piss out of your gang.'

Hadden drew her eyelids together. She would have preferred it if he'd said nothing to his brothers, but they would easily work out he had a source if he started drawing rabbits out of hats. 'Okay, but absolutely no names. Remember what we do means that we can have mutually assured destruction, right? You try to bury me then you go down at exactly the same time.'

'First of all, did the runner you lifted talk? He was one of yours at one time so he might turn.' Grainger felt nervous; he needed this, and it was dawning on him that this woman might be his only chance of getting through the shitstorm that seemed to be heading his way.

'He hates the job after what happened to him. He wouldn't even give the interview team his name. Does that help?' She felt that was too simple and it just couldn't be that easy if they were going to trade. 'You said "first of all", so what's second?'

'I need to know who you have inside Paul's team.'

'You have to be fucking joking! So you can rip the

poor bastard's heart out. No way. That's too much.' She couldn't hide her contempt – it was a request well beyond what she expected or was prepared to concede.

'In the same way I'll protect you to the last, it's the same for anyone else.' It was shite on a stick, but she couldn't really say anything else given he was putting his future health in her hands to do the same job.

Grainger took it like a slap across the coupon, although to be fair he knew it was a big ask when they hardly knew each other. Unfortunately he was desperate, but he couldn't show it or she'd take advantage – and why wouldn't she? He had almost no bargaining chips to lay on the table.

He began to sweat because without something from the meeting he was completely adrift. Despite the fact that what he'd been planning was beyond what she could work out, he needed what knowledge she had for reasons no one, including his brothers, could have imagined.

Grainger looked round; nobody was looking at them and the sound of the final minutes of the game would drown out anything they were saying. He was a gambler and about to play the first cards of the hand that would decide his future health prospects. 'I can give you something big: bigger than anything you're dealing with here.'

Hadden did her best to look unimpressed but she wanted to hear more. Sources or gangsters in custody promised the big one all the time – usually it was all bollocks and not worth the time of day. 'Okay, impress me. A clue. I don't expect you to throw it all on the table for me, but what does "big" mean? It had better be fucking monumental or that trade is off the table.'

He felt the palms of his hands go sticky and she saw the tension he just couldn't hide. She guessed he was battling even more problems than she'd realised, which was all to the good as far as she was concerned. He was robbing the profits and it sounded like he was more concerned about Paul Grainger than she'd realised; however, there was clearly something else going on, and she would have to do some more digging into what intelligence was available on him.

'It's guns. Guns for Belfast Loyalists. I know or can guarantee that if you want it, you can intercept a shipment to the team I do some business with.'

He picked up his drink, swallowed a mouthful and decided he was having a short the next round. His heart was beating the fuck out of his breastbone because he was playing the biggest game of his life and it certainly concentrated his mind. He always played the game with a bit of safety, but this was dark arts, where the stakes were all or nothing.

Hadden tried her best to maintain a calm exterior as this was quite an offer, and still might be fantasy, but if there was a possibility then she had to grab it. There was a lot to think about, because if it was true and it was connected to terrorism then it might be taken out of her hands. However, Loyalists were not in the business of going back to the Troubles as far as she knew so it was more likely to be organised-crime related. That could work big time, and why not? She asked the same question that anyone looking at the claim would make.

'Don't mean to insult you, Dominic, but the clue's in your name and background. Are you telling me that a boy from a good Catholic clan from the south would deal with these guys? Christ, this is seriously heavy-duty. Why?'

'I don't give a fuck about what happened over there. It's that simple. Republicans or prods – it makes no difference to me as long as the deal is right. Paul feels the past more than I do, but business comes first and God doesn't figure a lot in our lives, though I haven't introduced him to the boys over the water yet. Is that big enough for you then?'

He stood up. 'What you having? I'm having whisky, a double. Tell you the truth, I need it right at this moment.'

They both needed a lot and had a lot to offer each other. Hadden thought a turn like this would bury the damage done after the set-up. It had been a serious blow to her cred and this might just be the antidote. Arms trafficking was top-quality intelligence and would cover her in gold stars if she could pull it off. Yes, this might all work out fine. Hadden nodded. 'Sounds good to me.'

When he sat back at the table, the noise level had gone down. Some overpaid ex-players were analysing something or other on the telly and saying Messi was a genius like no one knew that already. Grainger had watched them while he was waiting on the drinks. The barman had cracked the joke he made almost every week. 'Could do that shift for half the price, state the blindingly fucking obvious – there, that's basically it.' He had laughed at his own joke and Grainger had managed a half-smile.

It was too quiet now for what they'd been discussing before he went to the bar. When she unexpectedly gave him a broad smile, he noticed she had almost perfect teeth. He might have expected a couple of fangs, but they were straight and even. He was impressed.

'What do you think then? Bit too quiet here now? We could go to my flat. It's only a short walk. At least it's private.' He didn't expect her to go for it but he wanted an answer if possible. The problems were closing in, and if he didn't go proactive, a chain of events might start that would be impossible to control.

'Okay. I'm still thinking but let's go there and see what we can work out. Two things though . . . You listening?'

He nodded as she narrowed her eyes and leaned forward.

'We're there for business. No fucking around, and believe me, I may have the body of a poor little woman but don't be fooled. You try anything and you'll wonder what happened to your arm, because I'll break it off and beat you to fucking death with it . . . Cheers.'

The more obnoxious she became, the more she attracted him. Despite realising that she was just playing her game, he had the feeling that the threat of physical violence might have substance. He'd never been threatened that way by a woman, and had never expected to be, but Hadden was no straightforward example of the gender. He wondered what she would be like in bed.

As they threw back the drinks, Hadden continued: 'Second thing is this. What you mentioned sounds good, but what if your name's all over it? Do I take you as well?' She stared at him for a moment, trying to see what was going on in his mind; watching for any little ticks and movements in his face that could expose a lie.

'It's workable. I arrange it through other contacts I use. Some straight and some not. For a job like this, they don't even know what it is they're carrying, and I'm far enough back for plausible deniability. Your side might suspect but they'll toil to tie me into anything. I make sure I have the goods on whoever I use so if they try and throw shit in my direction, it blows back in their face. These jobs are complex and I'm careful to stay back from the danger zones.' He seemed pleased with his answer.

'Okay, sounds good and I'll be covering your arse wherever I can as long as you're not overexposed. Hope you have a fresh bottle up there.' Her last comment threw him completely, her foot now running up and down the outside of his calf.

He struggled for a reaction; ordinarily he would have just taken it as a natural progression. This woman, however, didn't do natural progression. A couple of minutes earlier she'd been threatening to rip his arm off and now she was playing footsie under the table.

'You're some piece of work.'

He was relaxing and decided that he would play his game too. He kept letting her take control and fuck with his mind. Being no mug, he reminded himself that she was a bent shot so every bit as vulnerable as he was.

He'd seen her hold her expression still when he'd mentioned guns but there had been a glint in her eye. Fuck's sake, for a bizzie he was handing her a prize and a half. God knows what made her tick, but he suspected something not too dissimilar from every other player who wanted more than a nine-to-five job and two-and-a-half kids. It obviously wasn't money in her case. No, she wanted the glory. He got that.

He put on his best smile again – the one he reserved for his pick-ups – and the small lines round his eyes scrunched up in the way that most of those women loved. He grabbed her knee under the table and squeezed hard, making Hadden wince and the smile disappear.

'Just remember, Janet, that I fucking bite as well. I'll see you at the flat.' He stood up and headed for the door.

She hissed out a short breath and felt her heart race. She hadn't expected his reaction and ordered another double, throwing it over her neck before she left. The barman grinned and said, 'Take care.'

'Go fuck yourself,' was the reply he hadn't expected.

She walked out of the bar and took in a few deep breaths of the cool, damp air.

Frankie Mason had watched Grainger leave the bar on his own and walk past him on the other side of the road, so he wasn't heading in the direction he should have taken for home. The fact that two people had entered the boozer together and the female was still inside signified something: they were being careful. Why? He still had to find that out. Had anyone been offering odds, he would have put a few notes on their night being not yet finished. Maybe, like Grainger, she was married. But there was more to it, he was confident of that. His job was to stay on Grainger but the woman would appear, if not tonight then the next time, and her identity intrigued him.

Mason left his car and was able to keep Grainger in sight but a good distance ahead. Only a few minutes from the pub, he watched him turn up the steps to the flat and open the door with a key.

Nice place, Dominic. Very nice indeed, he thought. Arthur Hamilton had told him there was a flat, and he knew it was good property, but seeing Grainger go in gave him context in his mind. This flat was part of another life the top criminal was leading. His secret – or so he thought.

Mason walked past and managed to pull into a quiet doorway where he could watch for a while and any nosey bastard would just think it was some poor soul not allowed to smoke indoors. This street was quality.

The woman appeared before Mason had smoked half his cigarette. He stubbed it out and, although there was distance between them, it had to be the woman from the boozer. He watched the way she walked and moved. There was no chance of a photo, but this was still a result. She was looking along the numbers on the flats, checking. Mason guessed she hadn't been there before as she took the steps up to the main door and peered at the numbers on the entry system.

'No, you definitely haven't been here before, darlin',' he whispered into the night air. He watched her touch her face and hair, then do something with her skirt and mouth something indistinguishable into the entry-system panel. She went in.

Mason was pleased. Very pleased. Knowing she'd

likely be inside for a while, he headed back to pick up his car. It was getting late, and on this quiet street he could sit there long enough without attracting any attention. The feeling that he was in the middle of a rich vein made the decision about whether to hang around or call it a day a no-brainer: he'd stick with the job. A beer could wait, and it wasn't as if his flat was somewhere he was dying to get back to.

31

'What guarantees do I have with this deal, then?' He'd poured the drinks, which were home measures and a half. She tipped back the glass and didn't pretend it was too strong.

'Perfect, the right amount of booze to mixer.' She looked flushed, and they were both just a bit pissed but still on guard. 'No guarantees. As far as possible I look after you. One thing though . . . If you're recording any of this, just remember we both go down the sewers. I'm the only thing keeping Paul away from your little financial problems.'

It was partly his own fault – he'd given away that he was worried about Paul and had dealt her a face card.

'There's no recording,' he told her. 'Look, I need what you can offer and vice versa. I think, whatever your reasons, you want what I can give you and you're ready to risk it all. Strange one to me: you're not the usual piss-head or coked-up suit who needs the money just to keep functioning. In fact, I'd take a bet money doesn't mean that much to you. Anyway, we're in this together as the Tories keep telling us.'

'I would give you the name of the source inside Paul's

team, but what fucking good does it do to find someone I'm running with a severe case of death? Do you have any idea how much shit that would create for me?' She seemed to be discounting the proposal, but he'd already worked out that if the offer was right, this woman would go a long way to accommodate a deal.

'So you do run this character, but it wasn't him that gave your side the Leeds run?'

She had to be careful with her reply and stick to the original lie because it wouldn't do any harm. There was no way he could ever work out the truth. 'No, the source didn't give us that one. I told you, it was the Leeds team.'

He studied her as far as the excess booze would allow, unable to make up his mind whether that was true, but then for what he had in mind it didn't matter.

'Look, you already know I have Paul right in my coupon at the moment. I need to put him in his place and think we'll go head-on before long. He's my brother, but I want you to take him out at some stage. I'll help you. Let's face it, your side would love a rematch with a guaranteed result.' He raised his glass. 'How does that sound?'

She was interested, and the value of sealing the deal on running Dominic Grainger as a CHIS was going up as each minute passed. Getting him sewn up after what had happened would be a real bonus and a nice taster. That was the whole reason she was gambling: he had links to all levels of the crime and business world, plus a couple of politicians, and he could gift her the big names. She thought about the detective super who had ripped some strips off her back. Throwing Paul in the tin pail would be a nice prize, and she would find a way not to involve the same team in this one.

'I can do that, but what about this source? How do I know you just won't take care of him and stick two fingers up?' She raised her glass to him.

'Because I can't, for fuck's sake. If my problems come out in the open, my business and health are toast. This is survival. I want your boy for something else. To work for me. Handing him to my brothers wouldn't put another penny in the great big black fucking hole I've been digging for myself.'

She nodded, weighing it all up. There was risk, but then that's exactly why she was there. There was the thrill, her heart racing with the thought of the gamble she was taking. The exhilaration was worth it all, just to feel that alive.

'Okay,' she said. 'We have a deal. If it goes wrong then we're both fucked.'

She put the glass down. 'I'll be back to you tomorrow with the other handler. As I told you before, there has to be two of us for all official meets. That's when I become your main handler. We set things up and you tell us about the guns. Not on the first meet. We go through the business with you, threaten you about money laundering and you agree to sign on the dotted line. Second or third meet you give us the guns story officially. Before that you give me the whole story in private. Okay?'

He nodded, his breath shortening at the possibility of uncovering something the police had in their secret locker.

'It's Tonto. He's mine.' She stood up and for a moment considered giving Grainger the other thing he clearly wanted. But she had to keep that one dangling and she was tired. 'See you tomorrow.'

His lips tightened but he tried not to show surprise. Christ, they'd suspected the bastard, so Paul had been right again. On the other hand, Paul should have known that the boy had trouble stamped into his DNA and never taken him on in the first place. Every fucking thing that he touched turned to rat shit. Well, on the plus side it worked out perfectly for what he had planned, and he wondered what Hadden would think if she knew what he really had in mind. If she wanted to fucking swim in the sewer she had to accept the risks he and people like him took every day. He asked her some things about Tonto's habits and where he spent his time.

'Thought you'd have known all about him. He works for you after all.'

'He doesn't work for me, and I definitely don't need the hassle with the guffies my brothers employ. This is an exception. I told you, I have serious grief with Paul and the bastard will move against me if he gets half an excuse. I want somebody I can manipulate on their team. So I want to know where I can find him without making a fuss.'

'Like it. Devious but makes sense.' Hadden told him what she knew about Tonto's habits when he was away from the business. It was pretty straightforward: being a regular in the Jambo boozers, home games and a snooker club were the sum total of his social life, and he tended to be in the same places on the same nights if he wasn't dealing.

Grainger liked it. Tonto wasn't a loner but the next best thing, so he should be able to get a hold of him without witnesses. When he was satisfied, he stood up and offered her another drink.

She shook her head then walked over and ran her hand over the side of his face. 'We'll do good things together.'

Once again, he imagined her gasping for air, the small veins popping in her face and eyes as his hands squeezed her throat. That image was starting to become a habit.

'Okay, see you then,' he replied, putting on one of the lopsided smiles that women liked. 'You're welcome to stay if you want.' He knew as soon as he opened his gob it sounded feeble, but they were both half-pissed, so it was worth a try.

'Not tonight. Lot to do.' She turned at the door. 'After we meet tomorrow I'll see you again tomorrow night so I can hear all about the guns. Do we have time?'

'The deal won't happen for a couple of weeks. Just getting the logistics arranged.'

'Good. Who's the contact over there? I want a name to research before we move on this. You don't give anything away at this stage. Just a name. I gave you Davy McGill and all I want is a name.'

'Tommy Souter. He comes from the Donegal Pass area.'

Grainger felt naked for a moment. Exposed. The Belfast men were serious players, but it was all or nothing now. It was the same stakes for both of them and their fates had suddenly become intertwined. A complex game plan was in motion, and if any part of it failed, everything else would go with it. Hadden could solve part of his problems, but she couldn't replace the small fortune he'd wasted, and that would be a difficult one to resolve. Which was why he'd just traded the name of the Belfast man who'd cut his throat without a moment's hesitation if he knew what was taking place. Grainger was a problem gambler but this was the biggest bet he'd ever made, and he'd need some luck along the way.

He closed the door behind her, went back into the kitchen and poured another drink he didn't need. It was better to get fully pissed because he knew that, sober, the odds of it all coming off would seem crazy, and he needed to sleep. He didn't bother with any mixer in the drink, throwing it over in one, squeezing his eyes shut as he felt the raw spirit scorch its way down his throat.

'Aaaaaaah.'

Grabbing the bottle by the neck, he walked through to the lounge and switched on the TV. He tried to focus on the news but it was hopeless, so he put on some music and let his head rest back on the seat. Less than a minute later he was snoring gently and had the temporary relief he wanted that night.

Outside the flat, Hadden tried to straighten out her head. There was a lot to do but she seemed to have sealed the deal with Dominic. The arse of a head she was going to have in the morning was the least of her worries. If she could sign him up, get the Belfast man from him in front of the co-handler, maybe the bonus of Paul Grainger locked up . . . what a start that would be. Absolute gravy, she thought, and she'd paint it up as an organised-crime job to keep the terrorist units or the spooks well away from it.

'Fuck them,' she said to the empty street.

Not totally empty, though, because Frankie Mason was studying her, wondering what had taken place inside. They hadn't been in there that long, but if Grainger had been stamping her card maybe it was a quickie and she had to get back to her other half if there was one.

He scratched his chin. He was going to enjoy finding out who this one was, but he'd also have to report something back to Big Arthur in the next few days.

First things first, he thought, as he watched her swaying ever so slightly along the pavement, tapping numbers into her phone and putting it to her ear. He was still too far away to hear what she was saying and was reluctant to open the car windows. Anyway, by the time she reached the junction with Dundas Street, where she stopped and waited, Mason knew exactly what she was doing. A woman who was gently pissed and without a coat in the light cold drizzle no doubt just wanted to get home, and fuck the expense. Sure enough, the taxi arrived a couple of minutes later and she stepped inside.

It was an easy follow at that time of night when the old city was so quiet it was as if no one could be bothered to come out and play.

The taxi headed to Comely Bank and he watched it pull up in Raeburn Place, where she got out, paid the driver and entered one of the buildings. He said 'please' and hoped he'd get a clue to which flat she was in.

Bingo! The middle flat lights went on as she appeared at the window and pulled the curtains together.

'Good girl.' He clambered out of the car, walked to the main door and looked at the nameplates. 'J. Hadden. That'll do nicely, girl.'

He wrote the name and address on a small pad he always carried and thought that it had been a good day. He just knew that J. Hadden, whoever the fuck she was, would be interesting. The way she'd gone into the flat and pulled the curtains suggested she might be on her own rather than married. It was time for a cold beer and maybe a horror film when he got back to his own flat.

Janet Hadden looked round the barren place that was supposed to be a home. She hated it but knew it wouldn't matter where she lived. She was incapable of making the place homely. Decorating was more or less a complete waste of time. The walls were all emulsioned in the same neutral colour and there wasn't a single picture on the walls to show a memory or something that made her stop and think about the past. For her, the past meant nothing; it was something that had happened in another time, and she'd almost forgotten her family, as if they were just people she'd bumped into along the way. There was furniture, the basics that is, a TV she rarely watched and in the bedroom there was a bed and wardrobe but nothing else. The place was almost as sterile as a hospital ward. She only had two sets of plates in the kitchen because no one ever came round to visit, and she couldn't be arsed to spend the money on something she wouldn't use.

She kicked off her shoes, pulled open the fridge door

and stared at the contents as if there was really a choice. Fruit juice and half a dozen beers. Those was her reserves if she couldn't get out of the house for some reason.

She grabbed a beer and felt a stab of guilt as she pulled the ring from the can. Guilt – that was an unusual feeling for her, but it didn't last. She said 'fuck it' a couple of times and sat in the chair opposite the TV. Hadden didn't bother putting it on and watched her reflection on the dark screen as she raised the tin in a mock toast.

'Chief Superintendent Hadden.' She saluted. 'Maybe Assistant Chief Constable. Christ, that would do, Janet. What do you think?'

She raised her eyebrows as if she'd been asked the question. 'I think that would be a very good idea.'

She put the tin to her lips and the cold beer felt good. She put it on the floor and switched the light off, sighed and was asleep a few minutes later.

She woke with a start, frightened, and her brain refused to cooperate with her eyes as she tried to focus in the half-light. The curtains weren't quite closed and there was enough artificial light spilling in to make the place look grey and foreign to her. She felt panicked and for a moment couldn't remember where she was. Her mouth felt dry and that was the clue. Another fucking hangover on the brew.

'Christ.'

She shivered. Even at this time of year the house was freezing, because she hardly ever put the heating on.

She felt her way through to the bathroom, held her mouth under the cold tap, took the toothbrush out of the glass there, filled it to the top and went through to her bedroom. It felt even colder than the lounge so she didn't bother taking her clothes off. The bed was chilled and she shivered through the next twenty minutes until exhaustion took over and she managed to fall asleep again.

Across the city, Frankie Mason rarely slept more than three hours at a time, but it never worried him. Sleep always felt like a waste of time. He never felt that deep pleasure that most humans experienced of slipping between clean sheets or with someone who mattered and could share those night hours together.

He got back to the flat and made up some notes of what had happened and what he needed to do the next day. When he was finished, he stripped down to his underwear and struggled into the heavily stained dressing gown that he'd used for years and never bothered replacing, despite the fact he needed something at least two sizes bigger these days.

Once he was sure he'd done what needed to be done, he opened a bottle of dark beer. He usually tried to have no more than four or five before he eventually went to sleep. He watched the news, but it was all about Brexit and Tories stabbing each other in the back, and he was bored with the whole subject. He switched channels but all the news was about much the same thing.

He decided instead to put on a new horror film he'd been looking forward to. He loved the genre and always reckoned he could have done well on *Mastermind* if it wasn't for the general-knowledge side.

The phone interrupted his train of thought and he screwed his face up as he looked at his watch, wondering who the fuck called at 2 a.m. It wasn't like he had friends.

'For fuck's sake,' he muttered, picking up the phone. It was Arthur Hamilton. He straightened himself in the chair as if the big man could see him. There shouldn't have been any surprise because the same thing had happened in the past – Hamilton operated round the clock. If he wasn't in bed, he thought nothing of calling people who worked for him, and he expected no complaints.

'Any progress, Frankie boy? Just in from a piss-up and thought I'd give you a wee ring.' Hamilton sounded like he'd had one scoop too many, and he could be an even more obnoxious bastard with a drink in him.

'Goin' fine. Doing the phone stuff and that takes a bit of time, know what I mean? Interestin' boy though, an' as far as the lassies go he just loves to play. Think I might have a line on the female in the bar. Should have somethin' for you in a few days. By the way, you know the boy likes a bet? A serious bet, if you know what I mean.'

'Good man. Keep on this. There's a bonus if you get me some shite on this bastard.'

'Consider it done.'

Mason heard the phone die at the other end.

'Big Arthur Hamilton at war wi' Dominic Grainger. Fuck's sake.' It was something he did a lot, talking aloud to himself.

He reached for the remote and settled back as the title of the new horror came on and he leered at the TV. He loved slasher movies and apparently this one had a body count that could equal the Vietnam War.

Mason was as happy as a pig in shit, which was basically what he was. This was his favourite time of the day, where he could switch off from the world, just drink beer and watch stories where people were cut to bits.

Mason's world, however, was about to collide with a number of others, and while some slept soundly, others were disturbed knowing that events were not in their own hands. For the ancient city, this was nothing new; corrupt men and women would always struggle to gain advantages that would bring ruin for some and rarely make the survivors happy. Only the city really survived these little dramas.

32

Mason swore when the phone rang on the cabinet next to his bed. He looked at his watch as he answered the call. He'd slept half an hour more than he expected, which was unusual because no matter how tired or pissed he was, he tended to wake at exactly the same time. The film had been a beauty, so good he'd run it through his head a few times before he dropped off, but, unusually, it had disturbed his short sleep.

It was the subcontractor on the blower. He was having a plate of bacon and eggs before he went out on the job and the way he chewed and spoke at the same time annoyed Mason, who just couldn't understand food first thing in the morning anyway.

'Any instructions?' The guy seemed permanently in a good mood, which was something else that tended to annoy Mason, especially so early in the day. He held his temper in check because the subcontractor was on the money: it was early, but the first rule of surveillance was to be in place before the target moved or you'd be watching an empty house. He knew it was the subcontractor's great strength; he was totally reliable. Hand him the job and he was on it and, best of all, no questions asked. He simply wasn't interested in the whys or who the fuck was paying money to spy, he just did the job, took the money and spent his time off looking after his pigeons. The man was content, which was a gift few people were blessed with.

'Stay on the boy. There's a female come into the game and I'll take her. Keep in touch and let me know what he's doin' durin' the day. Speak later.'

He pulled himself upright and stretched his neck. He should have been on the go and in place near the female's gaff by now and reminded himself that Hamilton was the man paying the bills so he needed to earn his wages. Fucking off the big man wasn't really an option; he might have been semi-retired but Mason knew exactly what Hamilton had done in his day and, more importantly, who he was alleged to have done it to. He didn't want to miss the woman, who was in his head for some reason, and his interest was definitely up and running.

He put together some of the paperwork he'd been working on alongside the subscribers for Grainger's phone and if the woman didn't move he could do some work in the car, make a few calls and try and work out who she was.

Mason dressed, which didn't take long because washing and shaving wasn't a priority. The clothes he'd worn the day before were simply picked up from the heap they'd formed on a chair at the side of his bed. He swallowed an aspirin, picked up his laptop and headed for the door. At that time of the morning, it was a twenty-minute drive to Comely Bank from the scabby flat he occupied in Portobello.

When he arrived in Raeburn Place, which was already starting to heave, it dawned on him that he might toil to get a parking space where he could watch the mystery woman's stair door in comfort. He was already agitated because he was later than he should have been, which meant finding a place with a decent eyeball on her flat might require a minor miracle. It was a lottery: on the one hand traffic wardens would start hunting the area like starving dogs, and on the other, in common with so many parts of Edinburgh, there were certain streets where cars trawled endlessly, more like slavering predators, waiting for a parking space to pounce on.

He narrowly missed two spaces with perfect views of the woman's front door and was seriously considering a bit of road rage with one of the bastards, who sneered as she slipped into a perfect space when he made the mistake of driving a car length ahead to reverse in. The bitch in question had one of those cars that resembled a sewing machine on wheels and she seemed to be pissing herself in triumph as she swung into the captured ground Mason thought was his.

He wanted to kill her but reminded himself that he was on a job. Nevertheless, he decided it couldn't completely lie, so he reversed back, stopped parallel to the sewing machine and gave her the eye like something from one of his horror films. For a moment, he put on the face of the serial killer of people's nightmares, and he loved it when the woman went from pink to white, her triumph morphing into near panic as he held the stare. As a final gesture, he drew his finger across his throat and was about to drive on when he realised there was movement at the stair door he should have been concentrating on rather than terrifying a housewife in a sewing machine. He'd almost failed to notice the woman who'd stepped out into the cool morning sunshine and fumbled in her bag as if she might have forgotten something. He cursed himself again for being late on the job.

After looking both ways, the woman headed along

Raeburn Place. It was that walk again from the night before – the woman who'd been at Dominic Grainger's flat had a distinctive way of moving, even though she'd been under the influence. Everyone had their own form of self-propulsion, and although most people would never notice, Mason absorbed these signals instinctively. He was an expert people-watcher, fascinated by their interactions and the non-verbals they displayed every minute of their days. For him it was a vast opera without words, visible wireless traffic keeping people apart and private or bringing them together. These were signs that watchers like Mason could pick up, analyse and use.

Hers wasn't a steady walk, and her hips weren't swinging, but a definite impatience in the movement confirmed it was her; in fact, the woman almost flounced. Even at a distance the night before and with the car windows closed he had been able to hear the faint sound of her feet hitting the pavement. It was like she was saying, 'Here I come; stay the fuck out of my way or else!'

There was another bonus: she'd changed her appearance, and he guessed that at this time of the morning she had her real face on display. The woman the night before and in the photograph from the pub had much longer hair and glasses. It didn't matter; it was her.

He moved off slowly, sure that she would jump a bus or taxi and annoyed that he couldn't park. He would just have to try to stay with her, hoping she wasn't going too far. She kept walking, and when there was no sign of her looking for a taxi, he changed the bet to the local Waitrose store and guessed she was going to buy the lunch sandwiches or early-morning coffee everyone liked to be seen with.

But Mason was wrong again. He pulled into a bus stop and watched her hurry along the road as if she was late. *Can't be, Frankie boy*, he thought and shook his head, beginning to suspect that things were about to take an even more interesting turn.

He knew he was right when he saw her cross the road and turn right into Fettes Avenue. There was only one place she could be going and he moved the car away slowly, giving her time. He indicated to turn right after her, and when he was stationary at the junction he saw her crossing the road again in the broad street that was the foreground to the old gates at the front of Fettes College. As soon as she crossed the road, it was clear it wasn't the college she was making for, so unless he was completely off course that left one option, and she was heading straight for it.

'Well, I'll be fucked. Dominic, what have you been up to, son?' he said into the stale air of the car.

She headed into what had been the old Lothian and Borders Police HQ. The uninspiring square building had been the centre of a thousand dramas when it was the seat of power in the old force; now, however, it was just another satellite office in the Police Scotland structure.

Mason watched her drape an ID card round her neck and disappear inside. There were a couple of parking spaces opposite the building and he knew the charges were more reasonable there than in most parts of the city. He stuck some coins in the meter and switched the engine off. There was nothing else he could do there and he certainly didn't intend on watching a police office all day and risk a pull for his trouble. He just needed a bit of time to think what his next move was and what he was going to do with this dramatic little turn of events.

He ran through the story so far: Arthur Hamilton, who was a premier-league gangster, though semi-retired for sure, hires him to watch his son-in-law who's also a premier-league gangster, or reputed to be. His brothers were certainly in the game but street men. Dominic pulls this female who knocks the fuck out of a guy in a bar without breaking sweat. She turns out to be law and meets Dominic using a disguise. She's on her own so it can't be official. Plus, just to add a bit of extra heat to the situation, Dominic's in touch with some fucking Belfast prods.

This was a serious brew and he knew these were only tasters from a bigger story. He pulled out his laptop and googled the words 'Hadden' and 'police'. There were a few possibles.

He locked on to a story from a few years earlier where a female detective sergeant had made an off-duty arrest and disarmed a bam with a knife threatening some American tourists during the Festival. He started digging and felt the tension in his throat. There were a few articles, and it happened that Detective Sergeant Janet Hadden had ended up with a commendation, whereas the bam had apparently lost a couple of teeth and needed treatment for a fractured arm after the arrest. It turned out she was a martial-arts expert and the bam had given her a chance to prove how good she was.

Mason knew he was about to be introduced to the woman who was bringing in his wages and causing a few ripples along the way. He found one article with a picture. Not a very good one, but there she was: the woman he'd just followed to Fettes. There was almost no change in her appearance, and he stared at the unsmiling face in the newspaper shot, taking in every detail he could store away.

'Well, Janet. What's your game then, girl?'

He sat back and wondered what the fuck he should do with this. By rights he should have called it a day, gone straight to Arthur Hamilton and collected his bonus and a pat on the back. But his nose was twitching. There was a story here – a good one – and he could easily spend another couple of days before having to get back to the big man with a final report. He called the subcontractor.

'Anything doing?' He didn't expect progress at that time of the morning and there wasn't any. Grainger had arrived at his office as usual; his assistant had gone out and got the coffees as usual.

'I'll come and join you in a bit. We'll go two up on this today. Want to stick with him wherever he goes. It's Thursday so the weekend starts here for this boy.'

Mason lit a cigarette and watched a few cars leave the police car park. They had plain clothes in them and he grinned because the new all-transparent, caring, sharing force insisted that the word 'police' was printed in big fuck-off letters at the bottom of the front doors.

He'd known a few bizzies in his time and remembered the days when the suits he mixed with for business would spend half their late shift in the boozer. Mason used to trade information with DS Mick Harkins in those days, although he couldn't remember the detective ever buying a round for his trouble. It seemed like a thousand years ago and men like Harkins were now as long gone as the dinosaurs.

He wondered what the risks were if he kept on this trail without the okay from Hamilton. Maybe he'd get no further and whatever was going on would just stay an intriguing puzzle, beyond his time and resources. What could he gain by sticking his hooter in this particular midden? He had no idea, but information could be gold. What made things difficult was that everyone involved so far, and probably including Janet Hadden, was dangerous in their own right.

He sighed and lit another cigarette as he watched a traffic warden wander past, looking for his first victim of the day. He fucking hated them and stuck a finger up as the warden, in a seriously oversized uniform, peered into the car. The warden stopped only for a second before it dawned that he probably couldn't win this one and moved on.

Mason said, 'Fuck you, boy,' in what he thought was a Deep South accent. The horror he'd watched the night before had featured a fairly impressive Louisiana sheriff who'd turned out to be a night-time slasher.

Mason decided to give it another couple of days and then report back to Hamilton one way or another. He had a feeling he might get caught in some kind of civil war, but he'd see where it went first. Although his head told him to leave it alone, his gut wanted more.

The cigarette had almost burned down to his fingers when he tossed it out onto the road, started the engine and headed off. Everyone had their little secrets and this was a collection of beauties. He couldn't just ignore them now; he had to know or he'd always wonder what they were all hiding.

It was nearly 3 p.m. when Mason checked in again with the subcontractor, but there was nothing moving at Grainger's office. They swapped round a couple of times just to give each other a break and avoid any locals wondering what the fuck was going on. That wasn't usually too much of a problem – most times if someone took an interest they tended to think it was the police anyway.

'Still nothing doin' but should see the boy soon enough. Time for his afternoon bet— Wait one!'

The subcontractor cut off for a few seconds and Mason didn't need to be told that there had been movement of some kind. He didn't get too excited and guessed it would be Dominic taking a flyer.

'A female accompanied by a male into the office. Got a half-decent picture.'

'Describe her first.' Mason waited, feeling the old butterflies in his stomach. A good job still gave him a kick, and this one had so much potential. The subcontractor gave him every detail he had, and he was meticulous. Everything he'd seen was noted.

It's our Janet, he thought. Mason didn't say anything to the subcontractor, because he didn't want anyone else to know.

'I'll join you in a few minutes and you can show me the photo. I'll take over and you can have a break.'

When he slipped in beside the subcontractor he was struck by how clean the guy managed to keep his car. Mason's looked and stank like the dregs in the bottom of a skip, but this guy was good and his old army habits had never left him. He was disciplined down to his daily change of socks whereas Mason had left it all behind almost from the day he walked back onto civvy street.

The photograph wasn't perfect but it didn't need a second look – it was Janet Hadden alright, and with a guy in his early thirties. He was in plain clothes but had that look some cops just can't hide, no matter what they wear or do with their hair. He might as well have tattooed Police Scotland on his forehead.

So this visit looked official and again he wondered what the fuck this woman was about. Mason had taken time to think and the problem was that these things didn't tend to present a sudden revelation of the truth; you needed patience plus effort to get somewhere near the plans or subterfuge of other people. He had to face up to the fact that this might mean weeks and he didn't have that before he had to give Arthur Hamilton something worthwhile. It was frustrating but he might just have to bite the bullet and give up what he'd found in order to keep the big man onside.

33

Inside Dominic Grainger's office everything went like clockwork and Hadden had to admire his acting ability, which was almost as good as hers. The possible downside was that it meant he was probably a more devious bastard than she'd accounted for.

She'd taken along Detective Sergeant Tommy Bannerman, who was new enough in the department to keep quiet and just follow the leader. He was happy as a pig in shit that she'd picked him for what was potentially a beauty. A lot of work had gone into preparing the ground, and if they could get Grainger to bend over, he'd be co-handler on a big, big fish. It never dawned on him that he was playing the role of unsuspecting fool – just a bit player in the real drama that was taking place on a level well away from the light. He watched and listened in admiration as his DI seemed to hit Grainger between the eyes with threats over money laundering and involvement in his brother's criminal organisation. Grainger went through all the range of emotions he would have if any of it was real: he did a good version of anger, accompanied by some mildish finger-jabbing, before finishing with a wonderful transition into accept-ance that the cops were just too good for him.

'Tell me what's on offer here.'

When he heard those magic words, Bannerman could hardly contain himself. Since joining the unit all he'd done was run a couple of low-level dealers who did no more than rat on the odd competitor who was doing exactly the same as they were themselves. This was a platinum record, off the Richter scale and it was a shame he couldn't mention a word of it to anyone. Disclosure of a source's name was a hanging offence; he'd be lucky to get a jaggy suit back and was much more likely to be fired if he opened his mouth in the wrong place.

Within an hour they'd made the arrangements with Grainger and he was signed on and had accepted the rules. Bannerman almost went misty-eyed when Hadden stood up and hammered the new relationship right into Grainger's face.

'Remember, Dominic. We dictate and you comply. You step out of line and I'll have your arse in Saughton before you can say sorry. You understand?'

She was the conductor waving her baton and Grainger, the big name, was reduced to the equivalent of roadkill. Bannerman wanted to learn from Hadden and do what she could do. He was hypnotised by a form of magic.

'I'll have something for you later in the week.' Grainger looked defeated and intent on saving his own miserable skin.

When they walked downstairs from Grainger's office, Bannerman couldn't help himself.

'Good job there, boss. Christ, that guy could be pure gold.' He was like a child and Hadden was pleased she'd brought him into the job. He was a dipstick, which was exactly what she'd wanted.

'Let's not get carried away, Tommy. We play it by the

book, keep the pressure on the bastard and hopefully he'll play the game for us. Have to manage him carefully though and not waste him with a couple of good jobs. We want this one as a long-term investment, so we might have to ignore some of what he gives us for the bigger picture.'

He nodded and felt he'd suddenly entered a new world where the criminals and stakes were much higher. It was just what he'd always wanted and dreamed of: to be a cop who mattered.

34

Frankie Mason watched the two bizzies step out onto the pavement. The male of the species looked like someone had tickled his balls with a feather, though Janet Hadden was wearing a serious expression, which, in his short experience of her, seemed to be the face she wore most of the time. He stayed where he was, not wanting to risk going on her tail again. He called the subcontractor, who wasn't that far away, and asked him if he could pick them up.

'I'll leave them to you but guess they have a car somewhere nearby.'

He was right and got the call that they'd got into a set of wheels and headed off towards Fettes.

'Let them run.' Mason guessed they would be heading back to their office, but it didn't really matter where they were going because the last thing he wanted was for them to realise they were being watched. They were the bizzies for fuck's sake and would tipple it eventually.

Mason decided to stick with Grainger for the time being. It was now late Thursday afternoon, so with a bit of luck he would follow his natural habits and chase some skirt.

It would be something else to report back to Hamilton.

He opened a flask of coffee, wishing he wasn't so addicted to the stuff. His mouth hygiene wasn't the best, and his regular injection of a strong black variety left his gob feeling like a dog's arse, but he needed it in the absence of a proper diet. The endless intake of black instant and cigarettes usually left his gut feeling sour; it was only relieved by his one meal of the day, which he never consumed till later on each evening. The pain was really gripping his belly, so he swallowed two indigestion tablets and tossed the empty packet onto the seat next to him with the other ones.

Mason was struggling to stay interested and wondered why Grainger wasn't moving. He was stiff and wished he could go for a wander round the streets, nip into a boozer and taste a decent beer. The subcontractor was close enough and Mason had decided to keep him on for the night in case he needed him to take over if Grainger did a lot of diving around.

He was just beginning to wonder whether, somehow or another, he'd missed Grainger leaving the office when the man appeared.

'Thank fuck,' he muttered.

He called the subcontractor and told him that there was movement and to stay close enough so he could hand over to him if required.

Grainger strolled off and caught Mason out. He cursed as he remembered one of the golden rules of surveillance: don't presume, which was what he'd done. It was Thursday late afternoon and the intelligence so far had been that Dominic Grainger would head for the West End and the boozers where he picked up his women. That area was within walking distance, but Grainger was heading in the opposite direction.

Mason had risked parking in a space that was too tight

and struggled to get out before Grainger disappeared from sight. Fortunately, he caught a glimpse of his quarry and managed to get back on his tail.

A fast black let Mason out into the stream of traffic. *Christ,* he thought, *a fast-black driver that actually gives a fuck.* Normally they just ignored everything on the road and gave two fingers to the Highway Code or good manners.

Mason settled down and lit up a cigarette. The brief delay had worked out and put some distance and cover between him and Grainger, who seemed in a hurry now. He followed him till he was back in St Vincent Place, pulling out a set of car keys next to a smartish Jag parked in front of one of the garages at the rear of the street. The car was new to Mason, but he was pleased because it stood out and would be easy to follow.

'Where we off to now, son?' Mason was talking to himself again, due in large part to the lonely existence that passed for his life. Apart from work there was almost no close contact with people unless he counted the subcontractor or other people he brought in to support some of his jobs. It didn't bother him at all; in fact, he really didn't want to be close to anyone, because through his work and a lifetime of rejection he just didn't like the human race that much, and he was fine just observing them for a living. It tended to prove what he thought anyway: that close involvement was probably best avoided.

He had his love of booze, horror films and the work, and when he weighed it all up, it wasn't that bad compared with some of the lives he examined. When he needed physical contact, he was happy with the working girls who operated at the bargain-basement end of the game. What took place tended to be over and done within a few minutes anyway, at which point he was ordering them out of his flat. That wasn't a problem – most of the girls couldn't wait to escape in case they picked up a bug lurking in the discarded rubbish that lay for weeks between the clean-ups that he was eventually forced into.

Dominic Grainger was looking for Tonto. Although he worked for his brothers and had never spoken to him, Grainger knew him by sight – and, of course, by reputation. Hadden had given him more than enough information to track the boy down to the boozer he always frequented from a Thursday onwards. Grainger knew this marked the boy out as a fuckwit, because the smart gangsters never stuck to a script. Not having been gifted with endless patience for doing things he didn't enjoy, he prayed that he wouldn't have to sit waiting half the night to spot the boy. He wanted to grab him before the boozer rather than after, when he'd probably be half-pissed anyway.

Tonto's flat was only a few minutes' walk from the pub, so he decided to take a chance and rap his door first. It was a risk, but Hadden had told him that he was on his own, with no female or flatmate in the road. He knew guys like Tonto spent little time at home, but it was worth a try.

Getting into the stairwell turned out to be too easy – even though there was an entry system, it was fucked, and his nostrils signalled that the close was used as a local toilet. He screwed up his face and remembered when he'd stayed in something worse than this. He'd come a long way since then.

Tonto's flat was on the third storey and he spotted the boy's name scribbled on a bit of cardboard – 'Davy McGill, a Jambo till I dye' – which was stuck to the door with tape. He smiled at the spelling. The words were no more than he would expect, but then it was just the work of some half-baked twat, so who really cared? He guessed the only correspondence the guy would get was the odd summons or a 'what the fuck you up to?' letter from whoever he owed money to.

He stood at the door for a minute and realised how much he looked out of place there. The smart suit and just-washed look was a stand-out so he definitely couldn't be mistaken for a resident.

It was quiet enough and he couldn't hear anything from the flat opposite. He put the side of his head close to the door without touching it and listened. Guys like Tonto probably wouldn't answer unless they knew exactly who was calling. There was a spyhole but he didn't want Tonto seeing him, pretending he wasn't in and then asking questions. If it got back to Paul, he'd smell treachery a mile off.

If Grainger had been concentrating less on Tonto, he might just have heard the close door opening as slowly and quietly as Frankie Mason could manage. Mason screwed up his face as the knackered door scraped over a few inches of the close floor, making just too much noise. But he was careful and it was pretty well masked by the heavy traffic outside. He knew how it was done and he stood still, letting his ears do the work. He just about heard Grainger climb the last few steps before he'd reached Tonto's door and then everything went quiet. Grainger had either been spooked by the noise or he was waiting outside someone's door. He held his nerve and waited; if Grainger came back down the stairs he could be outside among the punters before he could be picked out. The building was only four storeys, but he was sure Grainger was on the third or top floor.

Grainger heard it clearly from inside the flat. The music was playing loud enough for him to be certain that someone, most likely Tonto, was inside – and the bonus was that the useless bastard was blissfully trying to sing along with it, ignorant of the fact that his future was about to take yet another unwanted turn. Grainger spat on the spyhole so it wouldn't look covered, just distorted, then he whacked the door a couple of shots. The singing stopped and the radio was switched off. Grainger listened to Tonto pad to the inside of the door and stick his peeper to the hole.

'Hello?' Tonto left it at one word.

'Davy. Just want a word. It's Dominic Grainger.'

Tonto had given away he was inside and there was no way he'd refuse the main man. If it was someone going to take him apart, the door would have been caved in and the malky already applied with maximum force.

'Right. Christ. Hang on.'

Tonto started to remove the chain and unlock the door. When he opened it, he was pale, confused and trying to work out why a man like Grainger would turn up at his place. He was framed in the doorway with only his vest and pants for cover. The circumstances were such that he'd lost the ability to move or speak, and Grainger almost found it amusing. This definitely wasn't a fucking joke though and he put on a friendly grin to reassure the daft twat.

'We can stand here all day, Davy, or maybe you can ask me in. If you were in trouble you'd be in a coma already, so relax, son.'

The sound of the conversation meant Mason knew he could nip up one flight of stairs. He always wore rubber soles for these situations, which he dealt with all the time, and though he struggled to control his breathing – the fags were taking their toll – he managed to keep it quiet enough not to attract any attention. He was pleased, because in next to no time he had discovered that whoever Grainger had gone to see was called Davy, hadn't been expecting a call and was definitely on the third floor. That was all good as far as he was concerned. He took his time going back downstairs and out onto the street.

35

Tonto seemed to break out of the spell he was under, managed to say, 'Oh, aye,' and stood aside.

The place was more or less as Grainger had expected – in other words it was a tip – but he'd seen worse, and at least there were a couple of seats free of debris and clean enough to place the arse of his expensive suit on.

He saw Tonto's phone on the coffee table and felt reassured it was where he could keep an eye on it till their business was done, just in case the boy decided to call one of his brothers. It lay among a collection of dead beer bottles, lighters, overflowing ashtrays and his keys, which were on a Jambo key ring.

Tonto said something about getting dressed and Grainger watched him through the open bedroom door as he pulled on a pair of jeans. He came back through and tried to light a cigarette, but his hands were shaking so much he was having a real problem.

Grainger picked up one of the half-dozen cheap lighters on the table, stood up and fired up the boy's smoke. He had him under control; it was so far so good.

'Make us a coffee, and relax, for fuck's sake. Just

want to discuss a bit of business with you. Hope I'm not keeping you back or anything? In fact, get yourself a drink of something.'

Tonto tried to smile and find the right words. It was as if the Jambos' manager had arrived at the door and offered him a contract as their star player.

'No problem, Mr Grainger. Got some nice stuff.' It sounded completely daft and how the fuck would someone like him have nice coffee?

He was still shaking like a 9 a.m. wino and dropped his cigarette on the way to the kitchen.

Watching him struggling to pick it up relaxed Grainger, who leaned back into his chair. This was exactly how he wanted it – the boy had been the right choice for what he'd planned.

Tonto managed to wash a couple of mugs, mix up a drinkable brew for Grainger and half-filled his cup with cheap whisky. After slugging a mouthful, he refilled his favourite but severely chipped Jambo mug. He looked a bit less robotic when he returned, and the whisky had already hit the spot, helped on by the fact that he'd hardly eaten anything for almost a day.

Tonto sat opposite a man who he regarded as in a different league. He hadn't been killed, so it definitely was a bit of business. On top of it all, he was an agent for Police Scotland and a big man had just walked into his life – so it might be the equivalent of a lottery win. He imagined Janet Hadden's coupon when he told her that he might get close to Dominic Grainger. That was right up to the point where Grainger told him he knew he was a fucking grass. It was confusing because he was smiling when he said it, as if he was really pleased.

Tonto's voice turned into something close to a squeak, which in the circumstances was kind of appropriate. 'Sorry, don't know.'

He'd only got the three words out when Grainger leaned forward, stuck his hand up in a *stop-right-there* gesture and dropped the smile – because he had to take full control of the situation so they could get on with the business. 'Shut the fuck up and take another drink.'

Tonto did as he was told and downed the lot.

'Don't lie. If you lie I'll make sure your fingernails are pulled out one at a time before a blowtorch warms up your goolies. By the way, I also know who you're grassing to. Bitch called Janet Hadden. Am I right or am I right?'

He sat back again; he didn't anticipate a fight.

'Empty the ashtray, Davy, for fuck's sake, it's annoying me.'

Grainger was just applying pressure, making the boy dance to his instructions; it was the equivalent of tying him up hand and foot so there was no way to escape.

Tonto went into robotic mode again and did exactly what he was told. His body was like ice and he was so frightened that, if Grainger had ordered him to, he would have done the Birdie Dance with a feather stuck up his arse for effect. He wasn't being killed, but it was like being naked in front of a man who knew exactly what his big secret was, and he wondered how the fuck that had happened.

He picked up the ashtray, took it to the kitchen, emptied it and when he placed it back on the table, he sat down again, avoiding Grainger's gaze. He tried to control his breathing, but it was difficult, and he wondered what the fuck he'd done to suffer what had happened since the thing with the mad Pole, Janet Hadden and now this crock of absolute vintage shite.

'Now, I want to hear you say it. Once we clear that hurdle we can move on and, trust me, there's a good offer on the table if you play your cards right.'

Grainger picked up his coffee and took a sip. He was enjoying the boy's suffering.

The thing about Dominic Grainger that nobody, even his brothers, understood was that he was a sick bastard in his own right; it was just that he had the intelligence to realise that to succeed in business, he needed to play the diplomat more than was his true nature. He'd worked all his life to suppress his urges, and the only time they'd really surfaced was in private with a couple of pick-ups who he'd slapped about – nothing serious, but when he did it, somehow it felt good. Like something he'd missed all his life.

It had grown in him like a cancer. He couldn't remember such feelings as a child, and it wasn't till his late teens that he had the urge to cause pain, but he always had iron control. His brothers were violent time and time again, and Dominic knew it was a defect that might destroy them in the world they inhabited. The most successful gangsters applied violence when it was necessary and not as part of the fun. That was how his father-in-law had succeeded: he knew that violence played a crucial role in the game, and opponents and friends recognised that. The gangsters who worked for men like Big Arthur Hamilton followed him because they were loyal, apart from the wages, and if someone needed a tanking it was their own stupid fault.

'Look, Mr Grainger, they had me wi' the baws?' Tonto started to shake again and was looking at Grainger for signs. Maybe it was a big lie just to get the confession and then the gorillas would walk in and pull out the pliers for some painful dental work with absolutely no anaesthetic. His speech was already slurring with the booze hit, but his mind was in overdrive.

'Fair enough. That's what I wanted to hear. Now you do know what'll happen if Paul finds out?' Grainger laughed, sounding friendly, like they were just chewing the fat because it was fun. 'Paul suspects you already, and tell the truth, you're walking a fine line. Now here's the deal. Okay?'

'I won't let you down, Mr Grainger. I'm your man.' Tonto would have done anything to please Grainger. There were a million questions in his head, but he knew enough about being a criminal that you should always shut the fuck up when the man with your balls in a vice wants to talk.

'Right, the thing is that Paul's causing me problems. He's my brother, but he's losing the plot. Agree?'

Tonto nodded, but then he wasn't going to disagree. As it happened he did agree; indeed, everyone thought Paul was going off the end of the pier. He was a fucking radge, and if the rumours were true he was back on the nasal dust.

'I want you to be my eyes and ears in Paul's team so I know what's going on. As regards the police, I'll tell you what you tell them. Alright?'

Tonto said, 'Definitely,' and his spirits started to lift. The top man was handing him a job that could bring big points and everyone knew that points win prizes.

'That's one part of it, but there's something else that needs done now, and I need someone I can trust. Can I trust you, Davy?' He waited, knowing the poor bastard he was screwing into the carpet couldn't refuse.

'Absolutely, Mr Grainger.' Tonto lit another cigarette and this time his hand was almost steady. It was like that moment after the cops had stuck the guns in the Pole's phizog hardly a minute after he was about to be killed. Absolute elation. One moment you think the miserable existence that passes for your life is about to come to a violent end and then a guardian angel steps in – or in his case, heavily armed angels. He felt like it was a pal talking to him and maybe this was it, maybe this was the moment when a top dog would see his potential and everything would change for the better.

'Now, here's the thing.' Grainger leaned forward and lowered his voice. Tonto's heart beat a bit harder – the man was going to confide in him! 'First things first, get yourself another drink.'

'I'm fine, man – that stuff's banged the brain already. Know what I mean?'

'I want you to have another drink, Davy. You hear me? I want you nice and relaxed. We're pals now.'

Tonto's head was mince but he was buzzing, so he did as he was told, emptied the remains of the whisky into his cup and in the space of a few minutes he'd arsed nearly half a bottle. He grinned because this was beginning to look like it might work out in his favour. He saw Grainger had taken to smiling again, so it was all good so far.

'Don't know if you're aware but the wife is doing my head in. Thing is, I like the girls just a wee bit too much. Know what I mean?'

'Aye, tell me about it, Mr Grainger. Had my share.' As far as Tonto was concerned they were definitely becoming pals. He nodded towards Grainger, acknowledging the burden the female gender imposed on the males of the species.

'Well, she's got the lawyers involved and tell the truth she wants the fucking lot. House and the suit off my back. It's a sin. I'm fucked if I'll let her walk away with it all. Spent a fortune on the bitch.' Grainger swore more than usual because that was the language in Tonto's world.

'Fuckin' scandal, Mr Grainger.'

'Call me Dominic.'

'Cheers, Dominic.' Tonto felt like he'd taken a Desperate Dan hit of smack. The top man had said 'call me Dominic'. *Fuck's sake,* he thought.

'I've bought the bitch a fortune in jewellery and always thought it was a safe place to put some cash. Thing is, I want you to break in and chore the lot.'

He sat back because it was a simple enough job.

Tonto had been a pretty useful housebreaker in his teens and had a gift for it. He'd given that up when the old Lothian and Borders force had taken housebreaking seriously and started to hound the guys trying to make a dishonest living. At that point, he'd moved over to dealing dope, as the cops were taking less and less interest in street-level business.

The request put so casually threw him for a moment; he blinked a few times and his elation turned to momentary confusion. Being asked to break into Grainger's gaff was the last thing he'd expected. His booze-addled brain was trying to make sense of it and decide whether it was a decent idea or a bit fucking mental.

'No' tryin' tae tell ye yer business, Dominic, but couldn't you just take it when she's no' in, or when she's in for that matter?' He hoped he hadn't made a mistake questioning his new friend, but it seemed reasonable and sometimes even the bosses seemed to lack common sense.

'Good question, Davy, but you know who her old man is?' He nodded to his co-conspirator to emphasise the point. 'She's a fucking daddy's girl by the way, and Big Arthur thinks the sun shines out of her arse. Know what I mean?' He winked at Tonto to prove they were now mates.

Tonto knew exactly who her old man was. He'd never met Grainger's wife or father-in-law, but everyone knew the reputation and legends. Big Arthur Hamilton was one of those characters from the past who couldn't possibly have done everything that was alleged in the stories that had grown arms and legs over the years. That didn't matter though – there was enough truth to establish him among the gangsters as a top man who'd had the nous and balls to branch off into a string of highly successful legal businesses. He got the point Grainger was making and didn't need it to be explained. If he ripped the stuff out of her hands or fucked her around then her old man would definitely come out of retirement and there'd be casualties, whereas if a housebreaking took place then they might suspect, but they'd be able to prove fuck all. He nodded back to Grainger. 'Understand, Dominic.'

'There's at least a hundred grand there. You retrieve that lot and there's five grand for you. But it stays between us. No one else involved and definitely nothing to your police handler. Okay?'

Five grand. Five fucking grand for a break-in that would probably take half an hour, and one of the owners was involved. That was serious money and would put him right onside with Dominic Grainger.

'I can do that. Just need to work out a few details.' Tonto felt nervous again but happy. Breaking into someone's home always got the adrenalin active, but when it was a homer it was usually a piece of piss. He'd done a few in the past when punters had wanted to skin a few grand off the insurance, and it had been the easiest money he'd ever made.

Grainger stuck his hand over the table. 'Do we have a deal?'

'No problem, Dominic. I'll sort this one out for you.' He took the man's hand and felt a serious grip. Grainger fixed him with direct eye contact for a few seconds and Tonto thought he saw something he didn't like – then it was gone.

Grainger squeezed and watched the boy wince. 'No one, but no one else hears about this or the deal is off and I throw you to Paul. We're pals, so you can't fuck this up.'

Tonto nodded like a child trying to please an abusive parent.

Grainger got up and said they could meet over the weekend and work it out. 'Early next week for the job in case she moves the stuff out.'

He was heading for the door when Tonto asked him the one question that he couldn't just leave.

'So, how did ye know about me and the bizzies?' He felt his stomach grip because he probably shouldn't have asked.

'I'm a businessman, son, and have contacts everywhere. That includes inside the bizzies. Life's a bitch, eh, Davy?'

Tonto might have been half-pissed but he knew Grainger was right: life's a bitch and no one had to remind him of that particular no-brainer.

Grainger stopped at the bottom of the stairs and took Tonto's keys out of his pocket. He knew he'd been too pissed to notice but would definitely miss them in the morning. It was a slight gamble but a drinker like Tonto, a guy who lived alone and in a midden, would lose stuff all the time. Plus, the chances were he'd have a spare. In any case, he'd have a copy made first thing and put them somewhere it would look like they'd been dropped. It was just a case of waiting till the boy left his flat in the morning. Grainger was sure that the first thing he'd do now was head out for even more bevvy so his head still wouldn't be clear in the morning. That's how the workers lived: shit lives with shit prospects and bosses who didn't give a fuck whether they lived or died.

He stuck the keys in his pocket and was sure the only thing he'd touched in the flat was the coffee mug. He would make sure to clean it when he came back the next day.

36

Frankie Mason watched Grainger step back onto the street and look both ways before heading back to where he'd parked his car. He threw his cigarette into the gutter, cursing the cold shower that had started to piss down and soak the thin jacket he was wearing, then crossed the road, went back into the close and started climbing the stairs as quietly and slowly as possible. It was Sod's Law but no reason to panic when he reached the second landing and heard the door upstairs opening. Whoever it was, they were coming down fast so it was too late to simply turn and do a runner. He walked up to one of the doors and stood his ground, waited till the last possible moment and rang the doorbell. Tonto ignored him on the way past and was on his way out onto the street when the door was answered by an old guy who was pissed out of his skull from a morning session.

'What the fuck ye want?' He looked angry, as if he had something more important to do.

'Sorry, got the wrong door, pal.' Mason said it over his shoulder as he headed upstairs, but the old guy wasn't amused.

'Come back here, ya bastard, I'll kick yer fuckin' heid in.'

Mason ignored it – it was just another old piss artist dreaming about past glories.

When he stepped onto the third-floor landing he saw one door seemed to have been patched up and there was no name that he could see. The other door had a piece of cardboard displaying Tonto's name and his allegiance to the Jambos. He was sure it was the flat that side anyway from the brief conversation he'd heard.

He stood for a minute and just listened, but he couldn't hear a sound. Davy McGill. The name sounded familiar, but that was the trouble with his line of work – he heard names all the time, and it was difficult to work out who was who. This was a piece of cake though; it was a shit close and the cardboard nameplate meant the tenant wasn't in the top one hundred rich list. Probably some guffy. He'd soon track down who it was.

He was pleased but asked himself the same question he was asking all the time with this job. Why the fuck was Dominic Grainger surprising some low life at his door?

He walked slowly back downstairs wondering what he should do for his next move.

The old piss artist was waiting for him; he'd decided he had a score to settle with the stranger who'd disturbed him. He couldn't remember what the problem was, but it didn't matter. He was behind his door and had left it open just a few inches as he got ready for action. He slugged what was left in the bottle and gripped it by the neck. 'I'll fuckin' show the bastard,' he mumbled.

Mason was too preoccupied and slow to react to something he should have seen coming. He was just past the piss artist's door and ready to hit the next set of steps when he heard, 'Right, ya bastard,' as the old boy came at him from behind. Luckily his swipe with the bottle missed the back of Mason's skull and connected with his right shoulder. It might not have bothered him too much in his younger day, but there wasn't so much muscle there now to take the blow and it hurt without breaking anything.

'What the fuck?' He turned to see the old boy had landed on his arse with the force of the swing and the fact that he was rat-arsed.

'C'mon, ya crappin' bastard.'

The old boy tried to get to his feet, but Mason had recovered himself and shook his head. He stepped back a pace, took careful aim and kicked the old boy in the gut. He folded up on the stair and said, 'Oh ya,' and lay still. Mason quite enjoyed the diversion despite the pain – it had been a long time since he'd won any kind of combat operation.

He felt that was enough action and headed downstairs again. He was about to step outside when he heard the shout from upstairs.

'Come back – I'll fuckin' murder ye.'

Mason thought about going back up and doing the boy again but shook his head and stepped out onto the street.

Sometimes luck just falls in your lap and the guy he presumed was Davy McGill was chewing the fat with a couple of boys no more than a hundred yards from the stair door. It looked like one of those everyday chance meetings, but it suited Mason just fine. He saw them shake hands then Tonto headed towards town and Mason followed on. There was nothing to lose by staying with him for a short time. He had to be careful; he wasn't sure if the boy had taken much notice of him, but he was confident he hadn't. He'd looked preoccupied on the stair and that might have something to do with Grainger and what had obviously been a surprise visit.

It was an easy bit of work in the end and Tonto dived

into a boozer no more than a five-minute walk from his flat. Mason knew it well enough and had sunk a few there in his time: working class, definitely not the high pretension of George Street drinkers. This was what was left of old Edinburgh's drinking culture. Jambo territory with cheap enough beer, the conversation was rough and the piss-taking only for the thickest skins.

Mason thought about it for a few minutes, trying to figure out what exactly he was trying to achieve. That was the problem – he hadn't a fucking clue, just the undeniable attraction that he was doing what he liked best, looking under stones at what was crawling about in the dark.

'Who dares wins, Frankie boy.' He grinned, thinking about the old piss artist on the stair. He could see the funny side of it now.

He pushed open the doors to the bar and because he knew the layout he headed for the far end, which gave him a good eyeball on the place, who was there and whatever else because he still had no idea what the plan was. This one was definitely suck it and see.

There was no sign of the boy, which meant he had to have gone straight to the cludgie. There was nowhere else.

He was on the money – he'd just been served a decent pint when Tonto emerged from the men's and headed for the opposite end of the bar to join a couple of boys straight out of the same tin.

Mason shifted to an empty table with just as good a view, pulled out his newspaper and settled down to watch for a while and keep his ears open. It was unlikely the guy would do anything but get pissed, but it didn't matter. By the time he was finished, he would know how the boy acted, his mannerisms, his walk, and who knew what else might come up once he'd had few drinks.

That was the first point of interest: Tonto started to pack away the bevvy as if there was no tomorrow and he heard his mates comment on it. He speculated again that Grainger's surprise visit might be something to do with the boy's rush to get rat-arsed. It was impressive – after the first three pints he started on shorts, and Mason saw him squeeze in another quick short at the bar when he was buying his round.

Mason enjoyed the beer but took it easy. By the time he'd read his paper it was decision time and he didn't want to just stare at the boy getting pissed. Mason saw an opportunity coming up – Tonto's two mates looked fed up with him because he was really too far on and starting to talk shite. They left him propped up on the bar talking to some of the locals, who'd listen for a while then quietly move to another part of the boozer or leave. The barman was getting fed up with him as well, and Mason decided to make his move. He finished his beer, walked to the large space at the bar next to Tonto and ordered a fresh one.

It was like taking sweets from a baby – all Mason had to do was listen to the twat talking shite. They were best pals in half an hour, or at least that's what Tonto and his overheated brain thought.

Once Tonto tried to impress him with the fact that he'd done time, Mason told him he'd done three stretches in Bar L. It made Tonto's night – he was new best pals with an older gangster.

The next hour gave Mason all the background he could have asked for but not a link to Dominic Grainger. When he managed to steer him towards what he was doing for a living, Tonto went off on a tangent and seemed to be completely wound up about Celtic and their fans. Mason knew he just had to be patient. He was tired but decided to stick with it, and when he suggested they get 'a wee carry out', Tonto looked delighted.

'Great idea, Shug.' Mason had told his name was Shug Gardner. 'Flat's just along the road. We'll get some beers an' a bag o' chips. What dae ye say, pal?'

'Great idea, Davy. Fuckin' nice one, pal.' Mason wondered why the fuck a smart face like Dominic Grainger would get involved with this boy.

It took an hour and a half of listening to absolute shite in Tonto's flat before Mason got the link. It wasn't much but enough. He tried time and time again to steer the conversation towards whatever the boy was doing to earn, then it came as Tonto tried his best to impress his new pal.

'Look, Shug. I work for the top team, awright?' He was starting to slur and Mason was on the point of heading home.

'Right, son, good for you. Had a feelin' you were nae mug.' He sighed, struggling to stay interested. Maybe this had all been a waste of time.

'I'm a right-hand man for the Graingers. Paul an' me are like that.' He tried to entwine his fore and middle finger but struggled to make it work.

That made the trip worth it and Mason grinned. 'Nice one. Hear a lot about them but don't know those boys. There's three of them though, eh?'

Tonto tried to focus. Sober he would have heard alarm bells, but he was too far gone.

'Naw, it's Paul an' Sean I work for. They're no' gettin' on wi' the top boy Dominic. Dinnae mention that though, Shug – know what I mean?' He tried to make the cut-throat sign with his finger, laid his cigarette in the ashtray, leaned back and was fast asleep and snoring in seconds.

Mason stubbed out Tonto's cigarette and stood up. It had been worth it. There was a puzzle but clues within it, and what had been said filled in a few corners. The boy worked for the Graingers but not Dominic.

He had a look round the flat. There was nothing too interesting and minimalist didn't quite describe the decor. The only area that seemed busy was the overflowing coffee table. There was a notepad and what seemed to be Tonto's tick list, with deals and money owed by the junkies he dealt to.

Mason's eye was drawn to the bottom half where a telephone number had been scribbled recently. He guessed it was a recent scribble because the pen was lying on top of the number and nothing would have lain on that table for long without being moved around for the next beer bottle or chip paper.

For a moment, he thought he recognised the number then realised it was Dominic's from the phone records. He made a note anyway and stuffed it in his top pocket.

Tonto was snoring for Scotland now and Mason wondered how much the boy would actually remember about him the next day. He almost felt sorry for him; he saw so many of these young men who took all the risks for the top gangsters yet still ended up broken in health or spirit, half the time doing long stretches they couldn't cope with any more. It wasn't his problem though.

He looked round the flat again to make sure there was nothing he'd missed that might come in handy. It had been a decent day's work but the feeling that he was walking into the wrong territory was annoying his gut like a bad curry.

When he stepped out onto the street he took a couple of deep breaths. He felt absolutely knackered and wanted to get back to his own place.

When he opened the door to his flat he headed straight for the fridge and pulled out a beer. He was choking for a cold one. He sat back on his seat and ignored the TV remote for a change. His head was swimming and his gut hurt like fuck.

'Jesus, I'm gettin' old,' he muttered.

Tonto's face came into his thoughts and he ran a number of scenarios through his head about what the fuck Dominic Grainger was up to, but nothing quite fitted.

For the first time in an age Frankie Mason never finished his beer and didn't even bother with a last smoke of the day, which had always been one of his limited pleasures. He fell asleep, exhausted.

37

Sometimes shit just happens, nothing to do with the stars aligning in a certain way or the gods ordaining that the fate of a number of human beings in Edinburgh should move at their discretion. It just happened that on one of those days, Jacquie Bell felt she needed a new story to bite into and decided to call round some of her contacts to see what was grubbing about in the undergrowth of Edinburgh's dark corners. It was good tradecraft for a journalist, but it started a chain reaction that no one could control.

Mason loved it when he saw something in the media that he'd dropped their way or sold depending on the paper concerned. He thought it was only right to take payment for the odd bit of sleaze or red-hot inside info. When it came to the quality stuff, he was careful to feed only one reporter and that was Jacquie Bell. She was the most respected crime reporter in Scotland and, for a few gangsters, bent civil servants and local politicians, the most hated. She was relentless when she sensed that a story had legs, and over the years Bell had invested in making contacts from all levels including public life.

Her great strength was that she made whoever she was talking to feel like they were all hers, and stunning, almost Mediterranean looks helped where charm or a few notes alone hadn't always worked. Every boss she'd had worried about how far she pushed in doors, and there had been enough threats to make most men in the trade look for a job with a lot less risk. But her confidence was endless, and when she'd had to face the bad men, she'd done it and survived. They might not have liked her, but they had to respect her.

She'd known Mason for years, and they'd traded secrets that benefited them both one way or another. The advantage for her was that like a few of her sources, he imagined them together. Not something that was ever going to happen, and for Mason it was rare because he never really cared that much about the opposite sex in an emotional way. Much of that attitude was due to a mother from Hell and the fact that almost all the women he interacted with were paid for their services.

Jacquie Bell was different and stirred something deep within him. He was streetwise enough for half a dozen people and knew she was never going to slip between the sheets with him, but it didn't change his desire. She made him realise why lonely fuckers took up stalking, and he had to suppress the drive to find out more about her, watch her house, see who or what was in her life that she cared about. Fortunately, survival was an even stronger instinct in him and he fought those thoughts that would never be anything more than fantasies. That was as far as he took it, apart from pretending it was Bell when his hookers were bringing him to a happy ending.

When the phone rang too late that night he groaned, thinking it was Arthur Hamilton again, but he felt his heart pick up the pace when he heard her voice. She was like the big man in that respect in that she didn't seem to live in the same time zones as other people. When she was on her game, she forgot all about time or that other people had lives.

'How's life, Frankie? Been raking in any politicians' bins lately?' She laughed and it sounded like she might have had a couple, which was par for the course. Something in her genes meant she could abuse her body on a regular basis, sleep for six hours and wake up looking like a star.

Mason dusted some crumbs off his lap as if she could see him and as if it would have made a difference. He was in his old dressing gown and had consumed a couple of slices of days-old pizza with his beer when he'd settled down. He'd dozed off before the call with a piece of crust and a layer of crumbs settled on him and the chair underneath, until the phone had startled him back into the world, sucking in air like a man about to drown. He'd been in the dream zone again.

The army life was long gone and he'd never shed a tear for the service, but the memories of Belfast and the Troubles still came back in his dreams. There was always one memory that seemed to override every other horror. His mates all said the same thing, and the police detectives he'd met through his investigations told him a similar story.

For Mason, it had been his second week in Belfast and a call from the peelers for assistance. A body had been found near the edge of the Falls Road and the locals were somewhere between pissed off and attacking the cops. The army had been called in to support the problem and it wasn't the most difficult operation – just another day in the Troubles. They'd whacked a few heads, and the local boys hadn't really been up for it that day anyway because the hard men were away on a job.

When they'd cleared the area, he'd caught sight of the

body and it had pulled him up for a few seconds before a bastard of a sergeant had told him to move his arse. He wasn't a fully fledged cynic then but getting there, and years in the army had put a shell round him that seemed rock hard. The body was a young man who'd been executed as a tout, and the strange thing was that, on the great scale of things, it hadn't been that messy. The boy's face had been close to beautiful, with a halo of wheat-coloured hair round a face that had seemed almost at peace, despite whatever had happened before death. All the damage had been to the boy's hands, legs and body.

It was as if it had been intentional to contrast the angelic face with the ravaged body. It was unusual for the paramilitary intelligence teams to leave a face untouched when there was treachery, so whoever had done this had been cruel to the extreme, but then it had been a war. It was simple: he'd been an informant and the wolves had uncovered him.

Mason had seen much worse in his time, but that face still came back to him in the night. Always the same, the boy pleading for Mason to help him. But he could never move a muscle to help as the victim pleaded with him over and over again.

He tried to focus on the present. 'Not bad, Jacquie, not bad at all. What about you?' His heart was still racing as he pushed the boy's face into a subconscious box and shook the booze haze from his brain. He didn't want to sound like an arse to this woman in particular.

'Busy enough but looking for a bit of fresh news to excite the punters. Anything good to tell me? There's a drink in it?'

It sounded lame but a simple offer of a drink turned him into a helpless teenager who couldn't do his lines. He would have sold his soul to be seen with her as partners, and for all his cynicism, every single time she called he thought that this time it might just happen. It was foolish but he was a man thinking through his trousers.

'Some good stuff, Jacquie. Definitely have somethin' for you.'

'Okay, Frankie. Usual place tomorrow round six?'

'Fair enough. Only thing is I'm on a job, but if I get held up I'll text.'

'Okay. Laters, Detective.' She had a remarkable ability to sound on top of the world even in the early hours of the morning and with several drinks under her belt.

Mason smacked his lips; his gob felt dry. He shook the can on the coffee table next to his seat and found it was at least half-full. He drank it in one go, looked at the clock and groaned because the new day wasn't far off and he felt shagged out. If he was going to meet Jacquie Bell, he had to make an effort, but there was no way to recreate himself to the body beautiful in less than a day.

'Fuck it.'

He pulled the ring on another can and swigged it back so he couldn't change his mind. Sleep wasn't going to be an option, and he didn't want to see the boy's face again in what was left of the night. The call had been the push he needed. His instincts were to follow up on Janet Hadden and whatever the fuck Dominic Grainger was up to, but the dream had reminded him of the reality of the world he lived in. He was sticking his nose right into the business of the Graingers, Big Arthur and perhaps some Loyalist nutters. He was tired and just didn't need the hassle. He decided to suppress his own instincts to find out what was going on, because this thing stank like a rotting corpse. Jacquie Bell had far more resources than he did, and although the story was just a collection of intelligence fragments, it was the type of thing she liked to know.

'She's fuckin' welcome,' he muttered, then emptied the can and headed for the fridge to resupply. He didn't usually do this kind of session, but something was jagging his brain and he wanted to get pissed enough to flake out. He could live with a hangover; in fact, he wondered when he'd last felt well and full of energy.

'Fuck it,' he said again, placing the cans next to his seat, and stuck a horror on the box. It was Mary Poppins compared with Belfast and the memories of the boy with the beautiful face.

38

Mason got to the meet with Jacquie Bell twenty minutes early. He wanted to check out his phizog in the lavvy mirror to make sure he looked his best. He didn't need telling that his best wasn't that impressive, but he'd done what he could in the circumstances of too much booze and only a couple of hours of restless sleep. The good suit that he kept for very special occasions and funerals had been brought into the light. He hadn't had it on for long enough because there were almost no special occasions in his life, and he didn't like anyone enough to turn up at their funerals these days.

Once he was in the hot shower, it had felt so good he'd wondered why he didn't do it more often in the morning. Shaving had been a bit of a trial though, his skin puffy from his body trying to cope with the toxins that had flooded his system when normal punters were tucked up in bed. He'd cut the spot where his top and bottom lips met and growled, 'Fuck it,' as the blood trickled down his chin.

The razor had opened up another cut on his chin and when he'd run his hand over his face, he'd still been able to feel little gardens of stubble concealed in the slack skin round his neck. He'd sworn again and given up.

Mason had lost a few pounds since he'd last worn the suit and it hung just a little too loosely to look tidy, but it was better than his everyday clothes. After he was dressed, he'd put two fingers between the collar of his shirt and his neck and remembered that the shirt had been just a bit tight when he'd first bought it. 'How's that?' he'd asked before swearing again, because he knew the answer. His lifestyle was shit and his body couldn't recover any more. For all the beer he consumed, he was losing weight because what little he ate was crap and he knew it.

By the time he examined himself in the mirror of the upmarket boozer, he looked a bit better, and the weariness of the morning had been helped by a couple of double espressos and a few smokes. His palms were sweating but otherwise he was okay.

He ran the comb through his hair again, turned his head to show his best side, and surveyed the punters but didn't recognise anyone he knew. It was George Street so it was mostly tourists and office twats talking bollocks. The girls working behind the bar seemed to drift back and forward as if he was invisible. Eventually there was no one else needing served, so one of the girls stood opposite him and waited with an expression that said nothing, let alone 'how can I help you?'

'Pint, darlin' . . . lager.' He pointed to the pump and the Polish girl looked at him as if he was on the barred list. It annoyed him because she seemed to have been all smiles for everyone else at the bar. When she told him the damage, he nearly choked.

'Jesus! That a joke, hen?' He knew what the prices were but just wanted to annoy the staff. The girl looked over at one of the barmen who was the size of a Princes Street statue. It seemed like his biceps were about to burst the sleeves of his polo shirt. The giant lived for these moments when all his work in the gym would prove its value. He gave Mason the *you want some of this*? look and flexed his pecs. Mason watched the chest muscles ripple but wasn't impressed because he'd seen it all before. Okay, the guy could probably wipe the floor with his face but so what?

'Nice tits, son, but I'm no' available the night.'

He looked at the girl again, lifted his glass and winked. He was streetwise enough to know that the barman could flex all he liked, but he couldn't beat Mason up at the bar for moaning about the price of the beer. If he did, he'd be locked up, and Frankie boy would get a fuck-off compi claim against the boozer. Lurch thought about it and realised that he wasn't impressing the guy, nodded to the girl to serve another customer and went back to cleaning the glasses.

'You causing bother again, Frankie?'

He turned to see Bell behind him, grinning from ear to ear and showing a perfect set of teeth that made him feel even more unworthy. At least she had to be impressed with his triumph in the pissing competition with the boy at the bar.

He straightened up a bit. Why not? He'd just taken the piss out of a fifteen-stone gorilla and it wasn't every day you got away with that in Scotland without a daud in the pus.

'You know me, Jacquie. Just trying to spread a little sunshine along the way.' She definitely brought out the best in him, and it was one of the rare occasions when he could be arsed to engage in banter.

They grabbed a table away from the bar and the odd glare from the bar staff, who were trying to work out how a bit of class like Jacquie Bell could be in the company of the smart-arse who looked far too down on his heels for their establishment.

She ordered a bottle of red for herself and a refill for Mason, and they chewed the fat for ten minutes, as she knew this was always a worthwhile investment in her sources. Soon Mason was flying from a couple of drinks and that magical feeling of attraction, even hope, and he wished they could just stay there all night then go home together.

'So what's doing in the sewers, Frankie?'

Bell's question quickly brought him back to the earth and he remembered that their relationship was always going to be just business. She was a real pro and the best in her trade.

He swallowed the remains of his beer and paused again, trying to work out whether to throw her a couple of bits of scandal or give her the Dominic Grainger thing, because that would really get her taste buds going. He wanted her company so much he made the mistake of going for the Grainger thing. It might not be a complete story, but there were enough tasters to get someone like her joining the dots.

'Listen, Jacquie, there's a job I'm involved in, might no' seem the scoop of the century but there's somethin' there. I'm leavin' it where it is, but see what you think.'

Bell poured her second glass of red and leaned back in her seat. Mason always came up with the goods, and she saw he was struggling with what to tell her. That didn't happen normally – he usually just gave her the package. But if he was worried then that was a good sign, because Mason normally didn't give a fuck.

Within the first three sentences of the story he'd mentioned Dominic Grainger and Arthur Hamilton, which meant she was really interested. She drank the second glass too quickly and went for a third.

When he got to the story about the woman in the bar, her gut told her she was right down there in the sewer, exactly where she liked to find her best stories.

She'd nearly finished the bottle when he said, 'That's it,' then picked up his beer and slugged it back, waiting for judgement.

'Jesus, Frankie. What do you think it all means?' It was rare for her to ask a source for their opinion because it was her job to pull the pieces together.

'Fucked if I know. I wanted to follow this through but tell the truth there's a bad smell from this one and I've got a feeling some poor bastard's gonnae be damaged in the end. Bent law, Big Arthur, the Graingers and fuck knows what Dominic was up to with that numpty Davy McGill. Bad mix.' He looked at his empty glass and half-stood up to get a round.

She pushed some notes across the table. 'Get another bottle for me and whatever you want. This is on the firm.'

'Yer on. Think I need a goldie wi' the beer this time.'

As he headed for the bar she pulled out the small notepad from her bag and scribbled a few reminders.

'Jesus Christ, who is this fucking detective?' she muttered. She had the tingles, the buzz she felt when a good one fell in her lap.

When Mason came back to the table, he looked more relaxed, but she'd noticed him having a fly one at the bar while he was waiting. He'd unloaded the problem but that was fine with her.

'Can I get those numbers from you, Frankie? The Belfast number and anything else you've dug up?'

'It's all yours, Jacquie. I'm seeing Arthur in the mornin' an' I'll just tell him what he wants tae hear about Dominic. I'll leave the Belfast thing out, but I have tae tell him about Hadden and this boy McGill.' He tossed his whisky back and his face reddened with the effect of speed drinking. 'That's where my bonus comes in.'

'Fair enough, Frankie. Cheers.' She was feeling the

effects of the booze as well, but it was worth it – this was what she lived for.

'Tell you what,' she added. 'I'll have a look at this but keep me informed and let me know what the big man's reaction is.'

'You know him?' It hadn't occurred to Mason that she would know Big Arthur, but it should have because the reporter had more intelligence than the police when it came to who was who and what they were up to. Then it dawned on him who he was speaking to. It made him a bit nervous, because the big man had a rep in his younger days as a puller of exceptional talent. Jacquie Bell was exceptional talent and fed on people like the big man. Mason didn't know and couldn't know that her taste was for her own gender, but she kept that one dark for professional reasons. That would have shattered the fantasies of a few men in public and criminal life.

'Met him a few times,' she replied. 'Man thinks he's chocolate but an interesting career.' She grinned and her phone interrupted the moment.

Mason's heart sank when she took the call. Even though she should have been half or three quarters pissed she snapped back to life because it was obviously work related and his little fantasy died again.

She swore when she put the phone down. 'Need to go to the office, Frankie. No rest for the wicked and all that.'

She stuffed the phone and notebook into her bag, pulling on her coat. 'Call you tomorrow, and let me know about the big man.'

For the first time ever she leaned over, threw an arm round his neck and pecked him on the side of his face.

Mason watched her back disappear through the doors and felt lost. It was a strange feeling and it only happened with her.

He glanced over at the barmaid who looked like she

had a pain in her arse and decided he wasn't paying over the odds for the next drink while she gave him the evil eye. It was time to move to a proper boozer with no frills and definitely no twats behind the bar, just good old Edinburgh piss-takers with a nice line in sarcasm.

He had no idea why he did it but he turned at the door and, because he knew the cow was watching, Mason grabbed a handful of his balls as if he was Michael Jackson in his heyday and gave them a shake in her direction. She looked like she'd seen the ghost of Jimmy Savile and turned to the hulk again for support. But by the time he looked round, Mason was back on the street and pissing himself laughing, though he had no idea why because he didn't do much laughing.

Jacquie Bell was already in a taxi, and that was when fate took a hand and shit just happened again. She was pleased with what Mason had told her, but investigating it would require a good bit of work and might not come to much. The majority of times what seemed like gold turned to shit and a lot of wasted time. But then the names were all good, so it had the makings of a classic if it didn't end up being one of those monumental misunderstandings with fuck all at the end of it.

That's when her phone went off in her bag and what might have been possible with Mason's story changed again. Another source was calling her about a historical child-abuse story involving an MEP and it was a beauty. It needed immediate attention, so she decided that Frankie Mason's saga could wait a couple of days and what difference would it make? It would, and lives would be lost and shattered, but she couldn't know that.

Shit just keeps on happening.

39

Big Arthur had told Frankie Mason to come to the house. He liked to show off his study, which was a monument to the wealth the man had accrued over the years.

The house stood on its own ground in the posher east end of Portobello, though he was originally from the other end of that part of town. He always liked to tell people he 'didnae have an' erse in ma breeks back then'.

The study was all dark wood and a desk that cost more than a small family car. The window to the side of the desk looked out onto the garden, and Hamilton loved to sit there and work on his family and local history. It had become almost an obsession, and it was where he was happiest when he was at home.

He'd never been a domestic type; the only reason he'd married his wife was because he'd put her in the club and her old man had threatened to throw him in the sea if he didn't do the right thing. His future father-in-law had principles. Hamilton had never forgiven his wife for that turn of events.

As much as he despised his wife, he'd adored his daughter Jude from the day she was born. It was a strange feeling – being that emotionally involved with another human being – and it only happened with her. One of the reasons he'd been so successful as a criminal and businessman was that he never let emotion cloud his judgement. Jude had turned on him for the problems with his wife, but he wished he could have explained that it was complicated and that his wife had deserved every blow – or at least that was how he justified it in his own head.

When Mason arrived, Hamilton was dreaming that he had reconciled with Jude and they were spending every hour together. Mason took a seat opposite the desk, admiring the bookcase and array of leather-bound volumes that the big man would never even open but were part of the image he liked to portray.

'Wee dram, Frankie?' There was a collection of the best malts on a table in the corner and crystal glasses to go with them. Mason nodded and Hamilton poured him a treble Speyside, then the same for himself.

'That do ye, son?'

Mason nodded again; he was glad to get the booze. He was nervous and didn't know why, because he'd worked for the man a few times over the years and it had all been good. He'd handed the problem over to Jacquie Bell and was about to tell him what he wanted to hear and a bit more about his son-in-law.

Some cases though just had the words 'best avoided' written all over them, and he still had the feeling that with the ingredients he'd seen, this was all going to end badly. He'd always followed these cases up to see what he could find for himself, but why had he walked away this time? He couldn't put it into words but it was there – deep in his instinctive defence mechanisms, he sensed something that would burn people when this puzzle came into the light.

'Right, Frankie, tell me what's what.'

Apart from the Belfast connection, he told Hamilton everything, including what he knew about Janet Hadden and Davy McGill. He'd swallowed half the whisky by the time he'd finished, but he was still nervous and struggling to contain it, though apart from keeping quiet on a single Belfast number, he'd done a good job. The problem was that as he spoke, he'd watched Hamilton's face darken and twist, and that was enough to put the wind up the hardest men.

'So he's a fuckin' grass?' Hamilton banged his glass on the desk and some of the gold drink flipped over the edge onto the precious wood.

'I'm no' sayin' that, Arthur, only that she meets the guy on his own and then wi' another bizzie.'

'I know exactly what it means, Frankie. Think I'm fuckin' stupid or somethin'?' Hamilton was angry and needed to put it somewhere, and Mason was all that was available.

'Sorry, Arthur. Didnae mean to offend.'

Mason looked at the floor like a beaten child and the big man cooled down because it was all an act. He didn't really do that level of emotion. He knew exactly what the meetings meant because Hamilton had been a grass himself since he was a much younger man climbing the ladder. Mick Harkins had handled him for years, until he'd retired and beyond.

'Anythin' else, Frankie?'

'Hate tae say this, Arthur, but think the lassie's been playin' away as well. Sorry.'

'Well, she would, wouldn't she? Married tae that bastard.'

Mason left the house with an envelope full of clean fifties and twice what he'd expected. The last thing the big man had asked him was if there was anything else and

Frankie had told him the lie. He wasn't sure if Hamilton had seen it or not, but he'd patted Mason on the back and told him he'd keep in touch.

Once Mason was gone, Hamilton sat back in his seat and wondered what his next move was. Nothing for the moment because what could he do? But he knew what the bastard was up to now and that a creep like Grainger would give him an excuse at some stage because he had to. Going to Jude was a waste of time because she would spit in his eye if he told her about the other women, and it looked like she knew anyway. He was armed though, and when Grainger made a wrong move he'd be ready.

40

Two nights later Tonto wiped the palms of his hands; they were damp with sweat, and the tension was getting to him. He was checking everything before he left his flat.

He nipped into the toilet again because he'd overdosed on coffee and his bladder was annoyed. When he was done, he sat back on the sofa and lit another cigarette, trying to calm himself. It had been a while since he'd been involved in a break-in. It had never really bothered him too much in the past, but given everything that had happened in his life, including prison, he'd lost a lot of bottle along the way, and the romance of being a young hood had passed with the years. Once the job was done, he'd feed Janet Hadden info about Grainger, but only when this one was in the bag. The job had to remain a secret between him and Grainger and no one else.

'Calm, Davy.' He'd said it a dozen times, trying hard to avoid swallowing some dope to take the edge off. He needed a clear head – he could not fuck up a job for Dominic Grainger.

He took a few deep breaths and told himself it couldn't go wrong because Grainger had gone over it again and again. In fact, Tonto thought that was a bit overkill because the job itself was straightforward enough. The alarm was going to be switched off, and Grainger said that wouldn't be a problem because even if the insurance company kicked off about it, he was still getting what he wanted. A small fortune in sparklers.

Tonto looked at his watch, stood up, pulled the rucksack over his shoulder and headed for the door.

An hour later, he'd parked the stolen wheels and was in the garden at the back of Grainger's home, pretty well concealed in the darkness and cover of some bushes. He waited; the good housebreakers always did it properly and watched for a while. See what moved, pick up the smells – especially anything that hinted of pork.

The garden was a beauty, and even though Tonto had no interest in the subject, he thought it was minted. He knew Grainger had a smart pad, but it was even better than expected, in the heart of Inverleith on the north edge of the city and double posh as far as he was concerned.

The place was dead and, apart from a couple of cars passing somewhere in front of the house, he heard almost nothing apart from the occasional puff of a light south-west wind against his cheeks. His bladder was still complaining about the caffeine OD and he had to go twice in the bushes, though he couldn't produce much more than a dribble. Sitting waiting had taken him back to the days when this was his main source of income, and he gradually relaxed, because doing an empty home, a guaranteed empty home where the owner was involved, was a dawdle.

Okay, Davy, let's get this show on the road, he thought and grinned nervously for a moment because this was going to pay big and the cash would sort a load of problems. Maybe a wee holiday down in Spain, where he could stay pissed for a fortnight and forget all his worries.

The windows were a piece of pish, wooden sash and case just to make it even easier than he'd thought, and there wasn't a sound from the house. Grainger had told him that his wife was away for a couple of nights so he was in the clear.

Somewhere in the distance he heard a dog barking, but whatever it was, it was small and too far away to have been spooked by him. It was just the night, and he was almost calm now the job had started because there was too much to think about.

Tonto wasn't a smash-and grab-man; he went through the steps he'd learned over the years and especially from the old boys in the pokey. Take it easy, don't rush. There were four windows to choose from and Grainger had suggested a downstairs spare bedroom. It was on a corner of the garden near a high stone wall and overhung by a couple of old trees. Even during the day it was almost in permanent shadow, and at night he could work with the trees covering him and absorbing some of the sounds.

He peered into the window and switched on a small penlight. The room was sparsely furnished with nothing more than a single bed, a small double wardrobe and a picture of a horse.

Tonto felt his nose run and drew his sleeve across his top lip. The adrenalin was pumping him into gear; he felt the high and a burst of energy.

The window was a pushover and he had it open in under thirty seconds. He checked everything again, put his head just inside and waited for a few seconds. He remembered the lessons: 'Take your time, son. Listen, sniff the air. One step at a time.'

The house was dead although he could hear ticking and it sounded heavy, like an old-fashioned clock of some kind. That was okay.

He pulled himself over the windowsill and stepped

inside, waiting again. Nothing stirred. He checked the window to make sure it would stay open in case he had to make a quick exit. Grainger had told him he was staying out that night so the job wouldn't be discovered till the next day, meaning he had all the time he needed. He'd change as soon as he got back to the flat and dump the gear he was wearing first chance.

It was only a break-in for fuck's sake, but he'd read about Locard's principle in prison and always remembered the lesson that everyone brings something into a crime scene and takes something away. In the past, when he was still a teenager screwing upper-class properties with a team from Drylaw, he'd been locked up twice on forensics and he swore he wouldn't be caught out like that again.

The hall area was half-lit from the street, but only through a small glass pane above a heavy old front door so no one was going to see him from outside. He was flying now and he caught sight of himself in a mirror and nearly panicked.

'Jesus!' he whispered at the sight of the man in a balaclava.

He grinned as his heart slowed again. The ornate staircase was on his left and he looked up, checking again. There were twenty-two steps to a mezzanine landing where he stopped again and waited.

Grainger had told him exactly where his wife's bedroom was and that he'd have to force a heavy wooden door in the room to get to the jewellery. There was no way he could just do the cupboard though; he'd have to rummage the whole place so it didn't look like he'd headed straight for the cupboard, which would flag it up as an inside job. First things first though – he wanted to get the jewellery into his rucksack, then he'd do the rest of the house.

He stopped below the landing. He could see the closed door that should have been her room if Grainger's information was on the money, and why wouldn't it be?

He climbed the last few steps and wished he could enjoy this much energy all the time. Most days he felt like shit, but this was like being young and back with the Drylaw boys again. All action and never a dull moment till the Gestapo had come along and thrown him in a cell. Arrogant fuckers, those crime squad guys – loved themselves right down to their Ralph Slater suits. If they were chocolate they'd have fucking eaten themselves.

He put the memories away, stood at the door gripping the handle and waited again. Something hit the back of his nose and tongue. It was almost nothing, but it was there. He couldn't place it, but it made him stop for a moment longer. It was familiar, but not enough for an ID. It was a signal though, and the first since he'd gone into the house.

He remembered the lessons: 'Remember, son, if it smells or feels wrong then it probably is just that. Get tae fuck!'

For the first time, he was aware that he was sweating, but he was confused because almost everything else was hunky-dory. Almost – was that enough? This job was for Dominic Grainger, after all, and he needed to get a result, so he had no choice.

What the fuck is that? he thought again, trying to identify the faint signals on his olfactory nerves, but there wasn't enough even in his heightened state. He was between a rock and a hard place. 'Fuck it,' he whispered then pushed the door open a few inches and waited. Nothing but that little signal that was firing messages to his brain to come up with an answer.

The room was huge, probably bigger than his flat, and tidy. He put the niggling signals to the back of his mind and concentrated on the job. There was decent half-light from a near-full moon coming through the window and he left the blinds as they were. There was more than enough cover that it would have been impossible for anyone to see movement unless they were in the garden to the rear of the house.

He stood in the doorway and studied the room for a moment. Straight ahead of him he could see what he took to be the locked cupboard where Grainger told him the box would be. To his right was a king-size bed with the window the other side of it. He noticed that the top cover seemed to have almost been pulled off to the other side of the bed. It was out of place because the room was immaculate, another signal he saw and ignored.

He spotted two three-drawer cabinets to his left and was tempted for a moment to go through her stuff to see what she wore. She was supposed to be a bit tidy, but that was going way outside the task, and even though there was a domestic war involved, Grainger would take it as a gross insult if he found out that Tonto had been anywhere near his wife's knicker collection.

He walked straight across the room to the cupboard and ran his hand over it. It was just too easy and his jemmy forced open the door in less than a minute. He was buzzing – it was a walk in the park for the money that was being offered.

He shone his torch across the shelves. They were packed mostly with shoes and handbags, which must have cost a small fortune as they were end-to-end designer labels.

Grainger had described the metal security box where she kept the gear. It had unusual decorative markings, and there it was on the top shelf between two handbags worth more than he earned in a good month.

He took it down and laid it on the floor. He tried the lid but it was locked, exactly as Grainger had told him it would be. He'd said just to leave it closed. As long as Tonto got the box, it was job done.

He put it in his rucksack and then all he had left to do was make a bit of a mess in a few other rooms so the job would look genuine.

He stood up and looked towards the window and saw what he took as a black smudge on the wall. It was another thing out of place. He stared at it, trying to make sense of the signals that were making his heart speed up. His mind was trying to avoid what he was seeing. It wasn't just a smudge, it was a heavy stain, and there was a trail running down the wall just where the top cover of the bed was pulled down. There was an explanation that he tried to accept and his breathing shortened. His instincts told him to run, but he couldn't – he knew that the mark on the wall only looked black because it was dark. Tonto swallowed several times and his mouth had gone bone dry as he stepped slowly round the bed.

'No. Please no.' He said it out loud even though he knew he was supposed to avoid unnecessary noise.

Jude Hamilton was on the floor on the other side of the bed and there was a halo of blood around her crushed skull. A hammer was on the carpet a few inches from her head. Tonto knelt beside her and shook her arm as if that would make any difference.

'Please.' He was pleading out loud to a woman who he knew was dead and he started to gasp for air as panic set in. The bed cover was pulled down and her right hand still gripped the edge of the sheet. There was blood splattered everywhere and the left side of her head was mush.

Tonto threw up but was still wearing the balaclava. Pulling it off, he turned away from the body and retched again and again into the corner of the room. He fell to his knees, spat a mouthful of rancid spit onto the carpet and sobbed like a child.

Time seemed to hold still; he had no idea how long he was there, but gradually his mind cleared and he knew he had to get out. He also knew enough about crime and punishment to realise that he'd gobbed up and spat enough DNA to put him in the pokey, but at that moment his flight instinct was overwhelming.

Mixed up with what he saw with his own eyes was unfathomable confusion. There was only one thing he could be certain of and that was that he was in a serious pond-sized pool of shit. A potent mix that made logical behaviour impossible. This was worse than the mad Pole; at least he'd known why he was chasing him that day.

He needed to get time and space to think this one out so he got to his feet, stuffing the reeking balaclava into the rucksack, when he remembered that he was supposed to do the rest of the house. That wasn't happening now, and he realised why Dominic Grainger had told him over and over again to trash the downstairs first.

He bolted and forgot all his training, right down to the spots of blood he was leaving every time his right boot hit the floor. When he got behind the wheel of the car he'd stolen, he lit up a smoke and stalled as he tried to drive away. The panic had settled, but he was still shaking, and all he wanted to do was get away from what he'd seen in the house.

41

Tonto dumped the car just off Slateford Road. Normally he would have taken it outside the city and torched it, but that was too much of a risk in a built-up area.

Climbing the stairs to his flat two at a time, his breath rattled in his lungs, and he stopped outside his door for a moment, listening as if someone might be behind him. It was quiet apart from the sound of his heaving breath.

He closed the door behind him and dropped his rucksack on the floor, squeezing his eyes closed and trying to make sense of it all. He pulled off his shoes and padded through to the kitchen but left the lights off. He let the cold tap run and he drank the water as if his life depended on it. The need for a drink or some dope was overwhelming.

He turned and froze solid when he saw the dark shape of a man sitting on the chair on the other side of the coffee table.

'What the fuck?'

'Sit down, Davy. We need to have a talk.' Dominic Grainger's voice was calm.

'How'd ye get in?' It was all he could think of as a reply.

'Keys, Davy. Think I climbed up the drainpipe? Put the light on and draw those scabby fucking curtains while you're on your feet.'

Tonto blinked when he flicked the switch and reality hit him right in his gut. He'd presumed he'd just lost a set of keys and was using a spare – he wasn't savvy enough to have realised they'd gone missing after Grainger had called the first time. He lost keys all the time and never saw it as a problem.

Grainger had a shooter pointed at him and he was wearing surgical gloves. He was smart enough to put it all together – it didn't take Sherlock Holmes to work out that he was the tit of the month in the biggest set-up of all time. He should have known, but it was all too late and he knew it, which calmed him down. There were so many times when he'd wondered what the fuck his life was about and the fear passed as he sat down and lit up another smoke.

'Want a drink, Davy? Help yourself, son.'

'Don't mind if I do, Dominic.' There was a decent shot of vodka left in a half-bottle he'd left on the table, and he didn't bother with a glass. He lifted it to his lips and swallowed the lot.

When he put the bottle back on the table Grainger leaned forward and put a syringe on the coffee table.

'Let's not fuck about, Davy. You know what to do.'

Davy McGill had lived a shit life and he knew it, but in those last moments he found a kind of dignity. Grainger had expected him to beg for his life, even though it was worth shitpence, but the boy decided in that moment he'd show the bastard what he was made of. He spat across the table but missed the man who was going to kill him. *Story of my fuckin' life,* he thought as Grainger lifted the gun a few inches higher.

'Get the fuck on with it, Davy.'

Tonto had fancied a shot of good dope and he guessed that what was in the syringe would be the equivalent of Semtex, so good enough. He was tired of hustling, running and of all those fuckers who seemed to use him like a football.

'Fuck it, an' fuck you.' He grinned across the table, rolled up his sleeve and gritted his teeth as he stuck the needle in his arm, pushing enough heroin into his bloodstream to kill a horse. The grin gave way as he experienced the biggest rush of his life, and he felt no more pain as his life drained away.

Grainger opened the rucksack carefully, saw the jemmy and box – which contained fuck all but crap – and was satisfied. Her prints would be all over it. The stink of spew hit his nostrils from the balaclava and he knew what must have happened. It was all good.

He lifted Tonto's left shoe and took out a hanky from a sealed plastic bag. It was soaked in her blood and he ran it along one of the treads. Just a smear was enough – he didn't want to overdo it.

He left the flat ten minutes later, stopped before he stepped out into the street and pulled a woollen hat well down over his head. Half an hour later, all his clothes were in a weighted bag at the bottom of the Water of Leith, and he was doing the rounds of the boozers to make sure he was covered as far as possible. It wasn't a foolproof alibi, but in any case, the bizzies would have a gold-plated culprit, even though he was dead. He just needed all the pieces to fall into place, and he hoped his recent streak of luck stayed with him. You always needed a bit of luck.

Grainger was an intelligent man and knew that the best-laid plans could always go wrong. He was tempted to go back to the house to check what exactly Tonto had done, but there was always the risk that he'd be seen and that would fuck the whole thing up. He needed to stay away from the house all night, which wasn't that unusual, and their gardener was due in the morning. If Tonto had done the window he'd described it would be noticed.

Jude always stayed in when the gardener was there and made him a coffee and sandwich. There was nothing else he could do but wait, and he was surprised how calm he felt. In fact, there were moments of elation when he thought about what he'd done. She'd despised him and it had been written all over her face right up to the point she'd seen the hammer. That expression had changed to abject fear, but it was only a moment, and she hadn't even had time to scream before he'd hit her the first time.

He had a couple of drinks in one last pub then called the escort.

'Any chance of an all-nighter?'

'That'll cost you and cash up front.'

'I'll be over in a bit.' He felt high and excited.

The escort treated him like shit as usual, but it didn't matter – he'd just taken the biggest gamble of his life, and there was nothing like it.

42

The gardener did everything according to Dominic Grainger's script. Tonto had left the window open and the gardener saw right away that it had been forced. He was a timid creature and tried the door a couple of times before deciding it was someone else's problem. He went to a neighbouring house to ask if they had a contact number for Dominic or his wife. The neighbour had the home number and tried that with no answer. She then went to have a look at the window and tried the doorbell again before calling the police.

Two policewomen arrived fifteen minutes later. There was no doubt the house had been screwed, but there was always the remote chance some horrible bastard was still inside. They called for backup, and two detectives who were in the area arrived. They both climbed in the window and a few minutes later one of them came back out and told the PCs to seal off the area as far as possible. They were experienced DOs and got the show rolling – within half an hour a major investigation team was gearing up to deal with a murder. They'd already worked out that the recently deceased was the wife of Dominic Grainger and hoped that he was the culprit. That would make a nice headline.

Grainger was in his office when his secretary knocked on his door and told him two detectives were there to see him. His performance was worthy of an Oscar, and he went to pieces before their very eyes. They were hopeful it was all an act and a bit disappointed when he said he hadn't been home the previous night. It looked like he had an alibi, and they did their best to hide the dissatisfaction.

'Look, guys, I might as well tell you that Jude and I had our problems and were planning to split up. Just one of those things, but she was a decent person and God knows she didn't deserve this.'

He managed to produce a few tears and even the detectives thought he might be telling the truth, but not quite. They asked him if he was able to provide a statement and Grainger nodded.

'I'll do anything to help, of course. I hope you get this bastard.'

43

When the detectives got back to the incident room in Leith, the SIO Ronnie Slade waved them into his office. He was one of the best in the business and he was flying through the ranks, not because of who he knew, but a successful string of major investigations. He was a good-looking man still short of his fortieth birthday, fit and easy company away from the job. His team would always go the extra yard for him, and the two detectives were there because they were the business as far as he was concerned, and the first names he asked for on a job.

'What's the story with Grainger then?' He was hoping they'd at least come up with a gut feeling that would do for the moment if nothing else. Nine times out of ten those feelings were on the money.

'Hard to say, boss. Puts his hands up that the marriage was on the rocks and he snivelled a bit, but he's a hard one to read. He's come up with an alibi or part alibi that he spent the night in some boozers and then with an escort he uses from time to time. He admits that he's been seeing other women and they've had problems almost since he married the deceased. I'm not sure about him – doesn't feel right to me.'

The older detective scratched the stubble on his chin and turned to his partner who just said, 'Agreed.'

Slade was happy with that and even a suspicion gave them something to look at. It was nearly always someone close, so why not with this one? They already had it that the marriage was in trouble, and that was one of the oldest reasons in crime investigations.

'Just to make it a bit more complicated, boss, do you know her old man is Big Arthur Hamilton?' The older detective knew Hamilton from the past and it was definitely worth calling it a complication.

'Yes, got it early on from the intel boys. Big Arthur in the mix definitely means it's a bit more complicated. Christ, he'll skin whoever it is if he gets to him before we do.' He chewed his lip; this was going to be a problem no matter what he did.

'Make sure Grainger's available as soon as we get the body moved to see if anything's stolen from the house.'

Slade told the detectives to get a hold of the escort and work on her story.

When they left his office, the lead SOCO came in to give him a heads-up on what they'd found at the locus. He poured out the coffees and loosened his tie. 'Give me some good news,' he said as he pushed the cup across the desk, which was already starting to disappear under paper. The SOCO was a stickler for detail and that's what they were there for. He knew that the tiniest clue could unlock a case that might have seemed unsolvable.

'I'll just give you the main points and a full report as soon as. Entry through the rear window – the marks on the wood look like a good old-fashioned jemmy. We've got fibres at the bottom of the window that might be from the culprit's clothes when he or she climbed in.'

Slade nodded – it was a good start.

The SOCO sat back and Slade watched the frown lines squeeze together on his forehead.

'It'll take time to examine the carpets – presuming that our man walked upstairs. Nothing at all obvious downstairs so if it was a break-in, it's surprising that nothing's disturbed, unless the thief got in and just didn't realise she was at home. Then the question is: where did the hammer appear from unless it was part of their kit? Anyway, from what we can see, there's blood and hair on the hammer and we have to presume that's the murder weapon.'

Slade nodded again.

'So the killer should have some blood on his or her clothing and hands?' The answer would be crucial in the early hours and days if they could make a quick arrest.

'Definitely. There's the blood on the wall, and it looks like she hit it on the way down.' The SOCO took a sip of coffee. 'In the corner nearest her feet there's the area where we presume the killer threw up and what looks like saliva next to it, so guess they were spitting after throwing up. There's a hair on the surface of the pile of sick and a good chance it's from the killer because the colour's definitely not hers.'

'So good chance of DNA?' Slade liked what he was hearing so far.

'Be disappointed if there's not. Now we come to the cupboard in the room. It's been forced, so maybe something away from there. There's spots of blood on the carpet going back to the stair and looks like the killer had some on one of their shoes. But then it gets complicated.'

There was always something complicated and Slade pulled open his notepad.

'The bloodstain from the killer's feet is going away from the body to the corner with the spew then to the door, so we can presume that's all after the killing. Fair enough, so he must have done the cupboard before the killing, because there's no blood near the door or the approach to the cupboard door. Thing is, where did she come from? She was in her PJs and dressing gown. Did the killer break in and go upstairs without knowing she was in? Did she hear something and actually go towards danger?' He shook his head. 'That only happens in movies.

'The killer seems to have gone straight upstairs to the cupboard. If that's the case, they had knowledge of the house. But nothing seems to have been disturbed inside the cupboard and that doesn't quite make sense, though half the time I suppose that's the case. Only other thing is that from a first look at the blood patterns, it looks like the killer hit her again when she was on the deck, so there was certainly an intention to finish the job.'

Slade liked the SOCO, and like the detectives who'd been in the room with him, he'd wanted to know what his senses had told him. Facts would get an arrest and conviction, but he knew that instinct had its place.

'So for the moment we'll take a close look at Dominic Grainger.' Slade smiled when he said it and saw the SOCO was trying too hard to make sense of it. 'We would look at him anyway but keep the options wide open. Always the same the first few hours – seem to be puzzles all over the place but it'll come. Go get something to eat and I'll see you at the next briefing.'

The SOCO closed the door behind him and Slade chewed through a chocolate biscuit, which was probably all he'd get for a while. Everyone and his auntie would be trying to speak to him, which made it difficult for an SIO to just get on with the job in those first few hours. Having a class deputy could make or break the job, but he had a good one, and she always took a weight off his shoulders when he needed it.

He'd worked with DCI Lesley Thompson in the past and she'd gone from someone regarded as weak and untrustworthy through a reincarnation into one of the most committed detectives in Police Scotland. She'd had her trials, especially when she'd been badly injured while she was working with Grace Macallan and too close to a car bomb planted near the old Lothian and Borders HQ. But she'd recovered, and although it had looked like she was going to get an easy seat somewhere at the back of the action, she'd forced her way back to the front line and was proving that she was a star. Slade saw so much of Macallan's influence in her, and as far as he was concerned, that was good for him.

He called her into the office and she came in carrying her own mug of coffee. Her hair was tied back and she looked like she was glad of a break as she'd been fielding all the calls that Slade had missed.

'How goes it, Les?' They were close, and he was the only one who called her Les.

'Well, considering a Grainger's involved and she's Big Arthur's kid, the reporters are going into a spin and I think there'll be a million theories in the morning. Gang war and all that.'

She sat down, leaned over and grabbed his last biscuit.

'You owe me ten biscuits, Ronnie, remember?'

She grinned, watching his lips purse, because he loved a biscuit so much he was constantly robbing everyone else.

'Any updates?' He knew that although he'd only been less than an hour with the two detectives who'd spoken to Grainger and the SOCO, the whole story could have morphed into something new.

'Big Arthur's been on the phone again and wants to speak to you personally. We sent two DOs and a family liaison officer to see him first thing to break the news, and he more or less threw them out of the house. Raging is the word so I'm not sure how we do this bit.'

She passed the ball that no one wanted back to Slade.

'Okay, Les. I could do without it because I could write the script, but let's do it together. I had a run-in with the big man years ago and don't think he's the type who forgives and forgets. Still, it's his wee girl, so let's give him the benefit. Suppose that's why I get paid the extra lolly. Make an arrangement at the same time for us to see Dominic before or after the big man. I want to be at the locus when we take him inside.'

'By the way, Ronnie, the SOCOs have got a couple of excellent boot prints in the earth near to the entrance point. Quite interesting apparently, with distance wear on the soles, so should be a good bit of circumstantial if we get the boy.'

'*When* we get him, Les. When we get him.'

44

Arthur Hamilton opened the door and for a moment Slade wondered whether the old gangster was going to start swinging. He hadn't seen him for years, but he still looked a handful, and guys like Hamilton never lost it. He remembered a piece of intel a couple of years earlier that a drunk bampot had started hassling him in Inverleith Park when he was out with his dog. The bampot had asked if he had any change and when Hamilton had ignored him and walked away, the bampot had put on a show.

'Naebody turns their back on Benny Elgin. Yer askin' for a severe punch in the pus, auld yin.' The bampot thought he was a hard man, even though he'd taken more second prizes than most.

Hamilton's spaniel wasn't going to do much to protect him, but then he didn't need the old dog for that. The bampot made the mistake of booting the harmless old mutt in the arse, and it rolled along the tarmac path, squealing like a child. Apart from his daughter, the dog was the only other living thing that Hamilton cared about. Years of experience had trained him not to react without thinking or weighing up the options but though the dog would survive, he turned round to face the half-pissed or drugged arsehole who couldn't see the red warning lights flashing. In his mind, the man was ancient and that meant he couldn't defend himself.

'You any idea who I am, son?' Hamilton looked to the left and right, making sure there were no witnesses close up. There were a few dog walkers, as there always was, but they were on the edges of the park, well away from them and close to the intersecting paths in the middle, which gave them some cover from the trees there. The dog was back on his feet and stood perfectly still, seeing something the bampot couldn't.

'Ye famous or some fuckin' thing? Just empty yer pockets an' let's see what ye've got.'

Hamilton didn't move; he just stared at the radge as if he was measuring him up, which was exactly what he was doing. He looked at the guy's legs and hips. There was almost no muscle bulk there, so he definitely didn't work out and was a lightweight. His shoulders were narrow and wasted.

Hamilton was old enough and wise enough to know that lightweights with a weapon could still hurt and he waited for a moment just after telling the would-be robber, 'No fuckin' way, son.'

A sensible robber would have worked it out by then, but the bampot turned up the heat by producing a set of dusters and pulling them over his fingers. That's when the lights went out, and when he came to about twenty minutes later, he couldn't remember seeing the blow coming. Three teeth were gone and his jaw was fractured. A couple of old ladies had called the police when they'd spotted him lying in the bushes, and he had the nerve to report it as an assault. The local guys recognised the description, and they'd seen Hamilton themselves often

271

enough walking the dog, so they applied common sense to the situation.

'One thing, my friend, before we go any further. Want to know who you're describing?'

Something like 'Aye' came out through the bampot's clenched teeth.

As soon as they told him, he withdrew his complaint, just before they booked him for possession of the duster.

Lesley Thompson had never met Hamilton before, but she could see what she'd seen often enough in the service. How loss can ravage a close relative in a matter of hours. He was a big man, but both eyes looked like they'd been bruised, and the rims were inflamed with the result of grief. He was wearing a short-sleeved top but for all his years his arms were still strong, and she saw the tattoo of a thistle and the words 'Scotland forever' just below it.

'Jesus Christ, the lassie's murdered and they send Ronnie Slade.'

'I'm the senior officer on this, Arthur. That's just how it is. Can we come in?' Slade waited but knew how these things played out – the man was making a show because that's what men like him had to do.

Hamilton waited for a moment then nodded them inside and led the way to his study. Even in grief, he couldn't avoid showing off his prized room.

They sat down and there was no offer of a drink to Slade, who decided he had to take control before this loose cannon started to go off in all directions. He tried opening up with sympathy for the man's loss.

'Shove it up your arse, Slade. I want to know what's happenin' wi' this. Suspects or anythin' – you better tell me or I'll make your life a fuckin' misery.'

'Why did you throw the detectives and family liaison officer out today? We need your help and we need your statement. If you really care, you'll work with us on this,

Arthur. Now are you going to help or what? Either way, we do the job, but we need you to help us here.' Slade had been ready for what Hamilton had thrown at him, but he wasn't prepared to lose control of the situation.

'I'll make enquiries, Slade, an' if I find the guy first, you won't need a trial for the bastard. You hear me, son?'

'That's what I expected, Arthur. Have it your own way but get this. Some might take the fact that you refuse to cooperate as suspicious. The papers for instance. How would the world see that one? You've always been a man with an image and people will see smoke even if there's no fire.' He leaned forward as the words left his lips.

Hamilton had made his display and he seemed to shrink a size.

'She was all I had left in the world. Only family an' no grandchildren. Jesus Christ.' He put his face into his hands. The fight had gone for the time being.

Hamilton cooperated from then, but every so often he threw a bit of abuse about, though that was a price worth paying as far as Slade was concerned. He still refused to have anything to do with a family liaison officer, but it was clear that he would make his own moves to find who'd killed his daughter and everyone knew it. If it was just some ned housebreaker, it wouldn't take a man in the know long to find out who was doing what at that level of crime. The tea leafs had to sell their gear, and it would be a piece of cake finding out who the current resetters were in the town.

Slade decided that it might cause offence but he would move to get a surveillance operation running on Hamilton. The executive would probably have a canary, but they'd look equally stupid if the killer turned up with his throat cut by the heartbroken father.

When he closed the door behind the two detectives, Hamilton wondered about calling his son-in-law, but that would stick in his throat, and no matter what had happened that bastard would bear some responsibility. It might be indirect in that the marriage was a sham, but if he'd been there, if the marriage had been sound, then in another life Jude might have lived and that meant Dominic fucking Grainger was liable.

Moral amnesia meant he missed completely the irony that he had been a violent fucker himself all the years of his marriage and his wife had decided she really was going to a better place when she was told she was dying.

He would have to speak to Grainger at some point but not just yet. If it was the last thing he did, he'd find the killer, whoever it was, before the cops did and look into his eyes while he cut him up as slowly as possible.

45

Ronnie Slade always made a point of not judging people before he met them and especially where it was a murder investigation. The fact that so many of the killers were one of the deceased's nearest and dearest made it tempting to focus too narrowly on possible suspects. This one was tempting – the intel was that Dominic Grainger was a major player but protected behind legitimate businesses. It was so often the case that the main men had multiple firewalls between them and the reach of the law. He'd admitted already that the marriage was broken and on the night Jude Hamilton was dispatched he was with a five-star hooker. Some detectives would have him convicted already.

Just after they'd left Arthur Hamilton's place, Slade took a call that Jude's body was at the mortuary and the locus was clear if he wanted Grainger to go there. He headed for the Leith office and said he'd pick him up himself then take him to the locus to see if anything was missing or out of place. It had to be done whether he was the killer or not.

First things first though, he would take him to the

mortuary to identify the body, because they wanted the post-mortem carried out as soon as. There had been a run of accidental deaths and suicides, so the mortuary was already stacking up with its never-ending business. Some of the more cynical detectives claimed it was Rangers fans deciding enough was enough as the Celtic just kept winning everything in sight.

He'd never met Dominic Grainger before and apart from a couple of photos in criminal intelligence briefings hadn't seen him in the flesh either. When Slade walked into the office in Leith, the family liaison officer who was with him stood up and said, 'Sir.'

'Get yourself a break and we'll take it from here.'

Slade looked at the man half the murder squad hoped was the killer so they could have a piss-up and get back to normal.

As the FLO left the room, Grainger got to his feet and offered his hand to Slade, who took it and gave him full eye contact as they gripped flesh. They were both strong men but knew enough about social interaction just to squeeze, but not too much. So many modern men seemed to think crushing someone's hand put them on top of the evolutionary pile.

Slade introduced Lesley Thompson and he watched as Grainger gave her a slightly altered expression with just a hint more of a smile and his eyes crunched a little at the sides. The detective realised Grainger was one of those men who, despite the situation and the fact he was about to view his wife's remains, still sent out those little signals to the opposite sex that he was interested. It was like voicemail – you got the same reply whatever the call. He just couldn't help it.

They sat round the table unloading the formalities and saying what had to be said procedurally. A lot of SIOs didn't get the importance of these little moments and what they could tell the investigator. Grieving was some-thing that took place on many levels inside someone close to the deceased, and even in Grainger's circumstances where the marriage was broken, the effect could be devastating on the surviving spouse. Some people were just plain relieved that the person they'd shared so much unhappiness with was gone. There was always trauma, the reminder for the ordinary man or woman that people died without warning and it would never leave the survi-vors unmarked.

But Grainger didn't seem to fit any of the templates Slade recognised, though that didn't make him the killer. His eyes were red-rimmed and he looked weary, but anyone would be when they'd been told their wife had been slaughtered and then had to sit for hours telling a couple of detectives all they could about the deceased, their marriage and all their little secrets. It might not all come out at the start but inevitable a major investigation team, backed up by the HOLMES system, would examine every detail of a possible suspect's life, and Dominic Grainger was all of that.

He shook his head at some inner thought every so often. It seemed almost timed, too regular, but it still didn't make him the killer.

After half an hour, Slade decided it was time to make a move and play out the next two acts.

'Look, we need to go to the mortuary to identify Jude. It has to be done. Are you okay for this?' It wasn't really a question; it had to be done, but there were conventions to stick to. No matter what Grainger was in his professional life, he was the victim's husband, and it wouldn't be long before Slade stood in front of the cameras and said the usual stuff about 'a heinous crime' and 'Police Scotland's thoughts being with the family'. All bollocks of course, but it was twenty-first-century PR and no career, no matter how efficient, would survive without that level of bullshit. Slade was a pragmatist, and as good a detective as he was, he could also communicate with the best of them, so he gave the hacks and the executive exactly what they wanted but never believed a word of it.

Grainger broke down at the mortuary after identifying his wife, and if he was putting it on, it was a class act. Slade always trusted women's instincts more than men in these situations, and when Grainger took a natural break for the toilet, he asked Lesley Thompson what she thought.

'Don't know, Ronnie, but just doesn't feel right to me. Can't put my finger on why though.'

'That's fine, Les. We keep an open mind and Christ knows he's the prime suspect till we can prove otherwise.'

They drove Grainger to his house to see if he could see something out of place or missing. If he was the killer, Slade knew this would be an interesting moment if he was the man.

When they arrived outside, the police presence was still significant – there was a uniform at the door and patrol cars each end of the street. The press had been sniffing around, but they had their pictures of the house and had mostly drifted away.

Grainger stopped at the front gate as if he'd been stopped by someone, and he looked from Thompson to Slade like a child looking for help.

'Don't know if I can do this.'

Grainger had completely immersed himself in the role of the distraught husband and it was part of his insanity that he became just that.

'We need you to do this, Dominic. If we're going to find this person, you might see something in here that means nothing to us.'

Slade glanced over at Thompson, who was frowning,

and he knew what that meant. She just wasn't buying it. Slade wasn't so sure, but if Grainger was the killer, they would need a convincing case to get him to admit anything.

Inside the house Grainger walked slowly, and the detectives missed the involuntary pause and surprise when he realised that the ground floor was undisturbed, apart from the obvious attention of the SOCOs. It was a small fuck-up, but he'd told Tonto over and over again to trash the ground floor first. His act was shaken. He hadn't planned for Tonto doing it the wrong way round, but he knew he should have factored it in. It was important that it didn't look like the killer had gone straight for the cupboard and box. His stomach started to jangle and he asked the wrong question.

'Was nothing disturbed down here then?'

As soon as the words left his mouth he knew it sounded wrong. He was asking the detectives something they couldn't know. There was just a faint hint in his voice that this was not what he'd expected and he watched the detectives picking up those tiny signals.

Slade kept reminding himself it still didn't make Grainger the killer. People said the wrong things when they were faced with the reality of a murder locus.

'That's why you're here, Dominic, to tell us what you see.'

Slade tightened his lips, his senses now heightened to a level where people can almost touch the energy in the room, their primitive instincts alert to the tiniest prompt.

They went upstairs and Grainger's gut tightened. From what he could see, nothing had been disturbed from the moments after he'd killed his wife, changed into a fresh sterile suit and shoe covers close to her body then left the house to change again in the cover of the rear garden.

He was finding it difficult to maintain the act he'd

played so well earlier on. He knew there were flaws in his plan and he needed to keep cool. The detectives were looking for clues, and they always went for someone close to start with. There was a culprit decomposing in his flat and he just had to ride it out till they found Tonto.

Before he'd left the flat, he'd turned the heating on full as he knew rapid decomposition would cause them a shitload of problems. It was a gamble, but he still had a good hand and he pulled it back together.

They'd stopped on the landing, just short of Jude's room, and Slade asked Grainger again if he'd noticed anything.

'Nothing so far; you'd hardly know anyone had been here.' He pulled out an already soaked hanky and blew his nose.

'We have to go into the room where Jude was killed now. There's still evidence in there and we need you to look carefully. Take your time and tell me what you see.'

Grainger stood at the door and studied the room carefully. Tonto had fucked up, but it was still all to play for.

He looked from left to right a few times. The cupboard door was half-open, and it had obviously been forced, but nothing else seemed disturbed. For a moment, he wished he'd made Tonto suffer a bit more. He did his best not to look towards the bed and the area where he'd sunk the working end of a hammer into his wife's skull. That moment was something he'd never experienced before: it was special, a rush. He'd never taken class A but he guessed it had to feel the same, from what users had told him.

'The cupboard's been forced. Do you want me to look inside?'

He glanced round at Slade, who was behind him and nodded without speaking.

Grainger took the few steps towards the cupboard.

Slade moved to his side and pulled open the door, as his hands were gloved up.

Grainger stepped inside. It was more of a box room than a cupboard. He stood in the centre and cursed Tonto again. Almost nothing was moved apart from the fucking box, but he was left with no choice.

'It's all her bags and shoes in here, but the only other thing was a jewellery box with some bits and pieces in it. Nothing special. It was mostly sentimental, that kind of thing. I don't see it.'

Slade was happy with that. If Grainger was the killer, he wondered why the whole thing was so pish poor and why he'd gone straight for the cupboard, unless there was actually good gear in it and he was having that for himself. The other option was that he'd had fuck all to do with it. Either way, it was still good for him because if the killer had it, then they might still get lucky if he or she still had it or tried to punt whatever was in it.

'We never saw that in there, Dominic, so might prove important. Thanks. You okay to carry on?'

Grainger nodded and thought, *You bet your life the box'll prove fucking important*. He had to work at not smiling at that particular observation.

They walked him round the bed so he'd come face-to-face with the dark staining on the carpet where blood, bone and some of his wife's brain matter had seeped onto the expensive pile.

He said, 'Oh God,' and turned away from the truth. 'I'm sorry.'

It was all he said and it told the detectives nothing. But they had something to work on with the jewellery box, and once they'd taken a description they decided it was time to call it a day. There was no photograph, but Arthur Hamilton had given it to her for her eighteenth birthday. There wasn't much chance he could add to the description or provide a photo, but the HOLMES system would demand it from the team. Nothing was left to chance.

They dropped Grainger off at a hotel he used for his favourite hobby, and he said he'd stay there for a few days till the house became available again.

'What do you think, Ronnie?' Thompson asked, because that was always the first question detectives asked each other when they left the spouse, whatever they might turn out to be.

'Whatever this is, it ain't a housebreaking gone wrong. Think we've a few surprises in store before we wrap this up.' He turned and smiled at Thompson. 'Anyway, time we both got a few hours' rest. I'll call the ranch and tell them I'll be in at six unless something turns up. I'll drop you off.'

'Hallelujah. I'm starving and going to empty the fridge when I get in.'

Grainger sat on the edge of his hotel bed and weighed up the game so far. He sank a gin and tonic then poured another one. There was always going to be some fuck-ups along the way and Tonto had made a bad one, but he was still in one piece, and sometime soon the police were going to be faced with a very dead but cast-iron murder suspect. That was the plan anyway. For a moment, he thought about getting hold of an escort but that would be stupid – tempting but stupid.

46

It was nearly twenty-four hours since Jude Hamilton had watched her husband's grinning face as he swung the hammer that would end her life, and Sean Grainger had decided enough was enough. The brothers were in full revenge mode and wanted everybody out trying to find out who'd killed Dominic's wife. For all the problems between Paul and his brothers, this was an attack on the family, a fucking outrage, and in the world of gangsters that had to be answered. If someone wasn't composted for what had happened, then there would be a credibility question on top of the existing problems of merchandise being lost to the pigs.

Sean and Paul had watched Dominic's tear-stained face and seen how racked with guilt he was. The marriage had been fucked and he quite naturally blamed himself for not being there. His brothers said the right things, that it wasn't his fault and, most importantly, that they believed him. Though Paul had doubts initially – he'd always known that under Dominic's snake-smooth exterior lay the heart of an absolute bastard – the act he put on was so good that he decided to give him the benefit of the doubt.

He couldn't really believe that Dominic would be stupid enough to do anything that might lead Arthur Hamilton to point an accusing finger at him anyway.

They had all their team out knocking fuck out of Edinburgh's housebreakers, trying to dig out whoever had committed this affront. They knew Hamilton would be doing his own thing, but they wanted to get the bastard first. Credibility was at stake.

The only problem was that Tonto wasn't answering his phone, and no one seemed to know where he was. Sean was hacked off because Tonto had been a good housebreaker in his time and would have been handy to have out there. The hours passed and Sean was close to blowing a circuit from spending so much time trying to find a member of his team who should have known what was going on.

'I'll fuckin' nut the bastard when I find him, Paul,' he said down the phone, ending the call as he walked into a close that stank like a jakey's oxter.

He was raging when he banged the door, and after two tries he opened the letter box. That's when the piss artist on the next landing downstairs appeared again, and the guy didn't know how to shut it. He'd learned nothing from the meeting with Frankie Mason – in fact he couldn't even remember it. It was just part of his life as a pish-heid, waking up with strange bumps, cuts and bruises anywhere on his body.

'Stop the fuckin' noise up there or I'll come up an' kick fuck oot ye!' He said it with real conviction and wasn't quite fully pished so the words were clear enough to Sean Grainger, who didn't need any incentive to go into action. His anger needed an outlet and the pish-heid had virtually called out 'come on down and get some'.

Grainger came down the stairs like a force of nature and didn't even wait for the pish-heid to raise his fists.

He cracked the head on him first, and as the man groaned then buckled, he hit him with another four good shots, two to the head and two to the body. The last two were received when the pish-heid was on the deck.

Grainger felt just a little better and turned to head back up the stairs. The pish-heid managed to crawl back into his house then onto the sofa that was home to more bug life than the Amazon jungle. He groaned, 'What a fuckin' life,' before swallowing the remains of a vodka bottle and staring at the TV, which was switched off.

Grainger didn't wait this time and crashed the door almost off its hinges. It was remarkable how quickly his senses told him to stay a moment as the heat and smell hit him like a blow to his chest.

'What the fuck?' He waited and the faint but heavy, sweet smell of corruption filled his nose and throat. The weather outside was mild, almost humid, and the heat was overwhelming. Sean Grainger was a hard bastard, but his instincts had warned him that something was wrong and he walked slowly, drawing the blade he always carried underneath his jacket.

When he got to the living-area doorway he saw the back of the sofa facing him and Tonto's head hanging to the side as if he was pished or in a heavy sleep. He knew he was dead, but he had no way of knowing what else was in the flat with him and took it slowly.

He walked round to face Tonto, almost gagged and tried to pull open the window, but it was stuck fast with years of badly applied paint. The gas heater was going full blast, and although his instinct was to switch the bastard off, he didn't want to touch more than he needed to, and he was a professional criminal – he knew the bizzies would be all over this at some point, joining the fucking bluebottles' feeding frenzy. He'd already tried the window and forced his mind away from the horror to wipe down the handle he'd touched. At worst, he would always have an excuse for leaving a print in an employee's flat.

Tonto's face was a bluish-grey colour; his tongue seemed swollen and protruded just beyond his lips. The empty syringe lay beside his hand.

You fuckin' idiot, Davy, he thought. He pulled out his phone, called Paul and told him what he'd found.

'Touch fuck all, Sean, and get your arse out of there. When you get clear make a call to the bizzies from a call box where's there's no CCTV. No names – just that they need to get there pronto. Fuckin' Police Scotland'll probably take three days, but there you go. Fuckin' idiot, that boy. Wonder why we took him on?' Paul was already raging at events and this was another dollop of dog shit on the existing pile.

In fact, the police didn't answer the call straightaway – there was a backlog of calls almost overwhelming the force resources. It was only when the two junkies who lived next door came home in the early hours, saw the crashed door and thought there was a chance of a quick rob that the police became involved.

The junkies went into the house, saw what Sean Grainger had seen and panicked. They did the right thing, because they knew the bizzies might blame them, and called the police, and after ten minutes of tortuous rambling and the realisation that the circumstances matched an earlier anonymous call, a car arrived and the uniforms started the wheels moving. It looked for all the world like just another OD, and there was drugs paraphernalia all over the house. The only problem was the wrecked door, and they handed it over to the suits to go through the motions. But it was a sudden death so there'd be a port-mortem anyway.

The DOs had a look through the house and when the

older detective opened the rucksack in the hallway, he felt the rush, plus a burn in his nostrils from the stink of the rancid vomit clinging to the balaclava. He saw the jemmy, the box and he was long enough in the tooth to realise they had themselves a full house. He'd read the intel from the murder squad.

'Think we have ourselves a dead killer and the goodies,' he crowed. 'Ya fuckin' beauty.'

Within half an hour, the place was a mass of activity and the SOCOs were starting to examine every inch of the flat. The pish-heid in the flat below came out, threw a few punches at the uniforms and was locked up for assault and breach of the peace.

Ronnie Slade had gone home for a break. His head was swimming with the day's events and he realised he was spinning an awful lot of plates with the involvement of the Graingers and Arthur Hamilton. When he took the call, he wished he'd jumped in the shower as soon as he'd arrived home instead of chewing a fish supper. His fiancée was away on business and the thought of cooking had been too much, so he'd reverted to the staple diet of the police service.

He arrived at Tonto's flat and thought it looked good, but he knew in his water this case wasn't straightforward, and when he took a call from the intel boys that the deceased had worked for Paul and Sean Grainger, he felt the fish supper gurgle deep in his gut. The death itself seemed to point straight at an OD, but there was still the why. The body was decomposing rapidly, although one of the DOs claimed to have passed Tonto in his car just two or three days earlier.

The DOs who knew Tonto from the past said he was a good housebreaker in his time, but not known as a particularly violent type, so he must have gone into panic mode during whatever had happened at the locus. Probably thought an arm full of smack would put him in a better place, and it certainly did that as far as a few of the cops were concerned.

Slade stared at the wrecked door and let his mind wander over what might have happened.

'What're the next-door junkies saying?' he asked Lesley Thompson, who'd arrived before he had and had spoken to the smackheads, who were coming down hard and close to the gibberish stage. They'd been taken to Leith as witnesses, but Slade made sure their flat was treated as a crime scene, and when he saw the state of it, he found 'crime scene' was a perfect description. It was a typical junkie pit – a wall-to-wall tip – and the toilet was more dangerous than Syria on a bad day. He couldn't rule out them being involved in whatever had happened to Tonto although he thought it unlikely. They seemed to be claiming that the door was caved in when they came home.

'Work the evidence, Les.' He knew that grinding through the evidence was an absolute necessity, and he never cut corners, no matter what his gut told him. Slade had already taken a call from the Assistant Chief Constable, who was happy as a pig in shit that it was solved and thought it a bonus that the killer was potted.

'That'll save a fucking fortune in court time so job done, Ronnie. Good man.' The ACC was more bean counter than policeman.

'There might be complications, sir. Couple of things don't make sense at the locus and we need to resolve them. You know the family connections of the deceased, so who can tell?'

'You know, Ronnie, you just worry too much and need to stop seeing bogeymen where they don't exist. Get this wrapped up. There's a million other things to do, like getting the arrest figures up.' The phone went dead without another word.

Slade shook his head, but he was a pragmatist and knew it was just the way of the world to have leaders driven by numbers.

'God help us,' he said to no one but himself.

He got a hold of a couple of DOs who were outside and told them to talk to Dominic Grainger, whether he was sleeping or not, to identify the box. There was always the possibility of a horrible coincidence and that the box in Tonto's bag could turn out to be nothing to do with the murder.

'Work the evidence, Ronnie,' he said again.

The two detectives went to the hotel where Grainger was half-drunk but wide awake and staring at the ceiling, his mind heating up with the mixture of alcohol and stress. There were still spikes of elation, similar to that moment when the roulette croupier spun the wheel and he'd put more than he could afford on those random numbers. Those numbers that any sane man knew did no favours for anyone. It was all that, but amplified by the fact that this gamble could either solve his problems or ruin him.

It was more than ruin. *Get this one wrong, Dominic, and you're fucking dead, son,* he heard over and over in his head as he moved between elation and near panic, picturing what might happen either way.

When the phone rang, he jerked as if a gun had been put to his head. It was the detectives and they wanted to see him. Grainger was sweating already in the clammy air of the hotel room. His instinct was to put them off, but he had no way of knowing what they wanted. Maybe it was to arrest him. Maybe it was to tell him about Tonto. Who the fuck knew?

'Give me five minutes and come up.'

He had no choice. He headed to the bathroom and filled the sink with cold water then lowered his face into it, hoping it would tighten the slack skin that had appeared below his eyes. He held it there for as long as he could until his lungs were bursting and lifted his head, staring into the mirror, where he saw the wife killer looking back at him. Jude's face came back to him; she'd said 'please' twice before he killed her.

He went back to the bed, picked up the empty miniatures and stuck them in the wastebasket, but the heavy, sweet stink of a drunk's breath was in the air and he knew it.

His head snapped back when the heavy knock told him they were at the door. They came into the room and he saw them looking for anything that might say guilty. The detectives' eyes were never still as they examined the room, and he knew it would all be reported back. They looked at each other for a moment as the stink of booze and sweat hit their noses. What were they thinking? Did they sense his guilt?

'What can I do for you?' It was difficult to hold the act because it had never occurred to him how lonely it would be carrying the knowledge of what he'd done. He was capable of almost anything, but it had always been for the family business or just slapping some female a bit when it was necessary. This was a new place.

'We wanted to show you a picture of a jewellery box we've recovered to see if you recognise it.'

Grainger held his breath. If they'd found Tonto then maybe his plan would start to come together. It was irrational, but he'd worried that no one would give a fuck about Tonto and he'd be one of those tragic souls who'd lie for months. It was a crazy thought, because with the heat in the room, they'd have to evacuate the building in a few days with the smell and what had been Tonto dripping through the ceiling of the bampot in the flat below him, though knowing that didn't stop the nagging insecurity.

'Of course, anything to help.'

They couldn't touch the box till the forensic examination had been completed, but the photograph would do for now. An ID would put them right on track and they could focus on Tonto as the main suspect.

Grainger's hand trembled as they handed the photograph to him and he felt his heart thump, even though this was exactly what he'd wanted. The finger pointed straight at Tonto.

'That's it, that's it. Where was it? Have you got the bastard?' He knew as soon as he said it that it wasn't working. He was full of booze, and the act only really worked when he was fresh and sharp, buzzing on all cylinders. The older of the two suits didn't like it and Grainger saw the edges of his mouth turn down in a barely concealed sneer.

'We can't tell you too much at the moment, just that we have this box and we should be able to give you more information in the morning. You know a family liaison officer is available if you need one.'

'No, thanks. It's fine. I just want to know what you found.' The game had changed and his head cleared because they had to look at Tonto rather than him as the killer. 'I'll call in the morning, if that's okay.'

'Of course, sir.' The detective looked like the word *sir* had stuck in his throat. 'We'll get back in touch first thing and I think we'll have more to tell you by then.'

When they left him, Grainger sat on the side of the bed and stared at the floor for a few minutes, then he pulled off his clothes and stood under the shower till his skin tingled with the effect of the freezing water. He made a pot of coffee and forgot to drink it as he stared at the ceiling again, but this time he saw the way ahead. He just had to play the game and it would all work out with that slice of luck.

About 4 a.m. he drifted off to sleep. The major investigation team were still operating, albeit at a reduced level, but the investigation was still moving forward.

It was about that same time that one of the detectives on the team called Arthur Hamilton, who was wide awake and sitting at his desk. The DO and Hamilton had done each other favours each way over the years. Hamilton picked up the phone knowing that a call at this time of the morning would mean something. He squeezed the handset tight when the DO gave him what details he had.

'It's one of Paul and Sean Grainger's team, but he's potted, Arthur.'

'The name?'

'Davy McGill. Wee housebreaker turned dealer turned worker for the Graingers.'

The line went quiet as Hamilton absorbed it and considered what he knew from Frankie Mason.

'Is that Tonto?'

'That's the one. You know him?'

There was no answer because Hamilton had ended the call. He was on his feet, his fists were clenched and it was the old rage in him, something he hadn't felt since he was a young man. He'd put anger away years ago because it was bad for business, but this meant someone was going to pay.

The first question in his mind was why the fuck was his bastard son-in-law visiting Tonto just before all this?

He started to punch the wall, trying to rid himself of what was going off inside his head. When he sat down again, his knuckles were raw and bleeding, but it didn't matter. He picked up the phone and called his man in Glasgow.

'I need a team of four – bad bastards. Call you back later on.'

'It's yours, Arthur. I'll fix it up first thing.'

That was all the reply Hamilton needed.

47

Ronnie Slade had given up trying. He'd slipped in and out of a place between sleep and the waking world without ever falling over into something that resembled a peaceful rest. It didn't bother him any more; years in investigation had taught him that this was just how it was. Hard grinding till the killer was arrested or, worse still, the long, ultimately depressing haul of an unsolved murder. Then the question of whether anything could have been done differently. He only had one unsolved case on his books, but he knew who'd done it – it was a gangland killing with no doubt who'd ordered the execution. There had been the arrest and the inevitable no-comment interview, but they were professionals – the body was never found and there was zero forensic evidence – so he could live with that one and it carried no stain.

The identification of the box was a positive step, and it should really have been a clincher, but there would be other forensic evidence coming, given the state of the locus. There was a balaclava in the rucksack covered in spew and the mess at the locus would probably tie in. In normal circumstances, he would have been flying, with a gold star for solving it and maybe a few days away with his fiancée at the end of it. But it just didn't have that feel.

The report from the detectives who'd visited Dominic Grainger with the photo had failed to help his mood. They didn't like the look of Grainger, but then why would they, he told himself. Peel away the smooth front and Grainger was just another gangster, and they were detectives. He wished he could put his worries away and just get on with it, but he knew exactly what was coming once all the forensic work was done. A partially completed jigsaw with a few pieces missing. There would be a picture they could explain, but what would those missing pieces have told them? He knew the reality was that, even in the best cases with a surplus of evidence, there were always pieces of the story missing.

He pulled the car up alongside the kerb a couple of hundred yards from the station and stepped out into the cool morning air. It was only 6 a.m. but the city was beginning to stir. He picked up a newspaper on the way and when he left the shop, he heard footsteps behind him; it was Lesley Thompson.

He grinned. 'Why do we bother trying to sleep, Les?'

'Beats having a normal life anytime?' She smiled back and he marvelled again at the way she'd overcome so many hurdles. She'd blossomed into the perfect second in command.

'I can't make the pieces fit in my head, Les. You know the feeling?'

'If it's any consolation, neither can I. Too many villains in this one.'

They walked into the station and found the incident room was quiet, with the team who'd worked through the night either already gone or about to leave. A DS gave them an update which wasn't too much because they needed the forensics to tell them the story of what had happened at the locus and they still didn't know who the fuck had kicked Tonto's door in. But they had Felicity Young starting the analytical work and hopefully she could piece the fragments of intelligence and forensics into something they could understand. Maybe they could come up with one of those missing pieces.

There was a mass of paperwork and notes they'd both neglected the previous day and they worked the next couple of hours to clear it before the phones started ringing non-stop again.

48

Janet Hadden hadn't slept any more than Ronnie Slade. The news that Dominic Grainger's wife had been murdered had nearly choked her. She wanted it to be just a housebreaking that had gone wrong, but there was no way she could make herself believe it. The very fact she was the wife of one of her sources was bad enough, and she knew exactly how it all worked. If there was no obvious candidate, then Dominic would be the prime suspect in the absence of anyone else. That was always the best bet, and she knew enough about Slade to realise he'd be looking very closely at Grainger.

She spoke to her boss, who seemed pissed off at her, but then that was nothing new, and having to answer questions on a source whose wife had been topped didn't ring his bell. She was sure that when Slade had time, he'd be all over the source-handling unit to see what they could tell him about Grainger. For the moment though, it would be absolutely need to know, so there would be no disclosure to the incident team. Slade and Thompson would be the only ones in the loop to protect Grainger, who, regardless of what might happen, was still an existing CHIS unless something changed.

Hadden chewed the end of her pen and tried to think how exposed she was to close scrutiny by Slade and a deep investigation into her recruitment and handling of the source. She tried not to think about it. She knew the relationship between Grainger and his wife was poison, but would he really kill Arthur Hamilton's wee girl? Grainger had to be smarter than that.

She reassured herself that if he was clear of suspicion then Slade wouldn't get far with the source unit. Protecting valuable human sources was paramount, and there had been too many fuck-ups in the past where detectives had exposed sources for all the old reasons – revenge, money or to fuck up a detective who owned a source better than yours. The source units had been created to remove these problems, and now the human assets belonged to the force and not to an individual officer.

'Fuck!' She stabbed the pen into the desk and rubbed her cheeks with the palms of her hands, trying to reduce the tension in her muscles.

She swallowed the remains of a can of juice and switched on her computer to see what had happened overnight. She checked the routines as she did first thing every day and overall there was no big news story apart from the sniping at Police Scotland, but that had become the norm.

The phone rang – it was her boss, who sounded even more pissed than usual.

'Have you seen the news?' The temperature of his voice was North Pole in mid-winter and she squashed the can, forcing what was left of the contents out through the opening and over the back of her hand.

'No. What's up?' She tried to keep the tension out of her voice but whatever had happened, it was clearly bad.

'Why don't you read the fuckin' thing, then my office!'

The phone went dead and she looked at the sticky

mess running off her hand onto the desk. She swore again and wiped it down with a dry tissue that didn't really help. Her fingers punched along the keyboard and she stared at the screen, occasionally scrolling to another page. Suddenly she felt cold and her skin seemed damp. She was frozen for a few moments, trying to convince herself she wasn't reading the words in front of her.

Tonto was dead meat and there seemed to be evidence that he was the killer. Hadden sat back in the chair as if someone had kneed her in the gut. All the little pieces spiralled aimlessly like floaters in her eyeballs until they settled into patterns and there it was. She'd been turned over. She'd handed Tonto over to Dominic Grainger and he'd conned her rotten. The poor bastard was dead and would never be able to answer why, but she knew exactly what had happened, and she couldn't do a fucking thing about it. Grainger had tied her into the scheme, and if he went down then so did she. The bastard had her exactly where he wanted, and she was his insurance policy all the way.

She held the back of her hands up and found they were trembling. Her boss was waiting to unload on her and she had to work out her own strategy. At the end of the day it was simple: keep Dominic Grainger safe and she was okay. Two sources were involved, one of them dead, but her proposal to sign up Tonto and move on to Dominic Grainger had been approved and was a classic recruitment exercise.

She calmed. Although it was a fucking nightmare, she steadied herself – it was just another problem to be dealt with. She drew her lips back, snarled quietly into the office, and hissed the words like a cornered animal.

'I'll fucking kill him.'

She stood up, opened the cupboard behind her and stared into the small mirror hanging inside the door. By the time she was finished, she smiled at her reflection and was back on course.

Dominic Grainger would be sneering into her face when she got a hold of him. She'd play along with that till this mess died down, then she'd see him burn – and she'd be the one to empty a can of petrol over him as he begged for mercy.

Her boss was true to form, but she was back to the Ice Queen and only stared at him as he ranted aimlessly. He really didn't have a point other than that the whole thing was going to cause him hassle and he had other things to do, like planning for his retirement abroad. When he ran out of steam, she spoke quietly and with absolute conviction.

'You're reacting all wrong to this one, sir.'

She waited till he had sputtered a bit and couldn't think of anything to say except, 'What the fuck do you mean?'

'All we've done' – she emphasised the *we* – 'is recruit a legitimate source in Davy McGill who was good in his short time. We had no more reason to worry about him than any other source, and he gave us decent results. We had planned to move on to Dominic and we did, and that went pretty smoothly. I might remind you that he's indicated that he may be able to give us a shipment of arms to Northern Ireland. That's headline stuff, sir.'

She watched him absorb the assurances; he was swimming in her direction with his big fat gob open.

'If we assist the investigation in any way we can and just present this as an unfortunate set of circumstances beyond our control then job done. McGill's dead, and if they have enough evidence that it's him, this'll be forgotten in two weeks. That puts Grainger back in the clear, and if we get the result on the firearms, then we're Scotland's favourite detectives – for a while anyway.'

She sat back, looking like she'd just spent a nice night

out with friends. Hadden was back in her other self, the risk-taker who lived for this game. Her boss looked like she'd just delivered him a life-saving drug.

'Okay, Janet, I get it. Let's hope it is McGill, and if it is and Grainger comes up with the goodies, then we're back in business.' He said it as if he'd just thought of it all himself.

'We've never been out of business, sir. After all, you signed all the paperwork for the recruitment, I know how thorough you are, and you'd never have let me near it if it hadn't been a solid proposal. I'll get back to work. I'll not contact Grainger yet but wait to see what we hear from Ronnie Slade. I would suggest you call him, offer every assistance and leave it at that.'

She turned to leave his office. Her boss stared after her and wondered just how thorough he had been with examining the Grainger recruitment. He pulled the collar of his shirt a couple of times; he always did that when he was anxious about something.

Hadden sat back in her office, and although she was tempted to call Grainger, it would have to wait because Slade had primacy as SIO on the murder and would not appreciate her pissing around someone so close to the deceased.

The phone rang and she expected it to be her boss, having now absorbed what she'd said and looking for more answers.

'Janet, thought I'd give you a call. Guess you've heard the terrible news.'

It was Grainger and he'd caught her on the back foot again. He was a much bigger bastard than she'd realised and she knew she would have to be absolutely ruthless and careful in whatever lay ahead of her. There were a pile of traps opening just with the call alone.

It was highly unlikely his phone would be bugged this early in the investigation, and as the husband of a victim where there was a dead culprit covered in evidence, the authority probably wouldn't be granted in such a short time. There was nothing in the information she'd read that made it look like anyone other than Davy McGill, guilty as charged. If the call was being recorded that might be another problem, but they were tied into each other, and for the time being he had her trapped anyway, so what could he gain? No matter what, she had to be ultra-careful till her chance came.

'What do you want?'

'Thought we might need to talk, Janet.'

'You know I need to get clearance from the man running this investigation – Ronnie Slade. Do you want to talk about the Belfast thing?'

She'd thrown the prompt, and if he took it, she would surely get clearance from her boss and Slade, though for it to be official, she'd have to take the co-handler.

'Of course, yes, that's what I want to talk about.' He'd taken the hint.

'This is a bad line. Call you back in a second.' She put the phone down without waiting for an answer, opened her bag and pulled the zip on an internal side pocket. She always kept a clean phone available, switched it on and called Grainger back.

'Meet you at the same place as last time . . . thirty minutes.'

'Look forward to it.'

The oil in his voice almost choked her, and she struggled not to scream down the phone that she was going to kill him, but her rage surged then calmed again.

'See you then.' She managed to make her voice as level as his. She was playing high stakes and felt a surge of energy pulse through her. She grabbed a set of keys and told her team she was off for an hour to keep a dentist appointment. It would do for the moment.

49

Jacquie Bell swallowed a couple of aspirin and lit up her first smoke of the day. She was behind and had overslept after a late night in the office, preparing a story that was looking good to go within a few days. It had been full-on and was a decent political scandal that would probably bring down a couple of Labour councillors and get her some serious brownie points.

She was still at home and flicking though her emails to catch up with the night hours. There were a few news clips about the murder of Dominic Grainger's wife. She'd been told the day before and had ground her teeth for a second thinking about what Mason had been on about, but she'd put it away as just a bad turn of events that had no bearing on what he'd told her. The previous days had consumed her as she dug up dirt on the political story.

Her phone trembled from missed calls, which was nothing unusual, but she blew a cloud of smoke and stopped halfway when she saw there had been one from Mason nearly an hour before. He didn't do calls that early so that meant he was worked up about something.

She hit the call button and Mason answered on the

second ring, so he was definitely agitated. That was nothing new for her either though, and she was a master at calming the panic-stricken.

'You seen this thing wi' Davy McGill, Jacquie?'

She stubbed the cigarette out on the saucer she was using for her coffee cup because he was in panic mode, and Frankie Mason didn't do panic unless there was a very good reason.

'No, been up to the armpits, Frankie. What's up?' She tried to sound apologetic and the tone of his voice meant she'd probably need to be, though it wasn't something she was good at. Bell normally controlled whatever situation she was in, and even in the middle of a serious shitstorm, she could sit back and stay focused.

'What's up? Davy McGill is what's up! Looks like he did Dominic's wife and he's fuckin' in the fridge now. OD. This is bad news, hen.'

Normally she would have told him to drop the hen bit, but this was more serious than respecting the female sex as equals. She lit another cigarette as he rattled on a bit.

'Calm it, Frankie.' But as soon as she said it, she knew she'd picked the wrong words.

'Calm it? Fuck's sake, Jacquie, you an' I know that Grainger visited that boy, and by the way Big Arthur knows. What do ye think that means, or will I draw a fuckin' map?'

Mason had never been lippy with the reporter in all the time they'd known each other, but he was right. Arthur Hamilton would draw one conclusion, and as far as they knew the police wouldn't have the information they had. Bell had a close relationship with police officers of all ranks, and particularly Grace Macallan, who was one of the few people she called a true friend. She could ignore this, but if it came out that she'd withheld information on what looked like a corrupt relationship between Janet

Hadden and the deceased's husband, the doors in Police Scotland would close in her face, and that was not an option.

In amongst that they'd seen a relationship between Grainger and the alleged killer, and unless the police found out some other way, Frankie Mason, Jacquie Bell and Big Arthur were the only ones who knew there was another suspect. It would all look bad. If Hamilton went off at a tangent, which he surely would, and Dominic was found with his eyes ripped out, then there were a series of possible endings which were all bad for her.

'Need to think, Frankie. Can I call you back?' She needed to buy time because she just didn't have a strategy worked out, and this would need smart management.

'Jacquie, listen to me. Arthur's been on the phone and wants to meet. I didnae tell him everythin' – never mentioned the Belfast bit. If he finds out I held anythin' back he'll take me apart, an' think I know somethin' else. I know this man. I'm fuckin' off tae a pal's place in East-erhouse. No way am I takin' ma chances wi' the big man. You can get me on this number.'

The phone went dead in her hand and she picked up the cigarette that had been burning in the saucer, half its length turned to ash. It dropped on the table when she lifted it, but that wasn't too much of a concern at that moment.

She ran her hand through the hair on the side of her head and remembered she had a shitload on with the political scoop.

'Fuck's sake, Jacquie,' she muttered, knowing she had to declare it to someone. Her editor would just prevari-cate and worry again that she'd taken the paper and herself close to a big black fucking hole and this time they might fall in. Hamilton would be out for blood because of his daughter – she didn't need that explained – and if

Grainger or Mason turned up dead or missing then the hole would just get bigger and darker.

She muttered, 'Fuck's sake,' one more time, took a killer draw on what was left of the smoke and dialled Grace Macallan's number.

As the reporter waited for Macallan to answer, across the city, Frankie Mason was stuffing half of what made up his wardrobe into a bag. He knew if he got into Easterhouse that was home territory for the subcontractor. He'd already called the man, and he was happy to accommodate him for old times' sake. As usual, he'd sounded happy, even though Mason was obviously in a spot, and Mason wondered what the fuck was wrong with the guy – why couldn't he just be miserable just like everyone else?

'Nae problem, Frankie boy, as long as ye take yer share o' the carry oot at night. Edinburgh gangsters don't get in here without a pass.' He had laughed at his own lines, which grated with Mason, but it was a lifeline, and he was a drowning man.

He'd put the phone down and prayed that the police would announce it was Tonto and a one-off so he could get back to normal. He'd told Hamilton he was working through in the west for a few days and he'd get back to him. He knew it didn't sound convincing because the big man frightened the life out of him, and it was hard to lie to a man who might just kill you. His daughter was dead and someone would have to go down for that one and unfortunately it might not be the right man.

That was the trouble with gangsters – they didn't hold fair trials.

He stuck his smokes, phone and lighter into his pocket then checked his wallet again. Mason looked round the flat then at his pile of horror DVDs lying on the table before heading towards the door, but when he pulled it open, he walked straight into a black leather jacket. In fact, there were two almost-matching jackets and he knew right away they weren't Jehovah's Witnesses.

'Gaun somewhere, Frankie?'

They knew his name and the man that had spoken had a broad Glasgow accent. It definitely wasn't some kind of social visit.

He stared at them, trying to find words, but nothing he could say would work – that was obvious. They were hard-looking, the same height and unusually did not have shaved heads. Pretty good-looking boys but it was there – he didn't need a business card saying 'Bastards 'R' Us'.

'What can I do for you boys?' Mason finally squeezed out a few words.

'Mr Hamilton would like a word. Funny that, because he told us you said you were through west. Got a helicopter, Frankie?' He looked at his partner, who sniggered like a kid – they obviously liked exchanging a bit of humour with their victims.

'Just had tae come back tae pick up a few bits an' pieces then back through on this job.' His eyes were wide and he wanted to run, but in his condition, he wouldn't get to the stairs before they were all over him. Doing the pishheid on Tonto's stair was one thing, but these were two piles of muscle who probably did three hours a day on weights when they weren't terrifying some punter.

'Lucky we caught ye then, Frankie, eh?' He grinned again at his mate who nodded in appreciation. 'Come on, the car's illegally parked.'

His partner grinned again and they helped Mason down the stair.

Before he shut the door behind him, they took his bag and threw it back inside.

'Ye'll no' be needin' that, Frankie.'

50

When Dominic Grainger answered the door to his flat, he looked like he didn't have a care in the world until he told Hadden to come in. He was either drinking for his breakfast or still half-pissed from the night before. When she stepped past him, she noticed the stale smell of the night's booze on his breath. It was mixed with peppermint, and he'd obviously tried in vain to cover it with a mouthwash.

'You stink, Dominic. Not the best time to fuck your brain up.'

She walked past him into the lounge and sat down, crossing her legs. She felt in control and didn't want anger to boil up, though she knew she was somewhere in the middle of a swamp and wasn't quite sure if she'd get out. But there was nothing she could do till she saw Grainger's cards on the table and found out what he had in mind. The bastard had obviously planned well ahead, but she'd promised herself that if he left an opening, she would sink her teeth into him and watch him bleed to death.

Grainger was a vain bastard and she guessed he would expect fear, panic and maybe some pleading from her, but she was fucked if she would give him any of that.

He waited, expecting her to say something as he poured them both coffee, but she just stared at him, unflinching till he was forced to speak.

'Not talking, Janet? Thought you'd have a million questions.'

His head throbbed and he wondered how much booze he'd put away into the early hours. It had been the wrong move, and he was surprised at himself for losing control, but he'd needed something to take the edge off.

'What do you want me to say, Dominic? How pleased I am to see you, God you look so well? I'm a fucking adult, so talk to me. Why don't you share your little fucking scheme and what part I'm supposed to be playing?'

The superior little grin that had been plastered across his face when she came in dropped like a stone, and he realised this was another small miscalculation on his part. Even small miscalculations could get him killed when it was a big stakes game.

It was a gradual process, but he realised she was a cold one – nothing really made sense about her and that was dangerous. He would make sure not to assume anything about her in future. The woman was a fucking reptile and she could be venomous if she decided to strike.

His brain was mud, but he knew he had to pick his words carefully to make sure she got the message and understood there was no exits available for her.

'It was just needs must, Janet, sorry an' all that. Thing is, I was in too much trouble. Wife, debt, gambling and a half-mad brother who really wants to see me on my arse. Had to make a move or string myself up. Just too many problems.'

He sat back in his seat. 'So now you know what

happened and that we're locked in.' He picked up his cup and took a sip, but the bitter coffee did nothing but foul his tongue.

Hadden filled in the rest of his script for him. 'So Davy gets to be a dead killer, you live happily ever after on the proceeds of the marriage and we're best pals . . . nice, Dominic, very fucking nice.' She picked up her cup, sipped the coffee and kept her eyes locked on him.

'Everyone's a winner, Janet.'

'Well, not your wife or Davy fucking McGill,' Hadden said, talking right over him.

'True, but that aside, once the dust settles down, I'll give you my brothers and the Belfast job. I really need them out of the way and then I can settle all debts.'

'You really are a piece of work, Dominic. I always thought I was the most devious person I'd ever met, but you run me close.' She grinned, but it was just the reptile baring its teeth again. 'So what now?' she asked.

'Now we wait. Let your boys do the business with Davy. No doubt at some point they'll talk to me again, but they'll not find a thing on me unless I've been very unlucky, but then you'll be able to warn me if I have.'

Hadden knew there was no point in debating. It was what it was, but she wanted to at least drop the seed of doubt in his mind.

'Dominic, if there's one thing I've learned in my career it's that there isn't a perfect crime. There's always a mistake, a trace, some tiny fucking detail that you never even realised was there. Just remember that.'

'I thought of that already. Truth is, Davy didn't stick to the script and ransack the place. Looks kind of obvious so I expect your Mr Slade to worry about that one if he's a good detective. But like I say, the main suspect is dead and you're my insurance policy. Come to think about it, that rule applies to you as well. Looks like you've crossed the line a few times before we met, so what mistakes have you made, Janet?'

Hadden grinned again. The words told her what she'd always thought – Grainger just didn't get her. That suited her just fine. 'I expect to fall someday, Dominic; that's the thrill for me. I'm just not like other people.'

She stood up and looked down at him, wondering which one of them would die first.

'I'm off. Going to see Ronnie Slade and find out what mistakes you've made. By the way, your first bit of bad luck is that Slade is a fucking Rottweiler, and if there's a problem he'll smell it. Trust me. I'll be in touch.' She headed for the door and didn't bother speaking again.

Grainger tried to make sense of what had just happened. He should have been in control, yet Hadden had taken his best shot and barely reacted. That wasn't what he'd expected, and he wondered who he should worry about most, Ronnie Slade or the woman who'd just walked out of the room.

His head thumped and he decided that the coffee was doing more harm than good.

The phone on the table started to buzz and he saw that he'd missed a couple of calls. One from his father-in-law and one from an unknown number, but there were no voicemails. His skin chilled at the sight of the big man's number, but the call had to come at some stage.

Grainger headed for the kitchen and swallowed a couple of aspirin before calling back.

'Arthur.' He left it at just the name. There was no way of knowing what the man was thinking.

'Dominic, how you doin', son? Guess it's a hard time for you and thought we could meet up.'

Grainger knew the bastard despised him, but that was okay – they could play this game as long as he didn't leave himself exposed, and there was no way they would meet anywhere other than neutral ground.

'It's hard, Arthur, but what about you? Know how close you were.' The words almost made him gag, but this was the fucking nonsense that had to be played as they circled each other, looking for a sense of what was in the other man's head or concealed in his hand.

'Let's meet up. There's a lot to discuss, son. The polis will wrap this up soon enough now they know it was that fucker that worked for your brothers.'

There it was – mention of his brothers was exactly what he wanted. He wanted the police and, if possible, Arthur Hamilton all over them.

'Where do you want to meet?'

Grainger looked in the mirror above his fireplace and saw someone else looking back. The man in the mirror looked years older than the face that should have been there. He was pale, his eyes muddy and dark, the skin beneath them almost bruised. For a man who cared so much about his looks, it unsettled him. It was as if the changes were a sign to everyone who saw him, a declaration of his guilt without words.

They arranged to meet in the High Street later in the day.

Grainger pressed the 'end call' button and said, 'Fuck you.'

He sat down and felt nothing but exhaustion. The overdose on drink hadn't helped. He stretched his neck and, leaning back on the soft cushions, stared at the ceiling, his eyes stinging and his lips paper dry.

51

Arthur Hamilton put the phone down and left the small office. He was in an old industrial site he owned and the boys had been working on Frankie Mason. Not too hard, because it wasn't necessary. The man couldn't take a lot of pain, and Hamilton knew that you applied only what was necessary. Mason was sobbing, with his head in his hands, as the Glasgow boys stood over him. He was more or less unhurt, apart from a few slaps to soften up any resistance. But there was none – Mason had already decided he'd do anything just to get away from his tormentors.

Hamilton walked over to the chair Mason was sitting in and pulled his face up so he could look straight into his eyes. Mason recoiled and sat back, trying to put space between him and the man who'd been his employer, but it was hopeless, and it felt like two spotlights were burying into his eyes and right into the back of his brain. All the little corners were illuminated and Hamilton just had to look to see them.

'Don't lie, Frankie. Right?' His face was no more than a foot from Mason's.

'No, Arthur. Christ, I've done the business for you for years. Just tell me what you want?'

'The fuckin' lassie's lying in the mortuary, Frankie boy. My fuckin' lassie, an' I want justice. Davy McGill's toast an' no problem there. Thing is, you told me that fuck of a son-in-law gave him a house call – right? Good job, Frankie, but in the search for justice, I want the truth an' exactly what happened. So first of all, is there anythin' you left out? See, I've known for years you like goin' a bit above an' beyond the call of duty. Think I'm a fuckin' idiot? Never really bothered before because it made no difference, but this is in a different league. I heard from all my wee spies that you tend to dig a lot deeper than I ever ask for, but I thought someday that might just come in handy.'

'I never used anythin' against you, Arthur. Honest.' Mason's tears mixed with the slavers that ran down his chin as he looked round the room for something, anything that could help him, but it was hopeless, and the two leather jackets were too much for him to handle.

He felt weak and tired; there was no resistance, but there wasn't much to give Hamilton. He'd already given him everything apart from the Belfast connection, but he couldn't stand the man's eyes looking into his mind. He told him about Belfast and what he had learned, for all it was worth.

Hamilton never moved, still staring into his eyes, searching. Even when Mason had said it all, the man still held his face between his hands, watching for evidence of a lie.

Finally, he stepped back and took a deep breath then worked his neck and shoulders to relieve the tension.

'Belfast, Frankie? There's a turn-up. Those Loyalist boys play a hard game, son. Fuckin' radges. Done a wee bit wi' them as well.'

He looked at the two leather jackets and nodded

for them to step outside. He pulled up a chair and sat opposite Mason, picked up his cigarette and lighter and offered them to him.

'Smoke, Frankie? No harm done. Right?' He smiled as if they'd just finished a nice game of dominoes.

'Aye, right, Arthur.' Mason was shaking and struggled to get the smoke into his mouth before lighting it. He managed to return a kind of a smile and started to believe that it was over.

'Honest, Arthur, there's nothin' else.' He heaved in the smoke and coughed out the result.

'These things'll kill you, Frankie boy.' Hamilton stood and picked up Mason's jacket, which was slung over a chair a few feet away. The contents had been emptied onto the seat before the leather jackets had done the business on him. The big man picked up Mason's phone and smiled at him again.

'Last numbers dialled. Show me, Frankie.' He stretched out his hand and waited. Mason cursed inside. His discipline was to clear the numbers every day, but sometimes he just forgot, depending how knackered or pissed he'd been, and he hadn't cleared the numbers for a few days. He took the phone, opened the dialled numbers and saw the name he didn't want to see screaming from the list.

'Have you told anyone else this stuff, Frankie?'

Hamilton stared down at the screen and his eyes narrowed when he saw Jacquie Bell's number. 'Jacquie fuckin' Bell! Jesus, that girl knows more secrets than God Almighty. Well, Frankie, I'm waitin'.'

'She knows it all. I slip her the odd story, Arthur. Just a bit of give an' take. Know what I mean?' He tried another smile, but Hamilton wasn't playing.

'Think I know what you'd like tae slip her, Frankie boy. So I pay you for a certain piece of work an' you go above an' beyond, give me part back an' toss the full bhoona to a reporter? Is that the story, Frankie? Last chance – is there anythin' else left out, because I'm sendin' the boys round tae your place, an' if they find somethin' you've left out, well, guess what happens?'

Mason's brain started to overheat, trying to think if he'd missed anything that would cost him at least his teeth. He was about to say there wasn't when he remembered the recording of Janet Hadden panelling the guy in the boozer.

Hamilton looked at him and could see the fear all over Mason's wasted coupon. There was no way he was holding out and he told Arthur Hamilton what it was.

'Good stuff, Frankie boy, an' I'll get the two fuckin' ninjas to pick it up. Where is it exactly?'

Mason told him and hoped he hadn't left anything out. For some reason, he said, 'Cheers,' as if the man who was scaring the life out him had just bought him a drink.

Hamilton stopped him with a single finger to his lips. Mason started shaking again because he saw what was in the man's face. He was in full revenge mode and needed to hurt people – that meant anyone involved in the story and definitely if they'd fucked him around. There was no major sin on Mason's part, and any other time he might have got off with a yellow card, but not this time.

Hamilton whistled and the leather jackets stepped back into the old building. Hamilton straightened his jacket and walked past them.

'I'm off home for a shower then a meet in George Street.' He stopped and half-turned. 'I want him hurt but no' the full malky. Need him again in a few days, right?'

The leather jackets shrugged. It was all gravy for them – pain or the malky, it was all in a day's work.

Hamilton looked back at Mason. 'You let me down, Frankie boy, but once ye've had a light pastin' I want you back on the case, right?'

Mason nodded like there was an alternative. Hamilton headed for the door and spoke with his back to them. 'When you're done, text me.'

He walked out of the building and headed for his wheels.

Mason wasn't restrained. He had no option but to try a runner, but the attempt was a joke, and he heard the leather jackets pissing themselves as he ran around the old workshop like a cartoon character. His chest was burning with the effort, but he dodged around till he stopped and faced the Weegies, heaving with exhaustion. One of them was putting on a pair of fighting gloves while the other one combed his hair for some reason.

'You ready, Frankie?'

Mason had been a soldier, a handful in his days and he knew it wouldn't make any difference so there was no point in pleading. He ran at them and managed to shout, 'Fuck you,' before he was caught with a beautiful right cross to the chin.

There was about thirty seconds of pain but none were killing blows. They were professionals; Hamilton had said a bit of pain but no malky and that's exactly what they were delivering.

Mason drifted into something almost pleasant, where there were just dull heavy sounds somewhere in the distance, and then he passed out.

Police Scotland got a call later in the evening that a man was lying on a grass verge not far from the Gogar Bank area of Edinburgh. It was quiet and isolated, though only a few minutes from the link to the bypass.

The uniforms thought at first that Mason was the victim of a hit-and-run, and when they were waiting for the ambulance to arrive he came to. His vision was blurred, but he could see it was the law and that he was alive – hurt but alive. He tried to say 'thank fuck' but it came out as 'hank huck', which was all he could manage through his swollen lips.

The older uniform was kneeling beside him and said, 'What's that, pal?'

'Hank huck am awight.'

The uniform looked up at his partner. 'Talkin' shite – maybe brain damage or somethin' like that?'

There was no brain damage, and for all his pain, Mason just wanted to live. The ambulance took him to the hospital where they cleaned him up then stuck a high dose of painkiller into his system, which did the trick. There was nothing too serious, nothing broken or burst inside. He was okay and the injuries would heal. Hamilton wasn't cutting ties with him so his life wasn't over. He fell asleep and didn't wake for fourteen hours.

When he was eventually released, he went home and groaned when he saw the mess that Hamilton's muscle had left for him. The bastards hadn't been content with the recording of Hadden and Grainger – they'd taken all his favourite horror films.

'Thievin' bastards.'

He was pissed off but there was no way he was making a complaint. He was alive and that was all that mattered.

He went to the fridge for a cold beer.

'Thievin' bastards,' he said again. They'd even taken his supply of cold ones.

He sat down on his chair, closed his eyes and was asleep in minutes.

52

Dominic Grainger stood at the door of the George Street boozer and for some reason the bar he'd been to so many times looked different, but he couldn't understand why. It was dark outside, and a freezing wind that had chilled the North Sea coast of Scotland for days was driving the rain sideways onto the Edinburgh streets. Summer seemed to be gone for the time being.

He walked into the lounge, which was quiet, almost silent, and a barman with a hairless skull stared at him as he walked in, leaving the night outside. The barman was drying a glass with a stained white towel and nodded when Grainger walked past him towards the tables that were mostly empty. The light was dim, almost gloomy, and the punters looked subdued when they glanced in his direction as he pulled out a seat and sat at a corner table. The barman appeared and didn't smile when he ordered a double vodka and tonic.

'You want anything to eat?' The barman's teeth were brown and discoloured, and Grainger decided he had to be addicted to red wine, tobacco and coffee to get them so heavily stained.

Grainger shook his head and wondered where the management had dragged this one up. The staff were usually female, east European and worth the effort. Grainger had pulled a couple of them in his time, and it was part of the reason he liked the place. It had to be the weather, or just his mood, but the place felt miserable, and even the music was fucking awful. It was some classical shite, and he couldn't name it, but it sounded like it was better suited to a funeral.

He saw a paper on the seat next to him and scanned the headlines, something about Brexit, but he couldn't concentrate and he pushed the red top aside as Arthur Hamilton walked through the doors. The barman smiled as though he'd just won the lottery.

'What can I get you, Mr Hamilton?'

Grainger had never seen Hamilton in this boozer and wondered why the fuck he was getting the VIP treatment. It worried him. He felt threatened for some reason, but it was vague and he was confused. His skull felt like it was being squeezed. The few punters that were there were looking over at him, and he wondered if they were all big fans of his father-in-law as well.

Hamilton stood at the table and stared for a moment, unsmiling. He was a big man in every respect, and Grainger looked at his arms, which even under his jacket looked pumped up – his fitness regime over the years had certainly paid dividends. He sat down and didn't offer his hand.

'Well, Dominic?' That was all he said and he held Grainger with his gaze.

The pain behind his forehead was almost intolerable, and then he saw something in the older man's eyes. The bastard knew, there was no doubt about it – the man just fucking knew. He felt light-headed and afraid.

'I'm sorry, Arthur. I know what she meant to you.' He

wondered if Hamilton had noticed the red-rimmed eyes, the black smudges underneath, the tremor in the hands.

'You know what she meant to me? That a fuckin' joke, Dominic?' Hamilton shoved his face forward a few inches. 'You killed her, son. Davy McGill was a numpty and you put the laddie right in the frame.'

Hamilton looked round at the barman. 'Hear that, pal? This fucker killed ma wee lassie.'

The barman nodded. 'I hear you, Mr Hamilton, fuckin' disgrace.'

Grainger felt the room spin. The other punters in the bar were all staring at him as he wondered how the fuck his father-in-law had set this all up, but there was more to worry about. Hamilton stood up and seemed to grow forever. Grainger was rooted to the seat as his father-in-law pulled out a handgun and pointed it right at his head.

'Fuckin' rat bastard, talkin' to the polis, betraying your brothers and puttin' Davy McGill an' ma lassie in the ground.' He walked round the table and pressed the muzzle against Grainger's temple.

'Please, Arthur. You've got it all wrong. Please.'

'Hear that, pal?' Big Arthur shouted across to the barman, who was smiling and showing all those brown teeth.

'Hear it, Mr Hamilton. Boy's got a fuckin' cheek if you ask me.'

'Think I agree, son. Anybody disagree?' He looked around the punters in the bar, who didn't move and said nothing. He shrugged at Grainger who was staring up at him.

'Looks like everybody agrees wi' me, Dominic.' He grinned, but there was no humour in it.

Dominic watched a slow-motion movie as Hamilton's finger started to squeeze the trigger. He tried to scream, but his throat was frozen and nothing came as the trigger reached its critical point.

There was a dull boom as the gun exploded, and a multi-coloured flash, and it was as if Grainger had left his own body. He watched his head disintegrate, covering Hamilton in blood, bone and tissue. All he heard was people laughing as if it was all a comedy.

He sat bolt upright in his chair and groaned with fear, looking round for the man who'd killed him. But he was in his flat; it had all been a dream.

He shook his head and looked at the clock. He'd only been sleeping for an hour and his brain pounded with the pressure of his guilt, which seemed to be growing inside him like cancer. He hadn't expected this and wondered where these demons were coming from as he headed for the shower. Guilt was a new emotion for him, and he'd never factored it into his calculations before.

An hour later Grainger stepped out of a taxi and headed into the George Street boozer where he bought his drink and grabbed a seat from which he could view the whole bar area, and a paper. There was just a scattering of drinkers, and it had started to piss cold rain, which had kept a few at home rather than heading for the boozers to watch the big game or the latest from Syria. Irrationally, he checked the paper a couple of times, as if he might still be in a dream, then wondered what the fuck was going on in his mind. The news did nothing but piss him off – whatever the story was these days, it was all bad.

Arthur Hamilton walked through the door. Old habits die hard and he scanned the whole place for problems, looking for anyone who was out of place or waiting for him when they shouldn't be. He spotted his son-in-law right away but finished checking before walking towards the table to join him. It had been a long time since he'd been in a city-centre boozer and he felt a twinge of sadness. The old Edinburgh he knew was gone or nearly gone; the place was a land of posh boozers where punters who'd lived in the city for five minutes talked shite – and then there was the streams of tourists.

Grainger was in the seat he would have picked for himself, but he wasn't going to sit with his back to the door, so he took the seat beside him, which stressed Grainger a bit, but then that was the idea. They didn't shake hands.

'Want a drink, Arthur?'

'Naw, it's okay, son. Never drink an' drive.' He held up his keys and shook them. 'I'll maybe go for a coffee. Hate the stuff but it keeps me goin'.'

He waved his hand to a waitress who came over and took his order. Hamilton settled back in his chair and gave his son-in-law the eyes.

'How you doin' then, Dominic? Polis been puttin' you through it, I suppose?' The question was loaded, but it was supposed to be. Both men were sparring and this was just an opening round.

'No, they've been okay, Arthur, just doing what they have to do, I suppose. The bastards!' It was meant as a bit of banter and what gangsters would have said in normal times.

Hamilton still didn't move a muscle and just kept his face expressionless as he watched his son-in-law like he was prey waiting to be dispatched if it twitched the wrong signal.

'You?' Grainger asked as if he cared.

'Fine, but that Ronnie Slade's the business. Wouldn't like to have come across that boy too much when I was in the game. Know what I mean? Anyway, we need to make arrangements, son. They've got the boy that killed Jude. Well, they've got the body o' the boy that killed Jude.'

Grainger knew that Hamilton adored his daughter, was almost obsessed by her in fact, but he seemed too chilled. He knew enough about the man to worry about that. He should have been distraught, but Hamilton was a control freak, and when he had to, he would put a lid on all the emotion boiling inside him, though it would need a release at some point. That control was for a reason and he would feel cheated that the main suspect was dead. Hamilton was using the word 'son' for the first time in their relationship and it was a sign of contempt. They both knew that, so there was no problem. But they had to keep playing the game till someone made the wrong move.

'Thing is, Dominic, they've solved the case – well, as far as the bizzies are concerned – so there shouldn't be much of a hold-up on the funeral. Take it you've been thinkin' about it?'

'Well, of course, Arthur, but need to get the nod from Ronnie Slade then I'll sort it.' In truth, he hadn't really thought much about a funeral and he should have. That was obvious to a blind man. He could have sworn there was a tiny red flicker in Hamilton's eyes. They talked over what would happen with the funeral and the arrangements.

'I'll pay of course, son.' Hamilton said it as if it was a given, and not up for discussion.

'It's fine, Arthur, I'll take care of it. She was my wife, so it's my place.' He watched the tiny spots of heat flicker again behind the big man's eyes.

'Thing is, son, there's only one of us loved the lassie. Know what I mean? So I'm payin'.' He stressed the last word, put his forearms on the table and, without another word, dared his son-in-law to argue. Grainger nodded and felt the edge of his eye tic.

'By the way, I meant to ask. Did you know that horrible wee bastard McGill?'

'Knew the boy by sight, Arthur. That's it.'

He felt his eye tic rhythmically, like it was sending out a message in Morse code . . . *I did it* in big fuck-off non-verbals. He tried to sound matter-of-fact but those same non-verbals were leaking stress and guilt.

'He did a bit of work for my brothers, but God knows where the break-in came from. He was in that game years ago, but just a message laddie for their team. My brothers are raging – just as well he's gone before they got a hold of him. Heard some story he was short of dough so maybe this is how he was balancing the books.'

He'd said too much – too pleading, too fucking mealy-mouthed.

'Aye, that's what happens.' Hamilton put the tips of his fingers together in an arch just in front of his face. 'Never trust anyone, son. When I was in the game, the ones I watched closest were the men closest to me.'

He picked up his coffee for the first time and screwed his face up at the taste. He stared over the rim of the cup at Grainger. He'd just watched the lie pour from his lips like vomit. Tonto was dead and beyond a torture session with Arthur Hamilton, but his son-in-law was here on earth. He put the cup down and smiled.

'Need to go, son. Places to go an' people tae see, right? You get in touch wi' Ronnie Slade an' find out what the Hampden is. Right?'

Hamilton stood up and threw a tenner on the table. 'That'll cover the coffee an' whatever you're havin', son.' He looked at his watch and said, 'Take care,' before turning his back and heading for the door.

Grainger leaned back, tilted his face to the ceiling and closed his eyes. He took a couple of deep breaths, trying to relieve the knots in the muscles of his shoulders and neck. The barman came to his table and he asked him for a double vodka and Coke to try to stop the pounding in his head.

'Gimme a beer with that as well, pal.' His palms felt wet and he could smell the dull, heavy odour of sweat, even though he'd showered before the meeting. His body was hot, stressed with the effort of coping with the toxins he was putting into it. He'd gone from a fitness regime and careful diet to the eating and drinking habits of a piss-head.

'Fuck it.' He tilted his head back and downed the vodka in one go.

He stared at a corner of the bar and tried to see where the holes in his plan were, but apart from Tonto not following the script, there was no clear evidence. But Arthur Hamilton saw inside him – he knew it despite the man's even behaviour. What would he do next? That was the problem.

If it was him, he'd suspect but wait for evidence. Hamilton wouldn't fly off the handle when there was so much police activity, but he'd be digging in the background, and if he could build a case, then he'd come for him. There was nothing to do but sit still, ride it out and hope the police settled for Tonto, then he guessed Hamilton would stay his hand. He knew he only acted where there was a good case – that's why he'd been a success both as a businessman and as a gangster.

Grainger had another round and the booze started to settle him, though it was new booze on top of what he'd had the previous night – it would only take the pain away for a few hours then the morning would bring a fresh dose of reality. He called Janet Hadden.

'We might have another problem, Janet.' He didn't wait for her to say anything first.

'What fuckin' problem do *we* have now, Dominic?'

Her voice was cold and any thoughts he'd ever had of a relationship, physical or otherwise, were over. That was obvious, but the images of his hands round her throat flashed though his mind again as he listened to her voice. He imagined his face close to hers, squeezing slowly and watching every little tremor as she died, the wide staring eyes pleading for life to someone who just wanted to take it away.

'What fuckin' problem, Dominic?'

He snapped back to reality with the repeated question and squeezed his eyes tight. He told her that he thought Arthur Hamilton knew.

'You need to stay focused and, by the sounds of it, leave off the fuckin' bottle. You stay pissed an' we'll both end up dead. You hear me? Now calm down an' I'll see what's happening on the investigation. You're starting to act like a fuckin' street ned. Man up, for fuck's sake.'

He heard the call click off. She was right and he knew it. Hadden was pissed off at him, but the call had steadied him and he just needed someone to pull him back. It was going to be okay – the big man was fishing and Tonto was still the man in the frame. Sit tight, that was the answer.

He waved to the barman for a refill and he grinned lopsidedly when a stunning young east European girl brought the drink to him. He said something that he thought might impress her. If she was up for a laugh and a joke then he might get her back to the flat. But her face couldn't hide her contempt, and she turned her back and left him.

'Fucking cow.' He grinned at a couple who'd taken a table near to him and had watched his attempt with the girl who'd served his drinks. 'Must be a lesbian. Right?'

He grinned again and watched the couple ignore him before they moved to another table. The barman appeared and Grainger held up his glass and asked for a refill.

'Think you've had enough, sir. Time to go home and sleep it off.'

He tried to argue, but it was just too much effort. He

told the guy who he was, but it didn't cut any ice and he said he wouldn't be back.

'Probably wise, sir.' The barman didn't seem too impressed. He was new and the name Grainger meant fuck all as far as he was concerned.

Waking up at 3 a.m. was a painful experience, and Grainger couldn't work out what had happened for a couple of minutes. Then his mind downloaded his situation and he groaned as he felt his head start to thump all over again. He still had his suit on, and when he swung his legs over the side of the bed, he realised he was wet and saw the dark stain at the crotch of his trousers.

'For fuck's sake.' He pulled everything off, filled up on cold water and lay on the sofa as the early-morning hours filled his mind with nothing but waking terrors. He was moving between periods of supreme confidence and terrible fear of the unknown. It was wrecking him, but he had no option but to stay the course and observe every move of the predators who watched and waited.

53

Grace Macallan had waited in her flat for Jacquie Bell. The call had been short, but there was enough in her friend's tone to suggest something was up, and she knew the reporter didn't do drama unless it was just that. Jack and the children were at their cottage in Northern Ireland and had gone ahead of her by a couple of days so she could wind up a case she was involved in. They'd planned the short holiday weeks ago, and she had the old nagging worry that something might interfere with their time together. The corruption case she'd been investigating had been an unpleasant one, and it looked like a young cop with what had been a promising career was going to end up in Saughton.

She saw so much of it now, and the world had definitely changed. In her early days in the RUC, drink had been the curse that had put as many men in their graves as PIRA, but now it was dope and debt. Everybody seemed to want it all before they had the means to pay for their dreams.

The young cop had started to take the occasional hit of coke and it had run out of control before he could work out that he was a serving officer and a dealer all at the same time. The gangsters had sniffed him out like rotting carrion and within weeks he was selling his soul and beyond saving.

Macallan had felt sick watching him disintegrate in front of her when he broke down during the interview and admitted it all. She knew there was a place for counter-corruption but hated it and wanted to move on or out of the job, which had become a preoccupation. She talked it over endlessly with Jack, who knew enough to be supportive, but it had to be her choice. She did have options though, and her background in counter-terrorism meant she was qualified to move into the hothouse created by the turmoil in the Middle East.

The doorbell broke her train of thought and she glanced in the mirror before answering. The years were there but she looked healthy, and if anything, time was adding to the character of her face. Jack told her he liked the changes that married life, motherhood and the love of a man had given her. She was happy in her private life, and the dark days of the Troubles and her early days in Scotland were like an old film where actors had played out the parts of the detectives and villains. She pulled open the door and grinned at Jacquie Bell, who held up a bottle of very expensive Amarone.

'This is sixteen per cent proof, Grace. Fucking grape juice laced with rocket fuel. Get the glasses.' She put the bottle on the hall table, hugged her friend and pulled back to take in the face she just didn't see often enough. They were both workaholics, always sacrificing something for the job, and in another life, they would have spent so much more time with each other than they did.

'You're beginning to look like a mother, Grace. In a good way. Christ, I never thought I'd see that tortured detective from Northern Ireland turn into an advert for domestic bliss. But there you go. Maybe you can advertise domestic products when you retire – baking an' all that shite.'

Macallan laughed and that was always a rare sight. 'You look good, Jacquie, but God knows how you do it.'

'Told you before, science has got it all wrong. Fags and booze – they're the answer to all the world's problems. If we all just stayed pissed there wouldn't be half the problems. Where's that hunk of a man of yours?'

They sat down at the kitchen table and Grace poured the almost syrupy Italian wine. They smiled at each other just before the glasses touched their lips. The mood had changed though, and even though Macallan didn't know what the problem was, she knew enough to understand this wasn't going to be good news.

'Okay, Jacquie, tell me the problem and then we can gossip later.' She wanted to get to the point and listened without interrupting as the reporter told her exactly what Frankie Mason had told her, and that she'd had to sit on it.

The smile gradually dropped from Macallan's face as she absorbed the story and what it might mean. When Bell finished and waited for a response, Macallan put the glass down and took a moment before answering.

'Christ, Jacquie. You sat on a story about what might be a corrupt relationship and you tell me now? You know the problems we might have with this.' There was annoyance in her tone but it was controlled; Macallan knew it was easy to be judgemental with hindsight. It was a problem, a difficult one, and her concern was that someone could take the wrong view of what Bell had done then try to hurt her.

'Sorry, Grace. Sod's Law – I get the story and something else comes up. I'm not claiming to have done the right thing. Look, you know I'm an unscrupulous bitch, and if it wasn't for you, I might have left it buried, but I have a bad feeling about it. Just the wrong mix of chemicals. Cards on the table, I know Arthur Hamilton, and let me tell you, that boy will want to lick some poor bastard's blood. He's a bit of an old smoothie now, but cut him open and he bleeds acid. Bad guy, Grace. If I need to take a kicking I'll have that, but over to you, girl.'

Macallan stayed quiet for a moment and studied her friend. She sipped the wine and wondered why she'd never drunk it before. It was like warm chocolate, with a delayed buzz as it hit the spot.

'Must get some of this.' Then she put the glass down.

'Right, Jacquie, it's late so I'll get in touch with Ronnie Slade in the morning. There's two things we have here: the murder, although for all intents and purposes it's solved from what I hear, then there's the possible corruption. We need to be careful because there might be an explanation for what Janet Hadden has been up to, though Christ knows what that could be.' Macallan knew it was pointless to press the panic button, and she believed her friend when she said she'd come forward only because of her.

'It's important to understand if anyone else knows apart from your source?' Macallan raised her eyebrows to emphasis the question.

'As far as I know my source was going to tell Arthur Hamilton everything apart from the Belfast thing. That was probably for my benefit – he thought there was a story for me.' She paused and a half-grin spread her lips. 'He has a wee thing for me.'

'Don't they all? It's your capacity for drink that impresses the boys.'

'Tell you the truth, Grace, Arthur Hamilton is a scary man, and if he suspects Dominic of being involved he'll shake the trees to get the evidence. I can't guarantee the source won't tell him it all, including the Belfast connection. It's the visit to Davy McGill though that's going to stir him up, and my source will definitely tell him that bit. As I said, he's a scary guy.' She tapped the table with her fingers and watched Macallan's mind working.

'Christ, if this thing about Janet Hadden is true then it's a weird one. God knows what that means,' Macallan said. 'But if anything else comes up, Jacquie, you let me know – and that means right away.'

'You have it, my friend, although I think I'll stick to pulling down bent politicians in future. I'm getting too old. Less hassle and more brownie points.'

She raised her glass to Macallan, glad she knew her. Grace was one of the few people in her life that seemed to be there just when she needed her.

She felt light now; the wine was working its magic. She was gasping for a smoke but knew that was out for Macallan, who always said she was just one lungful of smoke away from being hooked again.

'Why don't we finish this and I'll open something else? Stay the night, Jacquie. I need to chew the fat and drink. Don't do that enough these days. Being the perfect mum has its drawbacks.'

Bell raised her eyebrows mischievously. It was her go-to every time she liked to wind Macallan up. When they'd first met, they'd spent one night together when Macallan was still at a low point and trying to recover from the horrors of the Troubles. She'd never been able to explain why it happened, but Bell loved never letting her forget.

'There's a lovely spare room, Jacquie – you'll love it. Now tell me all about these politicians you've been harassing.'

It was the early hours when they both realised that the third bottle was done, there was still work to do and that they needed an early start. But they had needed that night and being able to talk without any guards in place. There were no great problems resolved, but both of them wondered how so much could have happened in the short years they'd known each other.

Macallan went out like a light, the night having purged some of her worries about the present and future, whatever they might hold.

Bell, on the other hand, leaned out of her window as Macallan slept and for the first time she could remember, she felt lonely.

'Getting too old for this shite, girl,' she murmured.

She blew a stream of smoke into the night and a tear bulged before zigzagging down her cheek.

54

As Jacquie Bell stared into the Edinburgh night and reflected on a past and present that she was beginning to question, Arthur Hamilton stood at his own window looking at the same night sky. He'd been there for hours, alternately sitting at his desk chair or standing behind the glass, trying to come to terms with what was left of his life. His daughter had turned against him, but he'd always dreamed of a reconciliation and that she'd come to realise that everything he had would have gone to her or the grandchildren he'd never know now. It hadn't occurred to him till that night that he was now the end of his particular line of forefathers. For such a hard man, he'd nursed all the same fears as the mere mortals he'd steamrollered over during his years in crime and business. He'd been robbed, and people just did not rob Big Arthur Hamilton.

Occasionally he groaned as if he was in pain; his heart felt like it was being squeezed and rage boiled inside him. He pressed his forehead against the cool glass and closed his eyes, trying to work out what the fuck life was supposed to mean for him now.

He played the recording again, watching the woman Frankie Mason had said was a detective knock fuck out of the punter in the boozer. *What the fuck was a DI doing in that position then turning up with a different look at Grainger's office?* he thought over and over again. She was bent in some way, no doubt about it, and he'd had a lot of experience of detectives on the take, but not the female variety wearing a fucking disguise. She was part of whatever had happened, guilty as fucking sin, and he just had to work out why, or if the worst came to the worst, make her tell him why.

'Fuck it.' He ground his teeth before and after the words left his lips, squeezing the crystal whisky glass in his hand until it broke. He let the pieces drop to the floor and ignored the blood running from the open cuts in his palm. The pain was nothing to the poison beating through his blood vessels and in his head.

Eventually he looked at his hand as if he'd just realised what had happened. The side of his dressing gown was covered in blood, and in the moonlight, there was a dark, almost black patch on the carpet. He wondered if it had been the same where his daughter had been killed.

'It must have hurt, Jude,' he said to the daughter who only existed in his imagination now.

Hamilton decided in that moment that he couldn't wait for payback. What happened to him didn't matter, and in a way he was free to carry out whatever action he decided, but he believed in the old adage that revenge is always a dish best taken cold. Dominic Grainger was guilty, but to what degree? He could wait to see if he could find out more about what his reasons might be. He would get Frankie Mason to look at him again, dig a bit deeper.

It was always the same reasons for most things: money, sex or revenge. His bet was money. Grainger gave the impression that he was a sharp, minted operator, but the private detective had told him that he was a gambler.

He thought back to what he would have done back in the day if a rival operator had killed one of his. It had happened, and in those days, he hadn't just taken out the fuck who'd left his brother in a vegetative state; he'd set fire to the family home. The boy's mother had barely made it out alive. Then he'd taken every part of their business, and it had sent a message to all the other predators who might have thoughts of taking on Arthur Hamilton.

There wasn't anything to suggest that Tonto was working under the direction of Paul or Sean Grainger, but so what? Guilt by association – it wasn't court-of-law rules of evidence, but they weren't in a fucking court of law, and better that an innocent man died than some guilty fuck got away with it. It didn't matter; there was enough to say Dominic Grainger was guilty of enough to warrant a death sentence. It needed blood.

He headed for the shower, and the plan that was forming played through his mind as he stood under the hot shower, watching the blood mix with the water then disappear down into the darkness of the sewers.

55

Macallan woke early and heard Bell coughing in the bathroom. She switched on the kettle and searched for the packet of aspirin she hadn't needed for a while. It was still early, but she knew Ronnie Slade would be in the office already if he was working a case. She had a lot of time for him and they'd been friends since they'd met at the locus of a shooting that was remembered in police legend as the Gunfight at Ricky's Corral. It had been a bloodbath, but as far as most detectives were concerned a bit of a result, because the Fleming brothers, two Leith villains, had been treated to the wrong end of a shotgun. Macallan had recognised Ronnie Slade as the real deal back then, and he'd proved her right. Apart from anything else, he had respect among the ranks, though it had come at a price. When there was a difficult case, the signal went up to get Slade, and it had already cost him a couple of serious relationships. But that was the price they paid, and she knew what that meant as well as anyone in the job.

When Slade answered, he sounded tired and claimed that he hadn't had his first shots of coffee to keep him alive another day. He was happy to hear Macallan; they hadn't seen each other for a while and had both been preoccupied with difficult cases.

'Jesus, Grace, it's good to hear from you. Hope this isn't an official call that I'm in the shit,' he joked. 'Enough problems as it is with this case. Anyway, what can I do for you? Hope it involves meeting up for a drink.'

She cut to the chase and gave him brief details without going too far on the phone. She heard something in his tone, and his brief questions suggested this wasn't a total surprise to him.

'That's roughly it, Ronnie. Know you have this one solved, but there's two issues here, and one of them is in my domain and the other in yours. Might be nothing but had to let you know. I'll put this on paper for your eyes only as soon as I get to the office.'

'Is this from an official source, Grace?'

'One of mine, Ronnie, and rock solid in the past.'

'Look, I'm having a closed session with Lesley Thompson and Felicity Young to go over what we have. The forensics are more or less complete, and we want to make sure it's all being covered. Truth is, Grace, it should be solved, done an' dusted on the label, but something just doesn't feel right with this. You know the problem – further up the tree want it run down and I'm fighting a losing battle. Come over to the briefing and see what you think.'

'Good for me, Ronnie, be great to see the old team again and no doubt Felicity will have a story. What time?'

They agreed to meet mid-morning. Macallan had some breakfast but couldn't convince Bell to have anything more than coffee plus a couple of bites of toast that were obviously grudged and just to keep her friend off her back.

'Honestly, Jacquie, I worry about you. The clock ain't going backwards, but then you know that.'

'I'll keep in touch, Grace, and be careful out there.' Bell grabbed her jacket and bag and was already on the phone when she closed the door behind her.

Macallan walked into Slade's office three hours later and her face lit up when she saw Lesley Thompson and Felicity Young get to their feet. There was a bond that stayed with them no matter how long it had been since they'd last seen each other. They exchanged a few stories, and Slade smiled but stayed well out of it. He knew what their shared experience meant and that it was special.

They eventually settled down and there was almost a discussion about Brexit until Macallan put her hand up and called time on politics till they got the job in hand done.

Slade took over, handing each of them a summary of the evidence and forensics from the locus of the murder. He kicked it off with a note of caution.

'Look, this is just a discussion, and I haven't explained why Grace is here, but we'll come to that. This is need to know and I trust everyone to keep it that way at the moment till we decide if we go any further. First of all, Felicity, can you run through what we've got so far from the locus?'

Felicity Young, who was known in the job as The Brain, was a superb analyst, but more than that, she never saw herself as separate, just part of the machinery of the team. Solving a case gave her as much of a thrill as the detectives, although she was less demonstrative about a result.

'First of all—' The analyst stopped and pulled the glasses off her nose. It was a habit they all recognised. 'McGill was at the locus, and we have more than enough evidence that he entered the house through the back window. It was easily forced and we have fibres on the ledge that match what he was wearing, plus we have good footprints in the soft earth at the back of the house that match his shoes. There are soil samples as well that match.'

Slade's phone went off and there was a bit of leg-pulling because he was hard on anyone who made the same mistake in a briefing. He refused the call and put his hands up. 'Okay, I owe you all a drink, but don't grass me up to the troops – I just forgot, right? Sorry, Felicity, and on you go.'

'He was in the bedroom and we have a number of confirmations of contact or close contact with the deceased. I don't want to run through them all, but there is cross-contamination of blood and fibres, plus soil deposits from the garden. He must have picked up blood on one of his boots and I'll come back to that. There's nothing on the weapon to tie him, but he was wearing gloves, and I'll come back to that as well. There's an area where he vomited and we have DNA plus a hair in the vomit that matches his. We think he took his balaclava off because it seems he vomited when he had it on.' She scribbled something on the margin of her notes before continuing. 'There is a pattern of blood back towards the bedroom door and stairs, consistent with coming from the sole of his boot. There's more but that's enough to say he was there – there's a full report from the SOCOs and lab we've read and you can have, Grace.' She looked at Slade, who nodded confirmation and took over from her.

'The thing here is that tied to what was found in Davy McGill's flat, there's enough to convict him in any court, but there are unresolved issues. There's the fact that Davy McGill was one of Paul and Sean Grainger's team and not known for this level of violence. He was no saint, but although he'd been a decent housebreaker years ago, there's nothing on intelligence that he was still at that game.'

'Before we go any further – Grace, can you fill everyone in on what you've been told then we'll get to the issues.'

Macallan told them exactly what she'd been told by Jacquie Bell, apart from who her source was. Thompson shifted in her seat; the seeds of doubt were growing arms and legs in her mind, though Young remained impassive, apart from fiddling with her glasses. Slade let Macallan finish then took over again.

'Okay, this might mean absolutely nothing, but the deceased's husband visited the alleged killer days before the crime, though according to him he only knows McGill by sight. He's a liar, but then so what? Now we get to the issues. Can you pick it up again, Felicity?'

The analyst sipped a glass of water and picked up her notes again.

'I'll go over a few things, but let's start with the gloves found in his rucksack. There's no blood, hair or material from the deceased, and if he had them on when he used the weapon there should at least be spattering on the back of the glove holding the weapon.'

She put her glasses back on and looked round their faces for a moment, letting the picture develop.

'Now we have the cupboard where the box was removed. If he'd gone to that after killing the deceased there would have been blood traces on the carpet from his boots. There aren't, so the hypothesis is that he went to the cupboard before she was killed.'

She paused again and waited for the question she knew was coming.

'So does that mean he must have broken into the house, gone upstairs and then been disturbed by the deceased?' Macallan asked the question the others in the room had already been struggling with. Slade came back in.

'Precisely, Grace. So where was she? If she knew there was someone in the house, why did she head straight for him? She was in her dressing gown, but the shower and bath were dry, unless she dried the whole place before she went through and just hadn't heard anything because she was in the shower. It's possible the place could have dried off in the time before she was found, but we have a statement that she was swimming at her club earlier on and had a sauna so would she shower again?'

He left the question hanging and nodded to Young, who was scribbling more notes. She removed her glasses and carried on. She was definitely warming to her subject.

'So the other question is: why did he head straight for that cupboard? There might be an explanation – it could signify prior knowledge, but then there was nothing of value in the box. One explanation could be that he went straight to the cupboard because he didn't know the deceased's body was lying the other side of the bed. We've checked and he wouldn't see her from that angle.'

'I'm looking at the photographs from the locus and there's bloodstaining on the wall. Would he have seen that?' Macallan asked. She had the buzz – this was what she missed. Examining the puzzles, looking at the fragments and trying to make a picture of the truth.

'He would, but it was dark, and we've looked at this as well, Grace. He might not have noticed initially, but we just don't know. In the dark, you can see the marks, but it would be easy to miss them when you first entered the room, especially if you were concentrating on the cupboard, which is more less right in front of you.' She looked at Slade, who nodded again to carry on.

'So there are some problems that don't seem to fit what we have. To be fair that's not unusual, and there are always issues that don't seem to make sense at a locus. So we have the question if he went for the cupboard first, why was that? Then if that was the case, why did the deceased head for the bedroom – unless she just hadn't heard anything?'

'That's possible, I suppose.' Macallan paused and concentrated, trying to paint the picture in her mind, to be there at the killing. 'If she came into the room and Davy McGill was there anywhere between the door and the cupboard, she would be running past him to the other side of the bed. Possible but seems unlikely.'

'Exactly, Grace, though the trouble is that sometimes victims act against logic. But there's more,' Thompson said.

'The next problem is that there's a repeated bloodstain on the carpet leading away from the area of the body and almost certainly from his boot. That's fair enough, and we also have a faint pattern on the carpet from the heavy soil contact on the sole. From the position of the blood transfer, we're pretty sure this was from his right boot. So far so good.'

She looked directly at Macallan. 'This is where we have another problem. All that's on the carpet is this blood from the right boot, and we can see the tread of the left boot, but no bloodstaining from that one. However, the left boot found at Davy McGill's place had blood on the sole. Do you follow that, Grace?'

Macallan looked puzzled, trying to see in her imagination why that could be.

'Not really, Lesley.' She tapped the end of her pencil against her notepad and then saw what the others in the room saw. 'Unless it was planted.'

'On the money, Grace.' Slade smiled; he had always loved working with Macallan. Her intense focus was something he'd always admired. It was always more than just a job with her, and he was driven in the same way.

Thompson broke the moment again.

'The lab have looked at it and they're unhappy, as the bloodstain on the left boot has no subsequent wear or contamination on the surface of it. In other words, why isn't it walked off, to some degree? If the circumstances had been different, they would have suspected a plant by the detectives.' She waited for a response.

'So will it hold up, Ronnie?' Macallan wondered where this was leading, and they hadn't even come to Janet Hadden.

'As evidence of a crime, let's say involving a third party? The answer is: not on its own. If, for example, Dominic Grainger is involved in some way then all he has to do is deny it. We have nothing else apart from doubts, but they're significant doubts, Grace.'

'Motive?' Macallan threw it into the room.

'Has to be something to do with money,' Slade said, and they could see it couldn't settle happily with Davy McGill acting alone. 'We have information, including his own statement, that their marriage was in trouble, and now it turns out he's a serious and pretty hopeless gambler. If this was some kind of set-up then it wouldn't explain why Davy McGill broke in and stole a box full of crap. The box was locked, so he wouldn't know what was inside, and maybe he thought there was something else or he was taking to order. Just don't know, Grace. However, we now have your story that he was in contact with Davy McGill, so we have to act.'

Thompson broke in and reminded them there were other issues. 'We still don't know who kicked the door in, and the junkies next door deny that. Then I suppose the question is: did Davy McGill kill himself intentionally or was he forced in some way? If the blood was planted on the boot then it must have happened in the flat.'

She let it hang there while they absorbed the information and made their own notes.

'Okay.' Slade took control. 'Let's get this thing organised.'

'There's confirmation from my source as well that the marriage was a sham, and with the gambling problem on top, there's definitely a motive. What do you propose, Ronnie?' Macallan felt like her skin was prickling with energy. She felt alive, high and she wanted to know what had happened in that bedroom.

'We'll have him in, but not as a suspect, just a witness clearing up loose ends. We bring him in as a suspect on this, he just needs to sit with his lawyer, who'll accuse us of harassing the victim's distraught other half. What about Janet Hadden?'

'I'll get her at the same time. Don't know her, but she has an impressive record, although apparently she can be a bit of a loner. Can't make any sense of this alleged incident in the bar. If she attacks a man in the bar while she's in Grainger's company, before she's registered the first meet with him, then I just don't know. Weird one, but sometimes these things fizzle out, and we have to give her the benefit of the doubt.'

Macallan made a couple of notes and they finished the meeting, agreeing to coordinate interviews with Grainger and Hadden.

56

Arthur Hamilton had decided to watch and wait. The atmosphere at the funeral had been ice-cold, even if it was the height of summer, although in Scotland that meant mostly pissing rain. Jude Hamilton was buried in Portobello cemetery on the eastern edge of the city. There were bursts of sunshine mixed in with downpours that had soaked the mourners, such as they were. It was a surprisingly small gathering, and in a way, it hit home with both Dominic Grainger and Arthur Hamilton that not many people really cared that much for them. There were more old-time gangsters there as a token of respect for the deceased's father than there were people who actually loved and cared about them.

The only acknowledgement between father-in-law and son-in-law was a nod each way. The tension was there and everyone saw it.

Ronnie Slade and Lesley Thompson stood well back from the graveside, but if they'd had suspicions before the funeral, the ceremony had done nothing to tell them they were wrong.

Hamilton knew what they knew and didn't need to

worry about the constraints of the law. He was waiting on Grainger making a mistake and exposing the lie – then he would make his move. All he needed was that final piece to prove what had happened, and once he had it, all of the Graingers were dead men walking.

Hamilton had nothing left but the memories and his name. The last witness to what he'd done in the past was dead, and he could pretend that he had honour.

He scanned the mourners and found it was the same as at the church service. Not a single tear; in fact, no one was even pretending. It made him angry because he knew his life and what had been his family was a failure in every sense of the word. His wife had died hating him, and his daughter had grown up carrying his secret like a loaded weapon. He knew other gangsters with children who'd gone on to university and become lawyers and doctors. The old men had wanted something different for their children and they'd achieved that.

The mourners started to peel away and he stared at the hole in the ground containing the battered remains of his daughter. He hadn't noticed Slade and Thompson coming up beside him.

'I'm sorry, Arthur. We've had our run-ins, but put that aside and I know what this means. Christ, I've seen enough of it in my time.'

Hamilton looked up and studied the detectives as if they were strangers. 'Is that the case closed then, Ronnie? Job done, eh?' His lips were tight and he wanted confrontation; it was written all over him.

'The job's never done, Arthur. We study the evidence till we're sure, then we close the books, and there's still work to be done.'

Slade hadn't intended saying anything, but he saw in Hamilton's face that things were moving out of control and the last thing he needed was for him to do anything rash before he had Grainger in. It was arranged for the following day and dressed up as a routine interview.

'Look, Arthur, if you have any theories of your own be sure and share them with us. Hate us to have crossed lines.'

'Crossed lines, Ronnie? You do what you have to do and I'll take care of my business, son. I mean, the case is solved, isn't it? Tell me it's solved, Ronnie.'

Slade felt his mouth twitch as he tried to control his non-verbals, but Hamilton read the signs. They both knew what the answer was, but there couldn't be any conformation on either part.

'Arthur, I'm telling you here and now: stay the fuck away from this and let us do our job. You interfere and you'll end up inside, that's a promise.'

Slade regretted it as soon as the last word left his lips. The old gangster had waltzed him and he knew it.

'Jesus, Ronnie, think I give a fuck what you might do? I'm just mournin' for the daughter an' mindin' my business.'

He turned his back on the detectives and headed for his car. Slade watched him go and shook his head. 'We better put this one to bed, Les, or Christ knows what'll happen.'

When Hamilton reached his car, he pulled out his phone and called Frankie Mason.

'I want you all over my son-in-law again, Frankie. Bring in extra help if you need it and fuck the cost. Ye hear, Frankie boy?'

Mason winced on the other end of the phone, but at least the big man wasn't threatening to kill him, and it was a big earner if he wanted that level of cover.

'I can bring in ex-army guys if you want. They're expensive but—'

Hamilton interrupted before he could get the rest of

the words out. 'Just fuckin' do it, Frankie, and stay on the bastard till I say otherwise, okay?'

Mason could hardly disagree; he didn't want a rematch with the Weegies Hamilton had brought in. For a moment, he considered telling Jacquie Bell but thought he'd shelve that for the time being. If he fucked up again with the big man, he'd be taking a rest under the waters of the Forth the next time.

Instead, Mason picked up the phone and called in some of his old team.

57

Slade sat over the table from Dominic Grainger and tried to appear as if it really was a routine interview.

'We've just some loose ends to tie up and thanks for coming in today.' The words nearly stuck in his throat because he knew that Grainger was wise to the move – had his lawyer with him.

Grainger and Hadden had discussed this eventuality and what they would say if it happened, so he felt confident enough and purposely ignored Slade when he was talking, staring directly at Lesley Thompson. He was playing games, and his lawyer shifted uncomfortably with the tension being generated across the table.

'Somehow, I'm just not convinced this is routine, Mr Slade, but fire away – I've nothing to hide.'

Slade knew exactly what he was doing, and regardless of the game, he ran through a series of routine questions that seemed to annoy Grainger. He wanted to control what was happening, but Slade stuck to his script and asked almost ridiculously trivial questions till the lawyer objected. The detective ignored him and carried on till Grainger was absolutely wound up. Then he fired the first bullet.

'Why did you visit Davy McGill at his home?'

It was a direct hit and they all watched the impact. It was a question Grainger hadn't expected because he'd been sure no one could have seen him that night, and in the brief moment that he was unbalanced and searching for a response, they noted the slight change in his colour, the way his eyes narrowed and the pause he needed to invent a lie.

He'd gone over this time and time again and he knew he would make a mistake, but it all depended on what they knew. If it was just that he'd been there, then there was an out. The detectives knew so there was no point in a denial, and he was smart enough to know the best course was to go with it.

His recovery was remarkable and Slade knew their victory wasn't going to come easy.

Grainger put his palms on the table and leaned forward.

'I'm sorry, I didn't want to mention this and I apologise. You might not know it but I have, let's just say, some problems with my brothers, and Paul in particular.'

Slade had interviewed or tried to interview the Grainger brothers because Davy McGill was on their team. Sean had said almost nothing and Paul had said 'fuck off' to every question he was asked.

Grainger had regained his cool. 'I might as well tell you that it was becoming serious and I wanted someone on their team to keep me informed. They always gave Davy a hard time, so I thought he was the man to help me out. In fact, he said he would. That's why I was there.'

Slade had to admit that he was good, and the man could think on his feet. He'd flinched at the question then rebounded like a professional. Thompson stepped in and fired the next bullet.

'We've been told that you met DI Janet Hadden unofficially in a West End bar. In fact, we were told that you were with her when she assaulted a man in the bar.'

Hadden and Grainger had discussed this one a number of times. There was always the possibility this would crop up somehow because of the barny and he took it easily.

'I remember a woman I was with kicking off. I'd just met her and after that incident I gave it a complete miss. Can't even remember her name and she looked nothing like Janet. Long hair and glasses, as far as I remember.' He sat back, looking pleased with himself.

Slade felt his own emotions rising. That was normal and he controlled it. Like every other detective, he sometimes wished it was like the stories from the old-time detectives around when he joined CID – no lawyer present and a smack in the coupon for every smart remark – but it was a new age of investigation and the fucking lawyers were always in the way.

Slade pressed him on the incident in the pub and started to feel the dead weight in his gut that the interview was going absolutely nowhere near a result. He'd guessed that was what would happen beforehand, but there was always that glimmer of hope that it would be like the telly and repeating the question a few times would get the suspect to break down and tell all. Real life just wasn't like that though – it needed more than raising your voice a few times to get the real pros to open up, and it was only a small percentage that ever did. Even then, on the rare occasions it did happen, it was usually because there was a mountain of corroboration to put to the suspect.

He threw the last roll of the dice and watched the reaction.

'Davy McGill seemed to go straight to that cupboard where the box was. There was nothing of value in it as far as we can see. That seems strange to us. Any idea why that might be?'

Grainger didn't answer and let the lawyer earn his crust.

'I'm sorry, Mr Slade, but that question sounds to me as if my client is a suspect. Is that the case? Because if so, we're on thin ice here. He volunteered to come in as a witness. Either detain him or back off!'

Slade didn't let the intervention move him. The lawyer was on the money, but he wanted to send a message that they had their suspicions, so he didn't answer – he just gave Grainger full-on eye contact and waited.

'You heard my lawyer.' Grainger's lips were tight and he saw the message in the detective's eyes – *if I get a fucking sniff, I'm coming for you.*

Grainger nodded; it was no more than he expected. He was flying, the nerves and fears gone in the bear pit. The detectives had given it their best shot but missed the target. They'd exhausted their questions and Grainger's lawyer began to act up because they were just going round the same circuit now.

Slade threw in the towel and asked Grainger if there was anything he wanted to know, though he knew what was coming.

'How did you know I went to Davy McGill's flat?'

Grainger had to get an answer to that one, and although he knew the detectives wouldn't tell him, he would have to work it out. He'd been exposed somewhere along the line, and he would worry that they were keeping something else up their sleeves.

That was exactly what Slade wanted and was as much as he could achieve. Davy McGill was still the guilty corpse and there was nowhere else to go. The real problem was that, no matter how he tried, this case was solved as far as most people were concerned, and some other cases were parked just round the corner. At any minute, he knew he might get the call to take over another major incident, and Davy McGill would just be another story for the detectives to chew over a drink in years to come.

Across the city, Grace Macallan had started her interview with Janet Hadden a bit later. There had been a bomb scare in Fettes and they were all taken seriously, especially since the explosion near the old HQ which had almost killed Lesley Thompson. The station had been cleared after the warning and it had created an awkward situation between Hadden and Macallan, as they'd had to evacuate the building to the same assembly point.

Macallan had known small talk was out of the question, so she'd made sure there was some distance between them. She had one of her inspectors with her, and she'd used the time they were outside to go over a few more points before the interview.

She'd glanced over at Hadden a couple of times and wondered why they'd never come across each other before. She knew her by sight, and she'd heard the stories that she was a bit of a cold fish, but very efficient and got the job done, though Macallan guessed some people would describe her the same way.

The all-clear was eventually given and they'd drifted back into the building and met up near Macallan's office. They did the formalities and Macallan found herself in a similar position to Ronnie Slade in that all they had was information from Jacquie Bell's source, who they didn't know. Macallan would have trusted her friend with her life, but they were on soft ground and would have to go easy.

When she was on the way back into the office she'd received a text from Lesley Thompson that said they'd scored a big round zero with Grainger and they were wrapping up, so this was the only lead they had left.

Hadden sat across the table almost expressionless and said nothing; she didn't need to.

'This is not a formal interview, Inspector Hadden, and we appreciate how difficult it can be running agents and that you get enough problems as it is. However, you must be aware of the murder of Jude Hamilton – or Grainger – and of course she was the wife of a source registered to you.'

Macallan looked up from her notes, expecting some reaction. Hadden just nodded and barely moved.

'There are some questions being asked of Mr Grainger, and I can tell you that he's being interviewed again by the SIO on the David McGill incident team.' She looked directly at Hadden when she said it and saw a flicker across her eyes. That one had touched a nerve.

Hadden felt her pulse rise when Macallan told her that Grainger was with Slade, but she realised very quickly that the words had been chosen carefully and she clasped her hands before speaking.

'Has he been detained?' She felt her heart thump, because if he had then events might spin out of control.

Macallan wished she could lie, but as they were on tape, she had no choice but to tell the truth, though she knew her answer would ease the pressure on Hadden if she was involved in anything with Grainger.

'No, he's just giving a further statement.' She watched Hadden unclasp her hands. 'In addition, the man suspected of killing her was also your source, and you must appreciate that this situation does cause concern.'

'I appreciate it's unusual, Superintendent, but they were recruited and handled properly so I understand the force will want to make sure everything was done properly, but I'm confident it was.'

Macallan went through every detail of the record of the original approaches to Davy McGill then Grainger by Hadden and her partner. The forms were immaculate; Hadden was almost obsessive about record-keeping, and she had to be.

'Whose idea was it to target McGill then Grainger for recruitment in the first place, Inspector?'

'Mine, but the proposal was supported by my supervisors, and we believed that because Dominic Grainger was an up-and-comer he could be a valuable long-term source. We thought if we managed to sign him on, he would be a high-grade asset for years to come. Davy McGill was a natural target to start with, and we wanted to get him on board to help us with intelligence on the Graingers and as a way of corroborating what we got from Dominic. There wasn't anything unusual about that strategy.' She stayed calm, knowing Macallan's reputation and that she'd be studying every move she made.

'I notice that one job based on information you received where Sean Grainger was the target ended up looking like a set-up.' Macallan saw another flicker – that one had rubbed a nerve – but what struck her most was that Janet Hadden had iron control, and she wondered what that meant in context.

'These things happen, ma'am. Sure you've had your own problems with sources in the past.'

Macallan flicked her eyes up at Hadden. It had been delivered quietly, but it was a dig in the ribs. Macallan wanted to tell her who was in charge, but she knew that she had to control herself just as tightly as the woman across the table. She was rarely guilty of pre-judging people, but she didn't like Hadden. It was impossible to say why that was, but it wasn't just the dig in the ribs.

They were fucking around and that was a waste, so Macallan got to the point. She put the story to Hadden that a woman had been seen with Dominic Grainger before he'd been registered as an informant, and before the first recorded approach through a phone call.

'I don't know anything about that, ma'am.'

Macallan watched Hadden touch her face in a nervous gesture.

'The source of this information has told us that the woman with Grainger assaulted a man in the bar, and that that woman was you.'

Hadden swallowed, and the edges of her nostrils flared for a moment, but she rode the little crisis, reminding herself that if this was solid, then she'd have been cautioned, so they were short somehow. Besides, she'd had a disguise on so there was speculation and then there was hard proof. If they had the latter, she'd already be staring at the ceiling in a locked cell, so unless Dominic had grassed her, there had to be a weakness in the story. Whatever, someone had seen them that night and remembered, but how the fuck had they identified her?

'I absolutely deny this and would like to know where it came from.' She held her nerve and knew to just say what she needed to say and nothing more.

Macallan pressed her along the same lines and that was enough for Hadden to know that was all they had. Someone had seen her, but they weren't sure of the information. She gave the same answers to the same questions. The interview was running out of steam, and they both knew it, but Hadden wanted to act the innocent but dedicated detective.

'Look, ma'am, I know this situation with Jude Hamilton throws up some problems for us but that allegation about me is malicious unless you have something else. The other thing is that Dominic Grainger is helping us with an arms-trafficking job and I hope we can still work on this. All I ever try to do is my job.'

She sat back and wondered again who the fuck had seen her and how they'd identified her. Could she have been followed? And if so, why?

When she walked out of Fettes, her face was twisted in anger. Her control had been dropped and she knew she would have to be careful; she'd seen the suspicious look in Macallan's eyes.

Macallan stood at her office window and watched Hadden walk across Fettes Avenue. 'Think I'll meet this one again,' she said to her reflection then turned, picked up her phone and called Jacquie Bell. She couldn't mention that the source had seen the woman going to Grainger's flat because that would have exposed the fact that either she or Dominic Grainger had been under some form of surveillance, even though it was a PI.

'Any chance I can talk to your source, Jacquie? Hadden denies all knowledge.'

'Leave it with me, Grace, and I'll see what I can do.'

58

Grace Macallan shook her head with the trace of a wry grin. She'd seen it all before and it was just Sod's Law interfering again.

It was the day after the interviews with Grainger and Hadden and she'd arranged to meet Slade and Thompson to debrief what had happened. Macallan had just taken a chair in Slade's office when his phone rang and looking at his face, she didn't need to hear what was being said to him to guess what was happening. A young woman from Livingston had been missing for over a week and it was looking serious. She'd been missing before, but there were bad omens on this one.

Slade put the phone down, glanced towards the window and shrugged as he turned to Thompson.

'They're making noises that we might be pulled onto the missing girl case – there's some evidence she was seen with an unknown male before she disappeared.'

'We're being punished for something in a previous life, Ronnie.' Thompson smiled as she said it – she'd picked up the same vibe as Macallan. She had a weekend planned with the new man in her life and she hoped this wouldn't mean cancelling the arrangement. He was the first man she'd been with since she'd been injured in the Fettes bombing. Her body had been scarred, and although her face had been more or less undamaged, it had taken her a long time to become confident enough again to share her time with someone else.

Slade knew exactly what the position was and said, 'Take the weekend, Lesley, whatever happens. You deserve it and no arguments, please.'

'The price of success, Ronnie.' Macallan had a moment when she wished it was her taking the call, but it passed as she saw the lines starting to cut in around Slade's eyes. She knew exactly how he felt. Weary but fascinated by the possibility of a new case. It was the drug again – always the next case.

Slade looked towards Macallan, and for a moment he seemed like the boy who'd let everyone down. 'Sorry, Grace, but if I get pulled away, this will have to go to a DI to tidy it up, but we'll cross that bridge when we come to it. Tell the truth, I don't know how much more we can do anyway.' He explained in great detail what had happened with Grainger and conceded that it had taken them no further forward.

'What did you think of Janet Hadden?'

'Well, I didn't get any further than you, and at the end of the day maybe the information is just wrong. It happens. I'm going to see if I can meet the source of the information and take it from there, but I'm not holding my breath. My gut feeling is not good. A couple of the questions hit a nerve with her, but that doesn't prove anything. That's as far as it goes, but I'm not giving up on it just yet. Want to bottom it out rather than it coming back again in future and biting us on the leg.'

They wound up the meeting. Macallan gave Thompson a squeeze then decided to stretch her legs and walk into the centre of town, where she could enjoy the warm sun that was giving the old city some respite from the previous days of rain. She bought a paper, sat outside a coffee shop and glanced at the headlines, which were constantly bad these days. The country was still obsessed with Brexit and the political parties were ripping themselves up, but the forecast was for a long dry spell and she decided that was the only good news.

She couldn't concentrate on any of the articles though, and her thoughts kept going back to Hadden. There was something wrong with the whole thing, but it might never come to light. If she was dirty, then it was an unusual one – most of the cases she investigated involved all the old motives of sex, money or revenge. Why would Hadden be corrupt? She was single, seemed to avoid relationships and, according to her research, was well off financially. She was doing well career wise but wasn't a flyer, although she couldn't help thinking that Hadden should be with her record. She sipped her coffee and answered her phone. It was Jacquie Bell.

'My source won't meet you. Honestly, Grace, he's terrified of what might happen if his name comes out. Did my best but if you want me to ask him anything just say. He's with me now.'

'Did you mention that there was a CCTV recording of what happened in the bar?'

'There was and he had it, but Arthur Hamilton has it now. Problem is, if you go to him about that recording, he's going to know exactly where that information came from.'

Bell then told Macallan to take care and finished the call.

The reporter was spot on, and Macallan knew there was no way she could put Bell's source at risk – and he would be given Arthur Hamilton's track record.

The other problem was that it looked like Dominic Grainger was going to provide information on arms trafficking to Belfast. That was a big deal, and the executive would love those kinds of headlines after so many failures for Police Scotland. It didn't help that Macallan's unit was getting nothing but grief over its own conduct into the search for leaks from the force.

She ordered another coffee and grinned, thinking that she'd never have ordered a second coffee in the past. There was always too much to do, but her driven nature had mellowed. Motherhood, marriage and too many dark memories had changed her into a different person.

She'd watched Andy Murray saying on the TV that his wife and child were his priority now, tennis came second, and she got that. She was becoming content, and for a detective that could be a disadvantage, although she believed it worked the opposite way for her. She called Jack, told him she loved him and to kiss the children and pat the dog for her.

Macallan lifted her face to the sun and thought about Slade and Thompson. They were the new stars in crime detection now, and Macallan wondered if she was getting past her best, although she'd been asking the same kind of question for years. Self-doubt was a burden she could never shake off. The job was a short life and you became a dinosaur very quickly, but that was how it had to be. There was so much damage done investigating the hard cases; they drained the soul, and it was natural that the best detectives burned out too quickly.

She picked up her bag and decided to walk back to the office. Work could wait.

At that same moment, Arthur Hamilton had been staring at his study window for over an hour, barely moving. Anyone looking at him could never have guessed at the rage coursing through his blood. He had nothing left, and he felt empty. A living daughter who hated him had at least given him hope of reconciliation, and he could dream.

Now the horizon was empty and dark, there was only the memories. He stood up and knew exactly what he was going to do. It didn't matter what happened to him at the end of it all, but that rage needed to be channelled.

59

Paul Grainger hadn't been too sure about the job originally, but it was a big earner because the Belfast team were taking twenty kilos of coke along with the guns. Dominic had reassured them that this would just be the first and they were willing to take regular deliveries, including as much counterfeit goods as the Graingers could supply.

'They're hard bastards to deal with, but handy to have on our side, and they have rock-solid systems to avoid the law. I want you two to do the business – it's that important. Sean, you go with the load, and Paul, you follow on and watch for any attention. I want you to meet the boys in Cairnryan and get to know them if this is going to be a new line of business for us.'

Dominic opened up a couple of beers and pushed them across the table. 'There won't be any problems this time, and we have a bogey run going in front that has a genuine load. A few of the team know about that one, but apart from the suppliers down south, only us three know about this load so we're solid.'

'We could certainly do with the money and getting

back to normal,' Paul said, staring at his brother. He still wondered about what had happened to Jude. It had brought a shitload of unnecessary attention from the police, so they'd done almost no business, and on top of the other losses, they needed a job to go right.

'Okay.' Whatever else Paul thought, he was lifted by the return to business. 'You alright with this, Sean?'

Sean nodded – like Paul, he needed some action. He was bored and pissed off with everything that had happened in the previous weeks. 'Tell the truth, brothers, I just want to get involved. Know what I mean?'

They left the office when they'd finished their beers. The job for Belfast would run the following morning.

Frankie Mason had a small team watching Dominic Grainger, and they followed him away from the office and straight to another meet. The watchers called back that he'd driven out into the country near Penicuik and met up with a woman.

Mason clenched his fist when they came back with the description – it was Janet Hadden again. He'd been working on more of the phone records for Grainger, and before Jude had been murdered, he'd noticed a couple of calls to an insurance company, though at the time he'd ignored it. He'd followed it up since the murder and found that there was a big fat insurance policy in play and Dominic was looking at a heavy-duty pay-off. It might mean nothing, just the sort of thing a smart businessman would do, but it was interesting, and he knew Arthur Hamilton would have his own view on it.

Grainger left the meet, went straight home and didn't leave again. Mason called the team off and phoned Hamilton. He told him what they'd seen and what he'd discovered about the insurance policy.

'Nice work, Frankie, and keep them on it.'

Hamilton had already decided that at some point he

was going to lift Paul Grainger because he'd been Davy McGill's boss man and he wanted to find out what the fuck he knew. Depending what happened with that, he was going to look into the eyes of Janet Hadden and find out what she was involved in. All he wanted was to squeeze whoever needed it till he understood what was behind the murder of his daughter.

'Put a couple o' the boys on Paul Grainger, Frankie, and don't ask why, right?'

'Fair enough, Arthur. Long as they get paid they're happy.'

Mason put down the phone, called his team and told them to split up and watch Paul as well as Dominic Grainger.

Hamilton sat at his desk and stared at the picture of Jude. His pulse throbbed like a hammer in his neck and he wanted to hurt someone – to do it with his own hands to relieve the pressure. He phoned his friend in Glasgow and started to put his game into play.

'The female that ripped off yer boy. I'm havin' her in. Take it he'd like a word wi' her?'

'Sure he will, Arthur.' The Glasgow man knew his son had been humiliated and would lap up the chance to get payback. He still didn't know that the woman was a detective and Hamilton would leave it that way in case he took the jitters.

'There's somethin' else, pal. I want the boy to bring some people wi' him when I get her in.'

When Hamilton told the Glasgow man what he wanted, he was surprised, but he'd seen it done before. It meant that whatever Hamilton had against this woman it was serious business.

'Fair enough, Arthur. Easy done.'

60

Arthur Hamilton took an early call to find Frankie Mason sounded stressed.

'The boys just called me and it looks like something's up. Sean's riding passenger in a lorry and Paul's following in a hired car. They're on the M8 heading west towards Glasgow. What do you think, Arthur?'

'What I think is the boys stay wi' them. If the bastards are up to somethin' I want to know what it is.'

'Cheers, Arthur, just wanted to make sure.'

Mason was terrified of getting anything wrong with the big man again, and he relaxed once he'd had the nod. He called the boys following the Graingers. They were relaxed – as far as they were concerned it was a good job and a good earner.

What those boys and Mason couldn't know was that they were being observed by the police surveillance team covering the Grainger job. The call had come to the operational commander that there were a couple of unknown cars and drivers following the lorry, as well as Paul Grainger. He took the logical conclusion that they were part of the team and it meant the surveillance team had to be even more careful than normal. It wasn't a great problem, because they knew exactly where the handover of gear was taking place near Cairnryan. They had a tracking device on the lorry with the gear, and this meant the police team could stay well away from following cars.

Later in the morning, Mason took another call that the lorry was heading down the Ayrshire coast road and there were no problems so far. Mason called Hamilton again, who sounded pleased.

'Sounds good, Frankie. Bastards are up to somethin' and I wonder if they're headin' for the Belfast ferry?'

'Christ, what do we do if that's the case, Arthur? It's a possibility an' there was the calls Dominic made across there.' Mason felt slightly panicked again but Hamilton was easy with it.

'Fair enough, Frankie. If they go to the ferry, just leave them there. If they can, stay wi' Paul though – I want to know where he is.'

Sean Grainger was unaware of all the players watching their movements as they travelled down the narrow coast road at the edge of the Firth of Clyde. He watched the sun shine down on the sparkling waves around the majestic island of Ailsa Craig and wondered how he could get away from the business without causing a bust-up with his brothers. Dominic wouldn't be a problem, but Paul certainly would. He lit up another cigarette and passed it to the driver before doing one for himself, then called Paul, who told him there were no problems.

When they pulled into the car park a few miles short of the Cairnryan ferry port, they saw a couple of cars parked where they'd been told they would be.

Sean jumped out of the cab and watched as the four Belfast men left their cars. Sean Grainger could handle himself, but they looked like serious people. He walked over to them, shook hands and then the mood changed. Despite what they were involved in, they cracked a couple of funnies and acted as if it was a day out at the seaside.

Paul arrived and they did the introductions with him. The leader of the Belfast team seemed relaxed and suggested they leave the lorry with the driver and his team and he could grab a coffee with the Graingers in a roadside cafe there. Sean almost forgot why they were there but was first to see the movement of people at the edges of his vision. There were armed police coming at them from all sides, and he knew in an instant they had to have been waiting for them. There was no way they could have got into position without prior warning.

Paul and Sean ended up on their bellies beside each other as the police team started to cuff them all up.

'Fuckin' grassed again, Sean,' Paul snarled. 'I'll kill some fucker for this. Swear to God.'

They had them all on their feet and lined up, with the Graingers and their lorry driver next to the Belfast men, as the police team covered them and secured the area.

Sean looked to his left and realised there were two men who didn't seem to belong. He looked at Paul and nodded towards the two men; Paul shrugged and managed to say, 'No idea, brother,' before one of the police team told him to shut the fuck up.

It was cleared up when a detective went along the line and asked everyone to identify themselves. When they came to the first of the two unknown men they got their answer.

'We've fuck all to do with this, pal. We were hired to follow these fuckin' cowboys from Edinburgh. Private contractors.'

The detective looked puzzled for a moment then realised they had a slightly more confused situation than

369

they'd planned for. He pulled the two unknowns out of the line and passed them to a couple of plain clothes who took them away from the car park.

The Grainger brothers looked at each other and knew that they'd been pissed on from a great height. The Belfast men stared at them as if they were responsible, and all the goodwill that had taken place at the beginning of the meeting was toast. Whatever had gone wrong had gone wrong on the Scottish side of the Irish Sea.

An hour later, Frankie Mason was sitting in his office, wondering why it had all gone quiet, when his door opened and he disappeared under the weight of some serious law men who hadn't called on a social visit. It took a few hours to sort out, but Mason and his boys hadn't committed any offence, though the detectives who interviewed him took a bit of convincing.

Mason refused to say who his client was because that was confidential, and he knew it was better to get a hard time from them then explain to Arthur Hamilton why he'd disclosed his name.

The detectives were pissed off with him, but they had the result with the firearms and dope so they could live with it, although they warned him they'd be back.

As soon as Mason was free, he called Hamilton and explained what had happened but that he hadn't given up his name.

Hamilton was pleased and intrigued. He told Mason it was all okay and that there was a bonus waiting for him.

'Want me to do anythin' else, Arthur?'

'Naw, it's job done, my son. Leave it for the time bein' an' I'll get one of the boys to drop an envelope off at your place.'

Hamilton sat back and wondered how he could have underestimated his son-in-law so much. He was sure the bastard had sold his brothers down the line. He'd already heard the news on the BBC that a major operation had resulted in the arrests of men from Belfast and Edinburgh, and that there had been a significant seizure of firearms and drugs.

'The devious fucker.' Hamilton said it quietly, but it proved Dominic Grainger was capable of anything.

Hamilton had been a ruthless gangster in the past, but selling your brothers to the law seemed a step even he wouldn't have taken in those days. As far as he was concerned, the evidence was mounting against his son-in-law, but the next step was Janet Hadden. She was bent law, so he could take a risk he wouldn't normally have contemplated.

He called the two Glasgow heavies who were on loan to him and told them what he wanted. They were both mad as fuck and thought it was a great idea. When they put the phone down they high-fived.

'Kidnap a fuckin' detective. Love it.'

61

Janet Hadden felt sick in her gut. She'd met Dominic Grainger at his flat and had been buzzing with nerves in case Macallan or some other team had eyes on her or Grainger after what had happened. She knew Macallan hadn't been happy with her, but the success with the Belfast job meant she had some brownie points again, and her boss back on board as a fan. She could have done without seeing Grainger, but he'd insisted and sounded as if he'd just won the lottery.

He was full of it, and she realised she'd gone from thinking she controlled him when he'd been recruited as a source to watching him completely turn the tables on her and everyone else. He was off the Richter scale, and she had no idea how to take back control.

He'd roped her into an indirect involvement in the deaths of Jude Hamilton and Davy McGill. She was in the middle of a nightmare, and watching the smile on Grainger's face almost made her retch. He seemed to act as if she belonged to him; she could see what was in his eyes and what he might try next with her. She wanted to kill him, but another body turning up with a direct line to her would bring her down.

When she left his flat, she headed to the nearest bar and downed some doubles, hoping the booze would calm her down. She had always had a plan in the past, but there was no way out of this mess as long as Grainger was alive, and there was nothing she could do about it.

Macallan would keep digging – she knew it, and there was no way of knowing what she might find.

Grainger had seemed relieved that at least they knew who'd been watching them. It had been private detectives, and Grainger had been sure his father-in-law must have had something to do with it. He knew that Hamilton had used Frankie Mason in the past, and it was just the kind of stroke the big man would have pulled. It meant he knew a bit and definitely suspected him now, but Grainger's view was that there was fuck all he could do about it.

Hadden knocked back her last drink and thought about the range of problems she already faced – and now Arthur Hamilton was on her case.

She walked away from the boozer. The street was empty, and the only sound she heard was the rhythmic tap of her shoes on the damp pavements. She never heard the man behind her and it all happened in the space of a few seconds: the hood, the tape on her mouth and wrists, terror and the realisation that she was bound up in the boot of a car. She was a detective, so this shouldn't happen, but all of her nightmares had become real. All she could hear above the rumble of the engine was the dull sounds of male voices and the occasional burst of laughter.

She had no idea how long she was in there; she seemed to lose all sense of time and wasn't sure if she'd been minutes or an hour trapped in the dark. A deep and terrifying dark.

She tensed as she felt the boot being opened. The voices

of the men were clear and pure Glasgow, and there was the draft of cool air on her neck as she was lifted to her feet and walked into a building of some kind. The sounds of their feet seemed to echo, which meant it was a big place, and it felt cold.

She was forced to sit and tied onto a chair. The hood was lifted and she blinked repeatedly to clear her vision. The place was in semi-darkness, but she could make out that it was a large garage or industrial unit. Arthur Hamilton stood in front of her and he nodded to whoever was behind her.

'Go an' get the kettle on, boys. You deserve it.'

She heard footsteps behind her, but they didn't go too far because she could make out the sound of a conversation and what sounded like a kettle being filled from a tap.

'You know who I am, girl?' Hamilton stood in front of her with his hands clasped behind him, like a teacher giving a lecture to an errant pupil.

Hadden nodded and felt sick with fear. Gangsters didn't abduct detectives – there was no script for this one, and she knew he would only do this if he wasn't worried about payback.

'Now I've dealt with a lot of your kind over the years and there was always limits, but you've walked into the wrong territory. Now you're goin' to tell me all about what you an' that fuck of a son-in-law of mine have been up to.' He pulled the tape from her mouth.

'I don't know what you mean. You've just fucked with the wrong detective.' The other Janet Hadden had taken over and she strained against the tape holding her arms.

Hamilton hit her a shot to the side of the head. He hadn't done it for years, and it felt good as the skin above her eye spilt and dazed her.

She made a low sound in her throat and felt a trickle of blood down the side of her face.

Hamilton leaned down and whispered in her ear exactly what was going to happen to her and all her fight was gone in a moment. She sobbed and told him everything he wanted to know. She knew resistance would only bring pain. There was no way out. He was happy for her to see his face, wanted it – that meant there was no happy ending and he knew part of the story already.

At the end of it all he nodded, satisfied – his son-in-law had indeed killed his daughter and Davy McGill.

'Well, I'll be fucked.' He felt the pulse bang at the side of his neck and he fought to control his rage, but he was determined that he would be cold and hard when he dished out the final sentence.

'What are you going to do with me?' Hadden said.

Hamilton's head snapped up; he had almost forgotten her as he imagined what he would do to his son-in-law.

'You've got a treat comin', girl. You helped that bastard kill the lassie. Maybe you never expected that, but you were involved.' He nodded to someone behind her.

The Glasgow gangster who she'd slept with, ripped off and treated like a numpty walked into her view. He grinned as if he was looking at his next meal. Hamilton walked out of her view and she heard him say, 'Enjoy it, boys. Remember. I want her alive when you're finished wi' her.'

The Glasgow man leaned over until his face was only inches from hers. He leered at her torment. 'It's payback, darlin'.'

He snapped the tape back on her mouth and waved to the men behind her. The gangster she ripped off like a fool wiped the back of his hand across his lips and two shambling junkies appeared from the shadows. It looked and smelled like they hadn't washed in a month, and they seemed completely out of it, both of them sweating despite the chill air.

'These two star turns are gonnae spend the next couple o' days wi' you and dae whatever they like, as much as they like. They've got every fuckin' junkie disease ye can think of: hep, AIDS – they have it all, and so will you by the time they've finished. First things first though – I'll have a go before I head back tae Glasgow.'

He told the two junkies and whoever else was there to fuck off and that he'd give them a shout when he was finished. He pulled out a syringe and her eyes nearly popped when he pushed it in her arm and watched her drift off the edge.

Two days later, Janet Hadden was found wandering about on the edge of the M8 and was almost wiped out by cars that had to swerve to avoid her. When the police arrived, they thought she was a junkie and couldn't make sense of a word she said. She looked like she'd been the victim of an accident or serious assault. She was taken to intensive care, but her mind was broken and would never recover. Even if she had been rational, she could never have told the police why Arthur Hamilton had taken such a course of action.

When Macallan heard what had happened, she went to see her and was shocked at what she saw. It didn't make any sense. The doctors said she was pumped full of dope and looked like she'd suffered a prolonged serious sexual assault, but unfortunately, she couldn't tell them a thing and was in deep shock.

Macallan stood and watched her for a few minutes, but while her eyes were open, she was somewhere else in her mind.

She drove back to the office and realised they were no nearer to finding out what was driving this train of events. She reported back to a meeting of senior officers who had no idea how to deal with it. Hadden had been reported missing when she hadn't turned up for work, but if she couldn't tell them what had happened, it was impossible to know where to start.

The press were all over it, but they didn't know what line to take other than investigations were being carried out and a dedicated team was trying to establish what had happened.

In Janet Hadden's mind, she played the old nightmare over and over in a loop. The sky was even darker, but she was trapped on the edge of the same cliff and the earth below her feet was moving as if it was alive.

62

Dominic Grainger wasn't surprised when he got the call from Arthur Hamilton. It had to come, and in any case, he was relieved that he could get a chance to gauge what Hamilton was thinking or up to. Grainger was beginning to feel the weight of what had happened falling off his shoulders, but the thing that still kept him awake at night was what had happened to Janet Hadden. No one had worked it out, and the police were keeping quiet. Hadden walked on the edge, and there was no telling who else she'd fucked about, but he still couldn't be sure. He'd contacted the co-handler, who told him they had made a new arrangement and Hadden wouldn't be coming back. That was the line they were taking and sticking to it.

'Thought we could meet up, Dominic,' Hamilton said. 'Some stuff we need to talk over about Jude's things and her estate. I'd made some arrangements for her but obviously that's changed.'

Hamilton sounded calm enough but that meant nothing. Grainger knew there would be something else behind the call, but as long as they met in a public place it was fair enough, and he was sure Hamilton wouldn't try anything without proof. He might suspect, but if there was something more than being seen going to Davy McGill's flat, he'd be dead already. The police seemed to have given up, and he'd heard that Ronnie Slade had been moved onto another case.

'No problem, Arthur. What about Leith Walk? Some nice boozers down there now.'

It was arranged, and Grainger made sure he had a couple of heavies with him, or at least close by if they were needed. He couldn't see Hamilton trying anything in a public place, but you never knew what would happen on the way there or coming away. It wouldn't be the first time. He'd decided to act like a professional now. His debts were all taken care of, his brothers were inside and probably wouldn't see the light of day for twenty years. The Belfast boys were pissed off at the loss of the gear and the fact that four of their men were inside, but it happened, and there had not been any serious follow-up by the police on either side of the water so it could just as easily have been a problem on the Northern Ireland side. The PSNI had agents everywhere, and bugging operations were routine. They were making their own enquiries to see if the problems were theirs.

Grainger had taken the biggest hit financially but he'd planned that, and it was worth it to keep his cover and make him look like the biggest loser. His mortgage was paid off, he would get the life insurance pay-off and he'd taken the sensible option of getting rid of the flat. He would get back into business full-time, where he belonged. His marriage had been the start of so many of his problems, and he wished he'd never set eyes on Jude.

He had a good seat at the back of the pub with a view of the boozer door and it wasn't too busy. The TV was blaring out a sports channel that no one was watching, and his two heavies were across the road in a car. Arthur Hamilton came in and went through the same routine as always – he saw Grainger but stood in the door, scanning the place for any sign of a problem.

Grainger raised his glass, but Hamilton didn't change his expression. He looked older; his build had always been square and strong, but now there was almost the hint of a stoop and his shoulders were more rounded. Bereavement could do terrible things. Grainger had to work to keep the grin off his face.

When Hamilton sat down, Grainger said, 'Drink?'

The invitation was ignored, and he realised that there was even a change in the big man's colour. He'd always had the perma-tan and got away with it, but there was a blueish tinge to his cheeks now, and Grainger realised that the man was hurt far more than he'd realised. It was a fucking result, as far as he was concerned.

'Let's cut the shite, son. Shove the drink. I'm here tae deliver a message.' His body might have looked weakened, but his voice was strong and full of the old passion.

Grainger was thrown for a minute, and he struggled to work out whether this was the pre-cursor to an attack or a rant. His father-in-law had hated him since they'd met, and that was no surprise. He nodded and said, 'What's on your mind, Arthur?'

Hamilton leaned forward, and those blue eyes that had been a striking feature of his looks bulged, red-rimmed and angry.

'I'll tell ye what's on ma mind. You killed Davy McGill an' ma Jude. Don't take the pish wi' a denial or I'll fuckin' do you here an' now.'

He pulled out a hanky and dabbed it across his top lip. Grainger was sure he could go pound for pound with a man in such decline, but Hamilton was an old-school street fighter and had the X factor when it came to a tussle. That animal instinct to rip the other man's throat out before he did it to you.

'You an' that fuckin' bitch Hadden are responsible, and you'll pay. She's been sorted. The difference is I let her live.'

Grainger sat back and realised that his optimism had been premature. He tried to take in the fact that Hamilton had the balls to lift a detective and leave her wrecked in the middle of the M8.

'Think you've got this all wrong, Arthur.' It was feeble and Grainger heard the lie in his own voice. There was a time when there was no point fucking around, so he sat back and waited.

'I've got fuck all wrong, boy. I could have had you picked up and tortured, but I want you to have a bit o' time to think about it. Sweat, sleepless nights, wonderin' when you get the message. Next time I see you I'll have you strapped to a chair an' a blowtorch in my hand.'

'Fuck you, Arthur.' Grainger had no choice but to push back. His nerves were shredded, but there was nowhere else to go, and he'd become angry himself that his plans had been fucked up. 'She was a fuckin' bitch, Arthur, an' a slag, your daughter. Want the truth? She was into black men. Imagine that, Arthur, picking up black men – an' half the time she never even got their name.'

Hamilton was already rising from the seat. His face was scarlet and there was a dribble of spit running down the side of his chin. He managed to say, 'I'll fuckin' kill you,' but the words were strangled and Grainger blinked as the big man seemed to do an almost comical dance before slumping forward over the table. His face was side-on, right in front of Grainger, who couldn't compute what had happened.

He was vaguely aware of people crowding round Hamilton and lowering him to the floor. People were firing questions at him and he looked blankly at them without saying a word. Then his mind cleared and he stood up and said, 'He's my father-in-law.'

A man seemed to have taken control and said he was a nurse.

Grainger looked down at Hamilton, who was making a sound as if he was being strangled. His face was distorted and Grainger heard someone say it looked like a stroke. Someone else said, 'It's awright, son – you have a seat an' we'll look efter the auld man.'

Grainger was ushered to a seat and people put their hands on his shoulders.

His mind cleared and he wanted to raise his hands to the heavens and thank God for his intervention. A stroke – a fucking stroke! *Jesus, what a result*, he thought. He wanted to do a little jig and dance round the shattered body of his father-in-law but that could wait.

The ambulance arrived and took Big Arthur Hamilton to A&E. A couple of the locals offered to drive Grainger, but he said it was okay – he had transport.

Grainger walked down Leith Walk to the car and one of the heavies asked, 'Where to, boss?'

'The off-licence. Want to get some champagne.'

Momentum had changed again and he was going to end up king of the fucking castle.

'Good times ahead, boys. Stick with me an' you'll never regret it.'

He arsed the bottle of expensive champagne at home and still couldn't take it in. He'd gone to the hospital after buying the booze just to make sure the bastard was really ill or dead. The doctor had looked serious, though Grainger could hardly resist slapping him on the back and saying 'nice one' when he was told it looked like Hamilton had suffered a massive stroke. He had a couple of shots of whisky after the bubbly and rolled into bed a happy man.

63

It felt as if the muscles and tendons of both shoulders were being ripped out slowly, the balls forced from their sockets as the men each pushed hard against an elbow to straighten his arms behind him. The pain should have been excruciating, but strangely enough there was nothing, and from that moment he was aware only of the wind whipping through his hair and the deathly quiet. His mind, like his ruined body, had passed that point of no return where fear had been replaced by an almost dreamlike state. He didn't give a fuck because there was no point, and he realised that they couldn't hurt him any more. The bastards who thought they controlled him were wrong.

Despite this state of mind, he was aware of a problem that needed to be resolved, which was that his whole body was hanging forward by about twenty degrees and seemed to be defying the laws of gravity. In fact, that wasn't really the problem at all; when it came down to it, the problem was that his feet were on a ledge, and the rubbish-strewn ground was way too far below him for Lady Luck to hand out any form of landing that wouldn't kill him. No chance of an expert parachute roll before springing to his feet like an acrobat and sticking two fingers up at them; with his luck, he'd land in a pile of Doberman shit. He was fucked and had always been fucked; he just hadn't realised it before. They were five (or was it a hundred?) storeys up on top of a disused industrial building in the middle of a wasteland which seemed to stretch out to the horizon without a break. It looked like those pictures of a World War One battlefield. He thought there would be a few seconds' flying and then it would all be over. Not so bad after what the bastards had already done to him.

'It's time tae go, son.' He said it through the blood that kept filling his mouth. For the first time in his life he was absolutely sure what he wanted to do. That was it: the meaning of life – the moment where you realised it was just another scene from Monty Python. Fragmented thoughts were fighting with each other to make it into the conscious part of his brain and he remembered the old line from *The Lion King*: 'I laugh in the face of danger.' People did it and found strength. There was an old school pal who was a genuine good guy, had never harmed a fly, who just kept smiling and saying 'fuck it' before he died of cancer. He'd hardly ever cursed in his life, so it had real effect. 'Fuck it' made sense to him after that. It gave meaning to what was left – he understood it – and the best bit was that the bastards who'd spent the afternoon taking lumps out of him didn't. How good was that?

They were so strong they didn't have to grip him hard, and instead of concentrating they were taking the piss out of him and hee-hawing to each other at his distress. They both froze for a moment, wondering why a man with his coupon rearranged and hanging over the edge of a tall building was laughing.

Dominic Grainger looked round and discovered it

was his brothers holding his arms. Where had they come from? He took them by complete surprise and stepped over the side onto thin air. They weren't prepared and he slipped through their greasy paws like the wind. He closed his eyes and flew like a bird. No one could touch him now.

He woke up screaming – it was just a dream.

He pulled his legs over the bed and rubbed his face with the palm of his hands. He felt like shit and the dream had frightened him, but he didn't know why because it made no sense. He usually had no problems with hangovers, but his head throbbed and he headed for the bathroom for an aspirin breakfast.

A couple of coffees and a shower cleared some of the pain, but the tension behind his eyes was draining. It was the impact of what he'd been through, and for the first time in his life he felt the years weighing on him. It wasn't that long ago that his energy levels had seemed endless, but now he felt nothing but almost painful exhaustion, and things should have been better than that.

He sat still for an hour, ignoring the calls coming in, and let the headache pass. The more he thought about Arthur Hamilton, the better he felt, though it was still hard to believe that his greatest threat was out of the game – that and he could benefit if the old bastard died because he had no other family to speak of.

He gradually worked up the energy to call the hospital and they said he could come in. The nurse on the other end was sympathetic and couldn't know that Grainger would have pissed himself laughing if he could, though for the time being he'd act the caring son-in-law.

When he reached the hospital, he sought out the lead doctor on Hamilton's case.

'Is there anything he needs, Doctor?' Grainger put on his concerned face.

'Nothing at the moment. He's a very sick man and will need a lot of care. The damage is significant – loss of mobility, speech – and it's highly unlikely he'll ever come anywhere near normal function again. We just need time to assess him and get him through this phase of the treatment.'

The doctor was impatient to be away, and that was always the case, but Grainger couldn't care less. He only had one more question. 'Can he hear me if I speak?'

'Of course, and it's what you should be doing. Sorry, I have other patients.'

Grainger wanted to say, 'Fuck off then,' but he just nodded, expressed heartfelt concern and shook the doctor's hand. The doctor clearly didn't appreciate the gesture.

He walked into the room and found it quiet, apart from the low buzz from the machines monitoring and keeping Big Arthur from dying. He was lying half on his side, facing the door, and he certainly wasn't the big man any more. He seemed to have shrivelled – even his hair had lost its volume and was lying in damp strands across his head. One eye was open, one half-closed and drooped at the outside edge, and his mouth was half-open. The veins on his hand seemed to stand out like blue strings, and he made a low groaning sound when he saw his son-in-law.

Grainger pulled a chair in close and put his face close to Hamilton's, but there was a foul stink on his breath and he drew back.

'How are you, Arthur? I've been worried about you.'

He looked round to make sure there were no nurses earwigging nearby. He moved his face close again and tolerated the stink because it was important.

'I fucking killed her, Arthur. It was me and I enjoyed it. She begged me, but I did it anyway. By the way, she told me years ago what you did to her mother, so we're not that different, you fucking hypocrite. I did McGill as well. Who gives a fuck?'

Hamilton tried to say something but all that came out was a gurgling sound in his throat. Grainger smiled.

'I know, Arthur – you'd love to kill me an' all that shite, but that ain't happening now, pal. You're not quite a vegetable but near enough. Good news is that I'm all your family now an' I'm going to take good care of you. See, I want you to live like this for as long as possible. I'll be able to visit you all the time, and you'll be able to look at the face of the man who smashed Jude's fucking brains in.'

He smiled, and added, 'By the way, I'm guessing that was a nice touch with Janet Hadden. Fuck knows what you did to her, but the bonus was you got rid of another problem for me. Well done.'

He stood up. 'You take care, Arthur, and I'll be back whenever I feel like taking the piss.'

He was about to walk out of the room but turned back for a moment. He leaned over again, close up. 'Next time I'll tell you all about Jude's tastes in men – you'll love that.'

He walked out of the room, enjoying the low moaning sound behind him, and stopped to speak to the duty nurse. 'If there's anything he needs, please let me know, and I'll make sure he gets it. I'm his only family now and just want the best for him.'

The nurse put her hand on his forearm and squeezed it.

'It's lucky he has you – so many of the people we have here have no one.'

'I'm so fond of him. God, he didn't deserve this.' Grainger struggled to keep the smile off his face – it was all just pure fucking gravy.

He walked out of the hospital and felt the cool air on his face. The crisis was nearly over, he was back in charge and he thought he'd treat himself to a visit to his favourite escort. He hadn't felt like being with a woman for weeks, but the urge was back and it was time to celebrate. There were always a few loose ends, but all in all he was on solid ground and the only way was up. He'd arranged to see Sean and Paul in remand for appearances' sake and it would be the right thing to do. He'd get the best advocate money could buy and enjoy the spectacle of the silk trying to defend against a shitload of evidence.

64

Macallan looked at the various reports in front of her and sighed. She was toiling to work up any enthusiasm, and what had happened to Janet Hadden sickened her, because it was connected to what they'd been investigating, though it was unlikely she would ever find any answers.

Ronnie Slade was on a new case, and she wouldn't be allowed to investigate any further, given her role in counter-corruption.

She looked at the names: Davy McGill, Jude Hamilton, the Grainger brothers and now Arthur Hamilton, struck down with a massive stroke. The last man standing was Dominic Grainger. She still didn't know exactly what had happened, but he'd grassed his brothers and some Belfast Loyalists. That took nerve or utter stupidity, unbridled ambition or complete madness, or maybe all of them. She tapped her pen against the top of the desk and called Dominic Grainger.

He seemed surprised when he recognised her voice. 'Why, I thought this case was closed and I'm very involved looking after my father-in-law, so I hope you're not going to waste my time.'

She told him it was just routine and tidying up a few loose ends. She suggested his office, and she knew she would have to be careful in case he was recording, but it wouldn't matter – she'd choose her words carefully.

After the call, he stared at his reflection in the office mirror – he looked like a city trader and felt like a million dollars. Macallan was coming on her own, so he didn't feel spooked – if there had been a problem, there would have been two of them. He'd googled her and was intrigued; he'd seen her name in the headlines before and meeting her would be interesting if nothing else.

His secretary showed her in and Grainger was impressed. In a way, she had that slightly plain, serious look that he'd found so attractive in Janet Hadden the first time he'd met her. He saw the ring on her left hand and felt slightly disappointed, though he'd enjoyed his share of marrieds in the past. He offered her coffee and she refused.

'What can I do for you, Superintendent?'

'I want to know if you can tell me who killed Davy McGill. I think it was you.' She paused. 'I think you had something to do with your wife's death as well, but can't prove it, of course, so thought I'd ask. There's no one here with me. I'm just curious.'

Grainger was thrown for a moment on how to react. It was a game, so he decided he was safe enough to play. He was strong again, and after the thin-ice risks he'd taken, he was back on top. In fact, all the threats to his safety had been eliminated.

'Sorry, Superintendent, I really don't know what makes you think that. I should be annoyed, but I've suffered so much recently that I won't react.'

'You weren't so upset that you set up your brothers. You're a rat. You know officially we call people like you agents, but behind closed doors your title is rat.'

Macallan kept eye contact and watched his every little gesture. She saw the anger in him rising like a tide that couldn't be controlled. She'd caught him unprepared and he was taking the bait. His lips tightened.

'You should be careful, Superintendent. People stick their nose in the wrong place and get hurt. Ask Janet Hadden.'

Macallan stood up. 'Just wanted to meet you face-to-face. I've been dealing with people like you far too long.'

Macallan couldn't hide the contempt she felt for the man behind the desk. 'Just wanted to ask, and in a way you've answered the question.'

Grainger shrugged. 'What difference does any of this make to me?' He tried to look mildly amused – in control – but he was far from it.

'It doesn't matter – you wouldn't understand anyway.' Macallan had seen enough.

'You played the game and lost. It happens.' Grainger said it almost like a child getting the last word in a play-ground fight. He tried to grin as if he didn't give a fuck, but his lips were tight and he was still trying to control the rage firing just under the surface. He hated it when he couldn't control a woman – any woman – and the look of contempt on Macallan's face bothered him.

Macallan had turned to leave then glanced back when she decided there was one last message to deliver. 'You're going to die, Dominic, not an old man in your jammies. It'll be somewhere cold and lonely, and you'll be terrified when they hood you because that'll be your last view of the world. Then you'll be left there till someone finds what's left by accident and they pick you up like just another piece of roadside crap.'

She smiled almost warmly. 'Remember what I've told you when the time comes.'

She left Grainger staring at the door. He felt chilled

despite the heat in his office. He looked down at his hands and saw they were trembling. What he hadn't realised was that Macallan was far from finished with him – her next and final move would be against him.

Macallan called Mick Harkins and had a drink with him. Told him she was retiring early, though he didn't seem too surprised or convinced as he watched a tear wobble its way down her cheek.

'Right thing, Grace – get on with it and don't look back.'

She kissed his cheek and headed back to Fettes while Harkins sat in the bar, lost in his thoughts about Macallan. He knew what she obviously didn't and shook his head several times. He'd said the right things to his friend, but he knew what walking away from the job meant when you were an addict.

We'll see, Grace, he thought and slugged back half his drink before nodding to the barman. He was tired but he needed a few more.

It stunned Macallan that after all years she'd been on the force, all it took was signing a small form and being told what she'd get for a pay-off. There were no bells and fanfares, just a small white fucking form that ended so many years in the game. She hadn't done enough years for a full pension, but it didn't matter and was the least of her worries. They were financially sound and had more than she could ever have wished for.

When she walked into the small admin office where she could sign the form, she felt sure about what she had to do. She thought she needed to be outside the job to commit the sin that was coming and was prepared to carry the burden in secret. Hopefully only she would ever know, though she knew it might haunt her. She wanted the paper signed as quickly as possible so she could make the phone call.

It was straightforward up to the point the girl on the other side of the desk pushed the form over the table that would end her career. She bit her lip and blinked several times at the reality of the exit door. She needed this bit to make what she'd planned okay, but she froze, and there was a cold knot in the base of her stomach. The job had been her life, and on occasions could have been the cause of her death. So much was tied up in it, and it felt like she was on the edge of a cliff. She tried to focus on Jack and the children until she heard the girl speak.

'Superintendent – are you alright?'

Macallan blinked again and her shoulders sagged as she realised she just couldn't scribble her name on the form. There it was again – she was a junkie – controlled by a job that in the end forgot the dinosaurs five minutes after they'd picked up their cheques. That was her truth: she was afraid of not counting, and she'd seen it time and time again – the old detectives who appeared at piss-ups where hardly anyone could remember who they were. The final humiliation of imagining you were indispensable and the gradual acceptance of the truth that you were flesh and blood – old flesh and blood.

'I'm sorry, but I think I'll leave this for the time being.'

She was embarrassed and got to her feet, just wanting to escape from the office and the look on the girl's face.

Macallan almost jogged out of the building and ignored greetings from a couple of detectives who passed her in the corridors. When she was outside, she found a corner behind some parked cars and felt sick, heaving in the cool air. It only took a few minutes till she was steady again and pulled herself upright. Her face was a frozen mask. She'd wanted to be outside the job to give her cover for what she was about to do, but she was just going to have to live with her actions. She knew it was horse shit to think that there was some moral cover when she would be the only holder of the truth. She would always know what she was about to do and that she'd be damned by it.

She searched her pockets for her car keys – there was no turning back. 'Fuck it,' she growled, walking off towards the street. Forget retirement. It had to come, but she was done worrying about it.

She called the number in Northern Ireland. They hadn't spoken for years but had been close during the Troubles and worked through dark times.

'Good to hear you but sure this isn't a social call.' The voice was even; he was the coolest man she'd ever known, even when PIRA had decided killing him was a priority.

'I need someone's number and then I want you to forget this ever happened.'

'Who?'

She told him and the line went quiet for a moment. 'Bad man, Grace. I'll call you back in an hour. Be careful.'

She headed back to her office to wait.

The call came back in exactly an hour and Macallan stared at the number she'd been given for minutes, wondering if what she was doing was the right thing.

'What's the right thing then, Grace?' She muttered the question to herself and felt the nerves in her gut rattle a warning at her conscience.

She was startled by a knock at the door. It was Elaine Tenant. Macallan knew what was behind the visit before Tenant sat down – she would know that Macallan was looking at retiring, but she let Tenant speak as she wanted to be sure of her answer.

'I want you to stay on, Grace. There are two good reasons. One is I don't think the force can afford to lose people like you – we're losing enough as it is. The second is I just want you to stay. This is a friend speaking, and I know you'll miss the job. Last point is that I shouldn't tell you this, equal opportunities and all that, but there's a chief super job going in one of the major-crime teams.'

Macallan felt the urge to grab the promotion, but she knew she would have good reason to fight such urges.

'I'm not going, Elaine. Thanks for the support though. I got as far as the pen in my hand and the exit ticket in front of me and I just couldn't do it. Weak or what?' She tried a grin but it was forced and obvious. She tried again.

'I just can't do it, Elaine. I want to but I can't.' Macallan choked back the emotion that was threatening to spill over. Tenant saw it and understood what she meant.

'Well, you're far too young to bake cakes and warm Jack's slippers. Please don't blub or you'll set me off.'

'Got time off due so I'm going to our place in Northern Ireland to spoil myself, Jack, the children and the dog.'

Tenant threw a few compliments at Macallan but knew she was just filling the air with unnecessary noise – her friend needed room, so she headed for the door.

'By the way, you going to the retirement do in the Bailie?' Tenant fired the question over her shoulder on the way out. One of Macallan's best DOs had his ticket in and was heading for the door she'd been afraid to pass through. It had the making of a major piss-up and all the legends were turning up for the pay-off.

'Done.' Macallan decided it was exactly what she would need. Tenant looked pleased and closed the door behind her.

Macallan looked at the Belfast number again and tapped the desktop. She picked up her car keys, drove across the Forth Road Bridge and pulled into a lay-by, dialled the Belfast number and put a cloth across the phone. She knew the accent that answered too well, rough east Belfast and not amused when she refused to say who she was. She did her own version of the accent and it came easy. She was sure he was going to cut the call, but she had his attention.

'You want to know why your boys were lifted and the gear lost?'

'Don't know what the fuck you're talking about. What boys and what gear?'

'Cairnryan.' It was all she needed to say.

'Why you calling me? I don't know fuck all about this, but say for the sake of argument I did. What's it to you?'

'The same man did the same thing to people I know.' It was nearly the truth. 'You can leave it alone or check it out.'

'Talk.'

Macallan talked and told him just enough about Dominic Grainger, but not everything. She knew how these boys worked – when they got on someone's case they were thorough if nothing else.

'You trying to say he grassed his own brothers.'

'That's it. Please yourself.'

She finished the call and closed her eyes. It was all wrong and she knew she would have moments of regret. The chances were that the Belfast man would see it as some sort of dark arts and leave it alone, but she knew what they were like if they got a sniff of treachery.

She broke the phone and tossed the SIM card into a bin.

65

When Macallan arrived at the Bailie it was packed and she shook her head self-consciously when the roar went up as she walked into the pub. News of the retirement then non-retirement had already circulated. They were all there: Mick Harkins, Felicity Young, Lesley Thompson, Elaine Tenant and her fiancé. The party was already in full swing, and she knew she was going to be stung at the bar. It was traditional, and Harkins reminded her she was on the bell for everyone because she had nearly retired, so it still meant her buying a drink. Ronnie Slade walked in just behind her, looking like he'd been dragged through a hedge. She smiled – it was the look of a stressed SIO. She ordered him a drink

'Where's Jacquie Bell?'

'No sign yet, Grace. Let's get wasted,' Harkins slurred, and they did.

After a couple of hours, Macallan realised she was more pissed than she'd been in a long time. It felt fine, and it was a load off her mind to call it a day. She stepped outside and called Jack, who was in their place in Northern Ireland; she was going to join him the next day. He asked her again if she was sure about the decision she'd made and didn't seem in the least surprised by what she'd done.

'Well, this do is costing a fortune, Jack, given I've not thrown in the towel, so I better stick to it now.' She said goodnight to the children who asked her why she was speaking funny. Jack took over and explained that Mummy was tired. She blew a kiss down the phone and headed back into the pub.

'Grace.'

It was Jacquie Bell, who was right behind her as she held the door open.

'Where have you been?' Macallan asked. 'You've missed umpteen rounds!'

'Covering a story that's just broken – they just fished Dominic Grainger's body out of the Clyde. Two in the back of the head, very professional.'

Macallan stopped at the door and stared at the reporter.

'Problem, Grace? You didn't fancy him, did you? Come on, for fuck's sake or Mick'll drink the kitty.'

Bell saw something in Macallan's eyes but decided her priority was a good piss-up – whatever it was could wait.

Macallan knew she would question what she'd done for the rest of her life, but it was what it was and the case was closed. The singing had started and she joined in.

EPILOGUE

When Grace Macallan travelled to Belfast the morning after the leaving do, she glanced through the paper on the short flight from Edinburgh but couldn't concentrate. The details about Dominic Grainger's death were sparse, but it didn't matter – he was dead. She walked through the exit gates at George Best Airport and watched the children running towards her. Jack was behind them, and she noted the ever-increasing grey strands in his hair, but it looked good – and at least he had hair. He grinned as he held her.

When he was released from hospital, Arthur Hamilton was put in a care home where he spent his days staring at nothing in particular and trapped in his own version of Hell. The only visitor he had was his friend from Glasgow, who saw it as a duty. When he whispered in the big man's ear that Dominic had been taken out, Hamilton had tried to make a sound, but it was nothing anyone would have understood. His mind was still active and he knew Dominic Grainger was the lucky one compared with his tormented existence.

Mick Harkins sipped his lunchtime beer and glanced

between the TV above the bar and the newspaper he read every day at the same time. Big Tam the barman noticed him muttering at something that had clearly caught his attention. Something in the news pissed off Mick every day.

'Listen tae this, Tam. The two PCs who ran away from their post at Tynecastle and failed to help Tonto McGill being threatened with an axe have made a claim against the force for post-traumatic stress and failing to protect them with adequate backup.' He looked up at Big Tam. 'I'm tellin' you, Tam, the job's fucked.'

The barman wiped the top of the bar and agreed with the ex-detective.

Harkins wasn't finished. 'Listen to this! PC Denholm was quoted as saying that his life had been ruined by PTS and he is unable to lead a normal life. For fuck's sake.' Harkins had lost it. 'That fuckin' man never did a decent stroke in his puff.'

Big Tam grinned and kept wiping the bar, deep in his own thoughts.

Janet Hadden never fully recovered: her mind was shattered beyond repair and the police were never able to find out what happened to her.

GLOSSARY OF TERMS AND SLANG

Bar L	HMP Barlinnie
Baws	balls
Bizzies	detectives
Burd	Scots version of 'bird' – female
Close	narrow alley to a courtyard or to the stairwell in a tenement
Deafie	in this context intentionally not hearing or pretending not to hear
Dubbed up	locked up in police cell or prison
Duster	knuckleduster
CHIS	cover human intelligent source (informant)
Chored	stole
Clarty	Old Scots – filthy
Co-pilot	cell mate

Cowp	Old Scots for fall over or a tip; in this context used to describe having sex
Fast black	taxi
FLO	family liaison officer
Footman	surveillance officer out on foot eyeballing the target
Game's a bogey	a phrase meaning 'it's all over'
Goldie	whisky
Hampden	Hampden roar, rhyming slang for score
Hee-haw	nothing; fuck all
Henry Halls	rhyming song for balls
Hibee	Hibernian supporter
HMP	Her Majesty's Prison(s)
Jaggy suit	police uniform
Jakey	a down-and-out
Jambo	Heart of Midlothian supporter
Lie down	remand in prison
Malky	to seriously assault or murder
MEP	Member of the European Parliament
Midden	Old Scots for a rubbish dump
Moody	false or imitation
Napper	head
Ned	non-educated delinquent (chav)
Numpty	Scottish urban term for someone who's not that bright
ODCs	ordinary decent criminals
Oxter	Scots for armpit

Peelers	slang for police in Northern Ireland
PIRA	the Provisional Irish Republican Army
Polis	Scots version of police
Pokey	prison
Pre Cons	previous convictions
Radge	nutter
Saughton	HMP prison, Edinburgh
Scooby	Scooby Doo, rhyming slang for clue
Scuddie	Scots slang for nude
Snash	aggravation
SOCO	scenes of crime officer
Stookie	Rigid plaster cast that immobilises a limb in the event of an injury, usually a fracture; can also be used to describe people perhaps not the brightest
Tin pail	rhyming slang for jail
UC	undercover agent
Uniforms	uniformed police officers
Wan	the way some Weegies pronounce 'one'

ACKNOWLEDGEMENTS

Thanks to the friends and believers who convinced me to keep Grace sleuthing. I'm glad I listened to you. To the brilliant people at Black and White who make it all happen.